CHARLIE'

By

George Donald

Friday 15 December 1989

There was no need to use the torch for the clear, moonlit sky provided enough light for him to work.

The ground beside the hedgerow had never been tilled and in the dead of night, he found trying to get a shovel into the compacted and frozen ground was a whole lot harder than he had anticipated; that and the buried stones that when he struck them with the blade of the shovel sent a painful jolt up his arms.

He had been at it for almost two hours and wished now he had brought a pickaxe with him.

Though the night was freezing cold a rivulet of sweat trickled down his spine, causing his perspiration soaked shirt to stick to his back.

He glanced with disgust at the pitifully small mound of earth he'd so far removed and spat a nicotine stained globule of saliva onto the ground.

"Bastard!" he muttered and panting with exertion, savagely struck again at the ground with the blade of the shovel, twisting the blade to disturb the earth that fell into the hole.

He stopped, his breath held as he imagined hearing a vehicle approaching on the lane nearby, but sighed with relief and decided his ears were playing tricks with his mind.

In the distance an animal shrieked and sounded remarkably similar to a crying baby; a fox he guessed though whether calling for a mate or simply crying out in the darkness of the night, he didn't know for his upbringing had not been in the countryside, but in the murky Victorian tenements of Glasgow council estate.

He staggered back from the hole, exhausted and letting the shovel drop decided to have a fag.

Hands shaking, he lit the cigarette and almost reluctantly, stared down at the body wrapped in the nylon sheet, the darkened splodge of congealed blood at the head.

Inhaling deeply on the cigarette, he nipped it and threw it into the hole, then testing the depth with the shovel, convinced himself it was deep enough.

Stepping down into the hole, he grunted with exertion as using both hands, he struggled to pull the body towards him and almost hysterically, laughed out loud when he lost his grip and fell backwards onto his arse against the narrow side of the hole.

Exhaling, he stood up and forcing himself to be calm arched his back for it had been some time since he had laboured like this.

Quickly, he began to backfill the hole and when that was done, lifted the sods of earth he had spitlocked and carefully arranged them on top of the earth to roughly camouflage the hole.

He needed a piss and grinning, peed over the disturbed ground; the final indignity for the body.

Finished and tempted though he was to use the torch to check how it looked, he feared that if he did it might be seen and cause someone to come and discover the makeshift grave.

Finally, he spent several minutes stamping down the sods and collecting the shovel, his coat and jacket from the ground, made his way towards the car parked fifty yards away in the layby.

In the lane, he stopped short of the car and glanced towards the light of the nearby town. He didn't really know much about this area, but guessed it might be Hamilton or maybe Motherwell, but it was far enough away from where…

The sound of an engine startled him and he hurried towards the car. Fumbling in his trouser pocket for the keys he fetched them out, but in his haste dropped them as the noise of the engine grew louder.

Though it was dark, he guessed the vehicle was now only about a minute away.

"Shit!" he exclaimed, trying to decide if he should hide in the darkness or try to find the keys then get in the car and drive away.

Almost in panic, he dumped his coat and jacket onto the boot lid then laid the shovel on the ground as he dropped to his knees and scrambled in the darkness with his fingers to find the keys.

Hands shaking, he grabbed the keys and standing, opened the boot of the Morris Ital, grabbed his coat and jacket and the shovel and threw them inside before slamming the boot down.

He could feel the stream of sweat making its way down his spine as he rushed round to the driver's door and got inside.

In the rear view mirror, he could see headlights approaching and hands still shaking, searched through the bunch of keys before finding the ignition key and jamming it in the lock, started the engine.

The radio burst loudly into life, startling him and halfway through that month's number one hit, Rick Astley belting out *'Hold Me in Your Arms.'*

He glanced again into the rear view mirror, but to his surprise and relief the headlights had vanished, presumably to turn off into one of the several lanes or farm entrances that he had passed on his way here.

Taking a deep breath, he sat back in the seat and rubbed a weary hand across his brow.

How the *fuck* had he got himself into this mess?

He deeply sighed.

No matter how he tried to come to terms with it, he was involved right up to his stupid bloody neck.

He sat for several minutes to regain his composure then risking switching on the interior light, checked his face in the rear view mirror.

His reflection showed a man whose pallor was pale and a thin film of sweat glistening on his forehead, nose and cheeks.

Taking his handkerchief from his pocket, he wiped at his face and glancing at the dashboard clock, reckoned he would be home by just after 5am.

In time to grab some sleep and get ready for the job.

CHAPTER ONE – Present Day

He sat back in his desk chair and arched his back to relieve the ache, then decided that a short walk around the grounds would probably make him feel a bit better.

Getting stiffly to his feet, he glanced with dismay at the personnel files in the overloaded in-tray and wondered how long it would take him to get through the bloody pile.

"Ah, well," he murmured, "maybe if I'm lucky some bugger will break in to my office and set fire to it."

Opening his office door, he smiled at his frosty faced elderly secretary and said, "Just taking a couple of minutes for a breather, Miss Forsyth. Be back in ten," then before she could argue quickly strode towards the door that took him to the corridor outside.

Not that she frightened him, but Charlie Miller had faced hardened criminals who would baulk at taking on the sixty-something Jean Forsyth, reckoned by some of his staff to have been ignobly dismissed from the teaching profession because of her bullying; not the pupils though, but the staff.

He recalled his first day as Detective Superintendent in charge of CID Training at the Scottish Police College located in the stunning nineteenth century Tulliallan Castle in Kincardine-on-Forth.

Introducing himself to Miss Forsyth, her hands politely folded in front of her, she sharply told him, "I attend to your correspondence, organize your working diary, vet all phone calls, set appointments for your meetings, book your flights, vehicles and accommodation for your necessary trips and ensure that all classified documents you are required to deal with are returned to the originating office or shredded."

Glowering at him, she added, "I do *not* make tea or lie for you when you wish to be indisposed."

Taken aback, he had stupidly replied, "So I suppose a cuppa is out of the question, then?" which earned him a sniff and glare before she returned to her desk.

Now eight months later, the fractious relationship with Miss Forsyth was driving him mad, though if he were honest with himself, it was more the job that the grumpy woman.

Walking round the grounds in the July sunshine, he smiled or nodded to the uniformed trainee constables he encountered, some confidently acknowledging him while the younger officers shyly returned his smile.

The detectives attending their various course, he was aware, were all currently in the classrooms and mindful that in forty minutes he was to deliver a welcome speech to the new intake, he decided he'd time for a phone call.

Fetching his mobile from his pocket, he dialled the number for his wife Sadie, a uniformed sergeant at Baird Street office in the city, and smiled when she answered.

"Hi, love, what you up to?"

"Oh, just finished putting a washing out then when mum arrives, I'll get myself ready for the late shift. You?"

He grinned before replying, "Dug a tunnel to escape the grey headed dragon and I'm taking a relaxing walk round the grounds before I've a meet and greet with a new class of detective officers at two. Any likelihood you'll get away early tonight?"

"Doubt it. We've a new initiative on this week. Our lords and masters have decided that the gangs hanging around at night and fighting in the Sighthill Park is not on, so I'm taking a couple of van load of overtime cops there to show a presence, as they say."

"Well, be careful," he said, knowing that his caution would fall on deaf ears because one thing his wife wasn't and that was a retiring butterfly. If there was trouble of any sort, Sadie usually found herself embroiled in the sharp end of it somewhere.

"Course I will," she coyly replied.

"How are the kids?"

"Fine, though Geraldine's complaining that her dad promised her new training shoes when I already said no. So, Miller, did you?"

"Ah," he grimaced, "I *might* have mentioned something about…"

"Charlie!" he could hear the annoyance in her voice. "I thought we had discussed this? We're supposed to be on the same page with her."

"I know, I know, I'm sorry," he drew a deep breath then hurriedly added, "Look, there's somebody waving to me, I'd better go. Love you," and ended the call with a sigh of relief, recalling the fly wee bugger had promised *not* to tell her mum.

Returning the phone to his pocket, he glanced at his wristwatch and decided there was time for a coffee at the canteen before his introductory speech to the new intake.

****

The two labourers stood in the field leaning on their shovels, sweating in the the heat while they watched the JCB operator use the backhoe of his machine to excavate the trench where the architects plans indicated the main sewage pipe was to be laid for the four houses planned for construction at that part of the site.

Waving his hands criss-cross to attract his attention, the elderly Irishman cheerily called out to the operator, "Time for a fag."

Grinning, the operator waved his hand in agreement and switching off the engine, climbed down from his cab to join the labourers. Enjoying their smoke, the three men stood discussing Celtic's chances in Europe when the younger of the labourers glanced into the excavated trench and eyes narrowing, held up a hand to quieten the other two.

"What the hell's that?" he nodded down into the trench.

The three men bent to peer into the last of the earth dug away and saw what looked like a greyish coloured sheet, torn away from the ground by the sharp teeth of the JCB's bucket.

Glancing at the two men, the elderly Irishman stepped warily into the trench and said to his younger companion, "Hand me the shovel, Frankie."

Carefully, he used the tip of the shovel to prise the earth away from around the sheet and saw that what was uncovered was only part of the sheet, that the remainder was still hidden in the ground and not yet unearthed.

Laying the shovel down onto the lip of the trench, the Irishman licked nervously at his lips and with a brief glance up at the two men, reached with shaking hands towards the sheet.

Crumbling soil fell away as he attempted to prise the sheet from the solid ground, but at last he managed to pull some of the sheet free. With a choked cry, he fell backwards, hurriedly making the Sign of the Cross for when the sheet opened, the Irishman saw what looked like the top of a head; a head with dark hair.

****

The Police Scotland control room located in Motherwell was first to receive the news of what appeared to be the discovery of a body buried in a field by the side of the B803 road that run between Glenmavis to Slamannan.

"And where exactly *is* this location?" the police operator asked.

His mobile in his hand, Jimmy Holden, the site manager now stood with the two labourers and the machine operator, replied, "It's the new building development on the Raebog Road. We're about 300 hundred metres west of the Stirling Road roundabout. Can you get somebody out here quickly? My guy's are held up until this is dealt with and times money you know," he added, ignoring the surprised expressions of the three men stood with him.

Flummoxed, the police operator rolled her eyes, shook her head and ground her teeth before replying, "As soon as I can, *sir*, I'll have someone with you."

Ending the call, Holden turned to the JCB operator and waving an arm to his left, said, "Likely the cops will want to cordon off this area, Wally, but there's nothing to say you can't continue to excavate the trench a bit further on, say ten metres, eh?"

The man called Wally exhaled and shrugging, replied, "You're the boss, Mister Holden," before returning to his machine.

In the police control room, the irate operator typed the circumstances of Holden's call onto her incident log and calling over her supervisor, made him aware.

****

The two uniformed patrol officers who attended Jimmy Holden's phone call arrived within fifteen minutes to discover Holden seated at his desk with an array of technical drawing and his white safety helmet in front on him and emblazoned with the legend, 'J Holden' written in black felt tip pen.

In his late twenties wearing a white shirt and dark tie, green anorak over blue jeans and Hunter wellies on his feet, Holden was on his mobile to his company manager and in the middle of explaining that, "There might be a wee hold-up till the cops' sort this out."

Seeing the officers enter the caravan and with the phone stuck to his ear, Holden offhandedly flicked a hand to indicate they take a seat, but wasn't prepared for what happened next.

Almost dragging Holden's mobile from his ear, the senior constable of the two, through gritted teeth, informed the site manager that if he didn't get his arse in gear and take them to where this supposed body was he might find himself being charged with either wasting the time of the police or perverting the course of justice in what could turn out to be a serious crime.

Though he was of course bluffing, the ashen faced Holden didn't know this and grabbed his helmet. Followed by the two cops, he sulkily stomped off with his hands deeply thrust into his anorak pockets to where the trench was being dug.

As they stumbled through the large building site across the broken ground and saw the JCB being activated, the older cop's eyes narrowed and grabbing Holden's arm to halt him, asked, "Are they guys still working at the site where you found the body?"

"Aye, time's money," Holden repeated once more before huffily adding, "They're a good ten metres away from where the body is though."

"For God's sake," the older cop furiously pointed to the JCB and turning to his younger colleague, said, "Quickly, hen. Go and tell that bugger to stop right now and you, ya fucking idiot!" he snarled at Holden, "You've called to say you've discovered a buried body and you're digging a trench right beside it? Are you stupid or what!"

The young policewoman raced across the ground, shouting and her arms flailing while she attempted to attract the attention of the JCB operator, but it was the elderly Irishman who seeing her approaching, made the cutting noise across his throat to stop the operator from any further excavation.

"Right, show me this body," the cop snarled at Holden before adding, "and God help you if you've interfered with a crime scene, pal, because I'm telling you; the CID will *not* be best pleased."

Holden's face paled and lips tightly closed wordlessly led the cop to the trench where he pointed down at the partially excavated sheet, turned back enough for the officer to see that what seemed to be the top of a head with dark hair exposed.

With a sigh, the officer pushed his cap to the back of his head then beckoning his young colleague towards him, reached for his Airwave radio and knew that it was going to be a very, very long day.

****

Hearing her mother's car draw up in the driveway, Sadie Miller kissed her daughters Geraldine and Ella cheerio before grabbing her handbag and meeting her mum at the front door with, "Sorry I'm rushing, mum, but I need to be in before any of my guys. I've a turn on tonight."

Hurrying towards her Honda Jazz, she called back over her shoulder, "When Charlie gets in, tell him there's a shepherd's pie in the fridge, but the greedy bugger's to leave some for me for when I get home."

"Oh, and hello to you too, dear," her mum Carol shook her head and smiled as she waved at the departing car, then turning to the two wee giggling girls, loudly clapped her hands together then bending down, grinned and in a conspiratorial voice said, "Now, who's for a juice and some of grandma's home chocolate cake?"

****

The police controller at Coatbridge police station acknowledged the cops radio message that concluded by requesting the attendance of the CID, Scene of Crime and grinned at the "…and every Tom, Dick and Harry too. Over."

Calling the duty officer to his desk, the constable told him, "You might want to listen in to this, sir," then phoned the Detective Chief Inspector's room upstairs to relay the message that a body had been found.

Seated at her desk wading her way through a pile of reports, DCI Lorna Paterson picked up the handset and rubbing at her forehead with the heel of her hand, snapped, "Yes!"

"Ma'am, it's Colin down in the control room. That's a report there's a body been discovered by workers in a shallow grave on a building site in a field off Raebog Road."

"What? Where? Rae where?"

"Raebog Road, Ma'am," the controller supressed his laugh for it was unkindly rumoured the gangly Paterson could not find her own arse unless someone gave her the nod where to look. "It's a B class road that runs between Glenmavis and the Stirling Road. You know, where the roundabout is?"

"Not a clue," she sighed, "but give me the details anyway," then almost as an afterthought, asked, "Is that part of our area?"

"It is, Ma'am," he turned and grinned at the Inspector, who bit at his lip and smiled as the controller continued, "Two cops are standing by the location. All I know is that when the workers were digging up the field, they found a grave of some sorts."

"Right," she searched among the files for her pen and pulling a notepad towards her, took a deep breath and said, "Details, now please."
****

"And so, ladies and gentlemen," Charlie Miller stared around the room at the two dozen trainee detectives, "in conclusion, I welcome you to your six weeks training course and would urge you to consider that if you *really* want to work long hours outside the normal shift pattern, forego your regular holiday breaks, regularly have rest days cancelled, incur the wrath of your wife, girlfriend, husband, boyfriend or partner because some poor sod has gone and got himself or herself murdered and you're missing a big event the same evening because you're out chasing a killer, miss your kids birthday, christening or school leaving parties, be accused in court of fitting up your prisoners, work dozens of hours in lieu of payment that you'll *never* have time to take off," he grinned cheerfully. Extending his hands, he added, "Then, ladies and gentlemen, welcome to the CID."

He was about to turn away towards the door, but stopped and turning back, added, "Oh, and by the way, that *is* assuming you get your head down and pass the course."

Following him to the corridor outside, his deputy, DI Mark Bennett, grinned and said, "Well done, Charlie. Scare the shite out of them the first day."

"Aye," Charlie breezily replied as they walked together towards his office, "I've always had this knack of knowing how to motivate people."

"Have you read through their files," Bennett cocked a thumb over his shoulder backwards towards the closed door of the class room.

"I've skimmed through most of them," Charlie nodded. "The ones I read seem to have a reasonable bit of experience either in plain clothes or attachments to local drug squads, that kind of thing. One though struck me as a bit peculiar," his brow furrowed before continuing, "Did you see woman sitting in the second row with the fair hair?"

"Aye, with the twinset and pearls and the tweed skirt and sensible shoes? She's dressed like she's somebody's granny. She must be what, nearly forty, but saying that," he smirked with a twinkle in his eye, "she's a bit of a looker and a fit looking bird for her age."

"Her file says her name's Alison Baxter and she's forty-eight."

"Forty-eight? Your kidding me! I wouldn't have put her at that age," his face reflected his surprise before he asked, "What the hell's she doing on a DC's course? What service has she got?"

They reached Charlie's office and making their way past Miss Forsyth to his inner office, he indicated Bennett come in before settling himself behind his desk and reaching for a file.

Nodding to the side table with the electric kettle and the mugs and coffee, he said, "Pour us both a brew while I read you details from her file."

While Bennett attended to the coffee, Charlie pulled a file from a pile on his desk then opening it, began to read, "According to this she joined the police, aged forty-three, she's divorced and no kids. Listen to this, though," his eyes narrowed as he peered at the file.

"It's a recommendation about her from her Divisional Commander at Edinburgh."

He cleared his throat and continuing reading aloud, "Constable Baxter has proven herself to be an astute and observant officer who in my opinion should be considered for CID selection. I understand that while she is of mature years," he grinned and said, "and she's not kidding."

He read, "Constable Baxter has impressed her supervisory officers with her ability to assess and evaluate the inquiries she has been delegated, very many to a successful conclusion.

Again, conscious of her mature years," he smiled at Baxter and added, "which is another way of saying she's getting past it, Constable Baxter has maintained a heathy fitness regime and I am of the opinion she will be an asset to any CID unit she is assigned."

"So, she's got a female pal who is a Divisional Commander, Charlie. Does that mean we're supposed to roll over and pass her as a DC, even if she does get through the course? I mean, there's a lot of young, sharp cops out there would give their eye teeth for a crack at joining the CID. Wouldn't a woman of her age not be content with some desk job?"

"Careful what you say out loud or you'll sound like an ageist git," Charlie smiled as he accepted the mug of coffee and watched Bennett sit down on the couch. "Talk like that will get you the rubber heels knocking on your door. We're supposed to be an equal opportunities employer these days and *that* means we have to be age, race, religion and gender accepting and most importantly, aware."

He sipped at the steaming mug of coffee and licking his lips, said, "Frankly, Mark, I don't care what age she is. If she can do the job…" he stopped and stared thoughtfully at Bennett. "You don't really care either, do you?"

The detective, whose face was so weathered it had been rudely said that a box of Pollyfilla wouldn't have made any impression, grinned and toasting Charlie with his own mug, replied, "Not really. With less than a year to go, it's really none of my business how the polis conducts its affairs these days. My service has taught me to be reasonably broadminded and not take people at face value. That said, I'll happily while my time away here and then take my missus and my pension to a sunnier climate. Besides," he shrugged, "maybe at her age Baxter *is* bringing something to the job; certainly experience of life I'd say," he smiled. "And that can't be a bad thing, can it? So, what did she do before she joined up?"

Charlie leaned forward and turning some pages forward, bent his head to read aloud and said, "Says here that prior to joining the police, Constable Baxter worked as a..." he stopped and stared at Bennett, his eyes narrowing as he finished, "a university professor who taught criminology, Forensic psychology and profiling."

CHAPTER TWO

The circus comprising of Coatbridge detectives, uniformed officers to protect and seal the locus, Scene of Crime personnel, the duty Procurator Fiscal Depute and most importantly, the local casualty surgeon, all assembled in the field at Raebog Road some thirty metres from the grave site under the command of DCI Lorna Paterson who glancing down at her mud caked designer shoes, regretted her decision not to bring her wellies.

While the uniformed officers were dispersed by their sergeant to locations in the field, the small group watched as the SOC, ably assisted by two detectives, erected a large white tent over the top of the trench where the grave was located.

"There's really no need for me to be here at this time, is there Miss Paterson?" pleaded the ruddy faced PF Depute who wearing her best court suit and whose buttocks were tightly clenched because she *really* needed to go to the toilet, was horrified at the thought of having to use one of the workers on-site portaloos.

"No, perhaps not," a distracted Paterson nodded and that was all the reply the PF Depute needed, for without another word, she was off without a backward glance.

"What about me?" asked the elderly casualty surgeon who bit down on his already well chewed pipe. "I see no reason to be here to pronounce life extinct on what is very apparently a dead body being exhumed from a grave."

"Yes," Paterson rolled her eyes and sighed. "If I need you I'll call," then almost absentmindedly added, "Thank you for coming out anyway, doctor."

Watching him stumble off through the building site, Paterson was distracted when her Billy McKnight, her Detective Inspector, a fair haired stocky man who at five feet eight was a good four inches shorter than his boss, said, "Ma'am? The SOC supervisor Jean Galbraith would like a word."

Making her way with McKnight to the edge of the trench, they entered the white tent where they saw Galbraith and her colleague stood in the trench, both wearing white SOC boiler suits and face masks while they examined the partially exposed sheet and head of the corpse.

"Should we be wearing white suits, do you think, Jean?" Paterson asked.

"Ah, Ma'am, I don't think it's worth the bother at the minute," Galbraith glanced at the partially uncovered gravesite. She pulled down her mask and took a gulp of air. "Bloody hot in these things," she shook her head. "Right, we're about to try and remove more of the soil from around about the body. It might take some time because," she pointed with a trowel held in her hand, "as you can see the soil is quite dense and that suggests to me it's compacted through several years. Maybe even decades," she shrugged. "Are you happy we proceed?"

"Wait a minute, Jean," Paterson's eyes narrowed. "Let me be clear here. Are you of the opinion the body was not recently buried here? That it might have been buried some time ago? Years perhaps?"

"Oh aye, definitely," Galbraith nodded. "Like I said if it was recent, the earth wouldn't have been so compacted, that's bound to have taken some time, though of course I'm not an expert. What *could* be worth considering is bringing in a Forensic anthropologist who might be able to have a better idea about how long this body's been here and if I might be so bold, you might wish to do that before we exhume the body. Let the anthropologist see the body in situ, as it where."

"Do we have such a person on call? To be honest, Jean," Paterson pursed her lips and shook her head, "I've never had the opportunity to call upon such an individual before."

"Oh aye," Galbraith turned to her colleague and asked, "What was the name of that woman we used when the wee girl's body was found in the golf course in that sand thing, the bunker, down in Troon?"

"Eh," the SOCO narrowed his eyes and slowly exhaled as he thought, then brightly replied, "Mason. Doctor Julia Mason. She works out of Dundee University I think, but the Forensic lab at Gartcosh should have her contact details."

"Oh, I've *heard* of her. So," Paterson glanced at McKnight before turning towards Galbraith, "you're suggesting we might lose valuable evidence if we proceed with the exhumation at this time?"

"My opinion, Ma'am, is better safe than sorry and yes, I believe it would be better to wait till Doctor Mason views this body before we proceed with taking it out of the dirt."

Paterson nodded and replied, "Decision made then. We lose nothing but some time if we defer the exhumation for now. Billy," she turned to McKnight, "contact Gartcosh and make arrangements for Doctor Mason to attend here as soon as possible. In the meantime," she turned back to Galbraith, "thank you and your team for your efforts, Jean. I'll ensure the locus is protected till such times we get Mason here. Can you make you and your team available when Mason turns up?"

"Of course Ma'am, However, there is one thing we can proceed with at the minute," Galbraith quickly said before Paterson left.

"Yes?"

Galbraith, wearing her blue coloured nitrile Forensic gloves, turned back the sheet to further expose the dark hair and said, "With your permission, we can get a starter for ten if I you're happy for me to snip a lock of the hair and submit it to the Forensic lab. That way they can run it through their DNA database just in case the body's DNA is already recorded there."

Paterson smiled and nodding, replied, "Good thinking, Jean. Go ahead and get it done."

She watched while Galbraith's colleague handed her a pair of stainless steel scissors from a small toolbox and when the lock of hair was carefully cut, saw it placed into a paper SOC evidence bag that Galbraith handed to McKnight.

"Billy," Paterson said, "have one of the guys run that directly to Gartcosh and ask them to treat it as a matter of urgency for identification purpose."

"No bother and there's one other thing, boss," McKnight said. "The site manager is kicking off and wants a discussion with you because he's moaning he can't continue with his trench digging. How do you want me to deal with him?"

"There's nothing to discuss," she shook her head. "This field is a crime scene and for all we know, there might be other bodies buried here so all work halts right now."

"Right," he grinned with a nod. "I'll be happy to let the cheeky bastard know."

****

Martin Cairney, the six feet four inch tall former rugby playing Chief Constable of Police Scotland, was at his desk in the temporary Headquarters at Dalmarnock police office, the twenty-four million pound office that replaced the former Headquarters at Pitt Street in Glasgow city centre, when his secretary knocked on the door and said, "That's Chief Inspector Downes asking if you're free for a few minutes, sir."

"Oh, does she wish me to phone her?"

"No, sir. Missus Downes is here in my office," the secretary smiled.

"Ask her to come in please, Jeannette."

Harriet Downes, known to most of her colleagues as 'Harry' and the officer in charge of the Police Scotland Media Department, entered and closing the door behind her, said, "Sorry for barging in, sir, but we've just had a call from a Lanarkshire newspaper about an ongoing incident that I thought you should be made aware of."

Indicating that she be seated in the chair opposite his desk, Cairney sat back in his swivel chair and arching his fingers in front of his nose, replied, "Go on."

Flipping through the pages of her notebook, Downes began, "Well, after I received the query from the paper, I contacted the local divisions and learned that the Coatbridge CID have been tasked to the discovery of a body buried in a field out somewhere between Glenmavis and Slamannan."

He wryly smiled and said, "I hate to admit it, Missus Downes, but I'm not totally familiar with the outer, darkest depths of Lanarkshire, though I am curious as to why you're bringing this to me. Surely if the local CID are in charge they can deal with this matter?"

"I realise that, sir, but the CID clerk at Coatbridge, albeit he does not have the full facts, was able to tell me that it seems this body has been in the ground for a number of years."

"A field you say. Tell me, how did the body come to be

discovered?"

"A building company are in the middle of developing the land for a housing estate and that is also causing problems because the DCI in charge, Lorna Paterson, has suspended all construction till the field has been properly surveyed lest there are more bodies."

"Is there anything to suggest there *might* be more bodies?"

"Not that I'm aware of, no."

"Hmm. That aside, I believe then that DCI Paterson is quite correctly treating the whole field as a crime scene?"

"So it would appear, sir."

"And what is your issue or rather, what is the problem?"

"The construction company have also contacted the newspaper," she grimaced and added, "taking advantage of the free publicity, likely, and informed the paper that they are considering suing Police Scotland for the time that we have suspended their operations. That and the newspaper are asking if we have any idea who the victim might be."

"Well," he smiled, "I do believe the Justice Secretary and his colleagues in Government would have something to say if we were to give in to pressure from a civilian company when there is a serious crime to investigate, so let's not worry too much about that. Now, do we know who the victim is?"

"Again, sir, not that I'm aware of though I have learned that DCI Paterson cannot move forward in her investigation till the locus has been examined by a Forensic anthropologist and that's what the paper also want to know; if Doctor Mason will be involved in the inquiry."

"Ah, I presume we're talking here about Doctor Julia Mason."

"So it seems, sir."

Cairney recalled the last time Mason was involved in assisting the police in a historical murder investigation that commenced when in nineteen sixty, a twelve-years old girl was abducted, raped and strangled in the seaside town of Troon. The murderer had buried his victim in a sand bunker of one of the prestigious golf courses for which the town is famous and after the discovery of the body ten years previously, Mason's skill as an anthropologist was instrumental in both identifying the child and providing evidence that led to the arrest of the now elderly man responsible. However, her subsequent interview with a National Sunday newspaper prior to the trial disclosed specialist knowledge of the crime that benefited the defence and almost lost the Crown their case against the accused.

"I wonder," he mused, "if there is there anyone else DCI Paterson might use in her investigation?"

"I'm sure there are many equally qualified individuals, sir," Downes sighed, "but before coming to see you I checked with the Forensic lab at Gartcosh to inquire if they knew of any such individuals only to learn that Doctor Mason is retained on contract to Police Scotland for such inquiries."

"What!" he thundered. "How the devil did that come about?"

"No idea, sir," she shrugged, "other than to tell you she was retained by the former Strathclyde Police as well as a number of sister Forces and now that we've united into our current Force, we've sort of inherited her retention, as it were."

"Well," he sighed, "I suppose we'd better make use of the bloody woman if we're paying her a retainer."

He took a deep breath and in dismissal, reached for his phone and said, "Thank you, Missus Downes. Please keep me apprised of any further interest in the media."

****

Finished for the day, Charlie Miller ensured he checked his schedule for tomorrow before switching off his desktop computer and grabbing his coat.

On the way past his secretary, he said, "Good evening, Miss Forsyth," and received the usual silent nod.

Walking into the corridor outside, his thoughts were his own and anything but complimentary to Jean Forsyth. Not for the first time he wondered what had caused the woman to be such a sour faced bugger.

Making his way to the car park outside and his dedicated bay, his eyes narrowed as he approached his old Volvo, for never in a thousand years and particularly after his despair that drove him to near-alcoholism, would he have imagined himself re-married with two children.

Albeit Geraldine was Sadie's daughter before they met, he loved the girl as if she were his own and now she had a sister, little Ella.

He glanced down at the small, white painted wooden stick planted in the ground at his parking bay with his name on it; Detective Superintendent C Miller, and slowly grinned. At one time when serving with Stewart Street CID in Glasgow city centre, he had thought his career was finished and he'd be lucky to hang on to his job, let alone his rank as Detective Sergeant.

Getting into the drivers seat he sat for a moment, savouring his life and wondering what he had done right to deserve such happiness. Even the attempt on his life that had left him partially crippled in his left arm wasn't enough to dissuade him that his life had taken an irrevocable turn for the better when he met Sadie.

Now he had just a few years left to serve and with luck would see his time out in his current job, boring though it might be.

Aye, he nodded to the rear view mirror, there wasn't much wrong with his life these days and starting the engine, smoothly drove away from his bay.

****

DCI Lorna Paterson had returned to her office and stepping out of her shoes, was staring at them in disgust when her partially ajar door was knocked and opened to admit DI Billy McKnight.

He grinned at her face as examining her shoes, she began to use a dinner knife to scrape the worst of the mud off into her waste bin then said, "I don't know what you're grinning at. Have you *any* idea how much these cost me?"

"You forget, boss, I'm married to a shopaholic *and* I've two teenage daughters."

"Aye, right enough," she smiled in surrender before asking, "What's the word from the Dundee office? Have they contacted this woman Mason yet?"

He drew up a chair and sitting down, replied, "As you know I tried phoning, but only got an answer machine, so I asked the local CID to get someone to go round to the Uni there and trace Mason and if they do get a hold of her, get her to phone me. I haven't heard anything back yet."

"What about the locus? Any problems having the uniform stand by it overnight?"

"The usual mumps and groans from the shift Inspector," he grinned, "but when I suggested if he's got an issue he speak with the Divisional Commander, he backed off."

"Okay, so we're up to speed. Now," she gave up her scraping and laying the shoes on the floor, walked barefooted to sit behind her desk, "it all hinges on this Doctor Mason arriving tomorrow and assisting us to retrieve the body from the ground. I want us to be prepared, Billy, so before you head off for the night, get the incident room set up and see what resources we can spare as an inquiry team. For the minute, it looks like it *might* be a cold case, so keep the team to the minimum for now. I don't want us to leave ourselves short for the day to day inquiries and the guys are already overloaded with work."

"Have you spoken with Miss Mulgrew, yet?"

"No, I wanted to know if we had Mason on board first," she sighed, "but I can't leave it any longer. The boss will not be a happy chappy if I'm remise in informing her about a prospective murder inquiry," she grinned, before adding, "That's of course it if *is* a murder. Who knows, maybe it's a Covenanters body. Those buggers have been turning up in graves all over Lanarkshire since the seventeenth century."

"Covenanters?"

"My God, Billy McKnight," she shook her head. "Do you not know your Scottish history? The Covenanters fought a religious war against oppression and got themselves well and truly skelpt by the Kings army. To even be associated with them was treason and so when a lot of them died from their wounds, their families buried them in secret to avoid persecution from the Crown. Even today, for instance, if you walk the field where the Battle of Bothwell was fought you can still pick up lead musket balls."

"Boss," he grinned at her, "every day with you is a school day, but I *really* think you should get yourself a life. However, the one thing that shoots that theory down is that Jean Galbraith is of the opinion the sheet the body's head appears to be wrapped in what seems to be a nylon material." He grinned. "I'm betting they didn't have nylon sheets in the seventeenth century, eh?"

"Cheeky bastard," she returned his grin.

They both turned at the door being knocked and when Paterson called out, "Come in," the CID clerk poked his head around the door and said, "Ma'am, that's a Doctor Mason on the line for DI McKnight. Shall I transfer the call through?"

"Please do," she replied and a moment later, she lifted her phone and pressing the loudspeaker button, said, "Good afternoon, Doctor Mason. I'm DCI Lorna Paterson. It's myself that's asked you to contact us."

"Ah, yes. How may I help you, DCI Paterson?"

In a short, summarised briefing, Paterson explained about the discovery of the body and the suggestion by the Scene of Crime supervisor that before there was to be any further disturbance of the body, Mason be permitted to view or even assist in the exhumation.

"Do you have any information about the body, DCI Paterson?"

"None at all," she began, then stopped and correcting herself, said, "That's not quite true. When the body was initially exposed it by the labourers who discovered it, it was found head first, if you follow me and revealed the body to be dark haired. I've had a sample of the hair seized and conveyed to our Forensic laboratory for DNA profiling in the event the victim is listed on our DNA database."

"And if indeed you have the victim identified, DCI Paterson, what further use to your investigation would I be?"

Paterson didn't miss the brittle inference that she might be wasting Mason's time and casting an irate glance at McKnight, replied, "Let's just say that I'm covering all my options, Doctor Mason, and as you are retained by Police Scotland I believe it is in the best interest of my inquiry to use your expertise in these matters. That and if there is anything of evidential value in the grave, you might be the very person to expose it."

McKnight choked back a laugh as Mason replied, "Yes, well of course, I understand that. Now, these exhumations sometimes carry over into days so if I were to arrive tomorrow, can I assume you will have arranged overnight accommodation for me?"

"That will be arranged if required, Doctor Mason."

"Good, then it only remains for me to request the post code for your police office to enter into my SatNav and I shall be with you sometime early tomorrow morning."

That provided, Paterson ended the call and staring narrow eyed at McKnight, said, "What were you guffawing about?"

"Use your expertise? You might be the very person to expose it? Well, a wee bit of grovelling doesn't go amiss now and then, eh boss?"

"Listen, moron, if she gets the job done, I'll grovel all she wants. Now, before we knock off for the evening, I've my call to make to Miss Mulgrew and you've the incident room and team to set up, so anything I've missed?"

He slowly shook his head and replied, "I believe you've got it all covered. One final thing though. The hair sample I've sent through to Gartcosh. Apparently the scientists knocked off early for the evening to attend a Forensics lecture in Glasgow. The receiving clerk told our man that unless it's an emergency, there isn't a budget to call out a scientist out of hours so it will be tomorrow before the sample is examined."

"No drama," she shook her head. "There's not much we can do this evening anyway, so excuse me and I'll get on with my call."

Walking towards the door he stopped and grinned when she asked, "Do you think I can claim expenses for getting these shoes cleaned?"

****

The drive from Tulliallan Castle to his home in Westbourne Drive, Bearsden usually took Charlie about an hour, dependent upon traffic conditions. However, that evening he arrived home in just over fifty minutes and turning into the driveway saw his mother-in-law holding both girl's hands and just about to open the front door.

"Had them out for a wee walk around the garden," she smiled as Charlie swept the toddler Ella into his arms and bending down, offered his cheek for seven years old Geraldine to kiss.

Pushing the door open with his knee, Charlie asked, "Are you stopping for some dinner?"

"No, if it's okay with you, I'll head off early," she replied as she reached for her jacket from the coat stand in the hallway. "I've a wee social on at the club tonight. The girls are fed and Sadie says to tell you there's a shepherd's pie in the fridge and you're in big trouble if you eat it all. She'll have some when she gets in."

She turned to the two small girls and said, "Right then, you pair of scallywags, give your old granny a kiss before I go," and bending down towards the children, received their sloppy kisses. Standing upright, she gave Charlie a peck on the cheek too.

They watched as she drove off then seating Ella in her high chair in the kitchen, Charlie turned on the cartoons in the front room television for Geraldine before preparing his evening meal.

He had just switched on the oven when his mobile phone rang and glancing at the screen, smiled when he saw the caller was Sadie.

"Hello, sweetheart, that's me not long in. Carol's just left and I'm about to eat a whole shepherd's pie to myself," he grinned.

"You'd better not!"

"Why? What do you mean?"

"Just try that, Miller, and you'll wake up tomorrow morning with no balls," she hissed, then asked, "Have you seen tonight's STV news headlines?"

"No, what's up?" he made a face that caused Ella to break into a fit of giggles.

"A body's been dug up somewhere in Lanarkshire."

"Did it say who it is?"

"No, no information other than police are investigating."

"Well," he sighed and fetched the pie from the fridge, "it won't affect me any more. I'm a clerk now, remember?"

"A well paid, experienced clerk," she laughed.

"Listen, not to worry you or anything," he soberly asked, "but is Carol feeling okay? I thought when I got home she looked a little drawn, a bit peaky."

"She hasn't said anything. Probably just worn out by the kids. That and she always insists on walking Ella in the pram to collect jellybean from school when I keep telling her to take her car."

"Yeah," he sighed. "Maybe that's it," then asked, "How about you? Out in the ground with your team yet?"

"No, it's too early for the bampots to be throwing bricks at each other. We'll wait till it gets a bit darker then head out."

"So, you're not certain if you'll get a flyer tonight?"

"I told you earlier today," she scoffed, "I'll likely be here till the early hours to ensure the parks quiet."

"Well, I'll keep your side of the bed warm for you."

"You do that. Right, time to go. Love you," and she was gone.

"Daddy," he turned to see Geraldine stood in the doorway, one hand behind her back and the forefinger of her other hand coyly rubbing at her bottom lip. "About those training shoes you promised me..."

****

He rewound the news item and with disbelief, watched it again then a third time.

It couldn't possibly be, not after all these years.

He had been so careful and after all, it was the middle of bloody nowhere!

How the *hell* could they have found it?

He paused the television and arching his back, deeply sighed.

He needn't worry, he told himself for there was nothing to connect him to it; nothing at all.

Nothing.

His eyes narrowed.

He hadn't thought about it for a very long time, what he had done. Staring at the screen, he peered at the field behind the reporter, seeing the white tent in the distance.

But there was nothing he recognised and after all, it was so many years ago and it had been dark, the middle of the bloody night.

No, he was safe, of that he was certain and with trembling hands, reached for the remote control and switched off the television.

CHAPTER THREE

Charlie awakened to the noise of Ella singing happily in her room and turned slowly to find Sadie lying facing him, her lips slightly parted as she quietly inhaled and exhaled and her eyes fluttering in REM sleep.

As slowly as he dared, he slipped from the bed and with his feet on the floor, was reaching for his dressing gown when behind him, she said, "Yeah, go on. Do what all the men do; leave the money on the bedside table," then softly sniggered.

He grinned and turning back towards her threw his arm around her to draw her close, his lips reaching for hers until she screwed her face and said, "You won't want to kiss me, I've got morning breath."

He ignored her and planted a smacker on her lips, then smiling asked, "What time did you get in?"

"It was after two," she wearily replied. "Bloody nonsense kicked off just after ten, last night and by the time we'd sorted the wheat from the chaff and processed the half dozen prisoners..." she sighed and yawned, "I was going to wake you, but to be honest, I was too tired."

His hand slowly moved to cup her breast and now wide awake, she coyly smiled and was about to slip her nightie down when Ella loudly called, "Mummy! Daddy!"

Disappointed, they grinned together and rising from the bed, he said, "Stay where you are. I'll fetch you a coffee."

When he left the room, Sadie curled up in the warmth of the bed and feeling the warmth of his hand that had lain on her breast, regretted not waking her husband when she'd arrived home.

Collecting Ella from her room, Charlie carried the little girl downstairs to the kitchen where after plonking her down into her highchair, switched on the portable television and the electric kettle. While the kettle boiled, her poured Ela's cereal into her bowl and spooned coffee into two mugs.

"Morning, daddy."

He turned to find a sleepy-eyed Geraldine standing at the kitchen door and with a grin, swept her up into her arms before setting her squealing delightedly down into the kitchen chair.

Pouring cereal into a bowl, he was placing it down before her when the BBC seven o'clock news commenced.

In the act of pouring boiling water into the two mugs, his attention was distracted by the second news item, a correspondent wearing a heavy anorak and wellingtons who reported from a side road in Lanarkshire that police were still actively engaged in removing what was presumed to be a body from a grave in a field. As he watched, the camera zoomed in and focused on a white SOC tent in the distance where a uniformed officer wearing a Hi-Vis fluorescent jacket was slapping her arms about herself in an effort to keep warm while she stood guard.

"Poor sod," he muttered, sympathising with the unknown officer's night-time duty stood in a field in the middle of nowhere.

"What's a sod, daddy?" Geraldine asked him.

"Eh, ah," he grimaced, "it's a bit of grass cut from the ground," he hastily replied.

"Yeah," she narrowed her eyes and stared thoughtfully, recognising with the wiles of a seven-year old that she was being fobbed off.

Rolling his eyes, he turned away and telling Geraldine to keep her eye on Ella, hurried upstairs with Sadie's coffee.

"Thanks, sweetheart," she sat up in bed to accept the mug. "The girls downstairs?"

"Yeah, they're at their cereals and I've switched the TV over to the cartoon network."

"What," she grinned saucily at him, "you think that will keep them amused till we…"

"No," he grinned back at her, "you know me. I like to take my time at these things. But tonight, if you get in early enough…"

"Call it a date then," she nodded and sipped at the scalding liquid. "Is your mum coming in early today?"

"Yes, said she'll be here sometime after eight."

"Right then, lie on. I won't leave till she arrives."

"Don't you need to be away for quarter to eight?"

"What's the use of being the boss if I can't take a little time to myself now and then," he smiled at her and turning towards the door, added with a scowl, "That's an order, Sergeant Miller."

"Oh, I like it when you're all masterful," she grinned at him.

****

As was her custom, DCI Lorna Paterson arrived early at Coatbridge police station and was at her desk by eight o'clock. The door was knocked and opened by DI Billy McKnight who carrying a sheaf of paperwork, said, "Morning, boss. Got the overnight crime synopsis and twenty-four-hour Force bulletins."

Dumping the paperwork onto Paterson's desk, he continued, "While you're having a shufti through this lot, I'll fetch us a couple of coffee's."

Five minutes later he was back to find Paterson poring over the reports and who absentmindedly took her coffee from him while she continued reading.

He sat quietly in the chair in front of her desk when at last, she sighed and sitting back, asked, "See the news this morning?"

"Aye, it looks like the media's been camped out overnight at the locus."

Before she could respond, her phone rang and answering it, he saw her smile and heard her say, "Morning, Harry. I'm just putting you on speaker. I've Billy McKnight here with me in my office."

Pressing the button, Chief Inspector Harriet Downes voice, cheerfully said, "Morning, Billy. That wife of yours still costing you a fortune?"

"You better believe it, Harry. Bloody woman will have my pension spent before I see any of it. How are you?"

"Fine, Billy. Now, down to business. Lorna. I'm getting some interest…no, a *lot* of interest from the media about your body in the field. Anything to tell me that I can issue in a press memo?"

"Sorry, but nothing yet, Harry. I've Doctor Mason arriving sometime today, hopefully this morning and then we can proceed to exhume the body. One thing that might benefit us is we've a sample of the body's hair being examined, again hopefully today, for any hits on the Forensics DNA database. If they turn up a name it will enable me to commence my investigation, but until then I'm stymied because I want Mason to be present when the body is dug up."

"Nothing to suggest gender yet?"

"No. We've only exposed the crown of the head and there's not enough of the hair exposed yet to indicate if it's a man or woman."

"Ah, well," Downes sighed, "you can let me know when you have an update or need me to issue and appeal. One thing you should know, Lorna. The Chief's aware and taking a keen interest that you're using Julia Mason to assist your inquiry. Try to get her to refrain from speaking with the media while she's working for you. The last time she did so, she almost cost the SIO the case at the High Court."

"No pressure then?"

"No pressure," Downes laughed and with a cheerio to McKnight, ended the call.

"Billy, when you're finished your coffee, get onto the Lab at Gartcosh and inform them of the Chief's interest and that we need a result on the hair sample as soon as. Maybe that will perk them up a little," she sighed and sipped at her coffee.

****

Turning into Coatbridge's Whittington Street, Julia Mason ignored the 'Police Vehicles Only' sign and parked her silver coloured Mercedes B Class car in a bay. Getting out of the car, a uniformed constable stared curiously at her and asked, "May I help you, Madam?"

Moving to the rear of the car, she opened the boot and officiously replied, "I'm Doctor Mason. I'm here to meet with DCI Paterson. Will you kindly assist me with my equipment?"

Indicating a large, black coloured pull along suitcase in the boot of the car, she waited while the young officer struggled to heave the heavy case from the boot then closing the lid, Mason said, "Lead on, if you please."

Minutes later, the red-faced officer was knocking on the DCI's door and introducing her visitor to Paterson.

Greeting Mason with a handshake, Paterson invited her to sit and while Mason did so, cast and apprising eye over her.

Assessing Mason to be in her early fifties, she saw a stoutly built woman, pale skinned, light blue eyes and sharp featured with short, curly hair that Paterson guessed was still blonde and likely thanks to a sympathetic hairdresser and if her plummy accent was any indication, a native of Edinburgh's Morningside district.

Her dark, pin striped trouser suit was to Paterson's eye, expensively tailored, but it was Mason's hands that surprised her. Smartly dressed as she was, her fingernails were bitten almost to the quick.

"Thank you for arriving so promptly this morning, Doctor Mason," Paterson beckoned her to take a seat and asked the constable to request DI McKnight join her.

Inwardly as she watched Mason sit, she formed the opinion she didn't like the woman.

When the young cop had closed the door, Paterson resumed her seat behind her desk as Mason, refusing the offer of refreshment, sharply asked, "Tell me about this body?"

In as much details as she could and passing Mason SOC photographs of the locus taken the day before, Paterson described the discovery of the body and the general location of where it lay.

"And you say it's wrapped in what appears to be some sort of nylon shroud?"

"That's our initial assumption, yes."

The door opened to admit Billy McKnight who was introduced to Mason.

"Perhaps without haste then," Mason said, "we might attend at the locus?"

"The sooner the better," Paterson replied with a tight smile and arose from her seat.

****

That morning within a conference suite at Gartcosh Crime Campus, Detective Superintendent Cathy Mulgrew, representing Police Scotland Specialist Crime Division jointly chaired a meeting with the Justice Secretary and which also comprised of representatives of the four partner agencies who also occupied the state of the art building; the Crown Office and Procurator Fiscal Service, the National Crime Agency, HM Revenue and Customs and the Forensic Services. The contentious subject matter of the conference was the budget allocated to each of the Gartcosh based agencies; however, Mulgrew decided before the meeting became too heated that a morning refreshment break might be called for and so after an hour of sharp tongued talking, adjourned the meeting for fifteen minutes.

She was about to speak with her colleague from the National Crime Agency when she saw her secretary beckoning her to the door.

"What's up?" she smiled at the middle-aged woman.

"Sorry to interrupt, Miss Mulgrew, but I received a call from Archie Young at the Forensic Lab asking that you contact him as a matter of urgency. Said to tell you it's about the hair sample from Coatbridge."

Mulgrew's eyes narrowed. Archie Young, a tall, fair-haired and handsome man in his early forties, had for some time set his sights on the attractive Mulgrew, even though she had patiently explained that not only was she gay, but was in a long term and happy relationship. However, it had not dissuaded the captivated man who had told her that he 'lived in hope.'

Her eyes narrowed.

Lorna Paterson had phoned her yesterday evening to apprise Mulgrew about the discovery of the buried body so she was aware of the hair sample being sent to the laboratory for DNA examination. Perhaps then, she thought, this was not just another of Archie's ploys to engage with her.

Mulgrew sighed before replying, "I suppose you told him I'm engaged in a meeting with not just *his* boss, but the Justice Secretary?"

"I did, but he says it's important you get in touch with him right away."

"Did he mention if it's time critical?"

"Eh, no."

She glanced at her wristwatch and biting at her lower lip, said, "Tell him that I should be clear of here within the hour," then wryly smiling, nodded towards the room of representatives and added, "unless of course there's a bloodbath before then."

The secretary acknowledged with a nod and was about to turn away when Mulgrew asked, "Did Archie mention if he had a result for the hair sample?"

"No, but he *did* sound rather agitated," she cautiously replied.

"Agitated?

"Well, more than usual," the secretary suddenly blushed and confirmed what Mulgrew suspected; the woman was aware of Young's crush on her boss.

"As I said, one hour," Mulgrew dismissed the woman with a polite nod.
****

Pulling into his designated bay in the car park, Charlie Miller got out of the Volvo and made his way to his office, greeting the passing staff and students with a polite nod or "Good morning."

Taking a deep breath, he opened the outer office door to greet his secretary and saw Mark Bennett waiting for him.

"Sorry I'm a little late, Mark," he smiled then said, "Good morning, Miss Forsyth."

"Sir," she replied and he wondered how it was possible with that one word the damned woman could be so...so...bloody frustrating!

Sighing, he nodded that Bennett follow him into his office and closing the door behind the DI, bade him sit.

"Why is it that there's such a temperature difference between your office and that office," Bennett nodded towards the door.

"What do you mean?"

"Her! Jesus, that woman's attitude is so cold it's unnatural," he pretended to shiver.

Smiling, Charlie sat behind his desk and asked, "What's going on today then?"

"Just the usual paperwork and you have the candidates to consider for the top prize for the senior course's final week."

"Oh, right, well, leave that with me. Anything else?"

Bennett's eyes narrowed. "This body that's been found over in Lanarkshire, the one on the news. Why don't we ask the SIO's permission for a site visit? Let the senior course have a look at it? Give them a day out?"

"Hmmm," Charlie pursed his lips. "Not a bad idea. Let me think on that and if it's doable I'll find out who the SIO is and make the inquiry. Anything else?"

"Yeah," he grinned. "Why don't we arrange a *real* murder one night here at the Castle and invite that old cow out there to be the victim?"
****

They arrived by police minibus at the locus shortly after the attendance of the Scene of Crime personnel led by Jean Galbraith. Passing through the police cordon and the accompanying pack of reporters and news cameras, Paterson ignored the calls for a statement and instructed the minibus be parked on the adjoining lane a short distance from the site of the grave.

She was pleased to discover that as requested, Billy McKnight had arranged for the liveried major crime vehicle to be situated on the lane.

The large vehicle afforded them not only privacy to change into the SOC suits, but was equipped to provide hot drinks and the use of a refreshment area within.

If expediency was necessary, the vehicle also provided the SOC officers the opportunity to examine in detail anything that they might recover from the grave site prior to that item being taken to Gartcosh.

Assisting Julia Mason from the minibus, McKnight called out to a burly constable and said, "Please take that," he pointed to the large pull along case, "to the big bus there."

When the constable pulled the case from the minibus and dumped it on the ground, Mason scowled and cried out, "Be bloody careful with that! There's valuable equipment inside!"

Red-faced, the cop turned to McKnight who shrugging, offered an apologetic smile, but Mason's rudeness wasn't lost on either Paterson or McKnight who with an unspoken glance between them, mutually agreed that the woman was worth the watching.

"Good morning, Doctor Mason, I'm pleased to meet you," Galbraith, already wearing her white boiler suit, moved forward with a smile and hand extended to greet the anthropologist.

Ignoring her hand, Mason glanced sharply at Galbraith and said, "I assume you are here to assist me. Where do I change?"

Taken aback by Mason's slight, Galbraith's eyes tightened as she replied, "The large bus there," and turning on her heel re-joined her team.

Paterson and McKnight followed Mason to the bus where after all three had donned boiler suits, they followed the SOC team to the tent covering the grave site.

However, before they commenced work, Paterson, her face tightly set, said, "Doctor Mason, might I have a private word?"

Arms crossed she walked short distance from the group where they could not be overheard and turning, calmly said, "I understand you have worked with the police on previous occasions, so let me be quite clear, Doctor Mason. Regardless of our designation or particular discipline within the Force, we work as a team. We do not have prima donnas and we treat colleagues with courtesy and respect. I saw the way you spoke to Missus Galbraith who I must inform you is a team leader and a highly respected Scene of Crime officer with many years of experience. While I accept, Doctor, that you are a leader in your profession, Jean Galbraith is as much a professional in her profession as are you. At the moment she is a member of *my* team and if you treat any of *my* team with disrespect, you can pack your bags and leave right now. Do I make myself clear…Doctor?"

Mason, her mouth grimly set, stared wild-eyed at Paterson before slowly nodding and turning on her heel, returned to the tent.

Taking a deep breath, Paterson followed her and nodding a greeting to the SOC officers who stood patiently waiting, tightly smiled and said, "Right, Doctor Mason, how shall we proceed?"

****

The meeting concluded with handshakes and vague promises of reviews, but no firm commitment that the five agencies budgets would be reconsidered; at least not in the foreseeable future.

Accompanying the Justice Secretary to the front entrance of the building, Cathy Mulgrew bade him farewell and was returning to her office when she remembered that Archie Young wished her to attend at the Forensic Laboratory.

But not before I pee, she thought and made her way to the ladies on the ground floor.

Five minutes later she was admitted to the reception area where after being shown into an interview room, the young woman smiled and said she'd call Archie through.

Stood at the second floor window, she stared down into the atrium below where some staff were enjoying their breaks in the large common area that was scattered with easy chairs and tables.

She turned as the door opened and a grinning Young, wearing a white laboratory coat, held a file in his hand and said, "Cathy. So nice to see you. You're looking lovelier than ever. How have you been?"

"Archie, I'm very busy. I hope you haven't got me here to tell me how lovely I look?"

"Ah no," he frowned and handed her the file that . "You are aware that yesterday evening we received a sample of hair…"

"Yes," she raised a hand to stop him. "I know about it. From the body in the field."

"Quite so. Anyway, I conducted a DNA test today and compared my findings with DNA that we have recorded on our database."

Her pulse quickened as she said, "You got a hit? A match?"

"Yes," he slowly drawled, "I got a hit. According to what was noted in this," he waved the file at her, "our test sample was some strands of hair obtained from a hair brush. However, when I checked the name of our sample against our files I discovered the name had a caveat attached to it."

"A caveat?"

"Yes," he nodded, "and when I opened the caveat I found a reference number and an instruction that anyone comparing the DNA sample recorded on the database must as a matter of urgency, bring their result to the attention of the head of Strathclyde Police Intelligence Department. As Strathclyde Police no longer exists, my dear Cathy, I believe that since the formation of Police Scotland," he stared pointedly at her, "the head of the Intelligence Department is now you."

****

An hour into the examination and after Mason had laboriously taken a number of photographs and soil samples, the swaddled body was beginning to appear in its fullness.

"She might be a bit of an arse, but she knows her stuff," Billy McKnight whispered to Lorna Paterson, for stood five metres away and watching Julia Mason at work he could not help but admire her handiwork.

That and all rudeness towards Jean Galbraith seemed to have disappeared as Mason coaxed and instructed the SOCO and her team while slowly removing the soil from around the body, confirmed now to be wrapped in a nylon sheet and the sheet found to be bound with a green coloured string.

"My hubbie's a keen gardener," one of the SOC team volunteered. "That looks to me like the type of string he uses to tie up plants. I'm not certain, but I think it's impregnated with some sort of oil or resin or something like that to stop it from rotting in the soil."

Laborious though the task was, Paterson and McKnight were enthralled as they watched the removed soil being sifted through a large round, stainless steel colander. The soil that dropped through was discarded and taken to a small dump a few yards away. Any small items were minutely examined and passed to Mason to confirm they were of no evidential value before also being discarded to the dump.

It took several hours to methodically remove the soil around the body and then when she was satisfied, Mason indicated that the body could be safely prised from the earth and removed to a large SOC Perspex sheet that was laid on the ground a few metres away.

Taking McKnight's hand as he helped her from the trench, a rosy-cheeked Mason puffed out loud before saying, "I would strongly advise that the body be conveyed to a mortuary before we attempt to remove the covering, Miss Paterson."

"I agree," Paterson nodded and beckoning forward the metal coffin known throughout the service as the shell, instructed the detective who was to accompany the body that it remain in the shell until such time the post mortem was conducted.

"What's that?"

She, Mason and McKnight turned as one to see Jean Galbraith pointing into the depression in the soil where the body had lain. Mason dropped heavily to her knees and while a SOC officer held her hand for support, leaned forward into the trench with her head a mere foot away from the item and said, "I'm not certain, but I believe it's the end of a filtered cigarette."

"Not a Covenanter then,' McKnight whispered to Paterson, earning himself a dig in the ribs.

After the item was photographed, the SOCO handed Mason a pair of plastic tweezers and very carefully, she plucked the crushed butt from the soil and placed it into a paper bag.

Paterson leaned forward to ask, "Would a cigarette butt have lasted that long buried in the soil, Doctor Mason? Would it not have rotted over the years?"

"It of course would depend on how long it lay in the soil, ground conditions, weather conditions," she shrugged. "However, while I cannot of course be more definitive, I would hazard a guess that the nylon sheet that covered the cigarette butt, as you refer to it, might have acted as some sort of damp proofing. There is no doubt, however," she shrugged, "that the find is of tremendous value. Indeed, it might itself lead us to determine when the hole was dug though not necessarily by the individual who placed the body there."

"You're kidding, right?" McKnight stared at her, confusion in his face.

"I believe your profession requires you to act on fact, Mister McKnight?" she raised and eyebrow towards him. "Who is to say that the individual who placed the body there did not in stumble across the hole and merely use it for his or her own purpose?"

"Aye, right," he mumbled, though not convinced.

"Well, we've got the body removed," interjected Paterson, "so all it remains is for us to have the PM and try to determine who the poor soul is. Right," she suddenly clapped her hands together. "Jean, I'll leave you and your team to continue here unless, Doctor Mason, you wish to also remain?"

"I will in the meantime. I assume the PM will not take place until some time tomorrow, so for tonight, you'll have booked accommodation for me?"

"Billy?" she turned to McKnight.

"All done, Ma'am. The Dakota Hotel at the Eurocentral. I'll have one of our guys remain here for now to bring Doctor Mason back to Coatbridge to collect her car and provide directions to the hotel."

"Okay, then, Doctor Mason, I'll leave word for you at the hotel regarding directions and the time the PM is arranged for tomorrow."

****

Making her way to the third floor of the building, Cathy Mulgrew swiped her security card that gave her access to DI Danny McBride's office.

With his family, McBride was abroad on annual leave, but as his senior manager she not only had access to his computer security codes, but also access to the list of confidential files McBride stored in the large floor safe in the corner.

She checked her mobile phone for the safe combination number and after opening it, removed the box of floppy computer discs and glancing at the scrap of paper with the reference number, searched through the discs until she found two with the same reference number.

Returning the box to the safe, she mentally made a note that she had been remiss by failing to instruct the floppy disc contents in the box be transferred to a more modern and accessible storage device.

That, she decided, would be Danny McBride's first task when he returned.

Lastly she removed a large, plastic zipped bag that contained a bulky laptop with cabling and locking the safe, returned to her office. Calling her trusted secretary through to her office, she instructed the woman to connect the laptop to Mulgrew's computer screen and after ensuring it was working, asked that she not be disturbed.

When the secretary had returned to her own office, Mulgrew inserted the first of the floppy discs into the laptop and using the mouse, opened the file to discover that as she thought, it contained details of the investigation; statements, briefing notes, the names of officers involved in the inquiry, lists of sundry information. The second disc was much of the same, both discs copies of all the work that had been done and logged on the HOLMES system.

Her hands clasped on top of her head, she read the final synopsis of the investigation and slowly exhaled.

Staring at the far wall, her mind was in whirl.

After all these years.

Taking a deep breath, she reached for her desk phone and glancing at her desk pad, dialled the direct number written there.

When the call was answered, she said, "Good morning, Chief Constable. It's Cathy Mulgrew, sir. We might have a bit of a problem."

"A problem, Miss Mulgrew? How so?"

"The body that was discovered in a field in Lanarkshire. It seems it's from nineteen-eighty-nine and if the DNA sample that was examined here at Gartcosh is correct," she sighed, "it look's like we've found Murdo Clarke."

CHAPTER FOUR

Charlie Miller had just finished speaking with Sadie on his mobile when his secretary called him on his intercom to inform him that Detective Superintendent Mulgrew wished to speak with him and could he phone her as a matter of urgency.

Charlie smiled and dialling the number of his good friend, greeted her with, "Don't tell me. You've decided to go straight, left Jo and want me to run away with you. But I have to tell you…"

"Like that's going to happen," she chortled, then asked, "Have you much on today? Workwise, I mean?"

"Nothing that Mark Bennett can't handle. Why, what's up?"

"How about this evening?"

"Again," he shook his head and pursed is lips, "nothing that I can think of. Sadie's on a back shift and her mum has the girls till I get home, but I'm sure she won't mind if I'm a little late."

"Good. The Chief would like to see you. How soon can you get to Dalmarnock office?"

Taken aback, Charlie's eyes narrowed as he considered her question and replied, "Depending on the traffic, say forty-five to fifty minutes maybe? Why, what's this all about, Cathy?"

"Better that the Chief tells you, Charlie, but I'll be there too. See you when you arrive. One thing. Don't say to anyone where you're going or why," she added before ending the call.

He stared at his mobile and mumbled, "I *know* where I'm going, but I've no bloody idea why."

****

Dragging her suitcase behind her along the corridor of the hotel's third floor, Julia Mason swiped her room card and with a weary sigh, pulled the case into the room and locked the door before fully collapsing onto the bed.

The early rise and drive from her home in Strathmartine outside Dundee to the Coatbridge police station had been hectic and though she would never admit to being a less than confident driver, stressful too.

As she lay on her back, she thought about the call to assist in the exhumation of the body.

This, she fervently hoped, might be the first step on her way back.

Her eyes closed as she thought of the previous weeks meeting with the Dean, the shocking news that following a board of inquiry her tenure might be revoked, that in all probability she might be dismissed and all because of that *bloody* student!

She swallowed deeply, her fists clenching and body tensing as tears of anger forced themselves from her.

It had always been her downfall, her quick temper and uncompromising character to accept anything other than her student's best.

Besides, she told herself, the idiot got what she deserved for being so stupidly incompetent, dropping a valuable piece of bone that shattered so completely and irreparably on the tiled floor; as did the student's glasses that flew from her face when Mason slapped her. Her mistake was slapping the woman in front of the rest of the research team.

And now this; the complaint that could see her fired and so ignominiously sent into scholastic oblivion.

When the call had come from the police, she saw no reason to inform them that for now she was currently suspended from her academic teaching duties for after all, the suspension had nothing to do with her anthropological skill; no, she decided, it was merely an administrative issue and nothing that need concern the police.

Her attendance at the gravesite had both thrilled and excited her for as she worked, she contemplated an idea she had been planning for several months.

Her autobiography.

She closed her eyes and smiled, for after all, if as she fully expected her tenure was to be revoked, then she would require some form of income.

Her experiences in Africa, exhuming and identifying the bodies of the genocide victims in Rwanda and her work in the Balkan states in the nineties, as well as her public success in identifying the young girl's body in the Ayrshire sand dune; she was certain it would make great reading.

And now this, her swansong.

Yes, she widely smiled.

The university and their idiot students could go and *fuck* themselves. Julia Mason still had her story to tell and all she had to do was ignore that silly disclosure the police had required her to sign.
****

When Sadie Miller answered the phone, she realised immediately that Charlie was on his hands free in the car and in a firm voice, said, "Where are *you* skiving off to, Miller, at this time of the day?"

"Hi, sweetheart, I'm on the M9 heading back to Glasgow. Dalmarnock office, actually. Cathy phoned to tell me the Chief wants to see me."

"The Chief?" her brow furrowed. "What about?"

"Dunno," he replied. "What Cathy *did* say was that I was to tell no one where I'm going or why."

"I know where you're going," she said, "but I don't know why."

"That's what I thought," he grinned.

"But you're telling me, a lowly sergeant?" she teased.

"Only because I'm frightened of you and I've never learned to breathe through a pillow and you'd get it out of me anyway."

"And don't you forget it, Miller."

"Oh, don't worry," he smiled, "I won't. Anyway, the reason I'm calling is to ask you to tell your mum that I'll likely be a bit late tonight," he paused then added, "And before you ask, I don't know why, but that's what Cathy told me; nothing else."

"Okay," her curiosity was killing her, but she knew that when Charlie knew, the one person in the world he trusted was his wife.

"But don't worry," he continued. "I'll be home in plenty of time for our date."

"Our date?"

"Aye, didn't you promise that tonight we'd…"

"Oh, that," she slowly drawled then with an embarrassed smile, added, "Just make sure you take your vitamins before you come to bed," and quickly ended the call.

****

"Boss?"

Lorna Paterson glanced up and beckoned Billy McKnight into her office.

"I've just been on the blower to Gartcosh and spoke to the Lab," he began. "They passed me to one of their scientists, a guy called Archie Young who did the examination on the hair sample."

"I know Archie," Paterson replied. "What did he say?"

"That's just it," McKnight's brow furrowed and his face expressed his confusion. "He didn't say anything. Told me that he couldn't discuss the result, that if I wanted any further information I was to contact Detective Superintendent Mulgrew."

"And did you?" she sat back and peered up at him.

"Her secretary said she was out of her office and didn't know when she would return, but would leave a message to ask her to phone me."

"That's odd. Archie didn't give you a reason why he couldn't discuss it?"

"No," he shook his head. "He apologised and though I tried to explain we needed the information as a matter of urgency, he simply told me he couldn't discuss it and again referred me to Miss Mulgrew."

"Hang on," she lifted her desk phone and after dialling the number of the Forensic Laboratory at Gartcosh, asked to speak with Archie Young.

"Archie," McKnight heard her greet him. "What's this all about, telling my DI that you can't tell him the result of your DNA emanation of the hair sample? What?" her face turned pale before she said, "Very well. I'll speak with Miss Mulgrew."

Replacing the handset, she said, "You heard that. He wouldn't tell me either. How very odd."

"Do you have *any* idea what might be going on?"

"None at all," she shook her head then thoughtfully added, "but if Cathy Mulgrew *is* suppressing the DNA result for our victim, there must be a bloody good reason."

The door knocked and the CID clerk stuck his head in to say, "Ma'am, you were on the phone when a call came in for you. Detective Superintendent Mulgrew's compliments and would you please meet her at Dalmarnock office as soon as possible."

Paterson turned to stare at McKnight then said, "Whatever it is, Billy, you're coming with me to find out, so grab your coat."
****

Cathy Mulgrew, her arms folded and tapping the thumbnail of her left hand against her perfect white teeth, paced restlessly in the entrance foyer at Dalmarnock police station, unaware she was being watched by the young male station assistant who was captivated by the glamorous senior detective.

The automatic door slid open to admit Charlie Miller who was about to walk to the desk, but seeing Mulgrew embraced her with a smile. "It's been nearly a month since I've seen you," he rebuked her, "and the girls keep asking for you."

"I know, I know," she grimaced, "but to be honest, works been that bloody busy. Tell you what. Jo and I are free this Saturday. Why don't we come over and take them off your hands for the afternoon?"

"That'll work. I'll put some lunch on."

She drew back and staring at him, replied, "Oh, oh. Maybe not, because something tells me you might not be at home," but before he could respond, she turned to the station assistant and said, "When DCI Paterson arrives, please inform the Chief Constable's secretary. Thank you."

Walking up the stairs to the Chief's office on the first floor, he couldn't help but ask, "What's this all about, Cathy?"

"The Chief will explain it all."

A minute later they were entering the Chief Constable's Suite and immediately passed through by his secretary in the inner office where Martin Cairney stood up from his desk. Taking Charlie by the hand, he said, "Thank you for coming so promptly, Mister Miller. Please," he indicated the couch, "sit down."

They did as they were bade and heard Cairney call out to his secretary, "We're ready for that coffee now, please," before he re-entered the room and sat in the armchair opposite.

"Before we begin, sir," Mulgrew held up her hand, "I've asked DCI Lorna Paterson, the SIO in the investigation to attend here at Dalmarnock. My intention is to speak to her and inform her she is to stand down from her investigation."

Charlie's ears perked up. Though they had not previously met, he knew that Paterson was the DCI in charge of the Coatbridge CID and if she was joining them, wondered if this was about the body found in the field?

"In that case, we'll have coffee and await her arrival and once you've broken the news to her we can brief Mister Miller," Cairney grimly smiled, before turning to Charlie and asking, "How is the arm, Mister Miller?"

"Oh, fine sir," he raised it and making a fist, bent it back and forth. "The occasional twinge in the winter months, but nothing a couple of Paracetamol won't handle."

"And little jellybean? How is her maths coming along?"

Taken aback, Charlie smiled, recalling the occasion when Cairney briefly visited him at home and responding to Sadie's call while he worked in the back garden, walked in to the front lounge to find the Chief Constable and his daughter discussing her homework.

"Geraldine continues to surprise us, sir. In fact…"

"In *fact*," Mulgrew interrupted with a smile, "She'll surprise us all when she's older and I've already got her marked down as a potential recruit for the Force."

"And you have another daughter, I believe?"

"Ella, sir. She's just turned two and a half."

"Children," Cairney slowly shook his head. "It's what keeps us young," then pretending to growl, added, "Until they turn teenagers then it's grey hair from the outset." Pointing to his head, he added, "Trust me on that score."

The secretary knocked on the door and leaning into the room, said, "Sir? That's DCI Paterson and DI McKnight at the reception downstairs."

"McKnight?" he turned to stare at Mulgrew who shrugged and responded, "DI McKnight is DCI Paterson's deputy, sir. I didn't ask him to attend, but though she can't know the reason for the meeting she obviously believes it's worth his attendance too. Unless," her eyes narrowed in sudden understanding. "She must have learned that I instructed the Laboratory not to disclose the result of the DNA hair sample examination."

"Well," Cairney sighed resignedly, "Mister Miller and I will wait here while you deliver the news."

Turning back to the secretary, he said, "Please have DCI Paterson and her colleague brought upstairs to a free room and arrange for some fresh coffee for Mister Miller and I. Thank you."

****

Mulgrew met Paterson and McKnight in the Chief Constable's corridor and escorted them to a side room where she asked them to take a seat.

Preferring not to sit, she stood with her arms folded and began, "The reason I asked you to attend here is as likely you will have guessed, related to your ongoing investigation; the body in the field." She took a breath and staring down at Lorna Paterson, formally continued, "For reasons that I am not at liberty to disclose; DCI Paterson, I am instructed to inform you that you are to stand down from the investigation."

"What!" Paterson shot to her feet, her outrage evident on her face. "Is this something to do with me personally for if it is…" blazing mad now, her face red with anger, she snarled, "I'll take it to the Chief Constable himself!"

"Lorna!" Mulgrew snapped at her then raising her hands, slowly said, "This instruction *is* from the Chief Constable and no, it's *not* a personal issue; it's nothing to do with you. What I *am* authorised to disclose is that the body is the subject of an ongoing and sensitive inquiry and…" she hesitated, wondering how far she should take this, then added, "the body has been in the ground prior to either you, me or DI McKnight here even *joining* the police."

Paterson, confused, slowly sank back down into her seat and shaking her head turned to McKnight who said, "What the *hell* is going on, Ma'am?"

Mulgrew sat down and shrugging, replied, "Like I told you, I'm not at liberty to discuss this further, but trust me; you're well out of it. Now tell me, how far have you got in your investigation so far?"

"Well," Paterson slowly began, "the body is exhumed and in a shell awaiting the post mortem that is booked for nine o'clock tomorrow morning."

"Where?"

"Monklands Hospital in Airdrie. It *was* my intention to attend with Billy here and I've also engaged the services of an anthropologist…"

"Doctor Julia Mason. Yes, I know about her."

"She will also be attending. The locus is still under guard by uniform cops and I've had the ground cleared by the Support Unit, but to be frank I don't foresee any further evidence coming to light. At least, not above ground," calmer now, she half smiled.

"The one thing of possible interest that we discovered at the site is still to be formally examined by the Laboratory; it's what appears to be a cigarette butt with a filtered tip that was found in the soil under the body. Chances are that it might have been dropped there when the body was being buried. The production is still with us at Coatbridge. Billy?"

"Aye, boss," he confirmed with a nod. "It's in a paper bag in your room."

As if with a sudden thought, Paterson's eyes narrowed and she asked, "If I'm not to investigate this body, Ma'am, who is?"

"The Chief has decided that Detective Superintendent Charlie Miller will conduct the inquiry, Lorna."

"The guy in charge of Detective Training at Tulliallan?" McKnight asked.

"Yes, that's him."

"Well," he pursed his lips, "I hear he's a good bloke though I don't know much of his career history other than…" he paused as his brow creased. "Didn't he get stabbed a while back? Something about an attempt on his life?"

"That's him and trust me, Billy," Mulgrew smiled. "Charlie Miller is *very* good at what he does."

"So, Ma'am, you want me to stand down. I get that, but what do I tell my team? Will Mister Miller be assuming command of them?"

Mulgrew didn't immediately respond, then said, "No, Lorna. This will be a discreet inquiry with the minimum of personnel involved. I'd say almost a one-man show if you like, though I do suspect he'll probably recruit at least a couple of people to assist him. As for telling your team anything, I'll leave you to decide what to say just so long as you do not disclose what we have discussed here. Either of you," she glanced meaningfully from one to the other.

"I don't suppose you can tell us who he or she is, Ma'am," McKnight smiled.

"Sorry, Billy, I can't. What I *can* tell you is that if Mister Miller's investigation proves successful, it very likely and unfortunately will hit the headlines."

"Well, I suppose we'll just need to keep guessing, then," he continued to smile then to Mulgrew's bewilderment, turned to Paterson and smirked, "See, I told you it wasn't a Covenanter."
****

When Cathy Mulgrew returned to the Chief Constable's office, she declined coffee and settled into her seat.

"Mister Miller, while I recognise the fine job you are doing at the Detective Training wing at Tulliallan, I fear I must recall you to operational CID duties for I require not just your investigative skills, but also I know you are an officer upon whom I can wholly rely upon. That said, what I am about to relate to you does not leave this room; however, it will be up to you to brief whoever you recruit to assist you in this investigation. On that issue of assistance, you have a free rein and my support. Now, I don't want to sound like Max Bygraves," Cairney smiled to Charlie, "but I'm going to tell you a story. There's no need to take notes, Mister Miller, because," he nodded towards a square, cardboard filing box sat upon his desk, "Miss Mulgrew has printed out all the statements and briefing notes that were at the time logged on the HOLMES system. I should add that we will retain the original floppy discs and I'll be grateful if you will treat the paperwork as confidential."

He paused and clasping his hands in front of him, he began.

"Back in the mid eighties, a gang of masked, armed robbers were plaguing not only the Strathclyde Police area, but all of the other seven Forces and twice even across the border into Cumbria. From Inverness to Carlisle, Aberdeen to Irvine, they robbed their way across the country. They targeted banks, armoured cars and building societies. Interestingly, they never stole jewellery or anything that had to be re-sold; only and always cash. Not every week or even every month; perhaps the sub-branch of an Edinburgh bank one week, then two months later a building society in Troon. Three weeks after that they're in Oban robbing a Cash in Transit vehicle."

"I recall that gang, sir. I was just about to commence my probationary training when they were headlining the local papers. "Didn't the police arrest them?"

Cairney shook his head and replied, "Not all of them. These guys, numbering four in total or so we believed at the time, were so successful that their accumulated ill-gotten wealth was assessed to be anything between one and two million pounds. A lot of money at any time, but particularly during the mid-eighties. Now, the gang were not beyond using violence to achieve their end and routinely carried handguns and sawn-off shotguns. They never actually shot anybody, but would beat down anyone who tried to interfere during the robbery and they did injure a number of innocent members of the public. Their MO was similar in all their robberies; one man did the talking, one man discharged a shotgun to frighten the victims, one man drove the getaway vehicle, always a four by four or estate car that was stolen locally to the premises they robbed," he added. "The fourth man secured the cash, whether it be a bag of money from a security guard or if it was a bank or a building society, they brought their own holdall bags."

He paused and reached for his coffee.

"As you can imagine, all of these robberies were not only well planned and presumably reconnoitred, but well executed too. Despite the best efforts by the eight Scottish Forces who were ably assisted by the Strathclyde Serious Crime Squad and the Scottish Drug and Crime Enforcement Agency, no one was able to identify these men. Of course, rewards were circulated both publicly through the media and among registered informants as to the gang's identity, but without success. As time passed, the rewards increased and while the names of several well-known criminals were bandied back and forth, there was never any evidence to connect these individuals to the gang. Surveillance was not an option because frankly we did not know who were were supposed to be watching."

"I presume because you use the plural 'we', you were involved in the investigation, sir?"

"I was, Mister Miller," he nodded, "albeit briefly. In 1988 I was a member of the Strathclyde Police Special Branch and involved in running sources, some of who had links to armed criminals. Needless to say my remit was terrorism, but there was always an overlap by the supporters of these organisations into criminality, particularly in the procurement of firearms. Now, to continue. As I said, this gang, nicknamed by the popular press who," he sighed, "*love* doing that sort of thing, were known as the 'Four Minute Gang.' The moniker applied because on every occasion they were engaged in a robbery they were in and out in less than four minutes. Always. Their discipline was impeccable and even though they might not be finished collecting all the money, they stopped when one member used a whistle. Upon hearing the whistle they cleared out and were gone."

"A whistle?"

"Yes," Cairney smiled. "A whistle."

"Sounds military," Charlie's brow furrowed.

"That *was* one of the suspicions, but without any named suspects we pursued a lot of time on that particularly fruitless line of inquiry."

"As I asked earlier, sir, I thought the police arrested them?"

"On the fourteenth of December, 1989, a police informant finally came forward to claim the reward. At the time," his brow creased as he fought to recall, "the reward being offered was if memory serves me correctly, fifty thousand pounds. The informant, who was later assessed to be a fifth gang member who sold out his associates, made his claim for the reward through his handler, DI Jimmy Dougrie. The informant told Dougrie that he had information that the following morning, about midday on Friday the fifteenth, the gang intended robbing a building society in Renfrew's Hairst Street near to the Renfrew Cross. Dougrie of course informed the incident room who organised an armed response."

He paused and said, "I was part of that armed response."

"I thought armed response were uniformed officers in those days, sir?"

"Yes and no. Armed response back then was primarily uniformed officers, however, because of the topography of the area," he paused to explain. "If you know Renfrew, it's a busy shopping area and at that time of the day, very crowded with local shoppers. Anyway, it was decided that to avoid being compromised by the gang the armed response would be detectives. Sixteen of us were drawn from different teams, though primarily the Strathclyde Serious Crime Squad. We armed officers were deployed in close proximity to the building society and including the rear office of the premises. Of course there were a large number of unarmed detectives as back-up, but…" he paused again, "here I must insist that this goes no further, Mister Miller. Our instruction that day from a senior police officer who I must decline to name, was if any of the gang showed *any* hostility or made any attempt to use their firearms, they were to be shot. No attempt to be made to arrest them. Shot."

Charlie stared at Cairney and blinking, repeated, "Shot?"

"Yes, Mister Miller. Shot. The senior management of the day deemed the gang were far too dangerous to be permitted to escape. Shot," he repeated with a nod.

"Wow. I've never heard *that* story, sir," Charlie was clearly flabbergasted.

"As it turned out," Cairney smiled almost in relief, "the four gang members were arrested without any firearms being discharged and in due course, received heavy sentences ranging up to and including twenty-three years imprisonment."

"Sorry, sir, you said the *four* gang members. What about the fifth gang member, the informant?"

"Officially, there was never any admittance by the police of a fifth gang member and those who were arrested denied the involvement of any other individual. In fact, other than denying any other associate, the gang refused to disclose any information at all. However, as you so correctly deduced, the unofficial belief at the time was the informant was fifth gang member, a man called Murdo Clarke."

"But never proven?"

"No, never proven; however, that's why you're here, Mister Miller," Cairney drily smiled.

****

In the passenger seat of the CID car on the way back to Coatbridge, Billy McKnight sighed and said, "Okay, boss, tell me what you're thinking."

"What makes you think *I'm* thinking anything?"

"Because usually you're rabbiting on about something; girly television shows, chic flicks or some new outfit you've bought to impress the latest man in your life."

"You make me sound like a right airhead, Billy. Hey, wait a minute, McKnight!" she turned and stared crossly at him. "Latest man in my life? You think I'm some sort of floozy or what?"

"No," he roguishly grinned, "of course not. Well, not that I'm admitting while you're doing eighty something on the motorway! But let's get back to the body. Now, all kidding aside, boss, you're about as smart a detective as I've ever met or worked for, so tell me. What *are* you thinking?"

"Okay," Paterson sighed, "I'm wondering how I can persuade this guy Miller to take me on as one of his team."

"Really? You've had to hand the investigation over and now you want to work for the guy, eh, excuse the pun, who's stealing your body. Besides, didn't Ma'am say it would probably be a one-man investigation?"

"Oh, I don't know, Billy, he's bound to need someone to spar with during the inquiry. You know what it's like; someone to bounce ideas off."

Conscious that McKnight was a nervous passenger she shook her head as she intentionally pressed her foot down onto the peddle.

"This body in the field has really got my curiosity going. I've never worked a cold case before and to be honest, I relish the idea of having something like this on my CV."

"Look, boss, you'll get the promotion that you deserve in time, but *not* if you don't fucking slow down!"

She glanced at the speedometer and saw she was touching ninety. Easing off on the pedal, she grinned and apologised with, "Oh, sorry."

"You'll lose nothing if you give him a phone," McKnight suggested. "Maybe start off with something like," then adopting a falsetto voice, continued, "Oh, Mister Miller. I've *always* fancied working with you. I'm a good girl really and always aim to please."

"Aye, right," she scoffed. "That's what kept us women back in this job, prats like women who used their sexuality to get on. No," she shook her head, "I think I'll ask to meet with him and suggest I bring the SOC photos and my observations at the locus. That might work," she mused.

"Might be an idea to do your homework before you phone," he said. "Find out what you can about Miller."

"Do *you* know anything about him?"

"Only what you do. He was stabbed a while back by a cop, a DS I think that guy was, who if I correctly recall was later charged with murdering his own wife. Don't you remember the court case?"

"Oh, he's *that* Charlie Miller," she slowly nodded and turned from the motorway onto the dual carriageway towards Coatbridge.

To McKnight's relief, Paterson slowed to forty and nodding, said, "That's what I'll do. I'll give him a call. After all, didn't Ma'am say Miller would *probably* be choosing his own team?"

****

Wearing her dressing gown and using a hand towel to dry her hair, Sadie Miller opened the door to admit her mother Carol who kissing her daughter on the cheek, called out, "Where's my little chickadee, then?"

Ella squealed with delight and almost lost her balance as she hurried to be swept up into her gran's arms and smothered with kisses.

"The kettle's just boiled, mum, if you want to brew the tea. I'll get into my uniform and be right down," Sadie grinned at the antics of her mother and daughter. "Oh, and another thing. Charlie might be a bit later getting in tonight. Some job he's got on."

She was about to take a step towards the stairs when she stopped and remembering Charlie's comment, asked, "Mum. Are you okay? I mean, are you feeling okay?"

Carol Forrest stared at her daughter and try as she might, couldn't stop from rapidly blinking as the tears welled up in her eyes.

"Mum?" Sadie stepped forwards to embrace her and anxiously asked, "What's wrong?"

Carol took a deep breath and slowly exhaling, softly replied., "I've just been to the doctors. An early morning appointment. I…" she paused, her lips trembling while the tears run unchecked down her cheeks as she stared into her daughter's eyes. "I found a lump."

CHAPTER FIVE

Martin Cairney poured them coffee from the fresh pot and continued.

"Before I answer your question about the fifth gang member, Mister Miller, please let me explain about DI Dougrie's informant, Murdo Clarke." He handed Charlie his cup. "In 1987, Clarke was employed by British Rail as a senior clerk and worked out of an office in the Central Station, here in Glasgow."

Charlie's eyes narrowed as he interrupted and said, "Presumably then as a British Rail employee, Clarke also had the privilege of free train travel?"

Cairney smiled and replied, "You're getting ahead of me here, Mister Miller, for I suspect I know what you're thinking; that Clarke was ideally situated to travel the country by train reconnoitring locations to be robbed."

He continued, "Now prior to 1987, Clarke had no criminal convictions, but early in that year had come to the attention of the police when two officers responded to a call to his home. Upon their arrival, they discovered Clarke in a drunken state and his wife," he glanced down at his notes, "Stacey Clarke, who was sporting a bruised face. Missus Clarke made a formal complaint and Clarke was arrested for domestic assault and locked up for the night. I regret," he sighed, "the paperwork for the case is no longer available and of course in those days' computers were in their infancy in the police service hence it likely that following a period of time, the paperwork was destroyed."

He idly stirred at his coffee and went on, "Aware that a conviction might affect his employment and hoping to make a deal, he requested he speak with an officer about a team of thieves employed at the depot in the station who were pilfering form Red Star, the British Rail parcel service. Normal protocol is that kind of information would be dealt with by the British Transport Police and I cannot explain why they were not informed; however, the officer who interviewed Clarke was then DS James Dougrie, but soon to be DI Dougrie. There is no record of what information Clarke disclosed about the thieves. What *is* recorded is that Dougrie formally requested Clarke be enrolled as a confidential informant. In due course the application went through. It might be of interest there is no record of Clarke being awarded any conviction for wife assault so we can only suppose whatever deal he made with Dougrie worked out to Clarke's satisfaction."

Cairney, his throat dry, sipped at his coffee then smacking his lips together, continued.

"Once again, I cannot offer any explanation as to why, but the informant log of recorded meetings between DI Dougrie and Clarke is not available. Whether destroyed or lost I do not know and for the record," he shook his head, "I am appalled at the poor administration of the system at that time. What I *can* tell you is that on the afternoon of Thursday 14 December 1989, Dougrie submitted a report of a meeting with Clarke in a café in Renfield Street and as a result of information later submitted by Dougrie, the following day while preparing to rob the Renfrew building society, the four gang members were arrested. Before you ask," he held up his hand, "there is no record of how Clarke came about this information."

"But it *is* significant that he had the information and yet only four were arrested," Charlie interjected.

"Quite so," Cairney nodded.

"And that, sir, leads me to suspect that as you obviously do, that Clarke was the fifth man who turned his pals over to us."

"Yes, Mister Miller," Cairney again nodded.

"Do we know where Clarke is now?"

"Well," Cairney turned to glance at Mulgrew, "if the DNA examination is correct as I suppose it must be, his body was exhumed from a shallow grave earlier this morning and now lies at Monklands Hospital. I understand the PM is arranged for nine o'clock tomorrow morning."

"Oh," Charlie said, "now that's a surprise. However, I'm beginning to understand. You want me to prove that Clarke was the fifth man?"

"If only it were that easy," Cairney sighed. "Mister Miller, the task I'm about to set you is a lot more complicated than that."

He rubbed at his brow with a meaty hand. "The day after the arrest of the four gang members, that's Saturday the 16th of December, Clarke's wife Stacey Clarke reported him missing. Obviously, because of the confidentiality of the informants' procedure, we could never publicly acknowledge that it was Clarke's information that led to the arrest of the four members of the gang. However, while it was suspected that Clarke *might* be the fifth man, his disappearance caused questions to be asked about his relationship with the police. What complicated matters was some bugger, though never discovered who, let it slip to a reporter of the 'Glasgow News' a week after his disappearance that Clarke was a police tout."

"Was it suspected at the time, sir, that Clarke had been murdered?"

"Yes, Mister Miller, that was at the forefront of the investigating officer's mind, the officer leading the hunt for the missing man."

"And who was the investigating officer?"

Cairney glanced at Mulgrew before replying, "Jimmy Dougrie."

Astonished, Miller said, "*DI Dougrie*? Clarke's confidential handler?"

"Yes, I regret it was and let me say," he held up his hand, "I have no idea why that came about. It was entirely the wrong decision made by a senior officer who though now deceased, I can only say was a bloody incompetent."

He shook his head and added, "Needless to say, when the article about Clarke being an informant and now missing was reported in the 'Glasgow News,' it caused all sorts of questions to be asked and not least of DI Dougrie's appointment as the investigating officer. However, being the bloody *polis*," his anger was evident, "not one senior officer at the time considered removing Dougrie from the inquiry and bringing in an impartial detective."

"I assume then with Clarke being reported missing, the reward money was not paid out?"

"It's on record that Missus Clarke did make application for the money, but as it was her husband who actually provided the information, the application was refused. However, by applying for the reward it does infer that she was aware of her husband's actions as a police informant."

Charlie sat back in his seat and considered what he had been told before asking his next question. "What happened to the money that was stolen? Was it ever recovered?"

"The four arrested men were of course found guilty at trial and their assets seized that included all monies in their bank accounts. Between them, the Crown recovered approximately," he glanced down at his notes, "one hundred and eighty thousand pounds."

"But didn't you say that they stole…"

"Yes, Mister Miller. Somewhere between one and two million pounds."

"Bloody hell! That means that money is still unaccounted for?"

"A nice lift if you can find it, Charlie," Mulgrew smiled.

"What?" he glanced from Mulgrew to Cairney before asking, "Is that what you want me to investigate? Where the stolen money is?"

"If you *do* find the money, Mister Miller, that would be a bonus, but that's not your primary concern. What I want you to do, Mister Miller, is as quietly as possible and without too much fuss, find out who murdered Murdo Clarke."

"That's a tall order, sir. I mean, we're talking cold case here of…" his eyes narrowed and he shrugged, "twenty-eight years? Most of the witnesses will be dead or very old and I'm already thinking the suspects must be one of the four alleged associates or someone they contracted to kill Clarke."

"Oh, we already have a suspect in mind and that's why your investigation must be completely confidential."

"And who is your suspect?"

Cairney sighed deeply before replying, "Detective Inspector James Dougrie."

****

She decided to dine in the hotel restaurant and after showering, she changed into a long sleeved, knee length loose fitting kaftan dress, a gift from a grateful Rwandan family whose daughter she identified from among a several hundred within a mass grave in the Goma region.

Patting her hair, she inspected herself in the lift mirror while descending to the lobby where she made her way to the bar for a pre-dinner cocktail. Seated on a bar stool while the barmaid readied her drink, her mobile phone chirruped in her shoulder bag. The number was unfamiliar to her, but recognised the STD code as the Dundee area and said, "Doctor Mason."

"Julia? It's Francis Mahoney, I called your home, but there was no reply," he loftily said.

Her stomach tensed. It was unusual for the Dean to call her at all. A by the book man, Mahoney would normally have his secretary phone or make an arrangement for her to call at his office.

"I'm out of town right now, Francis, for if you recall," her voice oozed sarcasm, "you suspended me. So, what can I do for you?"

"This is rather awkward, Julia. As you are aware, there has been a number of complaints."

"A number of complaints, Francis? I am aware of only *one* complaint and that from a careless and vindictive individual who seeks to earn herself a good grade by belittling *my* reputation."

"No, Julia, that is just one complaint. The other three…"

"Three! What the *fuck* are you on about, Francis," she bellowed into the phone, startling the young woman who was preparing her cocktail. "What! Are the arseholes coming out of the woodwork now that I'm not there to defend myself? Is it 'kick a dog when it's down' now? What *other* three complaints, Francis, you fucking cowardly *bastard*!"

There was a hushed, shocked silence before Mahoney, by nature a genteel man, sharply replied, "It will all be explained in your severance letter, Julia. You may expect it in the post. Goodbye."

Wide-eyed and red-faced, she stared at the mobile in her hand and thought she was going to vomit.

They had really done it; they had sacked her.

Bastards!

Almost in a daze, she wandered away from the bar, not hearing the barmaid call out, "Madam? Your cocktail," and ignoring the curious looks of the other guests as she wandered back towards the lift, all thoughts of dinner forgotten.

She could not recall returning to her room, was unaware of sitting on the bed, her mobile still clutched in her hand.

Then she began to weep.

A full half hour passed before she composed herself and stumbling into the bathroom, filled a basin with water and doused her face, the shock of the cold water causing her to lose her breath.

She stared at her reflection in the mirror over the basin and gritting her teeth vowed that she would not let those bastards beat her.

Never!

She reached for a hand towel and drying herself, returned to the bedroom where she fetched her laptop from its bag and signing on to a search engine, sought the phone numbers for local investigative journalists.

****

The shocking news of her finding a lump and her mothers visit to the GP had completely deflated Sadie Miller who beginning to grasp the enormity of the revelation, phoned her Inspector. Citing a domestic issue and reminding him of time she had lying in lieu instead of payment, he agreed with some reluctance she could forego that evenings shift.

Now seated with Carol in the lounge, she said, "Tell me exactly what the doctor said and what she plans?"

"You have to understand, dear, I was pretty shook up when I found it."

"Was it only this morning, mum? I mean," she didn't want to sound critical, but continued, "You're always telling me to check my breasts. I assumed that it was something you did regularly too."

Smiling through her tears, her mother replied, "It's the old do as I say, not as I do and unfortunately," she sighed, "I'm now paying the price. It was only last week when I noticed the lump…"

"Last week!" Sadie was aghast. "Mum, why didn't you go to the doctor then?"

"Well, I phoned, but today was the first available appointment, love."

"Oh, mum. I wish you'd told me sooner. We could have went private."

"Private?" Carol smiled. "Where would I get the money to go private?"

"It's not a question of money, mum. Charlie and I have the means so…"

"I'm not having you and Charlie paying for me, Sadie Forrest, and that's final," her mother huffed.

"Sadie Miller, mum," she smiled, "and tell me this. Would you pay for me or one of the girls if we needed to go private?"

"That's different."

"How is it different? We're family. If you try that on with Charlie, what do you think he'd say?"

Carol laughed softly and replied, "He'd tell me I was a bloody fool, that's what he'd say."

"Course he would. Now, tell me what the doctor has planned and," she held up a reproving forefinger, "if it involves any length of time, we're going private and that's final."

****

They had almost wound up the meeting and now it was Charlie's turn to ask questions.

"Do we have any information at all, any witnesses or evidence that corroborates the suspicion that Dougrie murdered Clarke?"

"None at all," Cairney shook his head.

"Then how did Dougrie become a suspect?"

"The suspicion at the time, Mister Miller, was that Dougrie persuaded Clarke or vice versa, we're not certain, to roll over on his associates and keep the stolen money for themselves."

"Which would suggest that Dougrie then became extremely wealthy. Did he?"

"Alas, no. As far as we are aware, DI Dougrie resigned when he," Cairney made quotation marks in the air with his fingers, "failed to discover the whereabouts of Murdo Clarke. Three months later, in fact and six years short of his thirty."

"Was he ever interviewed about his possible involvement in Clarke's disappearance?"

"That box," Cairney nodded to his desk, "contains all the statements taken at the time relevant to Clarke's disappearance and includes a taped interview," he smiled, "on cassette tapes I might add, when Detective Superintendent Grant McPhee interviewed Dougrie just a week before Dougrie resigned. Dougrie's official reason for resigning was he believed he was being scapegoated for Clarke's disappearance; in fact, he inferred he had suspected Clarke to be a member of the team and that Clarke was alive and had simply disappeared with the money. McPhee passed away a number of years ago, I'm afraid, so that's a dead end," then smiled at his unintentional pun.

"And Dougrie? Is he still alive?"

"Before you arrived, I contacted our Finance Department and learned that James Dougrie continues to draw his police pension and according to his file, he will be sixty-five years old. His current address is in the box."

"So, in essence, sir, you want me to make investigation into Murdo Clarke's murder and either clear or indict Dougrie for the said murder. What are my parameters?"

"You may draw upon any member of the Force to assist you, but I would prefer you assemble a small team. Any individual you recruit to assist you must be made aware in the strongest terms of the confidentiality of this investigation. If word gets out that we are investigating one of our own for a historical murder, the ramifications will be unthinkable. Not only will every case Dougrie was involved in be the subject of scrutiny, but…" he stopped and stared at Charlie before continuing. "I need not explain for I'm sure, Mister Miller, you fully understand."

"Yes, sir, I believe I do." His mouth tightened and his brow furrowed when he asked, "What became of the four men who were convicted?"

"You'll find their details in the box there," Cairney nodded towards it, "but if memory serves correctly, Alex 'Sandy' Murtagh died in prison, sometime in the late nineties. He was murdered in an argument over tobacco. John O'Connor was released on compassion in 2001, but succumbed shortly thereafter to cancer. Of the remaining two, Frankie 'Smiler' Colville was released in 2010 four years early for good behaviour while Tommy Craig, the brute force of the team who favoured a sawn-off shotgun, served his full sentence of twenty-three years and was released in 2012."

Charlie had one final question and asked, "Is there a time limit to my investigation?"

"Officially no, but I will be grateful if you consider the inquiry to take no more than a month. After that time, we will review the situation with the likelihood that I will order the investigation closed and the murder of Murdo Clarke will remain open and unsolved."

"No pressure then?" Charlie grinned humourlessly.

"No pressure, Mister Miller," Cairney returned his grin.

"Right then, as the body was discovered in the Coatbridge area, sir," he moved to lift the box from the desk, "I believe I'll make that my base of operation. Do you wish me to report my findings directly to you?"

"Perhaps given the circumstances, you will draw less attention to your activities if you were to report anything significant to Miss Mulgrew who in turn can keep me apprised."

"Will do, sir."

Cairney reached out his hand to shake Charlie's who awkwardly held the box under his left arm, hiding the ache as the old wound made itself known.

In the corridor outside, Mulgrew said, "I assume your DI, Neil Bennett will cope while you're away?"

"There's nothing he can't deal with and if the worst comes to the worst, he can always get me on the phone. He'll be fine," he nodded with confidence as they walked towards the stairs.

"Anybody else you have in mind?"

"I'd like 'Sherlock' Watson to perform the PM."

"How is Elizabeth? I haven't seen or spoken with her for a while. How has she been since her hubby buggered off."

"She's doing well," he replied. "Sadie sees her regularly and though she hasn't *said* anything, I suspect there might be a new man in Sherlock's life."

"Good for her. I never did like that ex of hers. Tried it on with me once," she grimaced and shivered before adding, "Sleazy git."

"Well let's face it, Mulgrew, you *are* one fine looking bird."

"You're only saying that because it's true. So, who else have you in mind?"

"If she's available, Jean Galbraith from the Scenes of Crime for the autopsy photographs."

"Well, you won a watch there. Jean was the supervisor at the site. I'll arrange for her to be at the PM. Anybody else?"

"Well, believe it or not there's a trainee detective just started on the latest course at the College. I was reading her file and she might be of use. I'm going to bring her in on it too and she can also act as my filing clerk."

"What? She's a *trainee* detective, Charlie. Is that wise?"

"Maybe not, but she has got good qualifications prior to joining the police that could give me an insight into anyone I interview simply because I'm going to be speaking to witnesses who will be trying to recall what happened in 1989."

They reached the foyer and stopped.

"What about the SIO for the Clarke's body. How did she take it, being told she was off the investigation? It's DCI Lorna Paterson, isn't it?"

"I suspect you might be hearing from her," Mulgrew grinned.

"Right, anything else I should know?"

"What about this woman, Mason, the anthropologist? Will you still require her at the PM?"

"Has she signed a disclosure form of confidentiality?"

"I understand she has, yes."

"Then she might also have some insight into how Clarke died or was buried, so it won't do any harm for her to be there too."

They parted with the agreement that Charlie would phone Mulgrew at the conclusion of the PM to report how Clarke met his end and with any information that he believed might be worth passing on to the Chief.

****

Seated in the second back row of the classroom, Trainee Detective Constable Alison Baxter idly drummed her fingers against the desktop while forcing herself to pretend interest in the instructors boring lecture on the rights of individuals being formally interviewed under caution.

Christ, she thought, I taught this to first year students and it didn't make her feel any better that the bloody idiot had so far misled the class on three points of law.

However, she had already made her decision that no matter what she heard during the course and in particular about points of law, she would remain silent rather than have her fellow students believe her to be some sort of smartarse.

The door was knocked and then opened by Neil Bennett, the Detective Inspector who was Deputy to the Detective superintendent in charge of Detective Training. With a smile, Bennett approached the instructor and whispering something, then turned to the class. His eyes singled out Baxter and beckoning towards her, said, "Miss Baxter, can I have a word, please?"

Curious eyes followed her as she walked towards Bennett who turning, held open the door and indicated she leave the room.

He joined her in the corridor and politely said, "Please follow me."

Trailing behind him, she decided that she'd keep her mouth shut, that she'd learn in a minute what this was all about and to her surprise followed Bennett to the Detective Superintendent's office where sweeping by the beady-eyed secretary Miss Forsyth, they entered Miller's room. To her further surprise, Bennett seated himself behind Miller's desk and indicated she sit opposite. Smoothing her skirt behind her, she slowly sunk in the chair and hands folded on her lap, politely stared at him though for some reason she couldn't explain, her stomach was churning.

He stared for a few seconds at the good looking woman with the collar length fair hair and wondered briefly what the hell this was all about.

"It isn't common knowledge yet," he began, "but while Mister Miller is deployed elsewhere, I'm currently acting as the head of Detective Training, Miss Baxter. Now, you'll be wondering why I asked you in here?"

"Yes, sir, I am a little confused. Is there some sort of issue?"

"I really don't know," he shrugged and shook his head. "All I can tell you is that Mister Miller phoned me ten minutes ago with the following instructions." He glanced down at a handwritten note in front of him. "As of now, you are to be seconded to him for an unspecified period of time."

"Seconded to him? For what purpose? What about my training course?"

"Look, Miss Baxter…" he sighed and leaned forward onto his elbows, "Can I call you, Alison?"

She slowly nodded.

"Alison, all I know is that Charlie Miller left here this morning in response to a phone call. What the call was about or who it was from, he didn't disclose, but what I do know is that he's a good man and very highly thought of by top management. Whatever he is doing and whatever he needs you for must be important enough for him to have me make you a hotel booking."

Seeing her eyebrows raise, he grinned and lifting the note from the desk, handed it to her and said with a wide grin, "Don't worry, I don't think it's a clandestine meeting or anything to do with him fancying you or anything like that. You've to pack an overnight bag and make your way to the Strathclyde Hilton Hotel, the post codes on there," he pointed to the note, "where there's a room booked in your name. I've had an overnighter there with my wife and it's got a top class restaurant. At nine o'clock tomorrow morning, you are to meet with Mister Miller at Monklands Hospital mortuary and again, the post code is on the note. I'd suggest you do *not* be late. Any questions?"

"Lots," she was now thoroughly confused, "but if you can't answer them, sir, then I suppose I'll need to wait till I meet with Mister Miller."

"That's what I like to hear," he sat back and sitting back with his

hands clasped behind his head, grinned. "Unswerving loyalty to the job even if you haven't a bloody clue what's going on."
****

Charlie Miller lifted the box from the boot of his car and turning, was surprised to see that not only was his mother-in-law Carol's car there, but so too was Sadie's Honda Jazz.

Opening the front door, he was about to call out, "I'm home," but almost immediately was assaulted by his daughter Ella who wrapped her arms tightly around his legs. A second later Geraldine bolted out from the lounge and throwing her arms about his waist, stared up at him and whispered, "Mummy and granny are in the kitchen, crying." If he were surprised at Sadie's car being there he was now worried that something was seriously wrong and awkwardly laying the box down onto the floor while Ella hung onto his legs, lifted the little girl into his arms. With a hand laid gently on Geraldine's shoulder, he said, "Why don't we go into the lounge and you can keep an eye on your sister and I'll find out what's wrong?"

"Okay, daddy," she nodded, her red hair framing her pale face for even as young as she was, she realised there was something amiss. The kitchen door was ajar, but he knocked on it anyway and pushing it open, saw Sadie, who wore jeans and a pale blue coloured sweater, and Carol sitting at the kitchen table nursing mugs of tea.

"Well," he forced a smile, "seems that Missus Miller has taken a day off. What's the occasion then?" but inwardly kicked himself for being so flippant for neither woman smiled.

"Sit down, sweetheart," Sadie arose from her seat and pecked him on the cheek before adding, "and I'll get you a cuppa. Mum's had a bit of bad news today."
****

Sitting in the doorway of his conservatory and looking out onto large and well tended garden at the rear of the house, he stared at the planters and the wilting flowers. He really should be doing something about weeding and replacing them them, but these days had neither the energy nor the inclination. There was a time, he sighed; a happier time, happier days.

A wasp buzzed by his hand that held the glass of fruit juice, presumably attracted by the sugary smell, but uncertain whether to land or not and with his free hand he idly waved it away.

The sun was almost fully settled now behind the roofs of the houses opposite and he considered that he should be hungry, but these days had no real appetite.

By now he had now missed the STV six o'clock evening news, but had no further desire to hear anything more about the discovery of the body; in his heart believing the body to be the husband of the woman for whom he had given up so much.

No; no desire at all.

CHAPTER SIX

Charlie Miller had a restless night, but no less than did Sadie who twice that he knew of arose to softly tiptoe along the hallway to peek in to the guest room where her mother lay asleep.

They had spoken late into the evening, he persuading Sadie and Carol that a nightcap would settle them while Charlie sipped at a glass of fresh orange and finally convinced Carol to stay over.

He knew he would not get out of the house without disturbing her and after his shower in the en-suite quietly opened the door only to see the bed empty. Getting dressed, he found Sadie in her dressing gown in the kitchen preparing him a light breakfast of bagels and coffee.

"Sorry, sweetheart," she smiled wearily at him and he could see she wasn't far from tears. "I didn't get the opportunity to ask you what's going on, what the Chief has you doing."

"No matter," he munched at a bagel. "I'll explain it all when there's time."

"But you're not going to the College today?"

"Maybe not for the next couple of weeks or so," he replied. "It's a kind of confidential inquiry, but I'll tell you about it when I get home this evening."

His face creased. "I'm forgetting. Are you going to late shift?"

"I think so," Sadie nodded. "The one thing my mum won't have me do is fuss around her. I know her, Charlie. She needs to keep herself occupied and will drive herself and me mad if she mopes about what's going to happen next week, that's assuming the doctor goes ahead and orders the ultrasound scan and mammogram," she drily said, for like most people Sadie knew just how overwhelmed the NHS was becoming.

"Look," her took her in his arms, "I know she protested, but what if we go ahead and contact Ross Hall ourselves, asked for an appointment and get it done as soon as possible."

Sadie seemed uncertain and replied, "I don't know how she'd react. Do you think we should?"

"Tell her it's an early Christmas present," he smiled before adding, "Whatever you decide, you know I'm one hundred per cent with you and besides, Carol means as much to me now as do you and the girls. Let's not fanny about with her health, Sadie, let's just do it," he urged her.

"Yes, you're right," her forehead creased, she nodded then glancing at the wall clock, continued, "You'd better get your backside in gear, Miller if you're heading out to…Airdrie somewhere, did you tell me last night?"

"Monklands Hospital," he confirmed with a nod and with a final slurp at his coffee, hugged his wife before heading for the door.
****

Seated in her Mini Clubman, Alison Baxter glanced at the dashboard clock and saw it was now twenty minutes to nine. After dinner last night she had used her laptop to research Monklands Hospital and finding a site map, was now parked adjacent to the building that was located at the rear of the hospital.

Sat in the car park and glancing through the windscreen at the overhead clouds, she again wondered what the hell she was doing here and why Miller had asked for her.

She glanced to her left when an old style Volvo estate car drew in a couple of bays away and her eyes opened when she saw it was him. He had just got out of his car when he heard his name being called and glancing across the vehicles, his eyes settled on Baxter as she stood by the door of her Mini.

"Mister Miller," she called again, then locking her car made her way towards him.

As she approached he saw that her collar length fair hair was tied back in a short French plait. She wore a white blouse with open neck, navy blue pinstriped suit with the skirt to the knees, short heeled black patent shoes and carried her handbag over her left shoulder with a black handled umbrella clutched in her other hand.

As he stared at her he realised that while not beautiful in the glamour magazine sense of the word, Alison Baxter was undeniably a very attractive woman.

"Miss Baxter," he formally greeted her and said, "I trust you didn't have too much difficulty finding this place?"

"The wonders of technology, sir. The SatNav brought me straight here from my hotel," she smiled.

He nodded that they walk and while doing so, said, "I trust the Hilton looked after you?"

"It's not the first time I've stayed in a Hilton," then thought, that sounded rude and quickly added, "It was up to their usual attentive standard."

She couldn't know Charlie didn't pick up on what she thought was a rude response and he asked, "Likely, you'll be wondering what the hell you're doing here?"

"It did cross my mind," she cheerfully replied and nodded her thanks as he courteously opened the entrance door to the mortuary.

Walking through the immaculately sterile corridor, he said, "Have you ever attended a PM?"

"Once, during my probationary period at the West End station in Edinburgh. An elderly woman who had fallen down her stairs at home. There was some question as to whether it was accidental or not."

"And was it? Accidental I mean?"

She didn't immediately respond and he was about to prompt her for a reply, when she said, "Her husband was in the early stage of dementia and allegedly struck her. Or so the CID assumed," she sighed.

He stopped and stared at her before asking, "But you think otherwise?"

Again she didn't immediately respond, but then replied, "I was in my first year of probation, sir. I had no opinion to offer and certainly, none that anyone would listen to."

"But tell me anyway."

"There was no trial. As I later learned, the prosecution and the defence had a closed doors meeting and come to an agreement. The old guy, who had no family to fight his corner, was shipped off to a secure mental unit at Carstairs. Problem solved."

He detected a hint of bitterness in her explanation and said, "That doesn't answer my question."

She stopped in midstride and turning to look him in the eye, replied, "I was of the opinion that the old lady who was in her mid-eighties, stumbled and fell."

She pursed her lips and her eyes narrowed as she recalled, "The stairs were steep and even when I was walking down them I almost went my length. I can't obviously say for certain, but…" her eyes narrowed as she bitterly continued, "the woman's death became a statistic for the divisional DCI who was able to report a solved murder. The husband was unable to either recall what occurred or, in the brief few moments I had the opportunity to speak with him, even understand that his wife was dead. So, yes sir, I believe it was an accident."

His head bowed ever so slightly as he shook it and quietly said, "I have no knowledge of the case, but I can tell you it has been my experience in the CID that there *are* officers who will sometimes make a decision based on what *they* believe happened and ignore anyone else's opinion. There are even some who will take the short route to a conviction rather than assessing all the facts of a case. Such officers are fortunately few and far between and I hope to God nobody believes I'm like that," he sighed before continuing.

"I'm sure in your short service you will have met colleagues who are intensely dedicated to this job and give their all just as you will have met some who are lazy and incompetent. The police," he sighed again, "recruit from the general public and while the majority of those who join are keen and eager, there are always a few bad apples. I'm sorry you had that unfortunate experience, but if anything I'm certain it taught you the difference between a good detective and a bad detective. What you have to decide is, which one you want to be?" he smiled at her.

"Oh, I've already made my mind up on that issue," she returned his smile.

He continued walking towards the reception desk and said, "What I intend today is for us to witness the PM then you and I will head to Coatbridge office. I've arranged a room for us to use and I promise," he smiled and defensively raised his hands, "everything *will* be explained there."

Charlie had just identified himself to the young man who seated at the desk greeted them and was about to speak when they heard a voice from behind say, "My, my, my; if it isn't my old friend, Alison Baxter."

They both turned to see a woman approaching from the entrance door and who dragged a black coloured suitcase on wheels behind her.

When Charlie turned to Baxter, he saw her face pale and her lips tighten.

"Julia Mason," she almost whispered.

Charlie guessed Mason to be somewhere in her late forties to early fifties. A stoutly built woman whose skin was so pale to be almost translucent, sharp featured with short, curly blonde hair that he guessed wasn't natural.

Realising that there must be some sort of history between the two women, he extended his hand in greeting and said, "Doctor Mason, I'm Detective Superintendent Miller. Thank you for…" but to his surprise, Mason ignored him and staring almost malevolently at Baxter, snarled, "I'm surprised to see you here, Alison. A little out of your depth, are you not?"

Ignoring the jibe, she replied, "Good morning, Julia. I can't say it's a pleasure to see you again."

"Ladies!" Charlie interrupted a little sharper than he intended as he glanced to them in turn. "While I can see you both seem to be familiar with each other, I will be grateful if you would keep your personal opinions for later. Doctor Mason, thank you for coming. Now, if you *don't* mind?"

While both women stood bristling, he confirmed with the young man that the pathologist and Scene of Crime woman had arrived and was shown a room where he and the two women could change into Forensic suits and nitrile gloves.

In the room, Mason opened her suitcase and extracted a small leather satchel. When she saw Charlie staring curiously at her, she explained, "My tools."

While the women tacitly ignored each as they separated to use cubicles to don the suits, Charlie realised there was little point in conversation and when they were ready led them into the examination room.

Stood similarly dressed but also wearing a Versaflo face shield with the visor up, Charlie's old friend Doctor Elizabeth 'Sherlock' Watson stood chatting to the SOC supervisor, Jean Galbraith who had a digital SLR camera hanging from a strap about her neck.

On the examination table under the bright harsh light, the body, now removed from the metal shell but still wrapped in the nylon sheet and bound by the green coloured string, lay on its back with the only visible sign it was once human being the shock of dark hair sprouting from one end.

Greeting Charlie with a smile, he introduced Baxter and Mason before introducing Watson and Galbraith, then said, "Ladies, before we commence this PM I wish to make it clear that this examination is to be treated as confidential. Jean, Miss Baxter," he glanced at both women. "You are bound by Police Scotland regulations and discipline code, so be aware this PM is not to be discussed without my express permission."

"Miss Mason," he nodded to her, "I understand you have signed a non-disclosure agreement so the same applies to you."

"Liz," he smiled at Watson, "Cathy Mulgrew sends her regards."

She returned his smile and then said, "While I appreciate that the post mortem I'm to conduct is a low key affair, Charlie, you must understand that if I were permitted the opportunity to avail myself of the deceased's previous medical history…" her eyes narrowed as she nodded to the body on the table and asked, "You *have* identified this individual haven't you? I mean, Jean was telling me that a sample of hair was taken at the gravesite, so I presume you have already had the sample Forensically examined."

"I'm sorry, Liz, but again, that's confidential."

"Oh, and that's why you won't allow me the services of a mortuary attendant while I'm conducting the PM?"

"I'm afraid so" he grimaced, then continued, "Before we begin, I'd like your observations, Doctor Mason."

Turning to Baxter, added, "Please take notes."

He didn't expect Mason to comment, but heard her say in a stage whisper, "About the only thing the bitch is good for."

He discreetly took a step towards Baxter who clearly heard Mason, then saw her draw a deep breath. Tight-lipped, she glanced at him and slowly shook her head to indicate she would not be provoked.

"For your information, Mister Miller," Galbraith said, "I've already taken the initial photographs."

"I'd be grateful if you'd continue snapping photos as the PM progresses please, Jean," he replied and again wondered what the hell the issue was between Baxter and Mason.

"What we have here," Mason began in a plummy, tutorial voice, "is a body wrapped in what seems to be a nylon sheet and bound by a green coloured string or twine, if you like. With your permission?" she turned to Charlie, who nodded.

Taking a small but extremely sharp knife from her leather satchel, Mason cut the binding along the length of the body and handed the bundle of string to Galbraith who placed it into a paper bag.

Selecting a pair of stainless steel scissors from her satchel, Mason walked towards the head of the corpse and explaining what she was about to do, began to slowly cut a straight line in the middle and down the nylon sheet.

"As you can see," she concentrated on her cutting, "the sheet has become stiff with age and is not as pliable as it once was." Nodding to Charlie, she said, "You might wish to have this photographed, Mister Miller. There seems to be a label at the corner here."

After Galbraith snapped off a couple of photographs and Mason was finished cutting the sheet, she began to fold the sheet down on either side of the body.

When she stepped back, the other four could not but help lean forward to stare at the mummified body of a male who was completely naked. His eyes were closed, but his lips had shrunk back to expose a set of yellowing teeth.

"It seems that the body is wizened and shrunk through the years and as you can plainly see, the skin is wrinkled. I would assess this to be the result of complete dehydration. This is only an opinion based on my experience," she turned to Charlie, "and of course because the body is organic, radiocarbon dating would certainly be more specific."

"I'd be pleased if you give me your best estimation, Doctor Mason," he interrupted while thinking, no way could he justify the cost of radiocarbon dating when he already had an approximate date of death anyway.

"Well then," she huffed and poking a stubby finger at the skin on the let arm, pursed her lips and replied, "I was at the location when the body was exhumed and saw the conditions in which it was buried so, I am of the opinion this body has been in the ground for no less than twenty years and certainly," she softly laughed as if at her own brilliance, "no more than forty years."

Which fits in nicely with the twenty-eight years that Clarke's been missing, Charlie thought, then said, "Thank you, Doctor."

He didn't really need anything further from Mason and in fact, could probably have done without her participation at all, but now she was here he decided he'd ask one final question before dismissing her.

"Now, as an experienced anthropologist, can you tell me anything about the body that we as laymen might miss?"

She stared at him for a few seconds, then turning, bent close to the mouth of the body and sniffed. "I can tell you he was probably drunk when he died," she shrugged.

"What!"

"Come closer," she beckoned him to her. "Take a deep sniff at his mouth. You can still smell the whisky he drank and for the smell to preserve for this length of time, I believe it is a reasonable assumption he had consumed quite a lot."

Reluctant as he was, Charlie moved closer and slowly exhaling, bent to within a few inches of the mouth and took a hesitant smell. "My God, you're right," he eyes opened wide in surprise.

"How the *hell* could that have lasted so long?"

"The nylon sheet is a synthetic material," she explained. "Unlike cotton that when worn permits the body to breathe, nylon retains smells and that's why it's unpopular as clothing other than perhaps swimwear. When this man was wrapped in the sheet, the smell of whisky stayed trapped with him."

"Don't suppose of you can tell if it was a single malt, blended or what," Watson, eyes innocently wide, commented from the other side of the table.

Casting her a reproachful glance, Charlie asked, "I'm still a little confused, Doctor Mason. Surely after that length of time the smell from his released bladder or bowels would have masked the whisky smell?"

"No necessarily," she shook her head. "When the bladder involuntarily released the urine would likely have soaked through the nylon material and into the soil below. When the bowels released the faeces would have through time turned to powder."

She glanced at Watson and said, "Perhaps you might assist me to turn him on his side?"

After the two women had turned the body and held it on its side, Charlie, Baxter and Jean Galbraith leaned forward to peer at the dark, powdery stain where the buttocks had rested.

"As I said," Mason smiled, a superior smile that wasn't lost on the rest, "his bowels have relaxed *post mortem*."

It was then that Watson leaned towards the head and pointing, murmured, "Seems to have suffered some sort of blow there."

"Doctor Mason," Charlie had made his decision. "I am indebted to your participation in today's examination of this unfortunate male, however, I see no further need to detain you," he smiled at her. "Perhaps I can walk you out?"

She stared at him as though he were mad before spluttering, "You mean that's it? You don't need my assistance any further?"

"Ah, no Doctor. You have already given me the information I require," he convincingly lied. "As you are aware, what follows now is simply Doctor Watson's autopsy and frankly, I believe it would be a waste of your time to remain for what is now a relatively simple procedure."

Beside him, he could almost feel Watson bristle at his 'simple procedure' comment and already was preparing his apology.

Mason's face clouded over and collecting her toolkit from the nearby table, snapped the leather case closed and turning, wordlessly stomped towards the door.

Charlie beat her to it and politely held it open before following her into the corridor outside.

"Doctor Mason," he began, but without turning she held up her hand and hissed, "My bill will be in the post."

He watched as she shoved open the door to the changing room and slammed it behind her.

Exhaling, he shrugged at the startled young male receptionist and returned to the examination room.

****

The two men drew up in the white van and glanced towards the door of the mortuary.

"Is that it, then?" the driver asked as he leaned forward to peer through the windscreen.

His colleague turned a page of his notebook and replied, "That's what she said. They should be in there now."

"How do you want to handle this?"

The passenger shrugged and said, "We wait it out then catch them when they exit the building."

"How will we know them?"

"Oh, I'll know Miller," the passenger confidently said with a nod. "He's got a thick file in the records department and there's quite a few photographs of him too. I had a look before we drove out here. The last time he came to our attention he'd been stabbed and nearly died. Quite the hero is our Mister Miller," he turned and grinned at his companion.

"Will he come across, do you think?"

The passenger shrugged before replying, "Even a no comment answer is almost an admission, isn't it?"

"So, we just sit and wait?"

"No, *I* sit and wait. You head over to the main entrance. There's a WRVS café there, so go and grab us a couple of rolls and a coffee each."

****

Sadie had allowed her mother to sleep late.

Sitting in the kitchen nursing a coffee while Ella played with a pile of Tupperware dishes on the floor, she glanced up to see Carol smiling wearily at the door.

"Your man's halves are a lot bigger than I get in the club," she said.

"I think Charlie thought you needed a good nights sleep, mum."

"Well," she settled herself down into a chair and reached for her granddaughter who climbed onto her lap, "he was right then, because I slept like a log. Did you get jellybean off to school okay?"

"No problem though she was sorry she didn't see you before she left. Mum," Sadie slowly began. "It's Wednesday today, right?"

"Aye."

"Well, Charlie and I decided to give you an early Christmas present. Before you got up, I phoned over to Ross Hall Hospital in Crookston Road and…"

"Sadie! Please tell me you didn't! No, I told you…" she waved a hand.

"Mum!" Sadie reached for her hand while Ella, wide-eyed, stared from one to the other, her bottom lip now trembling at the raised voices.

"Mum," Sadie repeated, but calmer now. "It's like Charlie said, you are family and we need you. If it was one of the girls…"

"Oh God, praise be it's not," Carol shook her head and with her free hand, made the sign of the cross on her forehead.

"Well, if it *was* one of the girls or it was me or Charlie, wouldn't you be the first to tell us to get it seen to as soon as possible?"

Carol bit at her lower lip then hugging the little girl to her, nodded and replied, "Alright then, but only if you let me pay something towards it."

Relieved, Sadie smiled and said, "That's a matter we can discuss when we know you're going to be okay. Now, like I was trying to say earlier, we've booked an appointment for you to be examined tomorrow morning and I'll be coming with you. Well," she reached across to tousle at Ella's hair and added, "if granny's not here to look after you we both will be coming with you, won't we sweetheart?"
****

Elizabeth Watson frowned at him when he re-entered the examination room and said, "Are you ready for this 'simple procedure' then, Mister Miller?"

"Sorry, Sherlock, I didn't mean to…"

She raised her hand to stop him and said, "I'm affronted, Charlie Miller. So affronted at the insult it's going to take a bottle of my favourite red to placate me."

He raised his own hands in surrender and turning to Baxter, said, "You'll have gathered that Sherlock here is not just an excellent pathologist and a blackmailer, but also a close friend as well?"

Ignoring Baxter and Galbraith's grins, Watson, bent over the corpse, murmured, "Sweet-talking me won't work, Miller. It's still a bottle of my favourite red."

He sighed and rolling his eyes, turned again to Baxter and whispered, "She won't let this go."

"I heard that," Watson stood upright and taking a deep breath, smiled humourlessly and continued, "Shall we begin?"
****

The two men watched as a woman pushed her way through the door and dragging a suitcase behind her, made her way to a silver coloured Mercedes car parked nearby. Amused, they munched at their rolls and continued to watch as the woman struggled to place the suitcase into the boot of the car.

"Know her?" the driver asked.

The passenger screwed his eyes and slowly shook his head before replying, "Never seen her before, yet her face seems familiar."

The Mercedes had been gone for almost ten minutes when the passenger sat bolt upright and loudly said, "Shit!" then howled as he spilled some coffee onto his suit trousers.

"What?"

"I remember who she is! The woman in the Merc! It's her! *She's* the anthropologist, Doctor Julia Mason! Shit!" he pounded angrily at the dashboard and to make matters worse, spilled what remained of his cold coffee over his already soaked trousers.

****

It was no use.

No matter how hard he tried he couldn't get the discovery of Murdo Clarke's body out if his mind and returning indoors, switched on the BBC's twenty-four-hour news channel then spent almost an hour flicking between that and SKY's news programme. However, neither channel reported anything about the discovery and almost in disgust, realised he'd have to wait for the lunchtime STV news.

****

"Well, there's no more that I can tell you, Charlie," Liz Watson stepped back from the examination table and raised the visor of her Versaflo face shield. "My conclusion is that this man received a blow to the back of the head, but the skull is intact. Whether or not the blow was sufficiently hard to render him unconscious, I can't say after this length of time, but there is what seems to be evidence of bleeding of the wound. I've scraped some samples of what seems to be dried blood that Jean," she nodded to Galbraith, "will deliver to the Forensic boys at Gartcosh."

She cocked her head to one side and added, "Though of course if you know who this man is, there is no need for any DNA analysis of the blood, is there?"

He didn't respond, but simply smiled at her attempt to elicit a name. Exhaling in frustration at his silence, she continued, "I can also tell you that this man was stabbed in the lower left back with a wide bladed knife, an upward thrust that pierced the intertransversaii muscles and penetrated his heart. I won't labour you with the details that I will include in my report, but suffice to say that whoever stabbed this man either had great strength or a strong determination to kill him."

"Could a woman have inflicted such a blow, Liz?" he asked.

"Yes, without a doubt but as I said, a woman must have been really determined to kill him."

"Is there a likelihood the killer could have first struck the man on the back of the head, perhaps to stun him before stabbing him? Say, to prevent him fighting back?"

"That would be speculation, but yes, it's a definite possibility." She pursed her lips before continuing, "There is something else, though I do not want to throw you off on the wrong track."

"And that is?"

"A number of years ago I assisted with a PM in Edinburgh. A Special Forces soldier murdered a man who was having an affair with the soldier's wife. Anyway, that aside, the deceased had a similarly inflicted injury and it was later proven in the trial that the soldier had been trained to kill an enemy by placing his hand across the enemy's throat or mouth, drawing his victim backwards against him then stabbing him with an upward blow to the back to pierce the heart."

"So you're saying this wound might have been inflicted by someone with similar training?"

"Yes and no," she slowly drawled and then beckon Galbraith towards her, smiled and said, "Jean, could you turn with your back to me, please?"

Removing her nitrile gloves, Watson placed her left hand lightly around Galbraith's throat and with her right hand, demonstrated the blow to Glabraith's back.

"What I'm suggesting is that the killer murdered this man by this sort of action. Do you see what I mean?"

"There's only one problem with that, Liz," Charlie frowned. "Your blow would stab Jean with your right hand in the right side of her back. The wound's in the left side."

"Agreed and that might suggest you're killer is left-handed or if you wish to be pedantic, did *not* stab the victim as I demonstrated but simply walked up to him when his back was turned and thrust the knife into him."

"Left-handed. Well," he sighed, "if anything, it gives us another bit of information to mull over. Now," his eyes narrowed as he leaned forward to inspect the entry wound, "I've seen stab wounds before, but that's an unusually large entry wound, is it not?"

"I measured it at four and a half centimetres, so I'm guessing it was a broad bladed knife. Maybe a kitchen knife?"

"Or perhaps a sword," Alison Baxter suggested.

Charlie turned to stare at her, then slowly nodded with a grin, "We're maybe talking Glasgow here so it's not beyond the realms of possibility."

"Is there any significance in the fact the victim is naked, sir?" Baxter asked.

"The only thing I can think of is they didn't want him identified."

"What about fingerprints?"

"I can answer that," Galbraith stepped forward. "Before you arrived I tried to take his prints with our handheld fingerprint scanner, but no luck I'm afraid. His fingertips were too wrinkled. With your permission, Mister Miller, I can use the old and trusted fingerprint powder. I didn't want to use it till Doctor Watson had completed her examination."

"There's really no need, thanks Jean," then staring at the women in turn, said, "I already know who he is."

"I knew it!" Watson nodded. "You undoubtedly have your reasons, Charlie, but can you tell us how accurate Mason was in her assessment about his length on time in the ground?"

"Close," was all he would admit to, before continuing, "I've made an arrangement for the body to remain here meantime, so I'll leave you to wrap up here, Liz. Miss Baxter and I need to get to Coatbridge office. Jean, can you hang on and assist Doctor Watson?"

"No problem," Galbraith nodded.

He beckoned to Baxter that they leave, but then stopped at the door and almost as an afterthought, turned and said, "Liz. If you get the opportunity, can you stop by the house tonight to speak with Sadie. I believe she needs to seek your professional advice on a personal issue."

Puzzled, Watson nodded and replied, "Yes, of course. I'll phone her when I'm finished here."

Striding along with Baxter in the corridor outside the examination towards the exit doors, Charlie was providing her with the post code to Coatbridge office for her SatNav when pushing open the doors, he was suddenly confronted by two men, one of who held a camera and was taking photographs of him and Baxter.

"What the hell…" was all he managed to say before the older of the two men, in his mid thirties, fair haired and almost as tall as Charlie, loudly said, "Mister Miller. Brian Hendry from the "Glasgow News.' Can you tell me anything about the post mortem examination you attended for the body that was dug up in a Lanarkshire field? Is this a murder investigation?"

Stunned at the unexpected confrontation Charlie tried to walk off, but was closely followed by Hendry whose colleague continued to take snaps of Charlie.

"Is this linked to gang warfare in Glasgow? Have you identified the victim yet?" Hendry persisted. "Can you tell…"

Without warning, Hendry suddenly pitched forward onto his face, his notebook flying from his hand as the photographer, his face pressed against the camera, stumbled over the top of the fallen man's legs and also fell heavily to the ground, the camera bouncing across the tarmac with a loud crack.

Turning, Charlie was astonished to see Alison Baxter, her umbrella held firmly in her hand by the tip while the curved handle was just touching the ground.

"Oops! So sorry," she called out to the tumbled men and slyly grinned at him as he realised she had tripped the reporter and caused him to fall.

"See you at the next venue, sir?" she called out as she walked off. He nodded and as he walked to his car, wondered what sod had contacted the 'Glasgow News' and now made his investigation all the more difficult.

CHAPTER SEVEN

The office located on the second floor of Coatbridge police station that was allocated to Charlie Miller and his inquiry team overlooked the car park at the rear.

"Sorry if it's a bit dusty, sir," the Duty Inspector apologised, "but we've no real use for this room now and as I recall, the last time it was used was for storage, so that's why there are chairs stacked here," he nodded to a pile in the corner. "I can have them moved elsewhere if you want?"

"No, leave them where they are," Charlie shook his head and laid the cardboard box down onto a desk. "We won't need the full use of the room and there's the three desks and a landline, so that should suffice."

"Oh, I was led to understand you would be bringing a full inquiry team?"

"For the minute Inspector, it's just Miss Baxter and myself. Now, is the key you're holding the only key for the door?"

"There's a spare in the safe downstairs, but that would need to be signed out."

"Good, then I'll take that one," Charlie smiled as the Inspector handed it over. "Miss Baxter will be down later to collect the spare later. Now, who can I borrow a kettle and a couple of mugs from?"

****

A couple of minutes later the Inspector returned with an electric kettle and two clean if slightly chipped mugs. When he'd left, Charlie opened the cardboard box and fetched out a jar of coffee and three plastic containers that separately contained teabags, sugar and fresh milk. Setting the kettle to boil, he turned to Baxter and indicating she sit, he pulled up a chair and said, "Right, I know you're desperate to know what's going on, but before we begin, let's set a couple of ground rules. For the duration of this inquiry we're going to be working as neighbours, so do you mind if I call you Alison?"

"No sir, of course not."

"Then I'm Charlie, unless there's some reason you believe you must not address me as Charlie or we're in the company of management and you believe it proper to observe the rank structure. Another thing is that from this point you will identify yourself as Detective Constable Baxter. Are you okay with that?"

"Yes, Charlie," she smiled.

The kettle whistled and he arose from his chair, asking, "Tea or coffee?"

"Coffee, always; just milk."

"Roger."

As he prepared the coffee's he asked, "Give me an overview of your experience as a university professor who taught criminology, Forensic psychology and profiling."

"Well," she nodded thanks as she took the mug from him, "after I graduated from the University of Edinburgh with my Honours in Criminology and Criminal Justice, I briefly toyed with the idea of joining the police, but to be frank the lure of money in the private sector far outweighed anything the police offered at that time. That and I was offered a position at a prestigious university in New York where I worked for almost ten years and during which time I obtained an Honours in Psychology. During that period, I voluntarily assisted the NYPD on a number of occasions with criminal cases where profiling the suspects and their MO's assisted in several convictions. As a result I came to the attention of the FBI and also assisted their New York office on several occasions, one of which during a high profile serial murder case I successfully identified the individual who became their chief suspect and was later convicted of multiple murder."

Charlie's brow furrowed when he remarked, "It didn't have any of that information on your file."

"I didn't admit to it," she tightly smiled. "When I applied to join the CID I wanted to be treated as a budding detective, not some hotshot with a 'seen it, done it' attitude."

"I can understand that," he sighed. "With your kind of background and experience, management would likely have whisked you of to some desk job. So," he nodded, "please continue."

"While in New York, I married a university colleague; however, after five years the marriage failed and I decided to return home to Edinburgh where I secured a teaching post at Napier University."

"What caused you to join the police? I mean, with your qualifications, you must have been on a hell of a better salary that even what I'm getting."

"I was bored," she smiled. "I'm forty-eight now, Charlie, and I needed some excitement in my life. As I said, I had this lifelong ambition and always toyed with the notion of joining the police, but the opportunity never really arose and when I turned thirty, I thought I had missed the opportunity. When I learned the police in Scotland had dropped the age limit, I had just turned forty-three and decided to go for it. Of course I realise that my career as a police officer is limited, but what working life I have, I want to enjoy," she smiled and he saw that she was indeed an attractive woman.

"Well," he shrugged, "here's hoping that what I'm about to tell you will not only make use of your talents, Alison, but that you *will* enjoy the investigation too."

The next half hour was spent bringing her up to speed with everything that he knew and concluded with him admitting, "I've brought you on board because of your qualifications and frankly, I've never been involved in a cold case like this. So, what's your thoughts?"

"You said the stolen money, apart from that seized from the four convicted men's bank accounts, has never been recovered?"

"Correct," he nodded.

"Then it seems to me," she shrugged, "that Murdo Clarke's murder has to be about one of two issues. Either the gang discovered he was touting to the police and killed him or perhaps had him killed or it's about the money."

She pursed her lips before continuing, "And *that's* assuming he is in fact the fifth man. AS for Dougrie being the killer, it seems to me that other than supposition there's no evidence to link the former Dougrie with the murder. Now," her eyes narrowed as she stared at Charlie, "let's assume Dougrie killed Clarke. Why would Dougrie murder his informant for any reason other than the money, but the fact the money remains unrecovered seems to me that if Dougrie *did* have access to it, he'd be long gone and there would be no need for him to continue to draw his police pension. No," she shook her head, "Without any other profile information about him or Clarke, I can't think of a reason right now why Dougrie would murder Clarke."

"Tell me this," she continued, "is there any indication that upon their release from prison, the two surviving members of the gang, Francis Colville and Thomas Craig, received any of the money when they were released from prison?"

"Not to my knowledge, but we'll find out in due course when we get round to interviewing them," he replied.

She screwed her face in thought and added, "There is one little detail that we might have overlooked too."

He stared quizzically at her as she continued, "Assuming the money stolen during the gang's robberies are all notes of different denominations, it follows that those notes will have been printed and in circulation prior to or at the latest, 1989. You agree?"

He nodded and inwardly realised he knew where this was going. "I'm going to sound like a smart-arse here, but unless you are already aware my knowledge already is that bank notes in the UK last anything between one year for five pound notes to five years for the higher denomination notes so…"

"So," he interrupted, "if whoever *is* holding the money decides to spend it, they'll be spending notes that are likely outdated and no longer in circulation and that should raise a few eyebrows. Smart thinking, Alison."

She slowly shook her head. "Yes, well, if whoever *has* the money hasn't used it yet, it begs the question, where is it? From what you told me my first instinct is that if we can trace where the money is or where it went, we've found our killer."

He smiled and nodding, continued, "I agree. We try to follow the where the money went. However, that's not our only problem at the minute. The reporter from the 'Glasgow News'…"

"He said his name was Hendry."

"Yes, well, somebody has leaked to this guy Hendry that we're investigating the exhumed body and that might cause us problems."

"How so?"

"For a start the media will go all out to discover who the body is or rather, was and if they identify him as Murdo Clarke, missing since 1989, they might turn their attention to why we're not conducting a full blown inquiry rather than the covert inquiry we are running. That and if the leak has information that Clarke was an informant, well…"

"They'll turn their attention to trying to discover who was running him at the time."

"Exactly."

"Do you suspect anyone in particular as the leak?"

"No," he shook his head, "but it has to be a cop who was either at the site of the exhumation or knew the body had been taken to Monklands Hospital for the PM."

"Will you go after the leak?"

"It's pointless now the cat's out of the bag," he sighed, then recalling the confrontation at the hospital, asked, "What's the issue between you and Doctor Mason?"

She didn't immediately respond, but then then said, "I had known

Julia during my university years, though she was a couple of years ahead of me. Ten years ago she was engaged in an archaeological dig in Queens, in New York. As I recall, it was a number of bodies unearthed from a building project and presumed to be a gangster killing from the days of alcohol prohibition. Anyway, her being in New York and knowing her slightly as I did, we got together socially. In those days Julia wasn't always such a..." she smiled. "How can I put this without seeming to be too bitchy? Such a...stoutly built woman. No, in those days Julia was a bit of a vamp; a man-eater, if you will. Very career minded too and used men regardless of their marital status and one of those men," she sighed, "was my husband. Of course, I didn't realise what was going on until it was too late and though he promised he'd end it; well," she smiled sadly at Charlie, "as far as I was concerned, his betrayal was unforgiveable. Of course, I confronted her but she was completely indifferent to the damage she had done to my marriage and though we we were never really friends as such, the animosity stayed with me and obviously, with her too."

He raised his hand and with a cheeky grin, said, "I'm a very happily married man, Alison, and comfortable in telling you this that you can take as a compliment. You've certainly weathered the years a lot better than she has."

She laughed and then asked, "You have children?"

"My wife Sadie is a uniform sergeant and yes, we have two girls. Geraldine whose eight and Ella, who's two and a half."

"Lucky you. I never had kids."

"They bring their own joy, but can be a worry too. Now, let's get back to business. James Dougrie. You agree he's our first interview?"

"Agreed. We have his address?"

Charlie stood and reached into the cardboard box and withdrew the cardboard filing box he had received from the Chief Constable.

"He's in receipt of a police pension and we have the last known address, so after we have a look in here," he knocked upon the top of box, "that's where we'll start."

****

They were discussing the statements and documents that were now spread across two of the three desks when the door knocked and was pushed open by a tall woman with black, collar length hair who dressed in a bottle green skirted suit wore steel framed glasses. "Mister Miller?" she asked.

Nodding, Charlie replied and correctly guessed, "DCI Paterson?"

"That's me. Lorna, sir, please," she extended her hand.

Charlie introduced Baxter and then said, "What can I do for you, Lorna?"

Paterson took a deep breath and replied, "I was rather hoping that you might invite me to join your team." Her face expressed her curiosity when she asked, "Is this it, then? Just the two of you?"

"Just the two of us," Charlie repeated, then apologetically added, "I'm sorry, Lorna. I'm working under direct instruction from the Chief Constable to keep this as tight as possible. However, if the need should arise where I require some further assistance…"

"I understand," she smiled. "You'll let me know?"

"I'll let you know," he nodded.

****

She was in her car when Chief Inspector 'Harry' Downes phoned her.

"Harry, what can I do for you?"

"Cathy, sorry to bother you when I can hear you're driving, but I thought I'd let you know ASAP. One of my team has had the 'Glasgow News' on asking about a post mortem that occurred this morning at Monklands Hospital. Do you now anything about it?"

Shit! Mulgrew thought, but replied, "That's a sensitive issue. What else did they ask?"

"They wondered if Charlie Miller had any comment to make. Said one of their reporters challenged him outside the hospital mortuary for an interview, but that Charlie refused to make any comment. I tried to contact him at Tulliallan, but I got his Deputy, a DI called Mark Bennett who told me that Charlie was unavailable and referred me to you. So, are you in a position to tell me something that will permit me to make some kind of response?"

"I'm just on my way back to Gartcosh from Glasgow, Harry, so let me get back to you, but for now tell them nothing."

"Will do," Downes replied and ended the call.

****

It had been a fretful day for Sadie Miller.

While her mother entertained Ella downstairs, a discreet call from her bedroom to the Chief Inspector at Baird Street had confirmed her taking off the next few days.

Now, with their coats on, she had persuaded Carol to accompany her to the local shops, "Just for some fresh air," she had brightly said, the real reason being she needed to occupy her mothers mind with something other than tomorrow morning's examination, for Carol was literally jumping about the house like a rubber ball bouncing off the wall.

****

He was in the pub in Rutherglen Main Street having quiet afternoon pint when big Alex, the heavily tattooed barman with the broken nose and scarred face genially asked, "Watching the game on the tele tonight, Smiler or did you manage to get a ticket?"

Frankie Colville, known as Smiler since he was at primary school, shook his head and toothlessly replied, "It's the television, Alex. Trying to get a ticket for a European game at Parkhead is murder and besides, I don't have that kind of money these days. So, it's me and a couple of cans of Tennants. What about you?"

"Oh, I've the late shift in here, so I'll likely catch the highlights when I get home. How's the wife these days?"

Colville shook his head and frowning, said, "Not good. The doc says if she keeps taking the tablets then it'll help, but," he shrugged, "I keep expecting to wake up each morning with her lying there dead."

"Can't be easy for you, Smiler."

"For me? No," he shook his head, "it's Elsie that's the one who didn't get it easy."

He sighed before continuing, "Not with me away serving all that time at the Ruchazie Hotel. How she managed to raise four weans on the pittance the social gave her, I just don't know."

"Aye, but still, it can't have been a picnic for you either. What was it, twenty years you served?"

"Twenty-one I did with four off on remission for good behaviour. At least I got out," he shook his head then added, "You remember Sandy Murtagh, don't you? He got himself killed up in Peterhead in an argument about a pouch of tobacco."

"What about the rest of your team. Do you see any of them these days?"

Colville shook his head. "Johnny O'Connor passed away with the cancer and fuck knows what happened to that headcase, Tommy Craig. The last I heard of him he was drinking in a pub over in Shettleston somewhere. Not that he'd want to stay in touch anyway, not after we all got banged up."

"You guys did some damage when you were in your hey-day though," Alex grinned.

"Aye," Colville forced a smile and lifting his tumbler to finish his pint, bitterly added, "but where the fuck has it got me, eh? I'm to old to be employed, my missus is on medication to keep her alive and my four kids have scattered away and never get in touch with me. Oh, they'll phone right enough," he nodded, "but if it's *me* that answers the phone all I get is, 'Is my mammy there?' because they'll not speak to me."

He slowly laid the tumbler onto the bar and with a farewell nod to Alex, lifted his plastic shopping bag from the floor beside him and made his way to the door.

****

Now on the A90 towards Dundee, Julia Mason still fumed at her curt dismissal by the police officer, Miller.

The fool just didn't appreciate what she could contribute to his inquiry.

It annoyed her that though he evidently knew the identity of the victim, he would not disclose the name and made it that little more difficult when she prepared her article for the 'Glasgow News.'

Her eyes narrowed as she recalled the conversation with the journalist, the man called Hendry. He assured her that he would be in attendance at the mortuary and they would collaborate to prepare the story.

Why he didn't turn up confused her for he had seemed keen enough when she phoned.

Distracted by her thoughts, she braked suddenly to avoid colliding with the large van in front and let forth a stream of abuse at the ridiculously slow speed of the van, banging at her horn as she sped past the slower vehicle.

Tears of rage and anger seeped from her eyes and she gripped the steering wheel a little tighter.

They were all conspiring against her, of that she was now certain.

Well, *fuck* them all, she thought.

She would come out of this with her book and perhaps, her imagination took over, television interviews to promote her autobiography.

****

"This cigarette butt that was discovered beneath the body," Baxter turned to Charlie. "Have the Forensics been able to obtain any DNA from it?"

"I've not had any result as yet..." He stopped and suddenly slapped his hand against his forehead.

"Stupid, stupid, *stupid*!"

"What?"

"I haven't spoken with Forensics to tell them I'm in the SIO so if there *is* any result, they'll send it to the SIO who commenced the inquiry..."

"DCI Paterson."

"Correct. What's her extension number?" he asked as he lifted the desk phone.

Baxter glanced at the list on the wall and replied, "Two-seven-five."

Seconds later, Charlie said, "Lorna? It's Charlie Miller. Have you guys had any result on the DNA test for the cigarette butt you found at the location?"

"See, told you I'm available to assist," she gleefully replied.

He sighed and said, "I take it you've heard something then?"

"My DI, Billy McKnight, just took a phone call from Archie Young at Gartcosh. Shall I come and tell you what he said?"

Charlie recognised he was being teased and with a smile replied, "I'll sit here with bated breath awaiting your arrival."

Minutes later Lorna Paterson knocked on the door and entering, grinned and waved a scrap of paper at Charlie.

"Here you are, sir."

"Charlie, please," he smiled tolerantly and took the paper from her hand.

Baxter saw his eyebrows raise and said, "What?"

"Good old Archie. The good news is he's managed to lift some DNA from the cigarette, but the bad news is that there's nothing recorded on the database to match it."

"Mind you," she replied, "if I correctly recall, the database wasn't set up until sometime in the early nineties. Still, if we obtain samples from the people we..." she stopped and turned towards Paterson who leaning with her back against the door, raised her hands in mock surrender and said, "Don't mind me. Feel free to talk among yourselves."

"You're not going to let this go, are you?" Charlie asked her.

"If the body was exhumed in your area of responsibility and someone else stepped in and took over as SIO, would you just ignore what's going on?"

Shaking his head, he smiled tolerantly and replied, "Probably not."

"Besides, I'm a woman," she loftily continued, "and it's my prerogative to be nosey."

That earned her another smile and he said, "I promise you, Lorna, if I can use you, I will, but right now you'll need to let me and Alison get on with what we're doing."

Again she raised her hands in surrender and replied, "Fair enough. You know where to find me," and left the room.

"Persistent, isn't she?" Baxter grinned at him.

"You think *she's* persistent. You should try working with Cathy Mulgrew," he pretended to scowl.

"Right," he abruptly stood, "grab your jacket and the address for our former Detective Inspector, Mister Dougrie. Let's pay him a visit and see what he recalls about the disappearance of his informant, Murdo Clarke."

****

She turned as one of her junior assistants called out, "Ma'am, that's another call from the 'Glasgow News' asking for information about the body that was discovered in Lanarkshire. Will I patch the call through to you?"

She sighed and nodding for the young man to do so, lifted her phone and said, "Chief Inspector Downes."

"Chief Inspector, it's Brian Hendry here at the 'Glasgow News.' I was wondering if you've prepared a press release yet about the…"

"I know, the body discovered in a field. No, Mister Hendry, that's still under consideration."

"What about Detective Superintendent Miller's attendance today at the Monklands Hospital mortuary. Can you comment on *that*?"

"Again, that is still…"

"Yeah," he interrupted, his voice betraying his frustration, "it's *still* under consideration. Well then, what *can* you tell me?"

She hesitated and rubbed wearily at her forehead. She hated being left out on a limb like this when her bloody job was to mediate between the police and the news agencies, for their cooperation and assistance was a vital source in gathering information or getting messages out to the public.

"Look, here's what I suggest," she slowly began. "I don't have all the facts yet and you certainly don't want to run a story without the facts, do you?"

"No, of course not, but…"

"Just wait and listen to me," she unconsciously raised a hand to stop him speaking. "Your paper is the only paper that's persistently contacted us regarding the body. Your rival newspapers seem to have dropped the story as a by-line. Now, if you refrain from hassling me and my staff about what's going on, when I find out more I will call you. Do we have a deal??"

"What, you'll phone me before you issue a press release?"

"Only if you keep the story off the front page like your rivals are doing."

"Okay, you've got a deal, but you *will* phone Chief Inspector, won't you?"

"Speak to your news editor. He'll confirm that I'm a woman of my word," she replied and with a sigh of relief, she ended the call.
****

He thought he heard the doorbell ring, but glancing at his wristwatch saw it wasn't that time yet and ignored it for the thought of getting out of the comfortable garden chair wasn't worth taking in another parcel for next door.

There it was again, the bloody doorbell and the sod was keeping their finger on the button.

He glanced again at his wristwatch and wondered; had he got the time wrong? No, he unconsciously shook his head. There were still several hours to go.

With an irritated sigh, he pushed himself up out of the chair and in doing so accidentally knocked over the glass of wine by his feet.

"Bugger," he angrily muttered, torn between reaching for the toppled glass or attending to whoever was at his door and giving them a piece of his mind.

His legs were stiff from sitting so long and he reached for his walking stick by the back door.

Slowly stumbling in through the kitchen door and making his way along the hallway to the front door, he unconsciously favoured his good hip and longed for the day the left hip would be replaced. With the bright light shining through the frosted glass in the double glazed door, he could see a figure silhouetted.

He exhaled, preparing himself for an argument and unlocked the door.

Pulling it open, his eyes widened in surprise and his rebuke was cut off short as almost unbelievingly, he said, "My God, it *is* you! After all these years!"

He didn't see the knife, only felt the sharp and excruciating pain as the blade was plunged into his stomach, withdrawn and plunged again as he began to fall towards his killer, the knife striking him in the chest where hitting a rib, the tip glanced off and entered his heart.

His hand reached out to vainly grab at something as he fell, but the knife thrust came again, this time catching him in the throat and preventing his scream from alerting anyone passing by who glancing over the five foot hedge might have seen a bloodied figure racing towards the garden gate as former Detective Inspector James Dougrie collapsed to his death on his doorstep.

CHAPTER EIGHT

The two officers who attended the elderly female neighbour's frantic call to Belmont Drive in the Giffnock district of Glasgow, discovered the body face down at the open door, the walking stick lying by his side.

"Better get the CID and some extra bodies here, hen," the older cop gravely said, who confirming the man was dead, quickly stood back from the body lest his feet contaminate the expanding pool of blood. "While you're at it," he added, "stand by the gate there. I know it's a quiet street, but there's bound to be nosey buggers so keep the rubbernecks away as best you can. I'm away round the back to check if there's anything amiss and if I can get into the house that way."

The young policewoman did as she was bid, her voice a betraying her excitement as she used her radio for this was the first time she had attended a murder scene and inwardly hoped she didn't mess up, that she remembered everything she had been taught about securing the locus.

My notebook, her eyes widened at the thought and removed it from her utility belt pouch. Forcing herself to be calm, she quickly noted the time of her attendance at the locus and with a backward glance at the elderly man lying dead, involuntarily shivered and notebook in hand carefully sketched a matchstick figure lying at the angle in the doorway as she saw it.

Awaiting the arrival of the supporting officers, her feet nervously drummed a beat on the pavement.

An old style Volvo estate car drove slowly along the road towards her and she watched with suspicion as it stopped outside the house. The driver, a large bulky man with a prominent scar three-inch scar that run down the right side of his cheek, got out and stared curiously at her as a woman with short fair hair exited the passenger side.

The man said, "Is there a problem here, officer?"

"Nothing to concern you, sir, so please move along," she politely replied and held up a restraining hand.

He glanced behind her and eyes narrowing reached into his inside jacket pocket from where he produced a warrant card that he held up for her to examine and said, "My name's Detective Superintendent Charlie Miller. Can I be of assistance to you?"

Her face paled and she replied, "I'm sorry, sir, I didn't realise…."

But Charlie held up his hand and with a grim smile, replied, "No problem, Constable, you're quite correct to ask who I am. And you are…?"

"Helen Wynd, sir. Sorry," she blushed, "I mean Constable Helen Wynd."

"Okay, Helen. Now, DC Baxter and I are here to visit with a Mister Dougrie."

Nodding at the body lying in the doorway, he asked, "Is that him?"

"I don't know, sir," she shook her head as she turned to stare behind her at the body. "My neighbour and I have just arrived minutes ago. Stuart, I mean Constable Bates, he's at the back checking the rest of the house."

At that and almost on cue, the older cop walked up the driveway at the side of the house to the front of the gate and seeing Charlie, approached to find out who he was before introducing himself.

"I've been in the house, sir, but there's nobody else there. I made sure not to touch anything. I did see a photograph of a cop in uniform; you know, the old tunic we used to wear I mean and having had a look at the deceased I'm of the opinion it's him," he turned and nodded to the doorway. "The body's still warm so I don't believe he's been dead for very long. Helen," he turned to his neighbour, "have you called it in?"

"The Inspector and some support is on it's way and the CID are being contacted."

"Who is the Divisional DCI these days?" Charlie asked.

"That'll be Gerry Donaldson, sir. Works out of the Helen Street office in Govan. Do you know him?"

"Oh, aye," Charlie smiled humourlessly, "I know Gerry Donaldson." What he didn't say was the the balding, heavy set man with the ruddy complexion mainly from broken veins in his cheeks that was the result of his regular overindulgence of whisky was not what Charlie would describe as a competent detective. He inwardly sighed for already he envisaged problems with Donaldson and the murder of James Dougrie.

The four turned as a police car with its blue light blazing screeched to a halt and watched as a thin faced, female Inspector with pale skin and three uniformed constables piled out of the vehicle. The Inspector strutted imperiously towards the four and in a high pitched voice, asked Bates, "What's the story Constable and who are these civilians?"

Bates, clearly fighting to avoid grinning, replied, "This is Detective Superintendent Miller, Inspector and his neighbour, DC Baxter." Startled, the inspector turned to Charlie and face reddening, said, "My apologies, sir. I didn't realise…"

"Your officers have it all under control, Inspector," he interrupted, "and a fine job they're doing too."

Unseen by his Inspector, Charlie winked at Bates before adding, "Perhaps you might wish to deploy your officers to completely secure the locus, Inspector, while I speak with Constable Bates and his neighbour and can I suggest deploying at least one constable round the back of the house. I understand the rear door is insecure and we don't want curious visitors, do we?"

"No, sir, and yes, of course," then turned away to bark orders to her three constables.

Out of earshot of the four, Charlie smiled at Bates and with another wink, asked, "Bit of a martinet that one?"

"You've no idea, sir," the cop sighed with a shake of his head.

"Give us a minute," he told Bates and beckoning to Baxter, they returned to sit in the Volvo.

Fetching his mobile phone from his pocket, he dialled the number for Cathy Mulgrew and when the call was answered, put it on loudspeaker and said, "Morning, Cathy. I'm sitting with my neighbour, DC Alison Baxter in my car outside James Dougrie's house in Giffnock."

"What's he saying?" she asked.

"Not a lot I'm afraid. When we got here there was two cops in attendance and what seems to be Dougrie lying face down in his doorway, stabbed to death. As far as I can establish, it only occurred within the last hour."

"You're kidding me!"

"Nope," he couldn't help smiling at her surprise. "The locus is being secured and the local CID are being summoned."

At that, he saw a grey coloured CID car draw up behind the uniform car and the DCI climb our of the passenger door while two other detectives also got out of the car. "As I speak, that's the CID arrived, led by Gerry Donaldson."

"Donaldson? Bugger. That will cause you problems," she replied.

"So, do I have the Chief's permission to continue with my investigation or abandon the inquiry and sit back and let him balls it up?"

Baxter drew him a curious sidelong glance, but he responded by shaking his head.

"Give me a minute and I'll get back to you," Mulgrew replied and ended the call.

"I'm guessing there's no love lost between you and Donaldson," Baxter asked.

"The man's a bloody bully and an incompetent," he replied. "He's notorious throughout the CID for claiming credit for his staff's detections and blaming them when *he* messes up. He always values opinions, though," Charlie shook his head, "as long as it's his own. A number of years ago he was briefly my DI at Stewart Street when I was a DS and let's just say him and I have had words in the past. His thirty years is long gone, but somehow he's managed to stay in his post. Probably got a pal in management somewhere," he growled.

They watched as Donaldson walked towards the garden gate where Constable Bates stood and after a brief exchange of words, saw Bates nod towards the Volvo.

Donaldson's already florid face turned a darker shade of red as he slowly walked towards the car.

Getting out of the Volvo, Charlie and Baxter met him on the pavement where Donaldson said, "Well, as I live and breathe. Charlie Miller. Long time no see. Who's this?"

"DC Baxter, meet DCI Donaldson."

"Sir," she formally greeted him.

He ignored her and his voice oozing hostility, asked, "Why are you here, Charlie?"

"I'm conducting an ongoing investigation. James Dougrie was a witness that I intended interviewing."

"What's the investigation about?"

"I'm sorry, but that's classified."

"I'll need to know if I've a murder to investigate," he sneered.

"And if I believed you would need to know, Detective Chief Inspector, then I would tell you," Charlie calmly replied.

The mobile in his pocket chirruped and snatching at it, he saw Cathy Mulgrew to be the calling number.

"Miss Mulgrew," he began, his eyes fixedly staring into Donaldson's, "I'm currently stood with DCI Donaldson at the murder locus of James Dougrie. Do you have some information for me?"

Aware of the hostility between both men, she quickly replied, "You have the Chief's consent to assume responsibility for Dougrie's murder and you are to continue with the investigation. Again, within *reason*," she stressed, "you are to use what resources you deem appropriate."

"Thank you," he abruptly ended the call and forcing himself to remain calm, said, "DCI Donaldson, on the instruction of the Chief Constable, this is now my crime scene. Please have your officers arrange for Scene of Crime, PF's department and the casualty surgeon to attend the locus. Thereafter I want you to return to your sub office at Giffnock where you will set up an incident room and await my arrival there. Is that clear?"

Donaldson, his face apoplectic with anger, staggered back a step. He wanted to scream and rant, but some inner sense told him he'd lose the argument, so turned and angrily beckoned to his two detectives. Muttering to them, he jabbed a forefinger in the direction of Charlie before snatching the car keys from one of the detectives. They watched as Donaldson got into the driving seat of the CID car and with a screech of tyres, roared away as the two bemused detectives stared from the departing car to Charlie.

"Well," Baxter quietly said, "I suspect you won't be getting a Christmas card from that ignoramus and if his breath is any indication, he'll be lucky to get to his office without being stopped for drink driving."

****

The secret was out.

No longer was Detective Superintendent Miller and his neighbour, DC Baxter covertly investigating a former police officer DI James Dougrie who in 1989 was secretly suspected by the police senior management of that time of the murder of his informant, Murdo Clarke.

Now, with the public and full blown inquiry into the murder of Dougrie, Charlie had little option but to prepare himself to address his new team at Giffnock office and after satisfying himself that there was no more he could do to the locus, left a Detective Sergeant in charge there to finish up and secure the locus.

With Baxter, he made his way to the Giffnock office.

On route she said, "I have to ask you this. Now that it's no longer a secret, what do you intend for me?"

"What do you mean?"

"Well," she slowly drawled, "I'm the fish out of the barrel here. You brought me in for my specialist knowledge and to keep your inquiry under wraps from the mainstream CID, but now…" she paused and inhaled before slowly exhaling. "Now I'm wondering with my lack of experience as a DC, what use am I?"

He turned to briefly glance at her before responding.

"Yes," he slowly nodded, "you might be inexperienced in a major inquiry, but you have other skills, Alison. Skills I can use and don't forget we're still investigating a very old cold case; so for now, you're going nowhere."

"Okay," she replied, though he couldn't know how pleased she was. "What do I tell my new colleagues?"

"Tell them nothing. As far as they are concerned, you're a DC and my…what is it they call those guys?"

"Aide-de-camp?" she grinned before teasingly adding, "Might set tongues wagging, you having a female personal assistant."

He returned her grin and said, "Well, we'll easily put paid to that. You can come for something to eat tonight before you head back to the Castle. Meet Sadie and the kids if they're still up."

"I'd like that, thanks."

****

DCI Gerry Donaldson hit Giffnock office like a bull on speed, shouting and cursing as without explanation, he ordered the few officers he found there to set up the incident room. A bully of the worst type, Donaldson believed his thirty-four years of service entitled him to be right about everything.

As the detectives and their civilian staff hurried to set up the incident room in the general office, Donaldson demanded that one of them fetch him a coffee and made his way to the DI's room. When the coffee arrived, he rudely dismissed the young woman then from an inside jacket pocket fetched a hip flask from which he poured a generous amount of whisky into the mug.

Downing the contents of the mug, he felt more relaxed and thought about the confrontation with Charlie Miller.

Who did the jumped up bastard think he was dealing with? Some by the book plain clothes plod?

Bastard!

Fucking bastard!

He took a deep breath and eyes almost like slits, was tempted to refill the mug with whisky, but stopped.

He'd taken a hell of a chance driving the CID car to Giffnock, for he always made a point of being chauffeured wherever he went.

It wouldn't do for some beastie, some uniformed Traffic cop to give him a pull when he'd had a little snifter. Whisky made no impression upon him, but those bastards were worth the watching.

The door knocked and a female DS poked her head through the door to say, "That's the room prepared, sir, and the HOLMES people have been requested to attend with their equipment. Anything else?"

"How the *fuck* do I know?" he roared. "Ask Miller when he arrives!"

The DS's eyes narrowed as she wondered who the hell Miller was, but wisely nodded and withdrew.

Left alone again, Donaldson continued to seethe and tempted though he was to just leave and have someone drive him to Govan, he decided he would not give Miller the opportunity to recall him him back to Giffnock and so remained seated as he plotted how he could get back at the bastard.

****

Martin Cairney, the Chief Constable, was fit to burst.

Shaking his head, he addressed Cathy Mulgrew and said, "This is getting out of hand. Our suspect for a twenty-eight-year old murder is now himself murdered. If the media get a hold of what's going on, they'll have a field day. Hell!" he abruptly stood up from behind his desk and hands tightly clenched behind his back, strolled to the window.

Mulgrew said nothing, believing it best he got it out of his system before she spoke.

He turned and calm now, asked, "What did Miller say about Dougrie's murder?"

"It's early days yet, sir. All he could tell me was the first indications is that Dougrie had been stabbed and within an hour of Charlie arriving at his house."

"Wait," his eyes narrowed. "Within an hour of Miller arriving there? Is there a possibility that whoever killed Dougrie knew that Miller was attending to speak with him?"

Mulgrew shook her head and replied, "While there is the strongest possibility that Dougrie's murder is related to the discovery of the body which," she stressed, "was the subject of some media attention, I seriously doubt anyone knew of Charlie's intentions to interview Dougrie today. That would mean…" she stopped and stared at Cairney. "Sir, you can't believe we've a leak in Charlie's team? My God, there's only him and his neighbour and she's not connected to the inquiry."

"No, not Miller and his neighbour, Cathy, but did anyone else know of his intention to interview Dougrie?"

"No," she shook her head, " I don't believe so. I'm convinced it's an unfortunate turn of events and likely related to the media item about the exhumation."

"Well, if nothing else and you *are* correct it tells us that whoever killed Dougrie believed him to have some information about the murder of Murdo Clarke and that's why he was killed; to prevent him disclosing that information."

"I'm sure that Charlie will have deduced that, sir. Now," she stood up from her chair, "it's my intention to visit him at Giffnock where he's setting up an incident room. Do you have any message that I should relay to him?"

Cairney stopped pacing up and down and staring at her, took a breath then slowly relaxed his body before replying, "Tell Mister Miller he has my full support."

****

When word of the murder of a former police officer reached the Media Department at Dalmarnock office, Chief Inspector Harry Downes groaned.

The death of one of their own whether serving or retired was always bad news but this, she shook her head as she read the note from her deputy. However, reading on she saw that the SIO in the investigation was Charlie Miller and rolled her eyes, for she suspected that this murder was somehow related to the 'Glasgow News' inquiry by the the reporter, Brian Hendry.

Lifting her desk phone, she dialled the number for Giffnock police office.

****

Leaning with his arms folded and backside against the top desk and with DCI Gerry Donaldson stood sullenly by his side, Charlie stared round the room at the half dozen detectives and the three civilian staff. A couple of the detectives' faces were familiar and presumed he recognised them from their attendance on CID course at the training college.

Realising from the few personnel present that Donaldson had made no effort to bring in detectives from the other Divisional offices at Pollok and Govan, he hid his irritation and forcing a smile, introduced himself and Alison Baxter to the team, adding that he hoped to learn all their names in the next day or two.

"Some of you might recognise me as the Director of CID Training at Tulliallan, but that means nothing here, guys, so please, do not presume because of my regular job title that I know everything. If any of you think I'm missing something or there is something I should know, come directly to me and tell me. Like they say, every day is a school day and I'm no different to anyone else. Now, looking about I can see you might be a little disconcerted by the lack of numbers in our team, but don't worry," he raised a hand as though to quell their concern. "There will be other officers joining us if not today, then certainly tomorrow. DCI Donaldson I'm certain will be able to provide additional support and I'm hopeful I can also procure some detectives from the Major Investigation Team. For now, though, we get the incident room set up and the door to door in Belmont Drive started. Right, I need an office manager so," he glanced around the room, "any Detective Sergeants present?"

A dark-haired woman in her mid-thirties, her hair tied up in a bun who wore a tan coloured blouse and dark brown knee length skirt, raised her hand and hesitantly called out, "DS Shona Mathieson, sir. I've been running the office here until the new DI is appointed."

"Okay, Shona," he smiled, "you're it. When we're done done can you begin with sending some of the guys out to knock on the doors in Belmont Drive, please?"

He smiled at the three civilian staff, all female typists, who stood quietly together and said, "I'll be grateful if you ladies take your direction from Shona. Have you all worked a major inquiry before?"

The oldest woman nodded and replied, "The three of us are HOLMES trained, sir."

"Good, eh, you are?" he smiled at her.

"Alice Brookes, sir. I'm the head typist and the senior HOLMES operator when there is a major incident at this office."

"Thanks Alice. You and your ladies will be vital to this inquiry," he smiled at them in turn, then clapping his hands together, continued to the team, "The victim, James Dougrie, aged sixty-seven, was a retired police officer so as a matter of priority we'll need to find out who his next of kin is for formal statements and identification."

He glanced at a tall, well built and dark haired, scruffy looking detective with piercing blue eyes and a days growth and said, "I apologise, but I don't know your name."

"DC Willie Baillie, boss."

"Hello, Willie. You look like a man who knows his way around. Will you take that job on, please?"

"Glad to, boss," Baillie smiled at the compliment.

He could not know it, but Charlie's easy going manner and respectful attitude towards the staff present had already won them over though, as he was to learn, their intense dislike of their DCI was such that any senior manager who treated them fairly was like a breath of fresh air.

"I'd like to give you a briefing, but to be honest at this time I believe we're better getting ourselves sorted out and by tomorrow morning I will be in a better position to tell you what I know. However, suffice to say that Alison and I didn't just happen upon the murder locus; we were there to interview the victim about his knowledge of a missing person from 1989 who two days ago turned up in a shallow grave in a field in Lanarkshire."

A buzz of excitement run through the crowd for most if not all had learned via the media of the exhumation of the body.

"Now, there's nothing to confirm that the MP's body and the murder of our victim today are connected, but I intend working on the premise that they are. As I said earlier, it's my intention at tomorrow mornings briefing to give you what I know, but for now we'll get on with the jobs in hand. Shona?"

He nodded to the DS who taking her cue, called the detectives to her desk.

Turning to the silent Donaldson, he said, "While I take charge as SIO here at Giffnock, Mister Donaldson, I'll leave you to run the rest of your Division. Now," he smiled humourlessly, "please don't let me detain you any longer. Thank you."

Smarting at the dismissal, Donaldson turned on his heel and wordlessly left the room.

It was only when Charlie turned around he saw that the team had all stopped to watch him and in an effort to lighten the moment, he grinned as he called out, "Okay, who takes my two quid for the tea fund?"

****

He decided to take the vacant DI's room as his own for the duration of the inquiry and it was to there the call from Chief Inspector Downes was transferred.

"Harry," he smilingly greeted her. "What can I do for you?"

"For a start, Charlie, tell me what the hell's going on. First I get a complaint from the 'Glasgow News' that you attended a PM today out at Monklands Hospital then snubbed the reporter who tried to…and wait a minute. What was that about your neighbour sending him flying?"

Charlie responded with a laugh before replying, "The guy was in my face and Alison Baxter used her umbrella to send him flat onto *his* face."

"Oh, serves the nosey bugger right. However, I understand you now have a murder to investigate, a former cop called James Dougrie. I thought you were still running the CID courses at Tulliallan?"

"I am or rather I was, I mean. I'm acting on the Chief's instruction regarding the discovery of the body in the grave and now copped this murder because the two are related."

"Bugger me, Charlie," she wiped a hand across her brow. "How the *hell* am I going to issue a press release about this?

"Well, you *are* the expert, Harry, but if I might make a suggestion?"

"Go on."

"The cat's out of the bag anyway about the exhumation, so why not just tell the truth, that we the polis are making inquiries into an historical missing person and I'm also acting as the SIO for the murder of Dougrie; two completely separate inquiries. I mean at my rank it's not unusual for a senior officer to be the SIO for two different inquiries. After all, it's the team who are really investigating the MP and the murder; I'm only acting as the manager for both teams."

"You mean, like a club coach who also runs the national team, something like that?"

"What do you think?"

"Sorry, Charlie, these guys are too bright for a ruse like that. They'll spot the lie as soon as I open my mouth. Besides, if your investigation involves both the MP and the murder there's always someone with a big mouth in the inquiry and if it did come out that we'd try to fool the press, they'd be all over us like a bad rash."

He slowly exhaled and then said, "I don't suppose there's any way round it, then. The Chief won't be happy, but there's nothing else for it then. Can you prepare some sort of press release that indicates Dougrie was a possible witness to the case of the MP, but we're not yet certain that both cases are related?"

"Leave it with me and I'll try to sort something out and when I've got it ready, I'll run it by you. In the meantime, I can't control the media so expect them to be camped on your door at Giffnock."

"Thanks, Harry, I know you'll do your best," he ended the call. Replacing the handset into the cradle, the door knocked and was pushed open by Cathy Mulgrew.

"I've just come from the Chief's office. Thought I'd pop in and see how you're doing," she smiled and drew up a chair.

"That was Harry Downes on the phone," he nodded to it. "She's of the opinion the media will soon tie Murdo Clarke's body and Dougrie's murder together, particularly if I'm SIO for both inquiries. I told her not to deny the connection between the two…"

"You didn't!" she was aghast, then shaking her head, slowly added, "The Chief won't like that, Charlie, not one little bit."

"Then tell me how I can avoid it, Cathy?" he angrily replied. "These guys aren't stupid! I'm the SIO for both inquiries and let's not forget, the newspapers keep records too and when it comes out that Clarke has been in the ground for twenty-eight years and Dougrie was the investigating officer for his disappearance…" he waved his hands in the air then taking a breath and calmer, said, "I'd rather face the Chief's wrath than publicly get caught out in a lie and that would *really* make the police look as if we were doing something underhand."

She shrugged and said, "When you put it like that I can see your reasoning. Anyway, to digress. How did Gerry Donaldson take the news that you're the SIO?"

"As you would expect, not well at all. He stormed out of here without a backward glance and there's no doubt in my mind he'll do his utmost to undermine the inquiry."

"You'll need to watch your team. He might have a tout in there somewhere."

"Aye, well as long as I play fair I won't give him the opportunity to stick the knife in. On that point, I've only half a dozen detectives on my team and I don't see Donaldson letting me have any from the Pollok or Govan CID, so what's the chances of you sending me some of the MIT to assist?"

"I'll speak with their boss and get it done. Say eight?"

"That will certainly be useful."

"What about Dougrie's killer? Anything yet?"

"Early days," he shook his head,. "but I'm convinced the murder is related to Clarke's. Hang on," he suddenly stood up from behind the desk and made his way out of the office, returning a moment later with a fair haired woman who he introduced.

"Detective Superintendent Mulgrew, meet Alison Baxter," and fetched a chair that he placed alongside Mulgrew's before resuming his seat behind the desk.

"Alison, I was briefing Miss Mulgrew…"

"Wait," Mulgrew held up a hand and turning to Baxter, her eyes squinted when she asked, "Are you Alison Baxter the criminologist who wrote, A Perversion of Crime?"

"Yes, Ma'am, that's me," Baxter blushed.

Startled by this revelation, Charlie stared as Mulgrew smiled widely and extended her hand, saying, "I thought I recognised you from your cover photograph. I read that last year. As I recall you were a criminologist tenured at a New York university and cooperated on a number of occasions with the NYPD and if I correctly recall, the FBI too."

"Actually, it was just a few cases."

Mulgrew turned to glance at Charlie and slyly said, "I bet this rough git didn't know he had a noted criminologist working for him."

"Actually, smart arse, I did and that's why Alison is here. She was to be my neighbour for the duration of the Murdo Clarke investigation, but I've decided to keep her on. I intend for her to be my expert profiler, if I need one," he grinned, "and hopefully she will pick up on what I miss or don't see."

"Well, I envy you, Miller, for I'm an admirer of Alison's work and I suggest you might want to read it to."

He sat back in his chair and clasping his hands behind his head, glanced from one attractive woman to the other before replying, "Why is it you women always seem to believe I'm some sort of dunderhead?"

Mulgrew's opened innocently wide when she replied, "Oh, because we're always right?"

"Aye very good," he sighed and a was about to add more when the door knocked.

"Come in," he called.

DC Willie Baillie entered and said, "Sorry to disturb you, boss, but I've been on to the local branch of the Retired Police Officers Association and managed to track down their secretary. She tells me that James Dougrie lived alone and was divorced, then his ex-wife died, but believed that he'd a daughter living in Paisley somewhere. I got onto the police pension people and they told me that a number of years ago he updated his next-of kin and so upon his death his daughter becomes his beneficiary. I've got her address and phone number," he laid a sheet of paper on the desk. "Do you want me to follow it up?"

Charlie stared up at the scruffy detective and smiled before replying, "Excellent piece of work, Willie. Grab a set of cars keys and I'll come with you. Alison?" he turned to her, "You can join us too. Cathy, sorry to run out on you."

"Don't mind me," she stood up from her chair and raising both hands, grimly smiled before adding, "I've a Chief Constable to placate."

CHAPTER NINE

Rather than phone, Liz Watson instead decided to visit Sadie Miller and find out what Charlie wouldn't tell her in the autopsy room.

Leading Liz through to the kitchen, Sadie said, "Thanks for coming by, Liz. Mum's away to the shops with Ella and then she's going to collect Geraldine from school. Coffee?"

While the kettle boiled, Sadie explained about the mother's finding of the lump, the visit to the doctor and the distress Carol was currently experiencing.

"I believe you're absolutely correct in getting it seen to as fast as possible," Watson sipped at her coffee. "It's the anxiety and fear of what might be and if indeed the lump is malignant, this dread is thought by some in the medical profession to exacerbate the condition."

"I was hoping when she returns you might have a word with her? I can offer you dinner if you wish to stay on for a while?"

"Yes, of course I'll speak with Carol, but you must realise that without a diagnosis, Sadie, there's very little I can tell her without causing her more worry. As for dinner," she smiled, "thanks, but I have made an arrangement."

"Oh," Sadie grinned, "is this the mysterious man I suspect you are seeing?"

"Might be," she airily replied then eyes narrowing, stared suspiciously at Sadie as she continued, "So, Sergeant Miller, what do you know about this body I examined today?"
****

Carol Forrest, with Ella in the buggy, stood by the school gates and scanned the advancing horde of riotous children until with relief she saw Geraldine coming towards her.

"Hi, Gran," the tousled headed girl greeted her with a grin.

Taking her school bag from her, Carol hung it across the back of the buggy handles and with a smile, asked, "I don't think there's any need for us to get back home right away, so how about the three of us hitting Carlo's Café for an ice-cream?"

"Yes, please," was the gleeful response and ten minutes later, the three were occupying a table; the girls with their ices and Carol with a coffee.

"So, how was school today?"

"Just the usual," Geraldine shrugged with the indifference of an eight-year-old.

"Oh, nothing to report, then?"

"No, not really."

Carols was about to sip at her coffee when Geraldine, her eyes screwed up, asked, "What's going on, Gran?"

"What? What do you mean?"

"Well," she shrugged again, "you and mum were really upset yesterday and you stayed the night. Is something happening? Are my…" he hesitated, her eyes clouding over and her lips trembling. "Are my mum and dad splitting up? Some of the kids in my class. Their parents have divorced. Is that what's…"

"No," Carol reached for her hand and squeezed it. "No, love, not at all. Your mum and dad love each other very much and they're definitely not splitting up."

"Then what *is* it?" she persisted, her face determined to get an answer. "What's wrong?"

Carol stared at her and decided that the little girl was far too shrewd to be palmed off with a lie.

"It's me," she forced a smile. "I'm not very well. No," she shook her head, "There's a chance I *might* not be well."

Sensing that something was amiss, Ella stared from one to the other,

her ice-cream forgotten and her lips puckered as she began to softly cry.

"Here, here," Carol lifted her from the high chair and sat her on her knee.

"Geraldine," she took a deep breath as she rocked Ella to comfort her, "I'm going to a hospital tomorrow to have a wee test done. I should be okay, but it's just a safety precaution. Do you know what a a safety precaution is?"

"Something to make sure you're okay?"

"Yes, that's it and you know what you old mum's like," she pretended to make a face. "Worries about everything."

"That's mum," Geraldine sighed with a world weary face and added, "I really thought it might be something bad."

Continue to smile, Carol thought, dear God, here's hoping it's not.

****

With Willie Baillie driving and Charlie using his phones SatNav, he directed the big man to Tannahill Terrace in the Ferguslie housing estate in the suburbs of Paisley where they drew up in front of a squalid four-in-block building with two upper and two lower flats. Exiting the car, they could see the lower flats windows were boarded with metal shutters while the upper flat through the wall from the address they sought was similarly boarded up.

"I wished we'd got her on the phone first to ensure she was in," Charlie muttered as he closed the car door.

"No guessing which house we're looking for then," Baillie replied as he stood back to permit Charlie and Alison Baxter to enter the garden path and make their way to the door set in the side of the building.

The gardens in front of the flats were overgrown and littered with household debris.

There was no bell, so Charlie knocked loudly on the door. His knocking set off a child crying and a moment later a woman with shoulder brown hair, tired eyes set in a weary face and wearing an old, but spotlessly clean white tee shirt over navy blue coloured tracksuit trousers with a crying toddler on her hip, opened the door. She stared suspiciously at them and her eyes settling on Baxter, said, "If you think for one minute you're taking my children, you've got..."

Charlie immediately guessed her concern and his hand raised as he interrupted her with, "Missus Gibson! We're not the Social!"

She stopped and stared at him, her widening and raised her free hand to her mouth.

"Oh, God! Oh, my God! Not Alex! Please…"

Confused, Charlie took a step forward and with his hands raised, said, "Missus Gibson, I don't know who Alex is, but we're here about something else. I'm a police officer and these are my colleagues. Can we come in to speak with you? Please?"

Numbly, she nodded and turning away from the door, wiped at her eyes as she led them through to the front room.

They stood in the room and the first thing they saw was that though the furnishings, carpets and curtains were inexpensive and well worn, the house was neat, tidy and appeared to be spotlessly clean and an effort been made to make it into a comfortable, child-friendly home.

Charlie saw a young man wearing army fatigues in a framed photograph hanging on a wall who in a head and shoulders shot and with his Tam o'Shanter hat proudly wore at a jaunty angle, grinned widely at the camera. Slowly nodded in understanding he exhaled and turning to the pale faced woman, said, "Alex is your son and you thought we were here with bad news?"

Biting at her lower lip while she continued to hold the curious toddler, she nodded.

"Before we begin, can I confirm that you *are* Jessica Gibson and your maiden name was Dougrie?"

"Yes," she hesitantly nodded, her eyes darting back and forth at the three of them.

"Can we all sit down, Missus Gibson. Please?"

Charlie elected to sit in one of the armchairs while Baxter and Baillie sat together on the worn couch.

The nervous woman slowly sank down into the second armchair and balanced the clinging toddler, who had stopped crying but stared fearfully at them, on her knee.

"Missus Gibson, I'm Detective Superintendent Charlie Miller and these are Detectives Constables Baillie and Baxter," he nodded to the pair.

He paused before continuing, "While we're not the Social and definitely not here about your son, I regret to inform you we *are* here with bad news, Missus Gibson. Your father, James Dougrie, is dead. He was discovered earlier today on the doorstep of his home."

He paused for a few seconds to let the news sink in then asked, "When was the last time you saw him?"

She took a breath and staring at Charlie, replied, "When my mother took my brother and me with her when she left him in, eh, I think it was…yes," she firmly nodded. "It was in 1989. December 1989, because I remember…" she blushed. "It sounds silly now, but I remember Stephen asking if we were leaving our home, how would Santa find us? And that," she shrugged, "was the last time I actually saw him."

He certainly didn't expect that response and quickly glanced at Baillie and Baxter before asking, "You've had *no* contact with your father since that time?"

She shrugged again and was about to respond, but the toddler struggled to get off her knee and setting him down onto the carpet, she said, "Connor, away and play with your cars, there's a good boy."

They watched the fair haired child waddle from the room, his disposable nappy hanging from his backside like a low slung backpack, then she replied, "Perhaps I *should* say that I've had no personal contact, but I am aware that he came to my wedding, though I didn't know about that at the time. My brother told me later that he saw my father standing at the back of the church, but I suppose I was too preoccupied being a bride to notice him. And then there were the birthday cards sent to my mother's address for me and Stephen, but they stopped when she died. I guessed he didn't know where to send them after that."

"Yet he had this address," Charlie told her.

"Did he? I never knew," she seemed surprised then shook her head as her eyes narrowed. "Why didn't he visit then if he knew where I lived?"

"That's a question I can't answer," Charlie replied.

"How did he die? I mean," she stared at them in turn and then as if in sudden understanding, said, "If you're the CID, it wasn't natural causes then?"

"I'm sorry to tell you this, but he was murdered on his doorstep where he was found," Charlie replied.

"Murdered?" she visibly paled, her hand reaching for her throat. "My God, dad would have been, what, in his mid sixties? Who'd want to murder him? Was it a robbery or something?"

"That's what we're trying to establish, Missus Gibson. If you haven't had any contact with him in all those years, then I can only assume you have no idea about his life during that period?"

"No, nothing at all," she shook her head. "I don't even know if he was aware he had grandchildren. I've three," she smiled. "Alex my oldest in nineteen. He's serving in the army over in…" then stopped and as if in explanation, said, "He told me I'm not supposed to say."

"That's okay," Charlie smiled. "We don't need to know that at the minute. But he is abroad now, yes?"

"Oh, yes," she nodded and that, Charlie thought, seems to rule the lad out as a suspect though he would as a matter of course have it confirmed.

"And the others?"

"Amy is eleven. She's in her last year at primary school and at a club in the school till six this evening. Connor," she smiled for they could hear the wee boy loudly singing in one of the bedrooms, "he's two past. My brother Stephen, he's living in England now and has one wee boy Amy's age."

"How long has Stephen been in England?"

"Oh, maybe thirteen or fourteen years. In Somerset. I have the address if you like?"

"We'll get a note of that before we leave," he nodded to Baxter who sat with her handbag on her lap and her open notebook on top of that.

"And have you been home all day, Missus Gibson?"

"Yes," she replied, then quickly shook her head. "No, not all day. I took Connor in his buggy to the Asda store in the Phoenix retail park to get some shopping."

"Did you walk or drive?"

"I walked. I can drive. I mean, I have a licence, but I don't have a car," she stared curiously at him.

"Do you have the receipt for the shopping?"

"Yes, but why…" her eyes widened. "You don't believe that I…"

He raised a hand to stop her protest and said, "We have to check. The receipt, please?"

She left the room and returned a moment later with her shoulder bag and fumbling inside, produced a receipt that she irately thrust at him. The time and date on the receipt clearly indicated she was in Asda at the time of the murder. Nevertheless, Charlie decided he would have someone check the stores CCTV cameras to confirm it was she who actually obtained the receipt.

Handing it back, he said, "I'm sorry, but at this stage of the investigation, everyone is a suspect."

She visibly relaxed and slumped down into the armchair.

"Do you know if Stephen has had any contact with your father?" he asked.

"I shouldn't think so," she shook her head. "We were quite close at one time. Even though now…" she didn't continue, but licking at her lower lip, then said, "I think if he'd contacted our dad he'd at least have the courtesy to tell me that."

"When your mother removed you and your brother from your family home, what was the address?"

"Oh, God," she unconsciously run a hand through her hair, "I was nine at the time and Stephen was seven. It was in Giffnock and the address was," she tightly screwed her eyes together, "Belmont Road or Avenue or something like that. I don't quite recall."

"Belmont Drive?"

"Yes," her eyes opened wide, "That's it. Belmont Drive. I haven't been in that area for a very long time. Why?"

"I just wanted to confirm your father remained at that address during those years."

"And you, Missus Gibson. Are you married or alone?"

"I was married…divorced now," she shrugged. My husband…he was a gambler and couldn't accept the fact we were having another child and so…" she shrugged and Charlie could see the admission was difficult for her.

"Children were…" her face twisted as she sought the word then said, "an *inconvenience* to him; to his social life and his…his addiction. Anyway, he blamed me for the pregnancy then upped and left. That was before Connor was born. We had a nice house in Linwood, but when he left…" and she paused.

Clearly embarrassed, she continued. "The truth is Mister Miller, he left me with a lot of debt and I lost the house. I wasn't able to work because of the kids and I couldn't pay the mortgage and he refused maintenance for the children. His children," she bitterly added. "I haven't had any contact with him for a number of years, but I'm in the process of trying to legally get some money out of him. In any event, I had to apply for a council house. And that's why I'm here," she slowly exhaled and glanced about the room, her voice unable to hide her distaste at her surroundings.

Charlie pursed his lips and turning to Baillie, nodded to him when he said, "Willie might have some news for you, Missus Gibson. Willie?"

The big, rough looking man smiled slightly at her.

"We got your address from the police pension people, Missus Gibson. It seems your father named you as his beneficiary. When I explained the circumstances of your father's death, the woman I spoke with," he fumbled in a pocket and produced a scrap of paper that he handed to her, "asked that you get in touch with her. From what I understand and please," he held a warning hand up, "do not take this as gospel because I might be out of date, but as your fathers beneficiary I believe you are now entitled to half his pensionable rights. That and, well, his estate will need to be disposed of and that includes his home."

He pointed to the scrap of paper and added, "I've written the name of the Police Federation representative on there. You might want to give him a call too and explain about you being your father's beneficiary. I've already had a word with the Fed rep and it seems like most cops, your father used the law firm the Federation have an agreement with to act for him in issues regarding his Will. As I understand it, the law firm will appoint a lawyer to liaise with you, though I don't know who that will be, but more than likely someone from the same firm. The Federation guy whose name and number I've written on there on there," he pointed to the paper, "he's expecting your call and more or less told me that everything is relatively straight forward regarding any inheritance. He obviously couldn't *officially* tell me who the beneficiary is, but…" he shrugged and left the rest unsaid.

Charlie quickly interjected by saying, "You need to understand that the house is currently part of my investigation, Missus Gibson, but I've no objection to you attending there as long as you give me some notice. In fact, though you haven't been there since you were nine, you might be of some assistance to me if you do attend there.

Perhaps you might," he shrugged, "possibly recall something of value that's missing. If that were the case it would maybe give us an indication as to why your father was murdered. Would you do that for me?"

She was clearly not just startled by Baillie's helpful information, but stunned at the realisation her father's home might possibly now be hers and one hand nervously at her throat, could only nod.

"As you will likely be aware, Missus Gibson, this is an early stage of the investigation. Right now we're seeking any information that can lead us to who and why your father was killed. Now," Charlie continued, "this is clearly a sensitive question I know, but I have good reason for asking. Can you recall *exactly* when and why your parents split?"

"Like I told you," she slowly exhaled, "I know it was December and it was a Sunday, because there had been a terrific argument and mum didn't take us to church and I didn't get to go to Sunday School and to me at that time, Sunday School was a big event. I had turned nine so as I was born in nineteen-eighty it must have been December nineteen-eight-nine. I remember that I was complaining and mum told me to…" she blushed. "You have to realise my mother was *never* a woman who would normally use bad language. Well, certainly not around me or Stephen. But that Sunday," she swallowed and was clearly embarrassed at the memory, "when I was quite honestly whining about not getting to Sunday School, she grabbed my arm and told me…well, she told me to shut the fuck up."

"So, sounds to me like she was pretty stressed, then," Charlie nodded.

"When you're nine, Mister Miller, nothing is as important as your own needs," she sighed. "I'm sorry to say I don't know what was going on between my parents, but whatever it was, I was far too young to understand."

"I understand your mother died a couple of years after she left your father?"

"Yes. Four years, actually; in 1993. Cancer. She had been a very heavy smoker. I was thirteen and Stephen had just turned eleven. We had no close family that would take us and the council placed us with a foster family and luckily, together. The couple were getting on in age, but were very kind to us and we stayed there till I left at eighteen to attend business college in Stirling where I went into the student accommodation and Stephen left our foster parents home at seventeen. We both stayed in touch with them," she smiled, "but they've both since passed away."

He was curious and asked, "When your mother died, why didn't you return to your father?"

She didn't immediately respond, but then her face paled and she replied, "My mother told people he was dead and made us go along with the lie. That if we returned to him she would never forgive us."

"I'm sorry for seeming so personal, but weren't you curious about him?"

"Of course I was!" she snapped at him.

Her outburst caused an embarrassed silence, broken when she said, "Sorry, but…" she fetched a handkerchief from the pocket of her tracksuit trousers and twisting it as she dabbed at her eyes, continued, "I'm sorry, I didn't mean to snap at you. But you needed to know my mother. She wasn't a pleasant woman. In fact, when she took us from our home I now know…now that I'm a mother and older, I mean; she took us not because she wanted us, but to hurt him. To hurt my dad."

Tears trickled down her cheeks and sniffing, she continued, "Now he's dead I can't even tell him how sorry I am. Sorry that I didn't contact him. Sorry he didn't know he's got four lovely grandchildren, my three and Stephen's boy."

Charlie quietly said, "You've given us an idea of when you left your father's house, but do you know why?"

She stared at him, then slowly nodding, replied, "All I remember is my mother shouting at him. Something about *her*, though I didn't know who *her* was. I realise now that it was because my father found someone else. Another woman."

Charlie's eyes narrowed and leaning forward, he asked, "Do you know anything about this woman? Her name?"

"No, I'm sorry. Like I said, all I remember about the day we left is my mother screaming at him that he could keep his…his bitch, was one word she used. I remember she used that word because in the taxi that took us away, I asked her what a bitch was and she told me a bitch was someone who ruined her marriage."

"Where did your mother take you? When you left the house?"

"First to her own mother's house, my grandmother that was, but we didn't stay there long. They were always arguing, shouting at each other, then to a flat in Shawlands. A ground floor flat. It was awful," she involuntarily shuddered. "Smelly and damp. That's where we stayed till she was admitted to hospital with lung cancer. The council took Stephen and me from the flat and housed us with the foster family."

They sat for a few minutes while she went to the bathroom to wash her face and compose herself and during that time, Charlie raised his eyebrows at Baxter and saw her nod that she had completed her notes.

He shrugged and quietly said, "I don't believe that we're going to learn much more here, guys. Is there anything I *haven't* asked?"

Baillie shook his head while Baxter, leaning forward, said, "If as we believe Missus Gibson is to inherit her father's property and that includes the house, it might be worth getting her husbands details for if even though they're divorced he might fight in the courts to get something from her inheritance and as his reason cite the years they were together. If he somehow found out she was the sole beneficiary, it could be a motive for murder."

"Good point," Charlie nodded. "Make sure you get the details when she gives you the brothers address in England. We'll need to eliminate both of them and the son as suspects from our investigation."

"Sir," she nodded.

When she returned from the bathroom with the wee boy again in her arms, Charlie said, "From what Willie here learned, Missus Gibson, it seems that you're the only beneficiary of your father's Will. Can you guess why he didn't include your brother in the Will?"

"No."

"Are you still in touch with Stephen?"

"I get a Christmas card and the children get birthday cards with money for a present, but other than that..." she tailed off.

"I'm pursuing a murder investigation, so I won't apologise for asking. Why don't you and Stephen keep in contact?"

She didn't immediately respond and it was obvious from her expression she was uncomfortable discussing it, but at last she replied, "My husband Peter or I should say, my *ex* husband; he's addicted to gambling. Horse racing, poker nights in the casinos in the city, any scheme or gambling that he believes will make him rich. When Stephen left to travel for work in England, he met his wife and together they set up a business. Quite successfully, as I understand it and unless things have changed, they were doing okay with a nice house and a good living."

She paused, then continued, "Peter's addiction meant we were always in debt and of course as with every addict, he kept promising that he would stop. Before he left me and without my knowledge, he borrowed two thousand pounds from Stephen for some bogus venture. Needless to say, he gambled the money away. Months later, after he'd left me and I was pregnant with Connor," she unconsciously ruffled her son's curly, blonde hair, "Stephen arrived at my door looking for Peter. We had a blazing row and even though I swore I didn't know about the loan he wouldn't believe me."

She glanced at Baxter as though being a woman, the detective would understand and said, "My hormones were going mad at the time and well, words were exchanged; things said that couldn't be unsaid."

She lowered her head and added, "We haven't spoken since."

"It might be worth phoning him now," Baxter softly said. "If nothing else, to let him know about your father's death."

Gibson nodded, but didn't reply.

"It seems to me," Charlie interjected, "that though I don't know how, your father knew of your circumstances, Missus Gibson, and by making you his sole beneficiary in his own way he's tried to make up for all those lost years."

"Right," he nodded to the other two, "I think we've heard enough for the time being."

They stood up from their chairs.

"DC Baxter will get those details from you, Missus Gibson," Charlie said, "and when you feel up to it, contact Alison to let us know when you wish to visit your father's house. In the meantime, Alison," he turned to her, "Willie and I will wait in the car for you."

They took their farewell of Jessica Gibson and walking down the garden path, saw a group of male and female teenagers running down the street while they jeered and taunted over their shoulders at the two detectives.

"Bloody wee shites," Baillie muttered then stopped dead and angrily growled, "Oh, the *bastards*!"

He pointed at the CID car where a half dozen fresh and deep scores had been dug into the paintwork and run the length of the car.

Staring at the departing youths, Charlie said, "I hope Missus Gibson gets in touch with the lawyer soon for even if there's some time for the execution of the Will, I've no objection to her moving into her dad's house. In fact, the sooner the woman and her kids are away from this dump," he sighed and slowly shook his head, "the better.
****

In the incident room at Giffnock office, DS Shona Mathieson checked the list of duties to be completed first thing the following morning, then answered the ringing phone.

"DS Mathieson," Gerry Donaldson's gruff voice bellowed in her ear.

"Sir," she rolled her eyes.

"Is Miller about?"

She cast a glance around the room and seeing she couldn't be overheard, replied, "No, sir. He's out on an inquiry."

"What inquiry?"

She hesitated, but there seemed nothing wrong in telling him. "DC Baillie discovered a next of kin for the victim. Mister Miller has gone to deliver the news of the murder, sir."

"Oh, he has, has he? Well DS Mathieson, listen very closely to me. I want to know *everything* that Miller does, do you hear?"

"Sir, I don't think I can…"

"Shut the fuck up and listen to me! You *will* report everything he does because when that bastard has returned to his fancy wee job, you will still be here and *I* will still be your DCI and it's *me* that does your annual appraisal. Now, I know you're ambitious and it wouldn't do your career any good if you were to be returned to uniform duties, DS Mathieson, so…do we understand each other?"

She swallowed with difficulty, her nerves tightly wound and gritted her teeth before she replied, "Yes, sir. I understand."

Her hands were shaking as she slowly returned the phone to its cradle.

"Coffee, Shona?"

She startled and in turn, made the young civilian typist jump back.

"Sorry, Shona, I didn't mean to…"

"No, you're all right. I was miles away," she forced a smile and added, "Yes, thanks. A coffee will be lovely."
****

Sadie and Liz Watson were still in the kitchen when Carol arrived with the two girls.

"Mum," Sadie helped Geraldine take off her school coat, "you remember Liz from our wedding day?"

"Oh, aye, of course," Carol smiled curiously at her before glancing at Sadie. Turning back to Watson, she asked, "You're a doctor, aren't you?"

"Some would say doctor, others tell the truth," Watson grinned at her.

"Do you have homework?" Sadie asked Geraldine as she lifted Ella from the buggy.

"Maths."

"Right then, while mum gets the kettle on, Liz," she gave her a discreet nod, "I'm just going to take these two through to the front room."

"And that, Carol," Watson winked conspiratorially at her, "is my cue to have a wee chat with you."

****

They had been gone just a few moments when Jessica Gibson's eleven-year-old daughter Amy returned home. The young girl almost immediately could see her mother had been crying and run to hug her.

"Is it that crowd outside causing bother again, mum?" she stroked gently at the loose hair on her mother's brow.

"No, dear," she sniffed and attempted smile, "it's not them. I've had some bad news. Get your coat off and put your schoolbag away. I've something to tell you."

****

Chief Inspector Harry Downes read and reread the press release and finally satisfied with her effort, took a deep breath and lifted the phone.

When it was answered, she said, "Charlie, it's me, Harry Downes. I've got the draft completed for the press release and want to run it by you." Her eyes narrowed. "Are you in a car?"

"Just on my way back to Giffnock office, Harry, but shoot. Tell me what you've got so far."

"Well," she drawled, "I'll keep it short. In the draft I've admitted the body exhumed is that of Murdo Clarke, reported missing in 1989 and as one of his many major inquiries as SIO, Detective Superintendent Charles Miller, that's you by the way…"

"I kind of guessed that," he grinned.

"Mister Miller," she continued, "is also the SIO for the murder of James Dougrie, a police officer who in 1989 was the investigating officer for Clarke's disappearance. It is not confirmed that both inquiries are linked, however, Mister Miller is appealing for anyone to contact the police who might have information about the disappearance of Clarke and the murder of Dougrie. That's it, short and sweet and this way we can avoid the media accusing us of any kind of cover-up about the relationship between Clarke and Dougrie."

"That'll do for me, Harry. Is it ready to go out tonight?"

"If you're happy with it, it will be on the evening news."

"Okay, on my authority, go ahead."

****

Sadie saw her mother and Liz Watson head for the front door and carrying Ella in her arms, asked, "You guy's done?"

"All done," Watson smiled then stopped as her mobile phone chirruped. "Excuse me," she smiled and fetching the phone from her handbag, scrolled down as she read the text.

"Seems like your man can't dispense with me these days," she sighed. "Wants me for a PM tomorrow morning at the Queen Elizabeth mortuary. Maybe this time," she winked at Sadie, "he'll tell me the name of the deceased."

They watched and waved as Watson got in her car and drove off.

"What was that all about?" Carol asked.

"Oh, just something Charlie's working on, mum."

She closed the door and turning, said, "You're not angry I asked Liz to have a word?"

"Of course not," her mother smiled. "If anything, she's given me an idea of what to expect tomorrow. Kind of taken the dread away a wee bit."

"You know you'll be fine," Sadie threw her free arm about her mother's shoulder.

"I know," Carol smiled, but her daughter could not have suspected how frightened she really was.

****

On his way home from the pub, Frankie Colville stopped at the butchers on the Main Street before walking the short distance to his tenement flat in Rutherglen's Hardie Avenue.

Unlocking the door, he called out, "That's me home, hen. I popped into the butcher's and got us a couple of chops. Give me ten minutes and I'll put the dinner on."

He shrugged off his coat and again called out, "Elsie? That's me home."

Still there was no reply and with a sense of foreboding, he laid the shopping onto the kitchen worktop and made his way to the bedroom.

Pushing open the door, he saw her lying as he had left her; in bed with that morning's 'Glasgow News' in her hands, her medication on the bedside cabinet beside her and the glass of water untouched. "Elsie?" his lips trembled as he reached forward to touch her cold hand and knew she was dead.

He slumped down to sit by her and spent several minutes staring at her pale face, then reached down and with his forefingers, gently closed her eyes.

He tried, but could not help the tears that run unchecked down his cheeks and with a final glance at his dead wife, stood and returned to the phone in the hallway.

Dialling the familiar number, he said, "Is that the doctor's surgery? It's Mister Colville, about my wife. That's right, hen, Elsie Colville in Hardie Avenue. Elsie's..." he sniffed and choking back more tears, braced himself and slowly exhaled as he said, "Elsie's died, hen. Can the doctor come over, please?"

CHAPTER TEN

Charlie dismissed the team for the evening after instructing DS Shona Mathieson that the answer machine would take any calls through the night.

"Right," he beckoned to Alison Baxter, "I know it's been a long day for you, but that offer of coming over to my place, having some dinner and meeting Sadie still stands. Besides," he shrugged, "I want a wee chat with you outwith this place to get your view on why you think Dougrie was murdered. You up for it?"

"Okay with me. How far do I have to drive to the Castle tonight from your house?"

"I usually do it between fifty minutes and an hour in the morning, depending on traffic. I know it's a bit of a bummer being accommodated so far away and having to get here each morning, but I don't think the polis budget will stretch to your continuous stay in the Hilton," he grinned.

"No problem," she nodded and asked, "Give me your post code for my SatNav."

****

He was on the way home listening to Smooth Radio when the six o'clock news opened with what was a reworking of Harry Downes press release and grimaced when it mentioned him by name. Switching the radio off, he pressed the button on his mobile hands free and was almost immediately connected to Sadie.

"Sweetheart, is Carol still there?"

"No, she decided to go home tonight. Says she'll come here tomorrow morning and we'll travel together to Ross Hall for her examination. Oh, and thanks for sending Liz Watson. She had a chat with mum and well, you know…" she trailed off.

"Oh, I asked her to phone, but that's decent of her that she popped by. Listen, I've one of my team coming over for dinner. A woman called Alison Baxter. Is that okay? I want a word with her tonight about the case and didn't want to speak in the office. I'll explain when I get in."

"Understood. Dinner will be nothing fancy, I'm afraid. Lasagne, chips and some rocket salad."

"I'm sure that will be fine and let's hope she's not a veggie. Right, I'll sign off now. See you in about twenty or thirty minutes."

He was about to end the call when Sadie said, "Charlie! I forgot to say. Cathy phoned and asked if you'd give her a call when you get home. She didn't say what it was about."

"Righto. Bye."

He pressed the end button and driving, reflected on his day.

Again he wondered who had tipped off the 'Glasgow News' about the PM at the Monklands Hospital mortuary and his involvement. So much for bloody secrecy, he sighed.

He unconsciously smiled for though it was not in Charlie's nature to be at all vindictive or even take pleasure in anyone else's humiliation, he had enjoyed telling Gerry Donaldson that he was taking over the murder investigation. He smiled when he recalled

Donaldson's face, so flushed it looked like his head was about to explode.

Thoughts of Donaldson turned his mind to his team. If his knowledge of Donaldson from his Stewart Street days was correct, he had little doubt that the DCI would try in some way to inveigle someone on the team to provide him with updates as to how the investigation was proceeding…or floundering, he sighed.

It had to be someone that Donaldson could bully, someone who feared him as a boss; someone whose career he held sway over. But who?

He sighed and gave up trying to imagine who it could be for that, he knew, would only make him suspicious of everyone and the team would soon pick up on his misgivings and that in turn could only be detrimental to the investigation.

No, he would need to ensure that he didn't foul up, give Donaldson no opportunity to criticise or undermine the investigation and the only way to do that would be to find James Dougrie's killer.

****

The elderly doctor stiffly stood up from the bed and replacing his stethoscope into his brown, shabby leather bag turned and said, "I'm sorry, Frankie, I really am. Your Elsie was a fine woman. Shame that she had to go so young. Sixty-nine, if memory serves me correctly?"

"Aye, doctor. She was two years younger than me. Was it the illness? Sorry, that's a stupid question. What I mean is, it wasn't me was it? The stress of being married to me. You know, what I used to do and being away for so long in the jail."

The doctor smiled and clapping a hand onto Colville's shoulder, replied, "It was inevitable, I'm afraid and while stress can be a debilitating symptom in itself, no Frankie; Elsie passed because of the illness. Not anything you did. My God, man, you've been at her beck and call since you got out. Don't think I don't know that. You did a fine job looking after her."

"It would have been a better job if I'd been here instead of being in the pub having a couple of pints."

"A couple of pints in how may days? It's not as if you're a regular. Any time I've attended to Elsie she did nothing but sing your praises about how well you looked after her, so let's not be silly. You are *not* to blame for her death so get that out of your head. Now, let's go through to the kitchen and I'll complete the death certificate,

Frankie. You'll need that for the undertaker. Have you thought about arrangements? What Elsie's wishes were?"

Colville led the way to the kitchen and while the doctor took a seat, he absentmindedly switched on the kettle.

"Arrangements? Oh. There's paperwork in the cupboard in the front room. Elsie attended to all that. You know, the insurance and the…" he stopped, unable to speak and his legs felt so heavy that he reached for the worktop to steady himself.

"Here, get yourself sat down, Frankie," the doctor quickly stood and grabbing at him, helped him to a chair.

"Is there anyone I can phone? The kids I mean?"

Colville turned to stare up at him and replied, "The phone books with their numbers is on the table by the phone in the hallway, doctor. Maybe if you could. It would sound better coming from you. The kids, they don't…"

"I know. They don't speak to you anymore. Elsie told me," the doctor sadly nodded.

While the doctor left to make the call he sat there and thought of his wife, his dead wife, and wondered what was to become of him now?
****

Tommy Craig had been approaching forty years of age when he was arrested with his three fellow robbers in 1989 and just recently celebrated another birthday.

Waddling along Shettleston's Tollcross Road from his lower ground flat home in Quarrybrae Street, he passed a few neighbours who heads down, wisely steered clear of him for the morose Craig was not a man who stopped for idle chitchat; not when he was on a mission and tonight's mission was a pint or three in the pub across the road from the old public library.

Known locally as Gumsy, though never to his face, the shaven-headed Craig had the physique of a man fifteen years his junior and continued to maintain a rigorous fitness regime, a practise he had enjoyed during his prison years. Though now sixty-eight, he continued after his release to train hard at a local council gym where he took delight in baring his numerous prison tattoos to the impressionable teenagers who he was aware whispered behind his back.

Craig, a bachelor all his days, secretly revelled in his reputation and though now as a pensioner existed on social welfare, he seldom wasted his money on alcohol and never on tobacco.

Craig believed himself to be the archetypical Glasgow hard man; afraid of no man nor anything and particularly, not the polis.

Head held high and wearing his old, second-hand army camouflage jacket, he gallusly strolled along and turned the corner into Crail Street, seeing but ignoring the group of teenagers who stood on the opposite path at the zebra crossing by the brown stone flats and who gaped at him.

He inwardly grinned as he continued towards Tollcross Road, believing the teenagers to be casting admiring glances at him, but would have been shocked to know they giggled among themselves, for Craig was so bandy-legged it was unkindly said of him that when he walked he had a foot on both pavements.

Though not a regular drinker, Craig had decided to celebrate with a pint for on this evenings news he had watched the article about the murder of the former CID man, James Dougrie, his belief being any dead cop was good news.

****

She had made better time than Charlie Miller and arrived in the expansive driveway where locking the car, she knocked on the door. As she did so it occurred to her that perhaps Miller had not told his wife he was bringing someone to dinner, but was inwardly relieved when the door was opened by a smiling woman with a toddler on her hip who said, "You must be Alison. Come away in. I'm Sadie."

Closing the door behind her, she followed Sadie through to the kitchen where Baxter saw the table had been set of four and a high chair positioned at one corner into which Sadie dropped her daughter, Ella.

"Charlie should be here anytime," she smiled. "Now, I know you're driving, so can I offer you a tea, coffee or juice maybe?"

Settling herself down into a kitchen chair, Baxter accepted the offer of a coffee and while Sadie dropped Ella into the highchair, called out, "Jellybean, come and say hello."

Baxter turned to greet the tousled haired Geraldine who shyly smiled before returning to her TV cartoons in the front room.

"I take it Charlie's not far behind you?"

"I thought he'd be here before me, but he did say something about needing diesel."

"That's Charlie," Sadie shook her head. "When it comes to filling his car, he's last minute dot com, always waits till the needle is bouncing off the red."

She handed Baxter a mug of coffee and seating herself down, said, "Charlie mentioned you're still on your DC's course, so tell me, Alison, how did you manage to wangle to get yourself onto his team?"

She took a tentative sip of the hot liquid before replying, "I'm still wondering about that myself. I can only assume it's because of my academic background," she shrugged. "Charlie told me that he'd consider me to be useful when interviewing some of…" she stopped and hesitantly asked, "Has he told you anything about the investigation?"

Sadie smiled and replied, "Not in detail, no, and I guess that you think before you say anymore, you'd better get his approval. Don't be worrying, though," she slyly smiled, "I'll just use my womanly wiles to get it out of him anyway."

Baxter grinned and nodding, said, "He did stress I'd to tell no one what we were doing so…"

She was interrupted by the sound of the front door closing and hearing Geraldine call out, "Dad's home!"

Seconds later the kitchen door was pushed open to admit Charlie with his oldest daughter's arms wrapped about his neck as she clung to him.

"Alison, glad to see you found us," he smiled before adding, "Let me get this monster off me and my jacket hung away then," theatrically sniffing the air, smiled and said, "we'll get stuck into dinner."
****

In her bedroom at home, Julia Mason was in the process of unpacking her overnight case when the telephone rang.

"Doctor Mason?"

"That's me. Who is this?"

"Ah, Doctor Mason, it's Brian Hendry from the 'Glasgow News.' I saw you leaving the mortuary earlier today, but I didn't get the opportunity to have a word with you," he blithely lied. " Now, do you have the time to talk about that interview you promised me?"
****

In her first floor, two bedroom tenement flat in Dixon Road in Shawlands, Shona Mathieson paced the floor of the neatly furnished front room and continued to fume over the phone call from her DCI, Gerry Donaldson.

There was no other way to describe it; the bastard was blackmailing her into being his tout in the investigation. Knowing his method from her years under his command, what worried her though was if Donaldson acted true to form he would have someone else in the team also acting as his eyes and ears and with two individuals providing him with information, would know if one or the other was either lying or not giving him everything they learned.

Bastard!

She stopped pacing and stared out of the bay window to the street below. Her partner Gary would be home soon and it occurred to her that she should discuss Donaldson's threat with him, but things hadn't been good between them in the last few months and though it pained her to admit it, she suspected he was seeing his former wife again.

She knew he was pissed off about the money he had to pay Margie for child support. Though they never discussed it, Mathieson was literally supporting him financially, for his business as a self-employed plumber was barely making enough money to run the van and pay his half of the mortgage; an agreement she had insisted upon when he moved in two years previously.

Always the realist, she knew their relationship was coming to an end, but neither she nor Gary wished to admit to it and as if she hadn't enough to worry about, now she had Donaldson breathing down her neck.

She wrapped her arms tightly about her and rolled her neck to ease the ache in her shoulders.

Like everyone else in the bloody police she moaned and griped about the job, but the truth was she really liked her job and believed she had the ability and determination to go further in her career; a career that was now threatened if she didn't do as Donaldson asked.

Still staring down into the street, she saw the white van stop and reverse into an empty spot on the opposite side of the road. The old white coloured Transit van with the 'Gary Menzies, Plumber' and mobile phone number sign on the side looking as tired and almost as ragged as the cropped fair haired man wearing the stained blue coveralls who emerged from the driver's door.

She watched as he moved to the rear of the van and pulled at the handles to ensure the doors were locked. Glancing up at the window, he gave her a nod and almost mechanically, she returned his nod with a wave.

Turning from the window, she made her way towards the kitchen to begin preparing their evening meal, but then stopped.

They'd eat, she decided and then have the talk that was too long overdue.

****

It was as Frankie Colville expected, for other than the Cooperative undertakers collecting Elsie, nobody visited the house that evening. No phone calls from his kids and none from Elsie's sisters or surviving brother. They would know, of that he was certain for his kids still kept in touch with their aunties and their uncle.

Her family not phoning didn't surprise him for right at the outset of their relationship none of Elsie's family had ever approved of him, but he had thought at this sad time at least one of his sons or both daughters would have lifted the phone to see how he was faring.

'We reap what we sow,' he shook his head at the old adage and was about to go to the kitchen to make some dinner when the phone rung. His heart leaped at the sudden ringing and he almost stumbled over a chair in his anxiousness to get to it.

"Hello?"

"Smiler, is that you?" asked the unfamiliar voice, a voice that sounded cheery and a little tipsy.

"Aye, who's this?"

"It's me, Tommy. Tommy Craig. Have you heard the news?"

Startled that after all these years, Craig had contacted him and so he stuttered, "What news?"

He heard Craig taking a deep breath and background noise that sounded as if he was in a pub, before Craig replied, "That bastard Jimmy Dougrie. Him that Murdo was supposed to be touting to. He's dead."

The room spun and with a shaking hand, Colville held onto the wall as he slowly sat down onto the telephone table bench.

"Dougrie, the CID guy. He's dead?"

"Aye, it was on the news and guess what else was on the news.

They've dug up a body from a field in the countryside somewhere and guess what?" he heard Craig giggle. "The news is saying it's been identified as Murdo."

He swallowed with difficulty before replying, "So, they found him then?"

He closed his eyes tightly at the sudden throbbing in his head before slowly adding, "What about the money? Did they find the money?"

"Oh, aye," Craig gleefully agreed. "They found him, the bastard, but they didn't say anything on the tele about the money. Now him and his polis pal can dance the fandango together in whatever hell back-stabbing bastards go to!"

Colville rubbed wearily with the heel of his hand at his brow and said, "Tommy, I'm a wee bit busy the now. I need to go."

"What? For fuck's sake, get your arse out here and meet me for a couple of jars, Smiler. I'm in a pub on the Tollcross Road. Jump a taxi and we'll celebrate, eh?"

He took a breath and slowly exhaled before replying, "Tommy, I can't because Elsie…" he took a deep breath, "she died today."

There was a stunned silence, before Craig soberly replied, "I didn't know. Look, give me your address and I'll…"

"I'm not taking visitors the now," Colville interrupted, then a little more contritely said, "Call me tomorrow when maybe I'll be feeling a bit better, eh?"

"Aye, I'll do that, Smiler. I'm awfully sorry, pal. I liked Elsie. She was a right diamond so she was. I'll phone you tomorrow," Craig said, then ended the call.

He continued to sit on the telephone table bench, his mind in whirl. He hadn't given Murdo or the cop Dougrie any thought in years; that was all in the past.

Now this?

His eyes narrowed.

Why would Dougrie's death be on the news? A body being dug up in a field, now that was news, but the death of a polis who must be retired what, ten years or more?

His eyes narrowed. The only reason Dougrie's death would be on the news was if it wasn't natural causes, so what the fuck had happened to him?

He drummed his fingers on his knees as another thought occurred to him.

He hadn't seen hide nor hair of Tommy Craig for years, not since they were sent down together; so, his brow creased and he wondered, how the hell did he get my phone number?

****

Cathy Mulgrew shouted to her partner Jo, "I'll get it," and lifted the telephone.

"Cathy? It's me," Charlie said.

"You just home?"

"No, I got in and had some dinner first. I was ravenous."

"I've still to get mine," she raised a one-minute warning finger to Jo, "so I'll keep this short. The Chief went ballistic when he learned that Clarke was identified in the media and even more so when Clarke was tied in to Dougrie. On that point, any suspects yet for the murders?"

"Early days," Charlie sighed. "How is the Chief now? Still raging?"

"No, not since I explained the theory that if we tried to hide anything and the press find out, they'll carve us a new one. I persuaded him that was the smart thing to do and I let him know it was Harry Downes idea."

"So, is that why you wanted me to phone you? To let me know the Chief's reaction?"

"Not entirely," she drawled. "I managed to get you six detectives from the MIT, but no more. The anti-terrorist mob is conducting a covert operation in the next week or so and because it's a twenty-four-seven operation, they will need everybody they can lay hands upon. If the worst comes to the worst I'll try to fleece the north of the city CID for some help, but don't hold your breath."

"Fine. Anything else?"

"Well, the main reason I had you call me is to tell you to watch your back. Gerry Donaldson has lodged an official complaint that you railroaded him and took his murder from him. Donaldson didn't go directly to the Chief. He's got an Assistant Chief in his corner. Tony Mulveigh. Do you know him?"

Charlie glanced behind to ensure the children weren't listening before replying, "Weasel faced bastard who transferred up from one of the county forces in England?"

"That's him. He arrived when the Forces united to become Police Scotland and at the time, the word was he was a political appointment by the UK Government to ensure that the Chief toed the line. I heard he covertly reports back to the Home Secretary at Whitehall, but," she sighed. "You know what rumours are."

"What's his connection to Donaldson?"

"They were in the army together, apparently. The first foot and mouth regiment or something like that."

Charlie grinned at her description and replied, "Thanks anyway, but I know him from old so I expect he's already got someone in my team watching me. Bloody politics. When will we ever get away from it?"

"Never, probably," and turning, saw Jo tapping at her watch. "Right, need to run, that's dinner on the table. Keep in touch."

"Will do," he ended the call.

He didn't immediately return to the front room where Sadie and Alison Baxter sat with their coffee while the children played at their feet.

His thoughts turned to Donaldson and his deviousness and again he wondered; who have you got watching me?

****

Unusually for Tommy Craig, he had sunk five pints of Guinness and inebriated as well as being short of cash, scowled and deciding enough was enough, made his way to the door.

The fresh air hit him like a hammer blow and steadying himself with one hand on the door frame, stepped out into the twilight of Tollcross Road.

Squaring his shoulders, he began to slowly walk in the direction of his home in Quarrybrae Street, subtly taking in large gulps of air as he did so.

He thought about his call from the pub phone, wasting fifty pence on talking to Smiler with the intention of having him join him for a drink, but only to learn that Elsie had died.

He had always had a wee fancy for Elsie, but the stupid cow only had eyes for that toothless bastard of a husband of her.

Now she was dead.

Big deal.

People always leave.

Parents, brothers, sister, wives, kids; it was all part of being a gangster. Nobody liked to hang around when the cops were always on your case and definitely not when you ended up doing heavy time.

He grinned again when he recalled the good news that Dougrie was dead.

They had known when the four of them together they had stood in the dock, that the absence of Clarke could only mean one thing.

He was the tout; the bastard who had given them up to the cops; given them up to somebody who he now was convinced was the CID guy Dougrie.

He remembered that day as though it were yesterday.

Smiler in the motor with the engine running in the car park next to the supermarket on the High Street. John O'Connor, tooled up with a handgun and doing his edgy under the tower at the Town Hall at Renfrew Cross while he watched the building society across the road. Him with the sawn-off acting as security and Alex Murtagh, the leader and whistle man, carrying the second handgun and the bags.

Clarke was the man who had recce'd the place, decided on the plan and then fifteen minutes before they left O'Connor's flat in Drumchapel, Clarke's wife phoning the flat to tell Smiler that Murdo had just been he had been in a bump in his motor, but that Clarke had phoned her to say he had recce'd the place and it was still a goer and they were to go ahead.

Lying bastard that he was!

The cops had been waiting for God knew how long and when they sprung their trap, he grudgingly nodded, it was perfect. None of the three at the building society stood a chance with gun barrels pressed against their heads and the polis screaming that they would be shot if they didn't get onto the ground.

Only Smiler had sussed something was up when he glanced into his rear-view mirror and saw four armed men approaching the car. He'd gunned the engine and drove off, but was stopped by armed Traffic cops before he got to the motorway.

Their brief carried the message between them and they had agreed that they would not give Clarke up as the fifth man, that they would bide their time and deal with the traitorous bastard themselves.

But then the day after their arrest learned he had disappeared and worse than that, so had the money; it was obvious to Tommy then, he had screwed them over for the cash.

He turned the corner and with a stagger, stopped and leaned against a wall for a breather.

And now Clarke had turned up in a shallow grave.

He grinned and rolling his tongue round his mouth, spat a globule of dark saliva onto the pavement and inhaling deeply, prepared to walk on.

It did not occur to Craig to glance about him for why would he, safe here in his own territory.

But had he done so, he might have wondered at the figure across the road who in the shadows of the passing buildings, kept step with his slow pace.

CHAPTER ELEVEN

It had been Charlie's habit as an SIO to be if not the first, then one of the early arrivals at the incident room and this morning was no different.

Driving to the Giffnock office, he pondered the conversation the previous evening with Alison Baxter.

While Sadie put the girls to bed, he had discussed their interview with James Dougrie's estranged daughter and sought Baxter's opinion of the younger woman.

"Well, I'm confident she had no knowledge of her father's death prior to you breaking the news. Her reaction was as genuine as I've ever seen. It *did* puzzle me a little that she had not shown more emotion, but I can only presume that the years of estrangement with her father had dulled any sentiment she might otherwise have had if they had they been in regular contact. That and if her story about her relationship with her former husband is true, I'm guessing she is probably suffering from depression and likely exacerbated by the circumstances she now finds herself in."

"So, you're of the opinion that we should discount Jessica Gibson as a suspect then?"

"I believe so," she'd slowly nodded. "That's not to say I'm one hundred per cent correct and that we don't check her out for any criminal convictions, but based on my experience…"

"No, I agree. I might not have your qualifications, Alison, but I got the vibes she wasn't holding back, that her response to the news of Dougrie's murder was genuine."

His mouth twisted as he'd recalled something else. "Tomorrow, I want you to speak with Shona Mathieson and ask her to raise two Actions. Tell her I've instructed you to follow up on the alibi for Gibson's soldier son. Let's confirm the boy is abroad and was at the time of the murder. The second Action is for her husband, see if you can trace him at the address she gave you and alibi him as well. If as you think though they are divorced and there's the slightest chance that because of their previous marriage he might be legally entitled to some of her estate, that's as good a reason for murder as any."

His brow had furrowed with a sudden thought and he'd added, "Take Willie Baillie with you. He's proving himself to be a sharper looking guy than he looks and let's face it," he suddenly grinned, "I'm saying that and *I'm* no male model."

"You're bang on there, Miller," Sadie had entered through the door behind him to join them, a grin plastered to her face. "Am I interrupting?"

"No, you're fine, hen," he'd indicated she sit. "Alison and I were just discussing the investigation."

"Oh, and am I privy to what's going on?"

"What," he'd pretended surprise, "you haven't already drugged my dinner or plan to torture me into telling all?"

"Charlie Miller! I *never* coerce you into disclosing privileged information!"

"Aye, right," he slowly winked at the smiling Baxter and added, "isn't there something about womanly wiles you keep telling people?"

"Is there anything else you wish to discuss," Baxter had asked, "or should I just go before Sadie beats you to death?"

"Oh," he'd snapped his fingers in sudden recollection, "I'd forgotten about the PM tomorrow morning. Ten o'clock at the Queen Elizabeth Hospital in Govan. I'll want you to attend with me. You can bring Willie and leave from there with your Actions, okay?"

"Okay," she'd nodded and lifting her handbag from the floor, got to her feet. "Sadie, thanks for the home cooked meal," she'd smiled, "and good luck tomorrow morning."

Sadie had shown her to the door and when she returned he'd immediately apologised, his embarrassment etched on his face.

"Sorry, sweetheart," he'd embraced her. "I've been that wrapped up in this bloody investigation I clean forgot Carol's going for the examination in the morning. How is she?"

"Worried sick and no less than me," Sadie had replied.

And now here he was, tapping his fingers on the steering wheel as he waited for the oncoming traffic from Braidbar Road to clear and permit him to cross over and through the opening towards the car park at the rear of the office.

Getting out of his car, he was greeted by Willie Baillie who wore a light grey coloured shirt, maroon tie and dark grey coloured suit and to Charlie's curiosity, seemed a lot tidier than the unshaven man he had been the day before. That, and as he neared, Charlie saw that Baillie had closely shaved and smelled of some kind of pine scent.

"Morning, boss," Baillie nodded to him.

"Willie," Charlie slowly replied, acknowledging his greeting with a smile as Baillie joined him in the walk towards the back stairs.

"I take it you'll be giving us an in-depth briefing this morning, boss?"

"What I know, Willie," he nodded, "but to be frank it's not a lot at the minute. Here's hoping we'll turn up something more positive during the course of the day. Speaking of which," he held open the top landing door for Baillie to pass through, "I'm going to neighbour you with Alison Baxter today."

"Oh, good," he replied and a little too hastily for it made Charlie smile and guessed that was why Baillie had turned out a little more presentable than yesterday, that Alison Baxter had apparently made an impression on the big, bulky man.

"Aye," Charlie continued, "your first job will be to accompany me to the PM at ten then on the back of what we learned yesterday from Missus Gibson, I've asked Alison to raise a couple of Actions for you both."

They turned from the corridor into the incident room to see that Shona Mathieson was already at her desk and poring over the reports from the door to door inquiries.

"Anything interesting there, Shona?" Charlie asked.

"Morning, sir. Just a couple of reports from neighbours describing the deceased as a man who kept himself pretty much to himself. None of the neighbours were able to tell us anything about visitors to his home and some of the more recent neighbours who moved into the area were unaware he was a retired police officer."

Charlie nodded and his eyes narrowed for it seemed to him Mathieson's eyes were red rimmed and her face pale. Either she'd had a sleepless night or something had upset her. He glanced about the room and seeing others starting to arrive decided now wasn't the time to ask.

"Before we have the briefing, Shona, pop into my office and we'll discuss today's Actions. Bring your coffee too," he smiled at her.

****

Frankie Colville reached across the space between the twin beds, only to remember with a start that Elsie was gone, the undertakers having collected her body the previous evening.

With a sigh, he turned onto his back and stared at the ceiling, unable to prevent his eyes from watering.

He lay like that for several minutes before his bladder insisted he get up and slowly rising from the bed, made his way to the bathroom to perform his morning ablutions.

Ten minutes later, he was in the kitchen preparing breakfast and almost as an afterthought, switched on the radio.

He was just in time to catch the eight o'clock news and spatula in hand, stopped and stood to quietly listen when the announcer reported that police were continuing to investigate the murder of Murdo Clarke, whose body was discovered in a grave in Lanarkshire farmland. As the report continued, he found himself sitting down, his eyes narrowing as the announcer continued about the murder of James Dougrie and described Dougrie as the detective who led the hunt for the missing Clarke.

The sizzling of the bacon in the frying pan disturbed his thoughts and rising from the chair, stepped back to the cooker.

He had not seen Murdo Clarke since…he rubbed wearily at his forehead, well, since that night.

As he turned the bacon his thoughts turned to that evening all those years ago.

Two nights before they were arrested.

It had been a Wednesday and he smiled. How could he ever forget, for it was the gangs second last night of freedom before they were banged up; Alex never to be freed and sixty a day John being diagnosed the lung cancer that curiously became his ticket to freedom on compassionate grounds, only to die a short time after his release.

Then there was that mad bastard Tommy who refused to admit his guilt and served the full term.

Twenty-three years for being a pig-headed idiot, boasting that Tommy Craig wouldn't give in to the bastards.

And what did it achieve?

Absolutely nothing.

But Tommy had no one to come out to, no wife and no weans.

But he had Elsie and so, he toed the line.

Kept his nose clean and his head down.

Yes, sir. No, sir. Three fucking bags full, sir.

Told them everything they wanted to know; well, maybe not everything, he wryly grinned.

Not about what happened that Thursday evening before the Renfrew turn that got them caught.

No, what happened that night might have got him banged up for even longer.

But his total compliance as a con had worked and the parole board cut his sentence by four years; four more years he had with Elsie, if not the kids.

And now, all these years later, they had found Clarke.

He lifted the bacon and laid it onto a sheet of kitchen roll to let the fat dry onto the paper before turning to fetch the bread from the breadbin.

The CID would come calling now, of that he was certain. They'd go and visit Tommy too, but knowing that arse he'd tell them nothing. Besides, he grinned, Tommy had nothing *to* tell them because in fairness he had never fully been in the loop and certainly not that Thursday evening. No, he was too loud in the mouth and particularly when he was angry; inclined to say things out of turn, attract attention when they didn't need it.

Stupid bastard.

Buttering the bread, he carefully laid the bacon onto one slice then closed it with the second slice.

His address hadn't changed since he'd been inside, so likely the CID would be calling anytime and glancing about the kitchen, thought he'd get the place tidied up before they arrived.

****

Arriving at her office, Cathy Mulgrew's secretary had the morning newspapers laid out on her desk, items of importance clearly indicated with a red felt tipped pen.

Seated behind her desk with a mug of coffee cooling at her elbow, her heart sank when the headlined front page of the first newspaper she glanced at, the 'Glasgow News', literally screamed about the scoop on pages two and three; an in depth interview with Doctor Julia Mason.

Teeth gritted, Cathy turned to the pages to see the bloody woman's smiling face greet her with the headline, 'How I Identified Murder Victim Murdo Clarke.'

No matter that the whole column was shite and that Mason must have learned Clarke's name from the subsequent media bulletin, Mulgrew fumed, it was clear from the lack of facts the woman had fabricated a story for the benefit of the newspaper.

Her phone buzzed with a message from her secretary to tell her that the Chief Constable was on the phone.

"Good morning, Chef Constable," acknowledging his call, she rolled her eyes.

"You'll have seen the newspaper then, Miss Mulgrew?"

"Reading it as we speak, sir."

"Bloody woman," he hissed.

"My sentiments exactly, but that said she doesn't disclose anything that we don't already know or have told the media. It seems to me she's seeking her ten minutes of fame, that's all."

"Well, prior to calling you, I contacted an old friend who tutors at Dundee University and while he was reluctant to disclose details, he assured me that Doctor Mason is no longer employed there. In fact," she heard him take a breath, "she has been declared *persona non grata* and as a result of that decision is unlikely to obtain any kind of academic position in the near future if at all. That and I have instructed our Finance Department that should Mason make any claim for services rendered in this inquiry, such claim will be refused on account of her having broken her disclosure agreement with this Force."

"I wonder how long her payment for her exclusive will last her," Mulgrew sighed.

"Not very long, I imagine," Cairney replied. "Now, is there any progress in Mister Miller's inquiry?"

"I haven't spoken with him this morning, sir, but needless to say when I learn of any development, I'll contact you forthwith."

"Please see that you do," he abruptly ended the call.

She sat for a moment reflecting on Cairney's call, then dialled Charlie Miller's mobile number and when he answered, asked, "Are you at your office?"

"Got here about ten minutes ago. I assume you're calling about the 'Glasgow News' exclusive by Julia Mason?"

"I've just had the Chief on about it," she replied. "There's nothing in the article that can harm your inquiry, is there?"

"Nothing," he confirmed.

"Any progress?"

"I've tracked down James Dougrie's estranged daughter, but I'm relatively satisfied she has nothing to do with his murder. That said, she has a soldier son who's apparently abroad and a husband who deserted her, but who might still be entitled to some part of what she is to inherit. I'm having both these men traced and either interviewed or eliminated from the inquiry."

"Anything else?"

"I intend tracking down the two surviving members of Murdo Clarke's gang and if I can trace his widow, interview her too. Needless to say, the door to door around Dougrie's house turned up zilch, so that is a washout. Why, do you have something for me or any line of inquiry I'm forgetting?"

"No," she unconsciously shook her head. "The Chief's looking for an update yesterday, so anything at all Charlie…"

"You'll be the first to know," he finished for her.

He was about to replace the mobile phone into his pocket when he had a thought and was about to dial when the door knocked and was pushed open.

Shona Mathieson, carrying her mug of coffee, stood in the doorway. Cancelling his idea of phoning Sadie, he waved Mathieson into the office and indicated the chair in front of the desk.

"You wanted to discuss Actions, sir?" she began.

He was about to respond, but his eyes narrowed when he saw that Mathieson seemed a little on edge and instead asked, "Is everything all right, Shona?"

Her eyes, bright with unshed tears, flickered before she replied, "I'm fine. Honestly."

But Charlie realised she was not fine and rising from his desk, stepped towards the door.

"Wait here," he ordered her and making his way to the incident room, called out to the officers present, "I'm in conference with DS Mathieson, so for the next ten minutes no interruption, please." Returning to the office, he closed the door and then reseating himself behind the desk, said, "If I ignored anything that was troubling my staff, for one it wouldn't make me a very good boss and for two," he smiled softly, "though you really don't know me, please be assured that I'm long enough married to know that when my wife tells me she's fine when clearly she's not, I should stop what I'm doing and listen. So Shona, tell me what's wrong and how I can fix this or how I can help you."

Perhaps it was his kindness or perhaps she really needed to cry, but to her embarrassment, Mathieson suddenly found herself weeping.

Leaving his chair, Charlie moved around the desk and handed her a clean handkerchief.

He didn't say anything or try to comfort her, but merely returned his chair and waited till she calmed.

Moments later, Mathieson took a deep breath and wringing the hankie in her hand, wiped at her eyes and said, "Sorry, sir…"

He waved away her apology.

"Thank you. I thought I was all cried out, but I think I needed that."

"So, Shona, what's wrong?"

She didn't immediately respond, but then said, "Last night, I split from my partner."

He waited patiently for her to continue and she said, "Over two years we'd been together, but it had been on the cards for a while. Anyway," she shrugged, "it's over."

"Obviously I don't really know you," he quietly replied, "but I'm sorry this has happened to you. Do you need some time off to come to terms with what's happened because it won't be a problem and nobody need know the reason why you're off?"

"No, sir," she shook her head. "I'd rather be at work and doing something than at home wondering what has gone wrong. But thanks anyway," she forced a smile.

"Okay, then, if you're determined to work why don't we make a start on what Actions we need to distribute to the team?" he smiled at her. Ten minutes later with the list in her hand, she was about to leave the office but turning said, "Thanks, sir, for…well, you know," she shrugged.

"Any time, Shona," he nodded to her.

In the corridor outside his office, she felt guilty that she had not disclosed Gerry Donaldson's threat, that if she didn't keep him apprised of what was going during the investigation, her career was at risk.

She glanced nervously at the closed door, but knew in her heart that when Charlie Miller had moved on, she would still be here and remain at the mercy of her vindictive DCI.

****

They had decided that Carol Forrest would drive to her daughter's house first thing that morning and then after dropping Geraldine at school, travel together in Sadie's Honda Jazz for the early morning appointment at Ross Hall Hospital.

"I know you'll be nervous, mum," she began, "but remember; this is just an interview and initial examination. They won't be performing any kind of procedure today."

"But isn't a biopsy a procedure? Liz said that…"

"Yes, what I *mean*," Sadie hastily interrupted, "is that you won't be getting kept in or anything. A biopsy will give the consultant the opportunity to examine the lump and discover whether or not there is any need for surgery."

"You mean he'll check to see if it's malignant or not?"

"Yes."

Carol smiled and said, "You're trying to keep me calm, aren't you?"

Tears bit at Sadie's eyes as concentrating on her driving, she replied, "To be honest, I'm trying to keep myself calm."

Before Carol could respond, her mobile phone chirruped and glancing at the screen, she smiled and said, "It's Charlie. Hello?"

"Just wanted to say hi and let you know I'll be thinking about you, today."

"Thanks. I'm in the car with Sadie," she turned to smile at her daughter. "We've dropped jellybean off and we've Ella in the back. Do you want to say hello to your wife?"

"No, you're okay. I'm about to give a briefing, but I didn't want to miss you before you went for the examination. Good luck, Carol, and let me know as soon as you hear anything."

"I will," she replied and ended the call.

Turning towards her daughter, she placed her hand lightly on Sadie's arm and said, "No matter what happens today, I know I've got you and Charlie to look out for me."

****

He wakened fully clothed on top of the unmade bed with a band of drummers beating a retreat in his head and a mouth as foul as a choked toilet.

Easing himself up to a sitting position, Tommy Craig immediately regretted the movement and as slow as he dared, stood. Using his hands on the walls to shuffle along the narrow hallway, he made his way to the toilet.

He knew from memory that if he didn't clear his stomach, he'd feel like shit all day and straddling the toilet bowl, used a hand to steady himself while he stuck two fingers down his throat and forced himself to vomit.

The thick bile, testament to his intake of Guinness, flowed from his throat like a black waterfall and splashed not just into the bowl, but also onto the linoleum floor.

His body shaking, he wiped at his mouth with the back of his hand and reaching across to the basin, inserted the plug before turning on the cold tap. When the sink was full he took a deep breath and doused his face into the freezing cold water.

Gasping for breath he sank back to sit on the edge of the bath, then lifting his head reached for an already stained towel to dry himself. His stomach rumbled to remind him if he intended throwing up again, he needed breakfast.

With a sigh, he made his way through to the kitchen, deciding he'd clean up the bathroom later when he had eaten something and tried to recall if he had bread in the larder.

Five minutes later with a mug of tea and a plate of toast, he settled himself down in front of the television and switched onto the BBC News 24. Ten minutes into the programme he listened to the announcer report once more the story of the discovery of the buried body in a Lanarkshire field.

The Scottish correspondent took up the story, repeating the Police Scotland press release that the body was now identified as that of

Murdo Clarke, a documented Glasgow man who had been missing since late nineteen-eighty-nine and was now being connected with the investigation into the murder yesterday of former Detective Inspector James Dougrie.

"Fuck me," Craig muttered in surprise, for it had not occurred to him that Dougrie's death could be related to that of Clarke. He'd always suspected it was one of the other three who had arranged to get rid of Clarke.

He remembered a week after they were banged up, reading the newspaper report inferring that Clarke, by then reported missing, had been a polis tout.

Now he wondered; did that confirm what he and the rest suspected; that Clarke was Dougrie's tout?

He'd always believed that the rest of the team had thought him stupid, always cracking jokes he didn't get, using big words to confuse him and smirking behind his back.

Yes, and maybe even keep things from him.

The question he now asked himself was, did the other three not just suspect, but actually *knew* that Clarke had been touting to the cops? His brow knitted as he tried to connect the dots.

Two of the three, Alex Murtagh and John O'Connor were dead.

So, it had to be Smiler Colville who done in Dougrie and if it was Smiler who murdered Dougrie, maybe it was him who killed Murdo Clarke too.

He grinned, for now it all seemed so simple.

Suddenly angry, he realised with Alex Murtagh and John O'Connor dead, the only person he could ask was Smiler and by God, he *would* answer and whether or not he wanted to.

****

Allocated their Actions, Alison Baxter and Willie Baillie made their way to the car park where with a grimace, he apologised, telling her, "Sorry, but the only CID car keys I could grab was the old Focus. It's a bit smelly because sometimes the plain clothes use it for surveillance duties. You know, chips, fried food, that sort of thing."

"I've smelled worse," she smiled as she opened the passenger door, then added, "Speaking of food, I haven't had anything other than a quick coffee before I left Tulliallan this morning. Is there a takeaway nearby, by chance?"

"Better than that," he grinned, then a little self-consciously, added, "I know a nice wee café on Kilmarnock Road that does a cracking breakfast, if you'll permit me to buy."

"Yes, why not," she smiled and would have been more than surprised to know the big man was smitten with Alison Baxter and relishing the opportunity to spend some time with her.

CHAPTER TWELVE

He raised his head when Shona Mathieson knocked on his door and said, "Sir, one of the analysts has obtained the address for Francis Colville, one of the two surviving gang members you were asking about. We're still trying to locate the widow of Murdo Clarke and awaiting a return call from the Department of Works and Pensions on that and a call from the Prison Service for an address for Thomas Craig, the other surviving gang member."

"Thanks, Shona. Is Colville living close?"

"Glasgow, sir," she glanced down at the Action in her hand. "Hardie Avenue over in Rutherglen. Do you want it allocated or…"

"No," he waved a hand. "I'll take a neighbour and go myself."

"What about the PM?"

"Bugger," he nodded. "I'd almost forgotten about the PM. Yes, I'll go after the PM. I'm meeting Baxter and Willie Baillie at the mortuary so I'll take one of them them with me to visit Colville. Anything else?"

"No, sir, other than to tell you that DC's Baxter and Baillie are away on their inquiry, but the rest of the team await your briefing in the incident room."

"Okay. Any word back from the Forensic about the Scene of Crime examination at the locus?"

"Nothing yet, sir. I'll give them a call when the briefing's finished."

"Right then, Shona," he got to his feet, "let's get it done."
****
Waiting in the room adjacent to the autopsy suite, Liz Watson was already suited up for the PM when Charlie arrived to find that Alison Baxter and Willie Baillie were also present.

Professionally and thoroughly, Watson concluded her examination within twenty-five minutes and turning to Charlie, said, "Not that you need it confirmed, but the cause of death was multiple stab wounds to the abdominal cavity on the right side of his body and one to his throat which I suspect he received when he fell forward onto his face. Three blows in all I count. I'll not go into too much detail, but suffice to say the blows were delivered with such force they pierced, among other organs, the stomach, right lung and liver as well as his oesophagus. Interestingly," she held up a pair of stainless steel forceps with a tiny sliver of metal firmly held in the teeth, "I recovered this from his heart. It seems to be the tip of a knife of some sort and as you can see," she beckoned that Charlie glance into Dougrie's chest cavity, "there seems to be a slight chip on his rib here where I assume the knife glanced off before entering the lung. If the tip is anything to go by I'm guessing the knife must have been very narrow. A stiletto, perhaps?"

"Maybe," he thoughtfully nodded, then asked, "What do you think might have caused the tip of the blade to break off?"

"Possibly the force with which he was struck," she mused.

He watched as Watson dropped the small metal tip into a paper bag held by Willie Baillie.

"You said the right hand side of his body?" and turning Baillie to face towards him, Charlie feigned a stab wound with his right hand and saw it would have struck Baillie on the left side. He then feigned a stab with his left hand and saw it would have struck Baillie on the right side of his body.

Nodding his thanks to the big man, he turned to Watson and said, "So, there's a possibility our killer *might* have been left-handed?"

"That would pretty much be my assessment, yes," she nodded.

"And there's the likelihood Murdo Clarke's killer was also left-handed?" he mused.

"As I recall, yes. Right, anything else?" she asked.

"No, I think you've covered it all for now, Liz."

He turned to Baillie and said, "Change of plan, Willie. You get both Dougrie's blood and DNA specimens with that blade out to the Forensic laboratory at Gartcosh as soon as you can. Ask them to try to identify exactly what kind of knife it came from."

Almost as an afterthought, he added, "While you're there, speak to a guy called Archie Young, he's one of the scientists and ask if there has been any update on the cigarette butt that was discovered beneath Murdo Clarke's body. Ask him to compare any DNA from the butt with the specimens from James Dougrie's body. Alison," he turned to her. "You come with me to Rutherglen. We've an address for one of the 'Four Minute Gang,' Francis Colville."

Finally, he smiled at Watson and said, "Thanks, Liz. I'll get your report in due course."

"Well, don't hold your breath," she sighed. "You're not the only detective that's in a hurry and I'm backlogged with paperwork. Besides," she pointedly stared at him, "I do have my non-criminal post mortem's to perform for the hospital too, you know."

"Would perhaps a bottle of your favourite red hurry things along?"

"I'll have the report on your desk by tomorrow," she winked at him.

****

Sadie Miller turned her Honda in through the gates of Ross Hall Hospital and parked under the canopy at the front entrance.

Minutes later she and her mother Carol, swinging the giggling Ella between them, were at the reception desk where the pretty young woman noted Carol's details before asking them to take a seat.

In the waiting area, Ella was delighted to discover a corner set aside with toys and books and hurriedly made her way there.

Seated together, Sadie reached for her mother's hand and tightly squeezing it, said, "I know you're nervous, but try not to worry too much. That's my job," she smiled at her.

They had been there just a few moments when a nurse pushed through a set of double doors and called Carol's name.

Leading her back through the swing doors, Carol turned to wave at Sadie, who forced a smile as she choked back her tears.

****

He rushed to the phone in the hope it might have been one of his sons or daughters calling, but was disappointed when the young woman from the local Cooperative Funeral Service wished to confirm details for the cremation that had been agreed would be conducted in three days time at the Rutherglen Cemetery, in Broomieknowe Road.

"I understand you do not wish a religious ceremony, Mister Colville?"

"No," he shook his head and continued, "my wife wasn't particularly religious, hen, so there will just be the service at the crematorium, if you don't mind."

"What about a humanist celebrant, Mister Colville. Would you consider that?"

"What's that? A humanist thingamajig, hen?"

"Well," the young woman drawled, "the simple answer is a humanist celebrant is an individual who usually is an experienced public speaker who will visit you at home, discuss some personal details about your wife and it's their job to prepare a simple speech that will give your wife a nice wee send-off, if you like."

"Does it cost much? I'm on the social, you see."

"No, you can agree a price when they visit and likely you'll find the insurance might even cover it. Shall I ask someone to contact you? We have a list of names of celebrants in your area."

"Aye, well, Elsie was a good woman and it's only right somebody does say something nice about her. Right, anything else?"

"Only to ask if you want your wife laid out for viewing here at our Queen Street parlour?"

"No, there'll be no need for that," he sighed. "Elsie wasn't one for showing off, you see."

"Oh," the woman was taken aback, then said, "All right. Now, about a purvey after the service…"

"You can stop right there, hen," he irately interrupted her. "None of my family nor any of Elsie's that she had left have had the courtesy or even the decency to contact me, so I'll not be feeding the buggers sandwiches and tea, okay?"

"Oh, right then, Mister Colville," the young woman took a breath before continuing, "Well, that seems to be all. The service is at ten o'clock, so we'll give you a phone call thirty minutes before the car's due to pick you up. Will there be anyone travelling with you?"

"Nobody, hen, just me. If the weans want to see their mother off, they can make their own way there."

The call had ended just seconds when it rang again.

Hoping it might be one of his children he eagerly snatched at it, but again was deflated to find it was Tommy Craig, who asked, "Are you in? I need to see you."

If I wasn't in I wouldn't have answered the bloody phone he thought, but instead replied, "Aye, if you must. Do you know Rutherglen?"

"Are you still in the same house?"

"Hardie Avenue, aye."

"Right then, I'll see you in about an hour," Craig replied before ending the call.

Replacing the handset, he wondered what the thick bastard wanted, but shrugging, decided he'd find out in an hour's time.

****

DC Willie Baillie had just arrived at Gartcosh and was signing for his visitors badge from the security officer at the front entrance when his mobile phone rung. Asking the security officer to hold on for a moment he glanced at the screen, but didn't recognise the calling number.

"Hello, DC Baillie."

"Mister Baillie, it's Corporal Martha Collins of the Military Police at the Provost Company, Edinburgh Castle" the young woman with a strong Geordie accent identified herself. "You called earlier to inquire about the whereabouts of Fusilier Alexander Gibson of the First Battalion of the Royal Regiment of Scotland?"

"Oh, yes, I did. Do you have that information, Corporal Collins?"

"Might I inquire why you need that information, Mister Baillie? Has Fusilier Gibson come to the attention of the police?"

"Not at all," he assured Collins. "Yesterday, his grandfather was murdered and as part of the investigation, we need to eliminate all family members as suspects; their whereabouts at the time of the crime I mean."

"Well, for the last two months Gibson has been on deployment in a theatre of operations, but I regret that I cannot provide you with his current whereabouts."

"Okay, but can you confirm that yesterday he was *not* in the United Kingdom?"

"Yes, I can confirm that yesterday he was *not* in the UK," she slowly repeated.

"Good, that eliminates him from our inquiry. One last thing. I'm not certain if he is yet aware of his grandfather's death, Corporal Collins, so I'll be grateful if you consider this to be a confidential inquiry.

"Can do," she replied.

"Then," he smiled, "that's all I need," and thanking the soldier, ended the call.

Turning to the security officer, he grinned and said, "Thanks, pal. Now, where do I find this guy, Archie Young?"

****

Shona Mathieson had just returned from a toilet break when her desk phone rang. Answering the call, she paled when DCI Gerry Donaldson said, "It's me, DS Mathieson. Do you have anything for me yet?"

Glancing nervously round the room, she saw nobody was paying any particular attention to her and quietly replied, "Nothing yet, sir."

"Yet I'm reliably informed that Miller is away to the post mortem for the man Dougrie," he hissed, "and then intends going to see a suspect. Is *that* correct, DS Mathieson?"

She felt a chill run through her. It was as she thought; Donaldson had someone else in the team touting to him as well.

Gathering her thoughts, she quietly replied, "I didn't see that as of particular interest, sir, and the man he's away to interview is not a suspect. At least, not that I'm aware of and as for Mister Miller attending the PM, it's just part of the inquiry."

"Don't tell me what's part of the inquiry or not," he snarled down the line. "I've been in this game for a long time, Mathieson. In future, I want to know every little detail of what that bastard's up to, do you understand, DS Mathieson?"

"Yes, sir," she gulped.

The line went dead and she realised he had hung up.

Replacing the phone into its cradle, she slowly glanced around the room and wondered.

Who else was Donaldson threatening and how the hell was she going to get herself out of this predicament?

****

Driving towards Rutherglen, Charlie glanced at Alison Baxter and asked, "Have you given this case any thought since last night? I mean, any ideas how we should progress an inquiry that's anything between twenty-eight years and one day old?"

"So you're absolutely certain the two murders are connected?"

"I'm in no doubt at all," he nodded. "It's too coincidental that James Dougrie is murdered just when the body of Murdo Clarke is exhumed and identified."

"That's not quite correct, Charlie," she raised her hand as if to emphasis her point. "If you recall, Clarke's name wasn't released till *after* Dougrie was murdered. The media only knew that a body had been exhumed from a field in Lanarkshire."

"And that," he slowly exhaled as he sped towards Rutherglen, "would seem to suggest that Dougrie's killer recognised or at least suspected the body was that of Clarke and believed that Dougrie might know or suspect something that would then identify the killer. What about that theory?"

"I can't argue with your hypothesis," she nodded. "However, it doesn't confirm that Dougrie was in any way connected with Clarke's murder."

"No, it doesn't," he agreed with a sigh.

Her mobile phone activated and accepting the call, he heard her say, "Hold on a minute, Willie. I'll put you on speaker so the boss can hear too."

"I'm still here at Gartcosh, boss," Willie Baillie's voice boomed. "First thing is I received a phone call from the Military Police regarding the laddie in the army, Alex Gibson. The woman I spoke with confirms he is abroad, but of course won't say where Gibson is. However, she did confirm he was away at the material time of James Dougrie's murder."

"Well, that takes him out of the frame anyway," Charlie replied. "Go on."

"I asked the corporal I spoke with not to disclose his grandfather's dead; thought it better he hears it from his mother."

"Good decision," Charlie agreed.

"I also received a phone call from the Clydebank office who checked their Voters Roll and as of the last census, confirmed Missus Gibson's estranged husband Peter was recorded as living at the address she gave us in Davidson Street. When I'm finished here, I'll take a turn over to there and see if I can locate him."

"Maybe go with a neighbour, Willie. What to do is return to Giffnock and by that time I'll be back and you can take Alison with you."

"Okay, boss," Baillie quickly replied.

Charlie kept his face straight for if his suspicions were correct, he guessed the big man would be delighted to go anywhere with Alison Baxter.

"What about the cigarette butt?" he continued. "Anything from Archie Young?"

"That's why I'm still here," Baillie sighed. "Apparently he's in a clean room testing something or other and can't leave for another twenty minutes. When I meet with him, I'll phone you if you want or let you know the result at Giffnock?"

"No, you're all right. Just let me know when you get to the office. Anything else?"

"Not at the minute."

Baxter ended the call just as Charlie turned onto Rutherglen's High Street and peering through the windscreen, absentmindedly murmured, "Now, where's Hardie Avenue from here?"

****

Shona Mathieson glanced up when Alice Brookes, the senior civilian member of the three female HOLMES operators called over from her own desk to say, "Shona, that's a Missus Gibson on the phone looking for Mister Miller. Says she's the daughter of James Dougrie. Can you take the call?"

"Yes, pass her through to my extension," Mathieson nodded.

Identifying herself to Gibson, Mathieson explained that Mister Miller was not immediately available, but understood from him that Gibson might be calling to arrange a visit to her father's home?

"Yes, Mister Miller said I was to phone first and I was wondering when would be convenient?"

She was about to reply, when she saw Brookes, who had her back to her, lifting the phone at her desk and for some odd reason, thought it suspicious.

"Eh, sorry, I was distracted there, Missus Gibson," she slowly said. "Now, you're looking for a time to visit your father's home?"

"Yes, will it be a problem, Sergeant?"

She continued to stare at Brookes and saw her replace the phone to its cradle before answering, "No, I don't think so. Mister Miller was quite specific that you were to be permitted access; however, he did stress that you would need to be accompanied because he wants you to check if if you can determine if anything has been stolen. Anything obvious that you might remember. Is that okay with you?"

"Yes, yes, of course. My only problem is that it would need to be while my daughter is at school and I would have to bring my toddler son with me. I don't have anyone who would mind him."

"When would suit you to visit the house?"

"Today, you mean? Oh, I'll need to get a bus to the city and the train to Giffnock, but then be back for my girl getting out of school at three."

"Oh, you don't drive?"

"I drive, but I don't have a car."

"Right," Mathieson's eyes narrowed as glancing at her wristwatch, she quickly thought before replying, "Give me your phone number and a couple of a minutes, then I'll get back to you."

Noting Gibson's phone number, she dialled Charlie Miller's mobile phone.

He had just arrived at Hardie Avenue and was locking the car when Mathieson said, "Sir, that was Missus Gibson looking for access to her father's house. She doesn't have transport so what I'm thinking is I can pop over, pick her up and go with her to Belmont Drive. That way I can be there with her when she checks the house to see if anything has been stolen. She has a time frame for getting home to be there for her daughter getting out of school at three."

"It would certainly be a help if she had a look in the house," he slowly replied, then said, "Good idea, Shona. Can you leave someone looking after your desk when you're out?"

"That's not a problem, sir," she glanced at Brookes whose head was bent as she sat at her desk typing out a report.

"Right then, get it done and let me know if there's anything of note, otherwise, I'll see you back at Giffnock after you return Missus Gibson home."

Inwardly pleased he supported her idea, she ended the call, got up from her desk and after making the arrangement with Gibson to pick her up, made her way over to Brookes.

Forcing a smile, she said, "Alice. That call you passed through to me. It was James Dougrie's daughter, Missus Gibson."

She leaned over and continuing in a low voice, said, "The boss has asked me to take Missus Gibson to Dougrie's house to check if anything had been stolen at the time of his murder, but he wants it kept quiet in the meantime. While I'm away fetching her, can you monitor the office and if anything crops up that you need me for, give me a phone on my mobile?"

"Of course, Shona," Brookes smiled widely.

The snare set, she fetched her coat from the hook on the wall and her handbag from her desk.

Striding towards the door a thought occurred to her and hand on the door handle, she turned to a young detective and asked, "John, you have kids. Do you have a child seat in your car?"

"Aye, I do," he smiled, his curiosity evident in his face.

"Can I borrow it for a couple of hours?"

****

Sadie had joined Ella at the play corner and though she smiled and helped her daughter with the building bricks, her mind was occupied by thoughts of what her mother was going through.

After what seemed to be an interminably lengthy time, the double doors opened.

With the same nurse holding her gently by the arm, Carol her face pale and a forced smile playing on her trembling lips, walked towards Sadie who got to her feet and gave her mother a hug.

Little Ella, uncertain what was going on, but sensing the tension began to cry and was lifted from the floor by Sadie.

"I'll just fetch your prescription," the nurse smiled and returned back through the doors while Sadie, hushing her daughter, helped her mother to a nearby chair.

A few minutes later the nurse returned and collecting the medicine from her, Sadie and Carol slowly made their way to the car parked outside.

While Sadie strapped Ella into her seat, Carol slowly buckled up and turning to her daughter, said. "Before you ask, the doctor was very nice, very professional and told me that he would phone me with the result of the biopsy some time within the next couple of days."

Getting into the drivers seat, she turned to Carol and taking a deep breath to control her emotions, replied, "Well, for the next couple of days you're going nowhere. Charlie insisted you stay with us and there's to be no argument. Right," she stared the engine, "let's get you home for a rest."

****

Willie Baillie was restless.

He'd been sitting in the small waiting room on the plastic chair that was far too narrow for his backside and decided that if he was to wait any longer, he'd head down to the cafeteria on the ground floor and get himself some grub.

However, just as he arose from his seat a tall, fair-haired man in his early forties pushed through a security door and asked, "DC Baillie?"

Being the only person in the room, Baillie refrained from pointing out the scientists astuteness and replied, "Aye, that's me. Mister Young?"

"Archie Young," he smiled and extended his hand before continuing, "I understand you've been waiting a for a wee while. Sorry about that. I was dealing with some hazardous material. Can't take chances with that stuff, eh?"

"No, of course," Baillie agreed but didn't have a clue what the hazardous material was and had no real interest either.

"I was delivering some post mortem specimens and a small tip of a blade to your guys here at the Lab and my boss, Mister Miller, instructed me to ask if you had made any headway with the cigarette butt discovered under Murdo Clarke's body?"

"Well, I did obtain some DNA from the butt, but no," Young shook his head, "nothing so far to indicate whose DNA it is."

"Unfortunate," Baillie replied, then added, "Mister Miller asked if you could compare the DNA from the butt to the specimen I brought over. James Dougrie, our murder victim."

"James Dougrie?" Young's eyebrows narrowed. "Wasn't he a police officer?"

"Regretfully, yes," confirmed Baillie.

"Okay, I can get that done. Do you want to wait for a result?"

"No, I've hung about here far too long. I'll get back and when you get a result, either way, please give Mister Miller a call."

As he turned away, he couldn't admit he'd much rather head back to Giffnock and meet up with Alison Baxter than waste more time at Gartcosh.

****

Frankie Colville had just finished washing up the breakfast dishes when the doorbell rung.

He wasn't looking forward to renewing his acquaintance with Tommy Craig, but was more than surprised to see a tall, bulky looking man with a facial scar at his door who was accompanied by a fair haired, good looking woman.

"Mister Colville? I'm Detective Superintendent Charlie Miller and this is Detective Constable Alison Baxter. I wonder if we might have a moment of your time?"

Though he had expected the visit, he was still taken aback and agreed before he had time to think about it. Stepping to one side, he wondered if he should have asked for their identification.

But it was to late now as the large man said, "Through here, is it?" and led them along the hallway towards the front room.

"Can I ask what this is about?"

"Can we sit down?" Charlie countered.

"Aye, if you must."

They sat together on the couch while Colville lowered himself into the armchair by the tiled fireplace.

"Do you live here alone, Mister Colville?" Charlie asked.

"I do now," he sourly replied. "My wife died yesterday."

Stunned, Charlie's mouth fell open but before he could respond, Baxter said, "We're very sorry to hear that, Mister Colville. Can I get you anything? A cup of tea or something?"

Surprised by her sympathy, Colville replied, "Eh, aye, okay then. You'll find…"

"It's all right, Mister Colville," she raised her hand and graced him with a dazzling smile. "I know my way about a kitchen," and left the room.

Smart move, Charlie thought, impressed by the way his neighbour handled the awkward situation and repeated, "I'm very sorry, Mister Colville. Had I known I assure you I wouldn't have troubled you at this sad time."

"So, why are you here, Mister Miller?"

Charlie shrugged and pursing his lips, replied, "You will know from the papers about the discovery of Murdo Clarke's body and the murder of James Dougrie. Clarke, we know from our records, was an associate of yours and suspected to be the fifth man of your gang. Dougrie," he shrugged again, "well, whether you knew it or not, he was the police officer running Clarke as an informant. Were you aware of that before it was inferred in the newspapers?"

Colville's eyes bored into Charlie's, then he sighed and replied, "You're right, of course. Murdo, the back-stabbing bastard, was the one touting to a cop, but none of us knew for certain it to be your man, Dougrie. When we were captured at the building society job in Renfrew and then Murdo got on his toes with the money, it didn't take a genius to work out he was the one who had fired us into the cops."

"So you believed Clarke had fired you guys in and was away with the money?"

"That's what we thought, yes," Colville carefully replied, but too carefully for Charlie's liking.

"Did you know James Dougrie, prior to you being arrested?"

"No," he replied, but again Colville responded far to quickly for Charlie to believe him.

Colville's eyes narrowed at the sudden flash memory of the arrest; the screaming and the shouting, thinking he had got away but then being dragged from the getaway car by the polis waving their guns and him almost shitting himself as he lay on the ground.

"So you're saying you never had any dealings with James Dougrie? Never met him at any time?" Charlie interrupted his thoughts.

"No, never," he firmly replied with a vigorous shake of his head.

"Here we are," Baxter interrupted his thoughts as she nudged open the front room door with her shoulder and carried a plastic tray in with three cups and saucers and two bowls with milk and sugar.

Setting the tray down onto a low table, she milked and sugared the tea before handing each of the two men their cups and saucer.

Resuming her seat next to Charlie, she smiled at Colville and asked, "Your wife, what was her name?"

"Elsie," he sighed and tightly smiled.

"Have you any family, Mister Colville?"

Sipping at his tea, Charlie guessed Baxter had some reason for her questions and decided to let her continue.

"Two sons and two daughters, but they don't get in touch," he shook his head. "They would speak with Elsie, but since I did my time in the nick…"

He didn't finish.

"And how long since your release from prison?" she sipped daintily at her tea.

"Me? Oh, I got out in two-thousand and ten, four years short of my sentence; for good behaviour."

"And the family haven't been near you since? That's a real shame," she loudly sighed before continuing, "Well, my boss and I certainly don't want to cause you any more problems, Mister Colville, but maybe you can answer a couple of questions for us before we go, if you don't mind?"

Disarmed by her politeness and charm, he replied, "If I can, hen."

"Can you recall the last time you saw Murdo Clarke?"

Staring at him, Charlie saw the slightest flicker of Colville's eyes and his head bowed slightly as staring down to his left at the fireplace, realised he was lying when Colville replied, "Oh, I think it must have been the night before the job; the one we got arrested for I mean. We usually met up to confirm the details of the plan, what our different jobs were when we got to the place. You know, who was doing what, that sort of thing."

"So if you were arrested on Friday the fifteenth of December, that would be, let me see," Baxter's eyes narrowed, "the night of Thursday the fourteenth of December?"

"If you say so, hen. My memory for dates isn't that good these days."

"And do you recall where you saw Clarke?"

"Oh, that was in his house with Stacey, his wife. Aye, in his house in…" he cleared his throat and his eyes tightened as he tried to recall the address, then said, "Barlia Drive I think it's called, up in Chateau Lait. Aye, that's it. Barlia Drive. They had one of them two storey council houses at the time."

"Chateau Lait?"

He grinned at her confusion and said, "You're not a local lassie, then. Chateau Lait. It's supposed to be French for Castlemilk. That's what the locals call it. It's a council housing scheme on the south side of the city near Busby.

"Oh. And does Murdo's wife…"

"Stacey."

"Does Stacey still live there?"

"I wouldn't know, hen. I didn't really know her that well," he shrugged, but not convincingly enough for Charlie. "I'd only met her a couple of times and I haven't seen her since…" he stopped and licking nervously at his lips, cleared his throat before adding, "Not since that night, I mean."

"Who else was at that meeting, Mister Colville?"

"Nobody else that I recall, hen."

Once again Charlie thought there was more that Colville wasn't telling them as Baxter asked, "I know it's being broadcast on the media, but obviously we need to trace Missus Clarke to officially inform her about the recovery of her husband's body. Would you have any idea how we can find her? Any family or friends you might know of?"

He shook his head before sarcastically replying, "The only thing I knew about Stacey was she liked nice things. It cost Murdo a packet to keep her in clothes and jewellery too, if I recall. She definitely liked the high life, did Stacey. Bit of a girl, if you know what I mean," he winked and grinned. "Now," he glanced at them in turn, "I'm sure you appreciate I have things to do…"

"Absolutely, sir," Baxter treated him to another dazzling smile before adding, "There's just one more thing I would ask of you."

"Yes?"

Head down, she searched in her handbag and brought out a clear plastic phial before telling Colville, "Though there is nothing to suggest you are a suspect in the murder of James Dougrie, however, we are taking DNA samples from every witness we interview. Do you mind?" she stood up and withdrawing a swab from the phial said, "It's painless, if you can just open your mouth, please?"

Perhaps it was his lengthy time in prison spent doing as he was told that indoctrinated Frankie Colville for without thinking he opened his mouth and permitted Baxter to obtain her sample.

"Thank you," she smiled and replaced the swab into the phial. Turning to Charlie, she asked, "Anything else, sir?"

Choking back his grin at her gall, he shook his head and said to Colville, "Thank you for your time, Mister Colville and again, our sympathy for your loss. I might need to speak with you again at some time, so do you have a phone number I can contact you on?"

"I'm not hard to find. I'm in the phone book," he gruffly replied.

"Right then," Charlie got to his feet and smiling, said, "We'll see ourselves out."

They were gone just moments and still seated, Colville wracked his memory for the night he had last seen Murdo Clarke. What could they know, he wondered and what the hell was that shite about a DNA sample? After all the prison authorities took a sample before they let him go.

He hurried to the front room window and from behind the curtain, glanced out at the detectives and watched them walking to their car. Good, he thought, for now he had a phone call to make.

****

In their car outside, Charlie clicked home his seat belt, but before starting the engine, asked, "Well? What do you think?"

Baxter squinted her eyes in thought before she replied, "He definitely knows something about Clarke's murder, of that I'm almost certain. Did you notice how he was a little nervous when I pressed him to recall when he last saw Clarke? There's a train of thought," she explained, "that a liar will turn their head and stare down to their left. Don't ask me to explain the theory behind it," she smiled, "but it's taught to the NYPD interrogators using cognitive interview techniques to distinguish a lie when an attempting to retrieve information from a witness and Mister Colville in there gave us the most perfect example of it."

"Yes," he replied, "I did see that. That and the throat clearing."

"Exactly. All it remains is for us to try to find out what lie he told or what he didn't tell us, but," she turned to Charlie, "I don't believe continuing to interview him in the comfort of his own home and particularly after just losing his wife would have been a good idea."

"No, you're right. That's not to say we can't invite him in to the office at a later date. What was that about taking his DNA sample? He should already be on the database because that's usually a procedure completed prior to a prisoner being released."

"I just thought it might rattle him a little because I'm in no doubt he'll be wondering why we need it and besides," she shrugged, "I don't suppose it will do any harm to submit another sample to the Lab anyway."

"The deviousness of women," he grinned at her and started the engine.

As they pulled away from the kerb, neither Charlie nor Baxter took any notice of the stocky built, older man who wore a second-hand army camouflage jacket and who seeing them exit the close, had stopped dead and hurried into bushes behind the garages opposite the close to avoid being seen.

CHAPTER THIRTEEN

Shona Mathieson stopped outside Jessica Gibson's house and with a wary eye on the teenagers who stared insolently at her from across the road, locked the CID car before knocking on Gibson's door.

She was pleased to see that Gibson, carrying her son in her arm, was ready and returning to the car, Mathieson said, "Please, call me Shona."

"That was thoughtful of you bringing a child seat," Gibson said from the rear as she strapped Connor in.

"Can't have me breaking the law and particularly when I'm driving the company car," Mathieson smiled.

She concentrated on her driving for the start of the journey, then said, "I hope this won't be too traumatic for you, Missus Gibson, returning to your father's house; particularly after what happened there."

"Please, Jessica," she replied before adding, "I've given it some thought and if I'm honest, I'm a little nervous. You likely know I hadn't seen or had any contact with my dad since I was a child. Mister Miller asked me have a look to determine if anything has been stolen at the time of…well, when dad was killed, but I'm not sure if I remember the house that well. My room, maybe," she smiled, "but I can't see anyone wanting anything from there. Besides, he might have decorated the place, changed everything, bought new furniture even."

"Maybe so, but we can always have a look anyway, eh?" Mathieson replied with an encouraging smile.

The remainder of the journey was completed with Gibson entertaining the fractious Connor, apologetically explaining, "He's due a nap. Do you have kids, Shona?"

"No. No kids, no husband and no partner," she dully replied.

"Lucky you," Gibson murmured, then almost immediately added, "I don't really mean that. My three are great, but I'm not sorry to see the back of Peter, my ex."

"Right, here we are then," Mathieson turned round in her seat and seeing the child had fallen asleep, softly asked, "Do you want to carry him in? I'm sure we can lay him down on a couch or somewhere while you check the house over."

Minutes later, the little boy carefully laid by his mother down onto a couch in the front room, they began their tour of the house starting with the front room.

"It's not how I remember it," Gibson quietly said as she lightly run her fingers across the furniture.

"Not that I'm any kind of décor expert," Mathieson turned her head back and forth as she stared at the walls, "but it seems to me this room has been recently wallpapered; certainly within the last year or two anyway.

As they progressed through the house they saw further evidence of redecorating, a new kitchen and a modern toilet suite in the downstairs cloakroom. However, when they climbed the stairs to the upper floor, they discovered that while a new suite had also been installed in the bathroom and the master bedroom was likewise newly refurbished, the rooms that had been Gibson's and her brother Stephen's remained as they were when their mother removed them from the house.

Mathieson turned and was abut to speak when she saw that Gibson, hesitantly stood in the doorway, was quietly weeping.

"God," she spluttered, her hand rising to her mouth as tears coursed down her cheeks, "it's like a museum. He didn't change a thing." Moving into her room she lifted a doll from a pram and trying to smile through her tears, wearily sat down onto the single bed.

Turning to Mathieson and almost as if seeking confirmation to her thoughts, she said, "He didn't forget about us, did he?"

"Apparently not," Mathieson shook her head, but also realised it was a waste of time asking if Gibson saw or recognised anything that might be missing. The renovation to the rooms downstairs seemed to confirm that.

However, staring at the bedroom bedecked in a young Jessica's favourite things, she thought whatever else James Dougrie had or hadn't done, he'd missed his children and this was clearly evidence of his unhappiness.

Curious, though, she wondered, that he hadn't tried to reconnect with them when they became adults.

She decided to give Gibson some privacy in the room and was on her way downstairs when her mobile phone received a text message. Opening the text, she read: *phone me* and though the mobile number was unfamiliar to her, had no doubt who it was from.

Her call was answered almost immediately by DCI Gerry Donaldson who barked at her, "You didn't think that visiting Dougrie's house with his daughter was important enough to inform me? Didn't I warn you that I want to know *everything* that's going on?" he hissed in her ear.

"I'm not in a position to speak right now," she calmly replied and abruptly ended the call.

Pokerfaced, her lips tightly closed, at least she now knew for certain who Donaldson's second tout in the office was.

****

Willie Baillie arrived back at Giffnock office to find that Charlie Miller and Alison Baxter had not yet returned from their inquiry. Helping himself to a mug of coffee, he was called into the incident room by Alice Brookes who seated at her desk, stared up at him and began, "Shona Mathieson put out an Action to trace Murdo Clarke's widow who was the one that reported her husband missing. Earlier this morning an e-mail with an attachment arrived from the Randolphfield office out in Stirling where all the records of outstanding missing persons are being stored. Stacey Clarke's statement was the attachment, but," she sighed, "her statement was initially noted by a uniformed officer, a man I should add," her voice betraying her opinion of men in general, "who for some God forsaken reason instead of her date of birth, he wrote 'over twenty-one.' Stupid bugger," she shook her head.

"Probably at the time he was being courteous," Baillie smiled then staring at Brookes, pointedly added, "You know how some women don't like giving out their age. What was the address?"

"The same one we had listed for Clarke at the time he went missing, but Shona told me that the voters roll for that address no longer shows anyone called Clarke living there. Shona also did a criminal record check and a PNC check for a Stacey Clarke."

"Let me guess, it turned up dozens?"

"Quite literally, yes, but assuming she's at least fifty or over fifty years of age, none that were registered as living in the Glasgow area."

"That doesn't really tell us much if we've no other details, though, does it?" he mused then continued, "Could be if they were friendly with their neighbours, there might be someone still in touch with Missus Clarke. Give me the last known address anyway and mark me and Alison Baxter down for an Action to speak to the neighbours."

"You sure that will be okay with Shona and the boss?"

"He's due back anytime," Baillie nodded, "so I'll square it with him when he arrives."

"Okay," Brookes agreed and wrote down the address on a fresh Action sheet.

****

It was on the drive home that Jessica Gibson, in the back seat entertaining her son who was now wide awake, nervously asked Shona Mathieson, "The detective who was with Mister Miller, I'm sorry, I forgot his name…"

"DC Baillie?"

"Yes, that's him. He was very nice and gave me a phone number for a lawyer in your union, I think it is."

"Oh, you mean the Federation?"

"That's it. Anyway, DC Baillie said I was to phone this man and when I did the lawyer put me onto his colleague who is dealing with the Will and she told me that if my father has left me the house in his Will she couldn't see any reason as to why I can't move in right away. Would that be all right do you think?"

"I'm sorry, I can't make that kind of decision, but I'll inform Mister Miller of what you were told and once he's satisfied the house is no longer of any evidential value to his investigation, I don't suppose he'd object."

Her brow furrowed when she recalled the teenagers hanging about outside Gibson's house and asked, "I assume you're very keen to move out of Ferguslie?"

"You have no idea," she sighed in response.

"Well, as soon as I get back to the office and have the opportunity to speak with Mister Miller, either I'll phone you with what he says or ask him to give you a call himself. How does that sound?"

"Please, yes," the relief in Gibson's voice was evident.

Feeling a little cheered that she might be able to help the woman, Mathieson smiled and concentrated on her driving.

It was when she turned off Underhill Road into Greenhill Road she remembered she had another pressing problem to deal with and with a quiet smirk, had an inspirational idea how that might be resolved.
****

The humanist celebrant glanced at his watch, his face displaying his annoyance.

He had arranged to be at Mister Colville's house at four o'clock and now here he was, stood at the door for almost five minutes and it seemed that nobody was at home.

Taking a deep breath, he sighed. Maybe he was being to harsh for the man had just lost his wife and perhaps had some pressing issue to attend to or simply had forgotten the appointment for after all, it wasn't unheard of for the recently bereaved to lose track of what was going on about them.

Removing his mobile phone, he dialled the home number Colville had given him and less than a minute later, could clearly hear it ringing from inside the house.

Bugger it, he thought and ending the call, stuffed the phone back into his pocket and made his way out of the close.

It did not occur to the man nor would he have even considered it, but had he turned the door handle of the ground floor flat he would have discovered it unlocked.

****

He stopped the car in the rear yard and switching off the engine was about to get out when Alison Baxter laid her hand on his arm and said, "Wait a minute, Charlie."

Turning to her, he saw her brow creased in concentration when she said, "Jessica Gibson told us that her mother blamed another woman for breaking up her marriage. I know the door to door is completed, but maybe we weren't asking the right question."

"What should we have been asking?"

"We should have asked if James Dougrie had someone else visiting him or even living with him after his wife and children left or perhaps some neighbour has knowledge of this mysterious woman."

"You're assuming that if indeed there was some sort of relationship between Dougrie and this third party, it was sexual. It might have been a work related thing or maybe just a friend."

She stared at him then slowly grinned before asking, "How many male and female relationships do you know that, outside work, are just friends?"

"Well, there's me and Cathy Mulgrew for a start," he began, but Baxter held her hand up and said, "Isn't Miss Mulgrew gay?"

"Yes, but that doesn't mean anything."

"Oh, Charlie, I think it does," she smiled tolerantly at him.

"Well, there's…" his mouth twisted in concentration, but he couldn't immediately think of any other female he had a good friendship with who wasn't either a family member, colleague or a friend to both him and Sadie. And so, shoulders slumped, added, "Okay. So James Dougrie was having it off with another woman. How do you propose we go about finding her and if we *do* find her, what do you believe she can add to our investigation?"

"Like I said, let's start with a door to door with neighbours who have been there when Dougrie's wife left in December nineteen-eighty-nine."

"Curious," he mused, "that such a lot occurred round about that time, eh?"

"Even more curious that though Frank Colville says he met with Clarke the night before the job, but there's no mention of that meeting in any of the missing person paperwork Dougrie had in the file. I don't profess to be an expert, but isn't it standard practise to document the MP's movements in the days prior to their disappearance?"

"I'd say yes," Charlie shrugged, "but my limited experience in dealing with MP's is that the questions asked are down to how committed the officer dealing with the inquiry is."

"Yet there's nothing to suggest that Dougrie wasn't competent. I mean, for heavens sake, he was a Detective Inspector."

And Gerry Donaldson is a Detective *Chief* Inspector, Charlie unkindly thought, but replied, "You're right. Perhaps it was an oversight or perhaps..." he paused.

"Perhaps?" she prompted him.

"The wife, Stacey Clarke, reported him missing on what date again?"

"The day after the arrests, Saturday the sixteenth."

"And we're presuming that is round about the time of his death, yes?"

Her eyes narrowed and she smiled before replying, "You think he might have been dead before the dates we're working on? Before even the gang were arrested? But if that's the case, then who provided the information to Dougrie? Wait a minute," she cleared her throat, "It was his wife who later tried to claim the reward money so evidently she knew that he had grassed up his associates."

"And of course we are presuming it *was* Clarke who gave Dougrie the information," Charlie reminded her, then continued, "That's something else we need to think about."

His brow furrowed when he continued, "Just something else we have to ask Missus Clarke when we trace her."

He opened the driver's door before adding, "But we're better doing that after coffee, eh?"

****

He hurried home, his bandy legs shuffling at a pace that left him breathless, a sense of dread at every corner. His mind was reeling, deciding he needed the long distance walk to clear his head and was better able to see about him than run the risk of the polis catching him on a bus.

He had waited for several minutes in the shadow of the bushes behind the garages facing Smiler's close, watching until the big man and the woman had left Smiler's close and driven off.

He needed to collect his thoughts, work out what he had to say to Smiler before banging on his door and had taken that time to find a takeaway café on Rutherglen's Main Street where he bought a beaker of coffee before returning to the close and seeing the tall detective leaving in the plain clothes polis car.

He inwardly shuddered when he remembered going into the close, to Smiler's door.

It had been a long time since he had been involved in such violence. Any kind of violence.

Now, here he was, a fugitive again, running from the polis.

Dear God, he thought, for he knew that for all his bravado, Tommy Craig could not, would not suffer another spell in the jail; no, he'd die before he'd let the polis and the courts send him back inside.

He'd head home, grab what few possessions he could pack into his old suitcase and catch a train to the Smoke down south.

****

Shona Mathieson turned into the rear car park and saw Charlie Miller's old Volvo nestled against a wall.

Good, she thought, she might get a response to Jessica Gibson's query about moving into the house, but before she spoke with Miller, she considered what she must do to get Gerry Donaldson off her back.

Telling to Alice Brookes to keep her confidence about taking Missus Gibson to her father's house, then Donaldson's phone call had confirmed what she had suspected; the senior HOLMES operator was his second tout in the investigation.

Now, if her plan was to work, she needed to speak to an old friend and scrolling down her phone directory, pressed the green button for the number she selected.

****

"I know you're just in, boss, but I wondered if I can have a word?" Willie Baillie caught Charlie as he entered his office.

"Alison, can you drum up a couple of coffee's," he called out to Baxter while beckoning Baillie to follow him into the room. Taking off his jacket, he hung it behind the door and indicated Baillie sit in the chair opposite.

"Couple of things to update you with, boss," Baillie begun. "We've had an e-mail with Murdo Clarke's wife's statement attached reporting him missing, but unfortunately, no date of birth for her and the PNC check came back negative. Shona Mathieson was out on an inquiry, so I asked Alice Brookes to raise an Action to speak with the Clarke's former neighbours up in Barlia Drive in Castlemilk so ask if any of them keep in touch with her. Alice is also going to get onto the council's housing department to see if Clarke applied for a move."

"Good, and the other thing?"

"I had a phone call from your man at Gartcosh regarding the cigarette butt."

He shook his head. "It's a negative for James Dougrie."

"Ah well, worth a try anyway," Charlie sighed.

"Do you still want me and Alison to track down Missus Gibson's husband at his address over in Clydebank?"

Charlie glanced at his wristwatch and seeing it was almost four o'clock, replied, "No, I'll get some of the others to do that. I want you and Alison to head back to Dougrie's house. I know the door to door has been done, but there's a couple of questions I want asked of the neighbours. Alison can fill you in on your way there, but let her have her coffee first."

The open door was knocked and he glanced up to see Shona Mathieson stood there.

"Right, anything else, Willie?"

"Not for now, boss," and nodding to Mathieson, left the room.

"Shona," he smiled at her indicating she come in and take a seat.

"Sir, I'm just back from returning Missus Gibson home. What a shithole that is," she shook her head.

"My experience has been it's not the area, but some of the small percentage of the people who live there that give a housing scheme a bad name. Anyway, how did you get on at her father's house?"

In short, terse sentences, Mathieson described the visit and how upset Gibson was when she found the children's rooms unchanged. "Curious that he never contacted them after his wife died," he said. "I thought that too," she nodded, then added, "Ashamed, maybe?" "Perhaps," he pursed his lips. "Was she able to recall anything about this woman he was alleged to have been seeing?" "I did ask, but no, nothing at all."

It took her a couple of minutes to express Jessica Gibson's wish to move into her father's house.

"I told her that you would need to clear the house as a crime scene before any decision could be made, sir."

"Sympathetic as I am to her current housing situation, Shona, I believe I'll need to run her request by the Legal Department first. However," he rubbed at his temple with the heel of one hand while glancing at his wristwatch, "As keen as you and I are to see her out of there it's a little late to get any of they shiny butts on the phone at this time of the day, so here's what we'll do. First thing tomorrow morning, I want you with my permission as the SIO to contact the Legal Department and inform them I have no further interest in the house. Willie Baillie has done most of the legwork, so contact the Federation lawyers to ensure Missus Gibson is definitely the beneficiary for the house and when that's done," he smiled, "tell her to get someone to help her move in."

"Yes, sir," she nodded with a smile.

"Okay, since you were away, Willie Baillie had an Action raised to try and locate Murdo Clarke's widow. However, I've sent him and Alison Baxter to speak again with Dougrie's neighbours to see if any of them recall this woman."

He stared keenly at Mathieson and with a smile, asked, "Did you enjoy your wee jaunt away from the office?"

She smiled and replied, "It was nice to get out into the fresh air."

"Well, in that case and mind," he raised a warning eyebrow, "I've no budget for excessive overtime, but do you fancy coming with me to Castlemilk to speak to the Clarke's former neighbours?"

"Oh aye, I do," she grinned.

"Good," the door was knocked by Alison Baxter who held a steaming mug. "Well," he added, "let me have this coffee and I'll be with you in ten minutes.

****

She needed to make the call and in the pretence of using the ladies toilet, checked both cubicles were unoccupied before dialling his number.

He answered almost immediately and she said, "I only have a minute. I've something to tell you that you'll want to hear so, can you meet me in half an hour? The car park at the Eastwood Council offices in Rouken Glen Road. Yes, thirty minutes then."

Ending the call, she felt a shiver of nervousness and with shaking hands, redialled the number from earlier to simply say, "It's done. Thirty minutes."

****

DCI Gerry Donaldson replaced the near empty pewter hip flask into his bottom drawer and licked at his lips. Popping a couple of strong mints from the tin in his drawer, he rose from his desk and grabbed at his coat.

In the general office he growled at the clerk and told her, "I'll be out of the office for a while. If I'm needed, get me on my mobile."

He was gone before the female constable could respond and staring at the closing door, almost guiltily she murmured, "And good fucking riddance."

Consciously aware that he had taken a more than couple of nips through the day, he decided to take a CID car to the meeting believing it would be less likely to attract the attention of the beasties than his own car.

Pulling out from the Helen Street office, he began to make his way to the car park at the Eastwood Council offices.

He couldn't imagine what was so important that made Shona Mathieson so reluctant to relate over the phone, but could only guess she didn't want to be overheard.

He loudly burped and tasted again the single malt and the peppermints, mentally reminding himself the flask was almost empty and he needed to take it home this evening to refill it.

A little under twenty minutes later, he turned from Rouken Glen Road through the lights into the council's car park, his eyes searching for Mathieson.

Stopping the car, he snorted. Bloody woman was late. Just typical of the split arse, he inwardly sneered and steering the car into a free bay, switched off the engine.

He released his seat belt and was sat there for no more than seconds, then startled at a loud rap of knuckles on the driver's window.

His head snapped round to see the fluorescent jacket stood beside the car and lowering the window, a police woman's head bent down to ask, "Good afternoon, sir. Do you have business in this car park?"

"You fucking idiot!" he sneered in reply, now seeing that a second police woman stood behind her. "Can't you see this is a CID motor? What's your name? Now!"

The heavyset police woman, a grey haired sergeant he realised with a slight scar above her left eye, bent down to squat beside his window and said, "My name's Cathy Pickering, but that's not really important. What *is* important is..." she bent her head forward and theatrically sniffing, pretended surprise when she frowned and asked, "My, my. Tell me this, sir, have you been *drinking*?"

A cold hand snatched at his chest.

He had been set up! The bitch had set him up!

"Do you fucking know who I am?" he blustered, his rage so intense that saliva dripped from his lips and his face turned as red as a tomato.

"What I *know* is you're the driver who I saw bumping the pavement when you turned into the road leading to the car park," pokerfaced, the sergeant calmly lied, "and I see you to be the driver of a CID vehicle; a driver who I suspect to have alcohol on his breath, so it's my intention to breathalyse you, sir. Now please, get out of the car."

"Fuck off! I didn't bump the kerb!" he snarled and pressed the button on the armrest to raise the window. However, Donaldson might have fared better had instead he locked the door for with surprising speed and agility belying Pickering's size and girth and ably assisted by her neighbour, she snatched open the door and grabbing at Donaldson, bodily heaved him from the car to fall onto his back to the ground.

"Now," the heavily built sergeant knelt down with her knee on the chest of the struggling detective, "since you are obviously resisting any attempt to comply with my request for a specimen of breath, I'm arresting you for suspected drink driving and failing to provide the said breath specimen when required," she grunted and reached towards her utility belt for her handcuffs.

It was moments later when he was securely handcuffed in the rear of the Traffic car and her neighbour stood outside, locking the CID car and out of earshot, Pickering turned to stare at the furious DCI and with a quiet smile, softly said, "By the way, my wee pal Shona Mathieson asked me to convey this message and I quote; fuck you, Donaldson."

CHAPTER FOURTEEN

"So, you're in digs at the training college then?" Willie Baillie asked, though his stomach was clenching he had decided to go for it.

"I am for the minute, yes," Alison Baxter replied.

"Well, by the time you get back there tonight the restaurant will be closed so when we're finished this door to door thing, we can catch a Chinese if you like?"

She fought the impulse to smile and turning to him, replied, "Are you asking me out, Willie?"

"Eh, well, no, I mean, yes and no," he blushed as he stared straight ahead through the windscreen. "What I'm saying is that it's gone six now and by the time…"

"Yes, I heard you the first time. Let's say we get the door to door completed by what, say the back of nine? Will there still be Chinese restaurants open, do you think?"

"Oh aye, of course there will. There's a cracking one on the Kilmarnock Road I use."

"What, with your wife?"

"My what?" he turned to her, genuinely surprised. "You think I'm married? Bloody hell, Alison, I wouldn't ask you to come for something to eat if I was married!"

"Girlfriend then?" she teased.

"No," he quickly replied and took a deep breath. "No girlfriend and before you ask, no, I don't live with my mother either."

"Oh, so you're single and fancy free then?"

"I'm single, but I don't know about being fancy-free," he grinned, suddenly recognising he was being teased. "I've plenty of fiscal commitments. The mortgage that would choke a horse and payments on my car, but no women in my life, if that's what you mean."

He stopped the car outside Dougrie's house and switched off the engine.

"You know I'm likely a few years older than you," she stared at him.

"And your point is?"

"Well," she drawled, "how old are you, Willie?"

"I'm forty-three or I will be come next March."

"Mmmm, I've over five years on you," she smiled.

"Maybe when you were nineteen and I was fourteen that might have mattered, but at the age we are today, I don't think it's an issue, Alison, do you?"

"Okay," she conceded, "perhaps you have a point."

His eyebrows knitted as he replied, "I'm asking you to have something to eat after we do this job, Alison, not looking for a lifetime commitment. Besides, I don't even know if *you're* in a relationship. Are you?"

She stared at him and then slowly shook her head before replying, "No, I'm not and I apologise for being so ungracious. Yes, something to eat after this and before I return to Tulliallan would be nice. Thank you, Willie."

"Okay then," his face lit up with a wide grin. "Right," he opened the drivers door, "let's get this done, eh?"

****

The first door that Charlie Miller knocked upon in Barlia Drive was opened just six inches by an unshaven, longhaired, middle-aged man wearing a Chelsea football top who used his foot to keep back a small, black and white collie dog that snarled at the large detective.

"Get back, ya bastard!" the man shouted down at the dog before staring curiously at Charlie and asking, "What is it?"

Staring down at the mutt, Charlie replied, "CID. I was wondering if I could have a couple of minutes of your time?"

"Naw," the man vigorously shook his head and slammed the door. With a sigh, he turned to Mathieson and quipped, "Not a fan of the polis, then."

The next couple of doors they knocked upon were just as unhelpful, but it was the fourth door that he knocked that proved to be the most fruitful.

An elderly, grey haired, thin faced woman with a cigarette hanging from the side of her mouth whose eyes narrowed at the sight of the two detectives, said, "The Clarke's? Aye, I remember them. She was stuck-up cow, but he wasn't so bad. Sometimes nodded when he passed me in the street with his wee girl."

"He had a daughter?" Charlie's eyes widened in surprise and turning towards Mathieson, he saw her shoulders shrug and her head shake, wordlessly indicating that she also was unaware of a daughter.

"Well," the woman shrugged, "I *think* it was his wee lassie. About eight or nine she was. Definitely school age because she used to wear a uniform. Shy wee thing."

"Can we come in and have a word, Missus...?"

"Missus Lennox. Sophie Lennox and aye, you can come in, but don't take any notice of the place," she turned away as Charlie and Mathieson followed her into the dank hallway. "The cleaning lassie from the social work hasn't turned up today."

The smell of greasy food and cigarette smoke was overwhelming, causing both detectives to take a gasp as they followed the limping woman towards the front room at the end of the hallway, seeing that she leaned heavily on a wooden walking stick.

Glancing about him, Charlie decided the cleaning lassie seemingly hadn't turned up all year.

The suffocating heat in the front room was overwhelming and more so because of the two bar electric fire that burned brightly in the hearth.

"My arthritis," Lennox explained. "The doctor says I've to keep warm."

Warm? Charlie thought. My God, you could fry an egg on the floor, but instead asked, "Okay if we take a seat Missus Lennox?"

He didn't wait for a reply, but sat with Mathieson down onto the couch, seeing her removing her notebook from her handbag that she laid down onto the floor.

"Aye, go ahead then," she replied with a suspicious stare as she slumped heavily down into a cushioned armchair.

"Now, how well did you know the Clarkes?"

Her bottom lip curled and she said, "Not that well. Like I told you, that Stacey Clarke thought she was a cut above everybody else, but Murdo," she slowly smiled and shook her head. "Is that his body that's been found in the field? It was on the news."

"Yes, I'm sorry to say it is Mister Clarke. Now, you were about to tell us?" he coaxed her.

"Oh, aye, Murdo. Bit of a lad if what I heard was right enough."

"And what did you hear?"

"Oh," her face expressed her doubt, "You're the polis. Should I be telling you these things?"

"Mister Clarke has been dead for a very long time now, Missus Lennox. I don't think he'll mind if you talk about him now."

"Aye, well, if you grow up in this area you learn not to speak to the polis," she explained. Taking a deep breath, she continued. "Like I said, Murdo was apparently a bit of a lad, you know, in bother most of his life, but I never heard him getting the jail for it, you know? Sometimes he and Jimmy…" she paused then explained, "Jimmy was my husband. Tuberculosis took him eleven years ago. Anyway, sometimes he and Jimmy bumped into each other in the pub and they'd have a pint together. Jimmy said Murdo always carried a wad of cash in his tail, a thick bundle of notes and was good for standing a round for his pals."

He decided to cut to the chase and asked, "After he was reported missing, did his wife remain here in Barlia Drive?"

The old woman's eyes narrowed as she tried to recall, before answering, "Not for too long. I can't remember exactly when she moved out, but I seem to think it was weeks rather than months. Probably found herself another man to keep her in comfort. Fancied herself as a bit of a looker, did Stacey Clarke," she turned her bottom lip up. "Always dolled up to the nines, she was. Younger than him, too." She nodded as she remembered and added, "Aye, by quite a few years I think.

Charlie fought back a grin at the old woman's description of her former neighbour, recalling that Frankie Colville had told him and Alison Baxter of Stacey's fondness of the high life.

"Do you know where she moved to?" he asked.

"No," she shook her head, "but a lot of her clients kept coming around, asking for her."

"Her clients?"

"Aye, she worked from home. She was a hairdresser, you see. Did you not know that, son?"

"No, I didn't," Charlie smiled, for it had been a long time since anyone called him son.

"Apart from her working from home, do you know if she worked from a…a…what do you call them?" he turned to stare at Mathieson who interjected with, "Do you know if she worked in a salon, Missus Lennox?"

"Eh, I don't know about that, hen. She was always talking about getting her own place, but not to me," she sniffed. "Never had the time of day for me, she didn't. It was one of the other neighbours she told that she was friendly with, but *she* moved away a couple of years ago as well."

"So," Mathieson continued, "you don't know if she ever opened up her own salon?"

"No, hen, I don't."

"Sir?" Mathieson turned to him.

He smiled and rising to his feet, said, "Thanks for your help, Missus Lennox. One last thing. Do you recall what the daughter's name was or how old she was?"

"No," she shook her head. "I never really spoke to the lassie, just a wee thing she was. Pretty to. Spitting image of her mammy, so she was though, though I hope she doesn't have Stacey's nature," she sniffed. "But I didn't know her name. Her mammy didn't let her speak to the likes of me," her face darkened. "She was about the same age as my niece Clare so aye," she nodded, "that would put her about eight or nine. I remember that the uniform she went to school in was the same uniform that my niece wore. Miller Primary in Ardencraig Road."

"Well, that's something if we need to find her," he tightly smiled and thanking the old woman once more, left with Mathieson.

In the pavement outside the house, he asked, "Any point in knocking a few more doors or do you think we should call it quits at that?"

She smiled and replied, "There's a few curtains twitching, so I don't suppose we'll learn much more than what we've got, sir.'

"Right, decision made then," he nodded to the CID car. "Let's head back to the factory and call it a night."

****

Alison Baxter and Willie Baillie fared no better and soon gave up knocking doors in Belmont Drive.

"Right then," he squirmed into the driver's seat, "what say you we head back, sign off and I'll take you to the restaurant for that dinner?"

"Sounds like a plan," she smiled and sat comfortably back in her seat, wondered that in such a short space of time she found herself working on a cold case and a murder and now with a man apparently interested in her.

And a *younger* man at that, she inwardly grinned.

****

They had walked together to collect Geraldine from school and treated themselves and the kids to takeaway chip suppers.

The children now in bed, they sat in the kitchen sipping at their coffee, but their visit to the Ross Hall Hospital had hung over them like the elephant in the room and once again, Carol reminded her, "Look, hen, there's no point in worrying about what the result will be. It is what it is. The doctor said he'll phone me with the result then send out a letter if he needs to see me again."

She had almost got to the point of pleading, but no matter how hard she tried, Sadie Miller could not convince her mother to stay overnight, with Carol pointedly telling her, "I'm not an invalid, hen. Besides, I don't mind the occasional night here if I'm watching the weans, but you know I like my own bed. That and I don't like being away from the house too long."

"But you'll phone me if you're not feeling well?"

Carol smiled and reaching across the kitchen table to gently stroke at her daughter's hand, replied, "I'm not feeling any different to how I was feeling yesterday or the day before, Sadie. Yes, it's maybe cancer," she'd shaken her head, "it's not the flu. If I'm going to go downhill, it won't happen overnight. There will be plenty of time for you to fuss over me, okay? Anyway, it's my turn to clean the church tomorrow morning and," she grimaced, "you know what Father Flynn's like if the marble on the altar isn't properly polished. That and I might just have a wee word with him, ask him to include me in his prayers."

Now she had been gone just twenty minutes and Sadie was feeling guilty; guilty that she had allowed her to go and wondering if she would ever have the strength of her mother.

If ever she needed Charlie, it was now and glancing at the clock, her eyes narrowed as she wondered when he'd get home.

****

He had reached the safety of his building and with a backward glance to ensure he hadn't been followed, Tommy Craig groped with nervous fingers in his jacket pocket for his house keys.

His legs shaking from his fast paced walk, he wearily pushed open the garden gate, but sharply stopped on hearing the shuffling noise coming from behind the high hedge that separated his path with the path that led to the door of his ground floor neighbour.

His eyes widened and his heart raced as he prepared himself to run back through the gate and out onto the street.

Then he heard the hacking cough and the tapping of a walking stick on the concrete path and with a relieved sigh, realised it was only the old woman who occupied the flat below his; the old woman with the sixty a day habit and greasy skin who smelled like a chimney and who persistently whined that he never took his turn cutting the communal grass in the back court.

He waited till she wordlessly passed him by, her eyes malevolently staring at him and he fought the urge to throw her to the ground and stamp on her till her body lay broken.

Turning away from her scowl, he sniggered at his own fright and made his way to his front door, calmer now, his hands no longer shaking as he inserted the key into the door and ensured it was securely locked behind him.

In the kitchen, he set the kettle to boil and made himself a strong black coffee.

The mug in his hand, his mind raced as he thought of his options, whether to run or deny he had visited Smiler.

No one had seen him, of that he was certain. He thought of the phone call he had made to Smiler from his mobile and his brow furrowed. If the polis did their check on Smiler's home phone and found his mobile number, the phone wasn't registered to him so they couldn't trace it back to him.

He thought again of what he had seen, the two CID coming out of the close and getting into their car. He should not have gone for that coffee. No, he should have gone straight into the close and battered on Smiler's door and demanded to know what the fuck the CID wanted, what Smiler had told them. But no, he banged a fist onto the kitchen table, making the mug jump and spilling some coffee.

He'd stupidly went for that bloody coffee.

When he'd got back he'd had to hide again when he saw the guy leaving the close, the guy who was dressed in a suit like a detective and drove the big black car. The big guy who had peered through Smiler's ground floor window before getting into the car and driving off.

Who the hell was he and what was he dong peeking into Smiler's window?

He'd waited a full five minutes before deciding he'd go for it, go and see what Smiler was up to and why the polis were so interested in him.

The close door wasn't locked and when he hammered on Smiler's door, he'd got no response.

But the bugger was in, of that Craig had no doubt and turning the door handle, stepped back in shock when it slowly opened.

It was what he saw that caused him to slam the door closed again and get the fuck out of there sharpish.

Now he had a decision to make.

Should he run or should he chance it and remain where he is, hoping that the polis knew nothing about him visiting Smiler?

But if he *did* run, he miserably thought, where the fuck could he go?

****

Driving home from her office, Cathy Mulgrew had a dozen thoughts going through her head, not least what was happening in Charlie Miller's inquiry.

Her priority at the minute was the investigation into the abuse scandal recently come to light in the Bellshill care home for the elderly and which was bound to hit the papers sometime in the next few days. She angrily shook her head as though to clear it, thinking of the years the corrupt bastard who had run the home and what she had gotten away with. At least now she was under lock and key and if the case went well, looking forward to spending the next few years care of HMP Cornton Vale.

Then, just as she was about to leave the office, the phone call from the Duty Inspector at Helen Street office to inform her that DCI Gerry Donaldson had been brought in by two Traffic officers accused not only of drink driving, but police assault and a breach of the peace.

It wasn't Mulgrew's responsibility to deal with the issue. No, that would be down to Donaldson's Divisional Commander; however, the Inspector, a former Detective Sergeant, said he had called her as a courtesy, though she suspected the bugger was really trying to ingratiate himself for he had previously made it known he was keen to return to the CID.

Still, she could not help herself and smiled.

It wasn't all bad news for Donaldson had been a pain in the arse for a number of years and though the lucky sod had survived a number of internal complaints of bullying and mismanagement, he was unlikely to survive formal charges of drink driving and assault.

Not if the arresting cops do their paperwork correctly, she mused. She pressed the button on her hands free for the home number and when Jo answered, said with a smile, "That's me five minutes away, sweetheart. How about drawing me a bath and pouring us both a glass of chilled white?"

****

When he arrived at the office with Shona Mathieson, the sergeant stood behind the uniform bar stopped him in the corridor and said, "Message from the Duty Inspector at Helen Street, sir. At your convenience, can you give him a phone?"

"Did he say what it was about?" Charlie asked.

"No, sir."

"Right, thanks," he sighed and turning to Mathieson, said, "Check there's nothing time critical on your desk, Shona and if it's clear, I'll see you in the morning."

"Sir," she nodded and made her way upstairs while Charlie turned into the uniform bar to use the telephone at the desk.

A well dressed, middle-aged, overweight and bald-headed man rudely pushed past him, muttering obscenities on his way out of the office.

Turning to the grizzled sergeant, Charlie cocked a head at the departing man and asked, "What's his beef then?"

The sergeant grinned and replied, "The stupid bugger got himself a Hawaiian shirt, a pair of shorts, flip-flops and handful of Viagra then him and his pals went on a weekend bender to Spain thinking they were the bees knees and that they'd they'd all get their Nat King Cole. On his first night there he ended up pished and had his wallet with all his money and credit cards stolen in a nightclub. Comes in here and says the Spanish polis told him to report it when he got home. Aye," the sergeant shook his head, "now he's away complaining and threatening to report *me* because I refused to take a crime report and send one of my guys over to Torremolinos to look for his fucking wallet."

Five minutes later, his call made to the Duty Inspector, Charlie made his way to his office where closing the door behind him, permitted himself a wide grin and with a nod of his head, muttered, "Never thought I'd be happy to say it, but well done the beasties."

****

They had met that afternoon in the youngest daughter's flat in Bridgeton and first discussed then argued among themselves that one of them at least should call upon the old bastard and find out how he was. That and learn what arrangements he had made for their mother's funeral.

In the end, they had decided that the oldest son Joseph and the youngest daughter Faye would go together, both agreeing simply because the the younger son and older daughter had refused.

Now here they were at their father's door, the house they had grown up in with their mother while their father languished in prison.

Curiously they turned to glance at each other when they saw the door was a few inches ajar.

Joseph took a deep breath and rapped his knuckles on the door.

"Just remember to keep the head, eh?" his sister Faye nervously reminded him.

A minute passed and he was about to knock again when Fay, fearing a confrontation between her father and Joseph and seeking an excuse to leave, suggested, "Maybe's he's out. Maybe he's up in the Main Street at one of the pubs. We could always come back tomorrow, eh?"

"Wouldn't surprise me if the bastard was away getting pissed," Joseph angrily replied, then using his fist, banged again on the door with such force it swayed open a further two inches.

Another moment passed and they were about to leave when Joseph irately pushed at the door that creaked as it swung open.

He was about to call out, but the words choked and instead he gasped as with a loud cry Faye collapsed into her brother's arms when in the darkened hallway they saw their father, Frankie Colville, lying on his back behind the door with the handle of a large knife protruding from his chest.

CHAPTER FIFTEEN

The detectives and the Duty Detective Inspector called to the murder locus at the ground floor flat in Rutherglen's Hardie Avenue, were not immediately aware their victim was in any way related to the murder investigation currently being conducted from the Giffnock office.

At least not at the time of their arrival.

The initial scene of crime and door to door inquiry for witnesses was carried out thoroughly and with due diligence, but nothing was discovered that indicated who murdered the hapless Francis Colville. His distraught children who discovered their father dead were of little use, reluctantly admitting that neither had any contact with him for several years and only came by the flat to ensure that one, he was okay and two, to elicit details of their recently departed mother's funeral service.

It was when they explained that their acrimonious relationship with their father was because of his criminal past and his involvement in a four-man gang who in the eighties had robbed several banks and building societies that bells began to ring at which point the Detective Inspector, aware from a confidential criminal intelligence bulletin released just that day, that the murdered Colville might not be an entirely innocent victim as was first assumed.

Their statements noted, Joseph and his sister Faye were permitted to leave to break the news to their brother, sister and the remainder of their family.

Returning to Rutherglen police office, DI Boyle printed out the criminal intelligence bulletin and mentally keeping his fingers crossed that he was correct, that his victim Francis Colville was indeed of interest to the Giffnock inquiry, contacted the Police control room at Helen Street to request the attendance of Detective Superintendent Charlie Miller at the murder locus.

****

Cathy Mulgrew had just stripped off her business suit skirt and was standing in her underwear when Jo, the telephone in her hand and an apologetic expression, opened the bathroom door to whisper, "That's Mister Cairney asking for you."

Sighing, Mulgrew took the phone and sitting down on the edge of the steaming hot bath, slowly exhaled before saying, "Evening, sir."

"Sorry to bother you at this time of the evening, Cathy and no doubt when you're at your dinner, but I'm curious to know. Any news on the Clarke investigation?"

"Nothing, sir. I spoke earlier today with Charlie Miller who told me that following James Dougrie's PM, he intended interviewing

Frankie Colville, one of the arrested gang members, but of course now released. I haven't heard from him since then, but if you want…"

"No, no," Cairney hastily interrupted. "Tomorrow will do. One other thing before I go. I'm afraid to say that DCI Donaldson of Govan CID has been arrested for an alleged drink driving offence. That and, well," he paused, "allegedly he lashed out at the arresting officers and kicked at one of them and spat at the other. Hard to believe, but though I don't personally know the man…"

"Oh, I can believe it," she quickly interrupted, surprised at her own spitefulness. "Gerry Donaldson is known to have quite a temper when he's had a drink, sir."

"Well, that said, Mister Donaldson has been suspended by his Divisional Commander pending his appearance on these charges, so hopefully the PF will take cognisance of his position as a senior police officer and fast track his appearance at court. Can't think what the bloody press will make of it when word gets out," he irritably muttered.

And likely Donaldson's staff will be lining up to let them know, she thought, but instead replied, "If he's any sense, he'll make application to retire before his appearance at court, sir."

"Only if I bloody agree," he snapped back, then added, "Sorry, Cathy. Bloody idiot should have known better at his age and rank. Anyway, that all said, tomorrow morning I want you to appoint a temporary replacement for Donaldson; perhaps you might consider one of his Detective Inspector's to act up."

"I'll see to it, sir, and if Charlie gets back to me this evening I'll keep you apprised."

"Thank you, Cathy, and goodnight," he abruptly ended the call.

The door opened with Jo extending her hand for the phone and who asked, "Everything okay?"

"Yes," she smiled, unaccountably pleased that the tiring day ended with the bullying Donaldson finally on his way to getting his comeuppance.

****

Willie Baillie handed his bank card to the smiling waiter and said, "I rather enjoyed that."

"As did I," Alison Baxter returned his smile and running her forefinger around the rim of her glass of soda water and lime, asked,

"So tell me. Why exactly are you treating me to dinner, DC Baillie?"

"Well," he couldn't help himself and blushing furiously, replied, "I just thought…"

He shook his head and shrugged. "No, I didn't 'just thought.' I wanted to take you to dinner, see if maybe we could, I don't know…"

He couldn't explain it, but suddenly found himself tongue-tied.

"Don't tell me you fancied me?" she pretended to be shocked.

"Well, yes, actually I did…" he rapidly blinked and added, "I mean, I do. Fancy you, that is."

She stared at him and slowly smiled before replying, "But you don't know me or anything about me."

"What's to know," he leaned back in his seat, forcing a smile as accepting the card machine from the waiter, he tapped in his four digits. They waited till the waiter had left before he continued, "To be honest, Alison, I'm not in the habit of asking women out. I'm a bit of a…I don't know. A quiet guy. Reserved, I suppose you'd call it."

"My mother always told me it was the quiet ones I had to watch out for," she quipped.

"Aye, well, this quiet one is exactly that. Quiet. So," he took a deep breath, "now that we've had dinner together, do you fancy doing it again some time?"

She didn't immediately respond, then slowly nodding, replied, "Yes, but next time I foot the bill. After all, it's…"

She didn't get the opportunity to explain for her mobile phone rung and fetching it from her handbag on the floor, he saw the curiosity in her face when she read the screen. Holding up a forefinger to warn him to be quiet she greeted the caller with, "Hello, sir."

"Sorry to interrupt your evening, Alison," Charlie Miller said. "Are you back at the training college yet?"

"No, sir," she flashed a puzzled glance at Baillie. "I'm still in Glasgow. I'd something to do," and grimaced, uncomfortable with the lie.

"Oh, right. I've just received a phone call. Frankie Colville has been found murdered. Can you meet me at the locus? His house, I mean."

She took a sharp intake of breath at the news and replied, "Yes, of course. Are you on your way there the now?"

"Yes, I'm just leaving the house. I'll see you there when you arrive," he ended the call.

She didn't have time to explain for seconds later Baillie's phone chirruped and she heard him say, "Yes, boss, I'm still up."

She saw his eyes narrow as he asked, "What's the address?" then said, "Got that, Hardie Avenue, Rutherglen."

When he finished the call he grinned and said, "Maybe I'll let you go first so we're not arriving together. Can't have tongues wagging, can we?"

****

After finally agreeing to have a blood sample taken by the casualty surgeon, the Duty Inspector deemed that Gerry Donaldson was not a flight risk and bailed him to attend court in four days time with the condition he did not drive during that period and informed Donaldson that his wife had arranged for a recovery vehicle to come by to collect his car from the rear yard.

Sullenly, he grabbed the sealed plastic bag containing from the charge bar that contained his wallet and the other items taken from his pockets, but then about to step towards the rear door at the charge bar, he stopped. Forcing himself to be polite, he turned to ask, "I know I'm not permitted to enter here or any police station during my period of suspension, but I've some personal items in my desk drawer. Can I collect them before I go?"

"Sorry, sir, I'm under strict instruction…"

"Look," he forced a smile, "I know the routine, but the Div Comm's gone home and if you want you can come with me, see that I don't cause any mischief," he grinned and shrugged.

The Duty Inspector bit at his lower lip then calling through the civilian male turnkey, told him, "Mister Donaldson has something to collect from his office. Go with him and if anybody asks…well, just say he's getting some personal items from his desk, okay?"

The young man turned to glance at Donaldson and nodding, followed the DCI through the door towards the stairs.

Donaldson didn't acknowledge the turnkey following him but quickly made his way to his office on the first floor and along the quiet corridor to his office. Opening the door, he turned to say, "I'll just be a minute," then closed it before the turnkey could argue.

In the corridor outside, the young man was at a loss what to do, whether to follow Donaldson into the office or wait where he was and in the end, leaned against the wall and convinced himself it wasn't his business what the ignorant bugger got up to.

Inside the office, Donaldson quickly flicked through his desk rolodex that contained the personal details of all the officers under his command and with a sly grin, finally found the address he wanted.

Less than a minute later he was out the door and with the turnkey hurrying after him, made his way back down the stairs towards the rear exit.

****

Shona Mathieson had poured herself a well deserved glass of white wine and now in the kitchen, hit the play button on her mobile phone message service.

The one message was from her friend, the traffic officer Cathy Pickering, who simply said, "Hi, doll. That wee issue we discussed. Take it as read you'll have no more bother with that, okay? See you, honey."

Closing her eyes, she leaned with her back against the worktop.

She knew what she had asked Pickering to do was immoral and deceitful, if not entirely legal, yet could not but experience a sense of relief that it was over. She had spent hours trying to persuade herself the end justified the means, asking Cathy to risk her own career to save hers. That was something she could never repay, but would not forget.

As for Donaldson, she gritted her teeth, she had no regrets. The bastard deserved what happened to him, for not only through her time under his command had he terrorised his staff, but during those years got away with drink driving. His drink addiction had been an open secret even among the senior management, yet nobody at the Govan office had the balls to do anything about it, so afraid were they of his long reach and alleged contacts in the police upper management.

Her decision to collude with Pickering to trap Donaldson hadn't been easy, but holding her career over her in an attempt to have her inform on a good man like Charlie Miller; well, that went beyond the pale and what finally pushed her over the edge.

She sipped at the wine and taking a deep breath, smiled.

Tomorrow, for the first day in a long time, she could look forward to going into work and not have to worry about any more threatening phone calls.

****

Identifying himself to the uniformed officer at the close entrance, Charlie passed under the blue and white tape and walking into the close was met by a short, grey haired man with a neatly trimmed grey beard wearing a Forensic suit who extending his hand, smiled and said, "Long time no see, you old bugger."

"Well, well, Alan Boyle," Charlie grinned as he pumped the shorter man's gloved hand up and down.

"I haven't seen you since you were a DC when we worked together at Stewart Street. I hear you're a DI now?"

"And *you're* now a boss. A Detective Superintendent no less," Boyle shook his head. "You must have listened to me all those years ago when I was showing you the ropes," he grinned at Charlie.

"Aye, well if I recall those days I was half drunk most of the time and you covered my arse more than once, Alan. For that I'll always be grateful," he smiled. "Now, I assume it was yourself who had me called out?"

"That's right," Boyle handed him a white forensic suit and watched as Charlie, tearing open the packet, removed his suit jacket that he handed to Boyle before climbing into the suit. "The victim is Francis Colville, resident of the house who was discovered by his estranged son and daughter. The casualty surgeon has attended and pronounced life extinct and the SOCO's are finished and just packing up, but I asked them to remain in case there's something else you might need done."

"How did you come to associate Colville with my ongoing investigation?"

"The confidential bulletin you had issued earlier today. The name seemed familiar and when his son and daughter told me about his past history, I put two and two together and here we are."

"Good man, Alan. Right, let's have a look at him," but before Charlie entered the house, he heard a familiar voice identifying herself to the officer at the close entrance. Turning, he saw Alison Baxter and introducing her to Boyle, then sniffed before asking, "Enjoy your curry?"

"Yes, I did, thank you," she unaccountably blushed.

Boyle stifled a grin and said, "The body's right behind the door, so unless Mister Miller wants you in the house?" he turned to Charlie, who replied, "No, Alison, there's no real need for you to come in." "In that case," Boyle continued, "you can see him if you stand out here," and with that pushed open the front door of the flat.

In the harshly bright light of the Scene of Crime halogen lamps, they could see the figure of Frankie Colville lying on his back, his arms raised above his head and his legs splayed. The black coloured plastic handle of what looked like a broad bladed kitchen knife protruded from the right side of his chest. Baxter guessed the knife must have penetrated Colville's lung for a thin trickle of blood escaped from his mouth and had trickled down the side of his face to form a small, dark coloured pool beside his head.

His eyes were open and his face registered what to Charlie looked like disbelief.

"The doc says there are two distinct stab wounds and that the knife stuck seems to have become stuck between the ribs at the second blow. SOCO have identified some blood drops on the carpet just inside the door that seem to have dropped from the blade when it was pulled out after the first blow." He used a finger to indicate the doorframe just inside the hallway and added, "There's also blood spraying on the left there that might indicate the killer was also sprayed with blood."

"Did his kids knock?" Charlie asked Boyle.

"They saw the door was slightly ajar and tried knocking at first, but when they didn't get a reply, the son pushed the door fully open. That's when they discovered his body. They didn't go into the house, but left the close to use a mobile to call us."

"If he's lying just inside the door, then it seems that he's likely opened the door to his killer," Baxter broke the silence.

"Seems that way to me," Boyle pursed his lips and nodded with a glance to Charlie.

"Can you check if the Yale is on, sir?" Baxter asked him.

For a brief few seconds, Boyle stared curiously at her then stepping into the hallway, stepped over the dead man and said, "It looks like an old fashioned lock, this one."

They watched him pulling the door open a few inches, then push the snib, hearing an audible sharp click as the bolt engaged and then holding the door with one hand, used the other hand to again disengage the bolt.

"No," he shook his head, "the Yale lock wasn't on."

"So the door was presumably closed over, but unlocked," Baxter mused.

"And you're thinking his killer wasn't a regular visitor," Charlie's eyes narrowed as he turned to Baxter, "that it was someone who knocked on the door rather than a regular visitor who might probably know from previous visits the door was unlocked and be used to simply strolling into the flat?"

"Yes," she agreed, "but I don't know how that might help us."

"And the Yale being unlocked would suggest that after killing Colville, the killer simply pulled the door over after leaving," Charlie nodded before asking Boyle, "Where are they now? The son and daughter."

"I had their statements noted and allowed them to leave to inform the rest of their family. Will that cause you a problem?"

"No, not at all," Charlie slowly shook his head. "If we need anything further we can contact them tomorrow during the day."

"I assume you'll want to take this on, boss," Boyle said, "if it's related to your ongoing investigation, so can I ask; do you have a suspect for the ex-cop's murder at the minute?"

"Well, we might have had," Charlie shrugged and nodded down to Colville's body, "but it seems somebody got to him before we did."

Behind them, Willie Baillie identified himself at the close entrance and joined the trio at the front door.

"Got here as quickly as I could, boss," Baillie said before asking, "What can I do?"

Charlie stared keenly at him, seeing what looked like a curry stain on the big man's white shirt and choking back a grin, grunted before replying, "Liaise with DI Boyle's guys, please Willie, and collect any statements they might have noted. I'll also need you to transport the body to the mortuary and get it signed in."

He snapped a glance at Baxter and thought, they're adults; if she and Willie Boyle want to spend time together, it was nothing to do with him.

Turning to Boyle, he said, "Right, Alan, as you so correctly said, I'll square it tomorrow with your Divisional Commander that I take over the murder as part of my ongoing investigation, but for now let's have a look inside the flat."

****

It was after midnight by the time Charlie returned home and exhausted, he locked the car, his eyes squinting in the harsh beam of the security light that activated flooded the front garden as he stepped towards the front door.

"Shit," he muttered for he was certain the light would have woken Sadie who was undoubtedly asleep in their bedroom that overlooked the front door.

As quietly as he dared, he unlocked the door and slipping off his brogues, tiptoed through to the kitchen where to guide him along the hallway Sadie had as usual left on the light.

To his surprise, his wife was sitting at the kitchen table and smiling, said, "What time of night is this to come home, Charlie Miller? Been out with one of your floozies, have you?" as she arose and wrapped her arms around his neck.

"You're the only floozy I'm interested in," he grinned at her, his head snuggled against her hair and smelling the scented shampoo she favoured.

She drew back her head and asked, "Have you eaten?"

"No," he shook his head.

"Sit down. I've saved you some lasagne," she replied and turned towards the microwave.

With her back to him, she said, "You got my text about mum?"

"I did. I suppose it's just a waiting game now," he sighed as he slipped off his suit jacket and hung it on the back before slumping down into the chair. "Is she upstairs?"

"No, she wanted to go home. You know what's she's like," Sadie turned and grimaced, her arms folded across her chest, "never wanting to make a fuss."

"Did the consultant give her any indication when the result of the biopsy will be ready?"

"All he told her was that when the result was returned, he'd have his secretary phone if he needed to see mum again. Otherwise, if it's good news he would have a letter sent out."

"And we're paying him how much for his bloody time?" he bitterly replied, but almost immediately saw the hurt in Sadie's eyes at his crass comment and standing up, made towards her to wrap his arms tightly about her.

"Sorry, love, that didn't come out the way I meant it to. It's not the money…"

"I know, I know," she sobbed into his chest, her tears staining his shirt as her body trembled.

They stood like that for several minutes, long after the bell indicated his lasagne was ready until at last she turned away and grabbing a sheet of kitchen roll to wipe at her eyes and her nose, made him sit back down.

His appetite gone, he toyed with the food while Sadie made them tea until at last he said, "Sorry, I'm not doing this grub any justice." Forcing a smile, he added, "But I'm desperate for a cuppa."

She sat down opposite him, cradling her mug in her hands and replied, "Leave it. I'm sorry, I didn't ask about your day. Stressful?"

"Interesting," he exhaled and explained he was late because one of the witnesses and possible suspect for his murder inquiry had himself been murdered.

"But there's plenty of time tomorrow to talk about that," he smiled. "Let's finish this tea and get to bed."

****

Tucked up in bed in the spare room of their Simshill home, Gerry Donaldson's wife Sylvia heard him come home and knew from the way the front door crashed closed that he was drunk.

But nothing unusual in that, she sighed and though the room was warm she shivered.

Lying there in the darkness, she nervously prayed that he would either fall asleep in the chair downstairs or if he did manage the stairs to the master bedroom, he would do so without the need to come into her room to tell her to fetch him food or, she involuntarily drew her knees together, whatever other demand he drunkenly made of her, but fortunately such demands these days were thankfully few and far between.

Wide eyed and now fully awake, she listened to him banging about downstairs and wondered where he had been till this time of the night.

Her heart leapt when she heard a dull thud on the outside landing and her head turned nervously towards the bedroom door, but sighed with relief when she heard the master bedroom door loudly close.

Hopefully tonight, she mentally crossed her fingers, he would as usual fall into a drunken stupor and permit her a full night's sleep.

It was hours later when she startled awake in the darkness and turning towards the digital alarm clock, saw it was just after five in the morning.

She lay still, certain she had heard a noise outside her room door and yes, there it was again; the creak of the second step from the top on the hallway stairs.

Now wide awake, she raised her head and listened intently, hearing someone moving downstairs.

It could only be Gerald or…she fearfully turned towards the bedroom door, someone had broken into the house.

As quietly and as slowly as she dared, she slipped from the bed and reached for her dressing gown on the chair by the wall.

Taking a deep breath, she turned the handle with nervous fingers and opened the door.

She stopped dead and stood still for there it was again, the sound of someone quietly moving downstairs.

Her heart racing, she opened the door a few inches, just enough to permit her to peek out to the darkened hallway where she saw a slash of faded light and realised the door to the master bedroom lay ajar.

Puzzled, she was certain she had heard the door banged closed when her drunken husband had retired for the night.

Stepping out into the hallway, she stopped and wondered.

Was that the front door closing?

Emboldened a little that the intruder might now have left, she moved across the hallway and opening the opposite door, peeked in to see the quilt turned back and the bed empty.

Confused, she quickly made her way across the room to the bay window where she sneaked a glance out from behind the closed curtains in time to see her husband's car with the lights out moving slowly across the driveway, then disappearing through the gate it was gone from her sight.

****

The alarm sounded, but Shona Mathieson was already awake and had been for almost an hour.

She hadn't slept well, turning over in her head the circumstances and the part in which she had played in DCI Donaldson's arrest.

She involuntarily smiled, aware it was always in the dark of the night that the worst thoughts haunted her yet convinced that Donaldson's arrest would stand up, that no matter how much he suspected or protested, he could not deny the evidence of the alcohol in his system and the statements of two Traffic officers who caught him behind the wheel of a police vehicle.

No, his arse was well and truly now hung out to dry.

A little more cheered, she arose from bed and after turning back the quilt cover made her way to the bathroom.

Ten minutes later, showered and dressed in a skirted business suit, she breakfasted on a bowl of cereal and a mug of tea before deciding to head into the office.

She was looking forward to that day, pleased that the Detective Superintendent had placed his trust in her.

It occurred to her to have a quiet word with the senior HOLMES civilian operator, Alice Brookes and tell her that she need no longer worry about Donaldson, but to do so would indicate that she knew or at least suspected of Donaldson's hold over the older woman.

As she sipped at her tea, her eyebrows knitted as she wondered; could it be that Brookes was complicit with Donaldson, a willing partner?

No, she unconsciously shook her head.

She had known Brookes for many years and could not believe Alice would willingly tout for him.

Finishing her tea, she placed the bowl and mug into the sink and run some cold water over them.

Fetching her handbag from the front room and her overcoat from the hall cupboard, she had a final glance at the flat before locking the front door behind her.

Making her way down the stone stairs to the first landing, she hesitated and eyes narrowing, stopped.

Opening her handbag, she breathed with relief for there were her car keys inside.

Continuing down the stairs, she reached the ground floor and was about to step towards the closed door when she heard a rustle from the rear of the close behind her.

She was almost half turned when the savage blow to her head stunned her and she felt her knees weaken.

She tried to call out, but realised she was falling face forward to the ground, her handbag slipping from her shoulder and instinctively, but vainly stretching out her hands before her as she attempted to cushion the impact of her fall.

As she fell, she saw the black shoe as the kick was aimed at her face, but was unable to turn away. Such was the force of the blow her head bounced back against the close wall before she again fell face downwards onto the cold stone ground.

The shock of the blow that broke her nose, fractured her right cheekbone and her eye socket also caused what was later assessed to be severe haemorrhaging to her right eye.

Completely helpless, she was vaguely aware of a figure standing over her, a man she thought it was whose heavy breathing was punctuated with some garbled words, but she could no longer hear for she had by now lapsed into a blessed unconsciousness.

CHAPTER SIXTEEN

Charlie Miller had fallen into a deep, dreamless sleep and but for Sadie, would have missed his alarm call.

While she quickly headed downstairs, he stumbled from their bed to the en-suite where with gritted teeth he braved a cold shower and was instantly awake, murmuring a quiet obscenity as the shock of cold water hit him.

Minutes later, suited and booted, he was downstairs where Sadie, cautioning him to be quiet because the children were still asleep, had prepared him a bacon sandwich and mug of tea.

"I'll try to get home a bit earlier tonight," he began then sighed as he added, "but no guarantees, hen."

"If you get the opportunity, give me a call anyway to let me know," she kissed him goodbye as grabbing at his overcoat, he hurried out the door.

****

On the road from Tulliallan College to Glasgow almost twenty minutes before Charlie Miller had awoke, Alison Baxter thought again of her evening with Willie Baillie.

The big guy certainly seemed to be as he'd claimed; quiet and a little reserved.

She inwardly smiled, for though there was no doubting his charm and she was particularly impressed by his apparent honesty that he was no ladies man, nor did he try to impress her as most of her dates did by regaling her with tales of himself.

If anything, her brow furrowed, he was far more interested in what she had accomplished, expressing curiosity about her ambitions and her decision in later life to join the police.

Yes, she smoothly overtook a trio of lorries meandering along in the inside lane and turning the radio up a little louder, decided Mister Baillie was worth another dinner date.

****

Without informing Charlie Miller, Cathy Mulgrew had decided that she would call upon him at Giffnock office prior to visiting Bellshill police office where DCI Lorna Paterson, the SIO for the breaking scandal of the abuse recently uncovered in the care home for the elderly, had set up her major incident room.

Now in her car, she quickly wound her way through the city causing more than one irate motorist to wonder at the mad woman driving the gold coloured Lexus car.

****

The Chief Constable, Martin Cairney, was by nature an early bird and a little after seven o'clock that morning found him seated at his desk reading through the Police Scotland twenty-four synopsis of crime and offences that his aide, a uniformed Superintendent, believed might be of interest to Cairney.

With a red pen held in his shovel like hand, he circled those few incidents for which he wished more information and placed a cross against the remainder, satisfied that he at least was informed of them.

His eyes narrowed when he read of the discovery of the body of a Francis Colville in his ground flat dwelling in Hardie Avenue. According to the summarised report, the son and daughter discovered their father's body and Detective Superintendent Charles Miller had assumed responsibility for the investigation.

He circled the entry and made a note on his desk calendar to phone Miller later that morning.

Continuing and although already aware, he read with distaste the entry regarding the arrest of Detective Chief Inspector Gerald Donaldson of the Greater Glasgow Division and after a moments hesitation, circled the entry.

****

Bernie Cohen, a retired bricklayer who resided on the ground floor flat in the close in Dixon Road, yawned and nudging his wife Isa, said, "Wee Jock's creating merry hell, hen. I'd better let him out into the backcourt for a pee."

"Take a bag with you in case he leaves a deposit," she mumbled and turned over to snatch another half hour's sleep.

Grabbing his dressing gown from the hook behind the door, Cohen opened the bedroom door to the hallway to find the small West Highland Terrier dog on his hind legs, scratching frantically at the front door.

"Come away from there, ya wee bugger, before you scrape the paintwork," he snarled at the Westie who ignoring his master, yelped and continued to scratch at the door.

Lifting the lead from the hallway table, Cohen unlocked the door and bending down to attach the lead, made the mistake of opening the door a fraction for within seconds, the Westie was through the gap and out into the close, barking furiously.

"Ya wee shite," he snatched open the door, but his mouth fell open for there not ten feet from his door and covered in blood, lay the body of a young woman.

****

As fate would have it, the civilian supervisor, Alice Brookes, was the first to arrive that morning at the Giffnock incident room.

Making her way around the room to switch on the computers Brookes was startled when from behind her, Willie Baillie greeted her with a loud, "Good morning," before making his way to the table that was set up for the coffee and tea.

"Did you hear about DCI Donaldson?" she carefully asked.

"Aye," his concentration was on filling a mug with coffee. "I heard the guys downstairs saying he was arrested for drink driving. Is that right enough?"

"That's what I heard too," she replied, her face pale and lips tightly set; however, her curiosity got the better of her and she asked, "Does that mean if he was arrested he won't be working until the case is resolved?"

"If the story is true, I don't think he'll ever be working again as a cop," Baillie grinned at her. "I'm guessing he'll be suspended and if he's found guilty at court, he'll be booted out. He'll lose his pension rights too, I bet."

"Really," she was genuinely taken aback.

"Oh, aye, Alice," he nodded as he filled his mug with boiling water. "He might have kept his job though not his rank if it was only the drink driving charge and he tried to use a defence about having an alcohol problem." Baillie pursed his lips and continued, "The Force might have recognised it as an addiction and in this day and age where addiction is a recognised illness, offered him counselling, but I heard downstairs he also assaulted the arresting officers and that's just not on. If he's convicted of assault and being a police, it's two bites of the cherry. First the court hammers you then, if the crime or offence is bad enough, the Chief Constable takes away your job and that means you lose your pension too."

He smiled and nodded when he added, "As for that bullying bastard, pardon my French, it's long overdue for him to get himself caught." He could not know that since hearing the news, Brookes stomach had been in turmoil. Now hearing that Donaldson might never again be in any position to threaten her, she quickly excused herself and made her way to the ladies' toilet where locked in a cubicle, she softly wept with relief.

****

The paramedic who was a member of the ambulance crew tasked to respond to Bernie Cohen's frantic nine-nine-nine call could see that the injuries to the unconscious woman's face were severe; however, it was the wound to the back of her head when it struck the close wall that caused him to be more concerned.

"We're taking her straight to the Neuro at the Queen Elizabeth," he informed the female cop entering the close minutes later as very carefully, the paramedic and his colleague stretchered Shona Mathieson into the back of the ambulance.

While her neighbour used his Airwave radio to update the control room of the incident, the female cop asked the visibly shaking Mister Cohen if he knew the young woman?

"Know her? Aye, of course I do, hen" he stared at her as though she were joking. "She lives upstairs, on the first landing," he used his forefinger to point upwards. "Nice lassie she is too."

"Oh, right," the young officer busily scribbled in her notebook before asking, "And her name is?"

"It's Shona. Shona Mathieson."

"And is it Miss or Missus Mathieson?"

Cohen stared curiously at the officer before replying, "Well, she had a guy living with her, but I don't think they were married. Anyway, do you not know her, hen?"

Puzzled, the officer half smiled when she asked, "Why do you think would I know her, Mister Cohen?"

"Well, Shona's one of yours, isn't she? She's a detective."

****

Following some morning craic in the incident room with his team, Charlie Miller asked the civilian supervisor, Alice Brookes, to take over the office manager's desk until such time Shona Mathieson turned up and instructed Brookes to inform Mathieson to pop in to see him when she arrived.

He had just settled himself at his desk and was preparing his morning brief when the door knocked to admit Cathy Mulgrew.

"Had the Chief on the blower last night, asking for an update on your investigation," she sighed as she dropped into the chair opposite. "I'm on my way to Bellshill, but thought I'd pop in and get you to brief me before I get back to him."

"And good morning to you too," he cheerfully greeted her before asking, "Coffee?"

"Yes and strong, please. Jo and I sunk a bottle of white last night. Well, truth be told," she screwed her face, "I did most of the sinking."

"You know about Frankie Colville being murdered?" he asked.

"I had a phone call first thing this morning from Danny McBride, my DI in the intelligence department. He's just back from holiday. He's not really up to speed yet, so I'm guessing it was one of his team who told him of my interest. Anyway he's now aware of your inquiry. As a matter of course, he'd received an e-mail copy of the Chief's twenty-four-hour synopsis and read that little detail out to me. Any suspects?"

"None so far, but if Colville was himself suspect for Dougrie's murder, it almost certainly rules him out," he replied with a wry grin.

"What caused you to suspect him for Dougrie's murder?"

"Well, revenge is my first inclination, but that said I'd have to wonder why it took him so long to get round to killing Dougrie. If I'm honest, I have a sneaking suspicion that Dougrie and Colville's killer is the same person though hopefully I'll learn more at Colville's PM."

"And you'll keep me posted?"

"Of course," he nodded.

"You'll have heard about that idiot Donaldson, of course?" she fought the grin that threatened to overtake her.

"For the first time in my police career," he smiled, "I applauded the beasties. If the rumours from the cops' downstairs are true, he apparently resisted arrest and lashed out with his feet and spat on one of the Traffic cops. Stupid bugger," he shook his head before adding, "but if truth be told, he's done me a favour. It's no secret his staff and I include the officers serving in this station, were all frightened of him. Not physically, of course, but he wielded their careers over them like a big stick. Anyway, the bullying bastard deserves all he gets and I've no sympathy for him."

"No matter what we think," she sighed, "the press will have a field day with it. That's the Chief's real concern," she paused before adding, "what his arrest will do for the public image."

"Right, enough talk about him," he started to rise from his seat, "hang on and I'll get a coffee sorted for you."

Seconds later the desk phone rung and casting Mulgrew an apologetic smile, he sat back down and lifting the phone, said, "Good morning. Detective Superintendent Miller."

She saw him frown and he slowly settled back into his chair before he said, "Hang on Alan, I've Cathy Mulgrew here with me. I'm going to put you onto speaker."

He pressed a button and said to Mulgrew, "It's DI Alan Boyle who's working out of Aitkenhead police office these days. You'll remember Alan from when we worked together at Stewart Street. Go ahead Alan."

"Morning, Cathy," Boyle's voice crackled across the line and it was obvious he was travelling in a vehicle.

"Morning, Alan. Long time no speak."

"Too long," he replied, then continued, "I regret I'm on with some bad news. Really bad news. I've just had word that two of our divisional cops attended what initially was reported as a mugging in a tenement close on Dixon Road, over in Shawlands. However, the victim has been positively identified as DS Shona Mathieson. I'm not privy to all the details yet. In fact, I'm reading from a note here, so bear with me. At the minute I've sent two of my guys over to the locus and the SOCO are on their way there now. Mathieson's been taken to the Queen Elizabeth Hospital over in Govan with what I'm told is a life threatening injury to the back of her head. The note says she's also suffered some serious facial injuries. Her handbag was there at the locus and appears to be intact, so I'm though I'm not ruling out a robbery it doesn't seem to have been the motive for the assault."

He paused for breath, then asked, "Charlie, I understand Mathieson works at Giffnock. Is she on general CID duties or is she one of your inquiry team?"

"She is one of mine, yes. My office manager in fact," he dully replied, his face pale at the shocking news.

"Look, Charlie," Boyle went on, "I know you've taken on the Colville murder as part of your inquiry. With respect, I believe you're too close to the victim to take this on so if you and Cathy are in agreement, I'll keep this inquiry. At the minute, I'm treating it as an attempted murder, so needless to say, if you or any of your guys have any information…"

"Yes, of course," Charlie unconsciously nodded as he interrupted.

"Sorry to butt in, Alan, but is there anything I can do at this time?" Mulgrew asked.

"Not that I can think of, Cathy, but I'm in the car on my way over to the hospital as we speak. If you want to meet me there perhaps we can discuss it over a coffee and hopefully, by that time I'll have heard more from my guys at the locus."

"Good idea. I'll see you there in about…wait a minute. What ward am I going to?"

"My information is she's been admitted to the Neuro, so I'll find out when I get there and leave word at the reception desk for you when you arrive."

"Right, I'll see you there then," she ended the call.

Charlie replaced the handset and staring at Mulgrew, slowly exhaled. "I really feel I should come with you," he said.

"To do what? Hang about a ward waiting on news that I can send you? No," she shook her head and lifting her handbag from the floor, continued, "You break the news to your team and get on with your inquiry."

She stopped at the door, her hand on the handle and said, "I'll let you know anything I find out. In the meantime, expect a call from the Chief. I'll phone him and tell him I've been diverted to another inquiry. See you later," she flashed him a humourless grin and was gone.

****

She had arisen early, tying back her grey flecked auburn hair and pulling on an old worn top and loose fitting skirt. Still, she wondered while she dressed, what *was* he up to going out at that time of the morning and with a heavy sigh, assumed it must be work related. Minutes later she was in the utility room next to the kitchen sorting out a wash prior to putting it into the machine when the noise of his car driving across the stone chips alerted her to his arrival home. Her wristwatch said it was just a few minutes before nine.

Her heart always beat a little faster while she worried what kind of mood he might be in or what kind of reception she could expect from him; whether he had been drinking heavily wherever he had been or just had his usual frequent sips from the flask he carried. She no longer quizzed him for more than once her face had felt his wrath when she said or did the wrong thing.

Thank God the girls are long gone and don't have to suffer with me anymore, she whispered a private prayer of relief.

Moving to the window, she sneaked a look out through the curtain and to her surprise, saw him disappear out of sight around the corner of the house. There was nothing there other than the bins and the path that round led to the front door.

Probably getting rid of his latest empty bottle she thought and returning to the wash basket, lifted the hem of her skirt to enable her to slowly kneel down onto the cold tiled floor and began to sift through the basket, separating the whites and colours from the darks.

****

Tommy Craig awoke with a splitting headache and slowly stumbled from the bedroom to the bathroom to pee. Filling the basin sink with cold water, he took a deep breath and quickly doused his head head twice then shook it vigorously, splashing drops of water all over the walls.

Maybe buying that half bottle of cheap whisky and the four cans of Guinness hadn't been such a good idea after all.

With both hands tightly gripping the basin, he closed his eyes and remembered what he had seen.

There was no doubt in his mind the man had done for Smiler. The detective who drove away in the black car; the same type of car the polis used.

Tommy's problem though was he couldn't go to the cops with what he had seen. No, he opened his eyes and stared at his reflection in the cracked mirror above the basin. Those bastards would as soon as fit him up for Smiler's murder as take the time to catch the real killer.

After all, why would they bother wasting their time looking for the detective in the black car when they had an old lag like him on a platter?

Bastards!

He involuntarily shivered, suddenly aware of the chill in the bathroom and him standing in nothing but his underpants and a vest that was soaked with drips of water.

He run a hand across his bald head and staring at his unshaven face and watery eyes, decided once more that another dunking would do him no harm.

Gasping for breath, he lifted his head from the water and reached for a soiled towel that hung on the edge of the bath.

They'd be coming for him now. Of that he was certain. He had nowhere to run and like it or not, he'd need to face them and have his story right, tell them a bit of truth and a bit of shite; just enough to convince them it wasn't him that murdered Smiler.

He thought again of the detective in the black car and evilly grinned. That's what he'd do.

Give them a wee clue that it was one of their own who did for Smiler.

His thoughts turned to the team.

With Alex Murtagh murdered in the jail, John O'Connor dead with the cancer, that touting bastard Clarke dug out of a hole in a field and now Smiler killed, that left only him from the 'Four Minute Gang'.

He grinned that the papers never really cottoned on to the fact there were five of them in all. Clarke might only have been doing the reccies, but he was still part of the team.

He stopped grinning and his brow furrowed when it struck him and he wondered; why had Smiler been killed after all these years and…he involuntarily shivered.

Who the fuck was out to get them?

****

Carrying his mug through to the incident room with him, a solemn faced Charlie Miller called the meeting to order and when the team had quietened, begun, "Before I commence the briefing, I have some bad news to disclose. Earlier this morning, though I have no firm details as yet, Shona Mathieson was discovered seriously injured in the close in Dixon Road where she lives."

A shocked murmur went round the room that stopped when Charlie raised a hand and continued, "From what I have been told by the investigating officer, DI Alan Boyle, Shona has suffered some life threatening head injuries and was been conveyed to the Neuro at the Queen Elizabeth where she is being treated as we speak. I have no update as yet, but will keep you apprised of her condition."

He paused and added, "There is no further information or any known suspect or suspects at this time, however, DI Boyle is treating the assault on Shona as an attempted murder."

"Any suggestion the assault on Shona is related to our investigation, boss?" Willie Baillie called out from the back of the room.

"Nothing, Willie," he shook his head, "but it's early days so I'm not ruling anything out."

A young redheaded DC raised his hand and when Charlie nodded at him, said, "Shona has a partner, sir, a guy called Gary, though I don't know his second name. Is he in the frame?"

Charlie knew that Mathieson and her partner had just split up, but that had been shared by her in confidence and now he wondered; was the young guy onto something?

"Like I said," he patiently repeated, "DI Boyle is in charge of the investigation and to my knowledge there are no suspects at this time, however…Tony, isn't it?"

"Yes, sir. Tony Muirhead."

"I suggest at some point today you contact Aitkenhead Road with anything you know of Shona's partner and either speak with DI

Boyle or leave him a message."

"Sir," the young DC blushed as he nodded.

"Well, ladies and gentlemen, while I'm certain we're all worried about Shona, it won't catch us a killer, so let's get on with the job in hand. Alice," he nodded to the civilian supervisor, "though it's not strictly procedurally correct, I want you to take on the role of the office manager. There's nothing in the rule book that says a civilian can't do the job and I'm relying on your HOLMES experience to carry it off. Think you're up to it?"

"Yes, sir," she flushed with embarrassment, yet pleased at the responsibility she had been assigned.

"Right then," he continued, "as you might have heard when you arrived in this morning, one of our witnesses and former member of the robbery team, Frankie Colville, was in the early evening of yesterday discovered murdered in his flat. Like James Dougrie, Colville had been stabbed to death. While there is at this time no evidence to indicate the murders are connected, I am assuming responsibility for Colville's investigation and running it in parallel with those of Dougrie and Murdo Clarke. It doesn't take a genius to work out that all three men are related in some manner through the Four Minute Gang."

He paused and took a sip of his now cool coffee.

"The surviving member of the robbery team is a man called Thomas Craig. We have a release address for Craig from the Prison Service that is somewhere in the Shettleston area. Alice," he turned to stare at her, "please dig out the address and raise an Action for Craig to be interviewed. In fact," his eyes narrowed, "mark the Action to me." His head swivelled as he sought out Baxter in the crowd and seeing her, said, "Alison, have Alice raise an Action for you to track down Murdo Clarke's widow, Stacey. If you have problems, you can read Shona Mathieson's statement from the Clarke's neighbour, Missus Lennox, who told us the Clarke's daughter was at the local primary so try and track her down through the school records."

"Sir," Baxter acknowledged with a nod.

"Alice, I want you to create an Action for Willie Baillie and me to attend Colville's PM this afternoon with young Tony," he smiled at Muirhead. "You can accompany us and seize productions, okay?"

"Yes, sir," the young DC's eyes lit up.

"As for the rest of you, I want you to continue with the Actions you've been allocated and people," he held up a hand and wryly grinned, "I know some of the Actions might seem to be boring, but every piece of this jigsaw will complete the picture, so no moaning to Alice, okay?"

"Right, any questions?" his eyes swept the room. "No? Then get to it. Willie," he called out to Baillie, "can you come with me to my office please?"

Minutes later, the two men were seated opposite each other.

"It's a bad business about Shona," Charlie shook his head.

"What's your gut feeling, boss? Is it related to our investigation?"

"Who knows?" he shrugged then added, "But that's not why I want to speak with you. Sad though it is what happened to Shona leaves me without a Detective Sergeant. You've what, twenty years in?"

"Twenty-one now, boss. Twelve in the CID."

"Twenty-one and twelve. Then, Willie, I think it's about time you took on some supervisory responsibility," he paused. "I want you to assume the acting DS role for now. That okay with you?"

Baillie didn't immediately respond, but then smiling, replied, "I'll be pleased to, Boss."

"Right then, for your first task DS Baillie, you can accompany me to interview this guy Tommy Craig."

****

The police grapevine quickly got to work and word soon spread throughout the city cops that one of their own had been the victim of an attempted murder.

Those officers who knew Shona Mathieson well or even slightly were outraged at what happened to her.

Those officers who did not know Mathieson were aggrieved that a police officer had been attacked at her home and many armchair warriors boasted their grisly descriptions of what they would do if they were the one who was fortunate enough to arrest the bastard that did it.

Before long, the rumour mill spread almost as quickly as did the news of the attempted murder.

Though it was broadly suspected that Mathieson's assailant who carried out the attack had been someone she had previously arrested, one gossiping cop, hoping to be thought of as 'in the know', maliciously threw a spanner into the work by lying that he had been told her assailant was the wife of a police officer with whom she was conducting an illicit affair.

No matter what story was bandied around, the investigating detectives trudging up and down the adjacent tenement closes and knocking on doors were unable to find an eye witness to the assault. Neither did the SOC officers find anything of evidential value at the locus and so after receiving the bad news and with a weary expression, DI Alan Boyle frustratingly closed his mobile phone and continued his vigil at the Neuro Department where the surgeons worked tirelessly to save the young woman's life.

****

The team had permitted themselves ten minutes of quiet discussion among themselves while they attempted to come to terms with the grim news of Shona Mathieson's assault.

It was the young detective, Tony Muirhead, who suggested sending her flowers and quickly collected money from everyone present. Knocking on Charlie Miller's door, Muirhead informed him of the collection and accepted Charlie's twenty quid contribution towards the flowers.

In the incident room, Alison Baxter, a phone clamped to her ear, began the laborious task of tracing Stacey Clarke, starting with the Department of Work and Pensions where she politely reminded the young call centre operator that the request had been submitted earlier, but no reply received.

"That's Clarke with an 'e', Miss? Right, let me see," he drawled "I'll just pop you on hold while I go through the file of women with the surname Clarke with an 'e' and approximate age of…did you say she's between fifty to sixty years?"

"Yes, we believe so," she agreed.

"So we're starting here at nineteen fifty-seven then," he muttered to himself, before continuing, "Okay then. I'll not bother with the forename because sometimes this bloody system doesn't get the spelling correct and if you enter the exact match and there's a different spelling…" his voice lowered as he tailed off.

Minutes passed and she was beginning to suspect the bugger had cut her off when the operator came back onto the line to say, "Sorry. I can't seem to trace a Clarke with that approximate age, Miss. I also tried Stacey Clarke with different spellings for Stacy, but no joy. Are you certain those are the correct details, the age and that, I mean?"

"It's what I've got," she sighed, "but thanks for trying anyway," and ended the call.

Her brow furrowed when a shadow loomed over her. Glancing up, her head almost collided with that of Willie Baillie's who was just about to lean over her.

Smiling, he quietly said, "Thanks for last night. I had a really nice time."

"Me too," she returned his smile and was about to say more when Charlie Miller, stood in the doorway, called out, "Can I have everyone's attention, please?"

Once the hubbub subsided, he continued, "Due to the unfortunate circumstances of Shona Mathieson's assault, it has left the inquiry without a Detective Sergeant. I'm already working without a Detective Inspector, so in Shona's absence, I've decided to appoint Willie Baillie as the acting Detective Sergeant," then grinning, added, "Any objections, put them in writing."

The laughter confirmed what he thought; he had made a good and popular decision.

"Willie?" he smiled at the burly man, "Ready to go?"

"Right with you, boss," Baillie blushed at the smiles, grins and backslaps then winked at Baxter before he left to join Charlie in the corridor.

"Couldn't have happened to a nicer guy," she heard one detective say while another commented, "Long overdue, too. Would have happened a lot sooner if it hadn't been for that ratbag Donaldson sticking the mix in for the big guy."

Returning to her task, she was surprised to know how pleased she was for Willie.

Taking a breath, she returned to staring at her handwritten notes and realised that she had little option but to do as Charlie Miller had suggested.

She would attempt to track down Stacey Clarke through her daughter's school records and grabbing her handbag and a set of CID car keys, began to make her way down to the rear yard.

****

Unfamiliar with the area, Baxter used her mobile phones SatNav to direct her to Miller Primary School in Ardencraig Road, however, the fifteen-minute journey took almost twenty-five minutes because of the morning traffic.

Arriving at the school gates, she carried on up the lengthy driveway to the front of the modern school and parked in an empty bay in the staff car park.

Pressing the buzzer for entry, she was directed by a staff member to the office where presenting herself, she was directed to a middle-aged woman who introduced herself as Marion Wilson, the Deputy Head Teacher.

"It's a bit of a long shot I know," Baxter begun, "but I'm engaged in an inquiry about a family called Clarke. I've been told that a daughter of the family attended the school in the late eighties, a girl whose surname was Clarke and I apologise; I don't know the forename."

Wilson blinked several times behind her large framed glasses and with a bemused look, replied in an obviously affected plummy accent, "The old school was demolished in the late nineties and," she waved her hand about her, "as you can see, we're relatively modern now. As your inquiry is from the *eighties*," she grimaced, "we certainly won't have been computerised and I really don't think we'll have kept paper records from that far back, Miss Baxter. Sorry."

"What about staff? Is there anyone here who taught in the school about that time?"

"No, of that I'm certain," Wilson shook her head. "You see I'm the longest serving member of staff here, having arrived in nineteen-ninety-four," she smiled with a hint of pride.

"Oh, well," Baxter smiled, "at least I've tried. Thanks for your time."

Wilson entered the code to permit Baxter to exit the building and was walking towards her car when she heard her name called out. Turning, she saw Wilson stood holding the door ajar and beckoning her to return.

"I'm not certain if this will be of any use to your investigation," Wilson hesitantly began, "but there is one woman who might be able to help."

She followed Wilson through the building to the school cafeteria where a half dozen women were preparing that afternoons lunch.

"Missus McCracken," Wilson called out to a small, rotund woman with tight grey curly hair and a florid face who wore a spotlessly white chef's jacket, white cap and apron, though Baxter could see the apron was dotted with food stains and her fingers heavily stained with nicotine

As the small woman waddled over, Wilson said, "This is Miss Baxter from the CID. She was asking about a pupil who attended the school here in the late eighties. If I'm not mistaken, Missus McCracken, weren't you employed here at that time?"

"Aye, Missus Wilson, I started as a cleaner back in eighty-four, but it was the old school then of course. Then I got a job here in the canteen…" she smiled as though embarrassed and glancing sharply at Wilson, corrected herself with, "I mean the cafeteria. Anyway," she took a deep breath and from the rattle in her chest it seemed to Baxter that McCracken was a heavy smoker, "what can I do for you, Miss?"

Baxter explained that she was trying to locate a family called Clarke whose daughter, aged eight or nine years old, attended the school in the late eighties.

"Oh, you mean wee Mhari Clarke? Her mammy was Stacey Clarke? That wee girl?"

Baxter's eyes widened. "You mean you remember Stacey Clarke?"

"Remember her, hen? Christ, you don't forget that bugger Stacey," she vigorously shook her head then almost guiltily, glanced at Wilson.

"Perhaps if I were to leave you with Missus McCracken?" Wilson tightly smiled at them both and made her way out of the restaurant.

"Can we go out for a wee smoke?" McCracken asked, nodding towards a fire door and without waiting for a response, led the way through the door to where the large steel bins were lined up against the back wall of the cafeteria.

"What's this about, hen? Is it anything to do with the body that was dug up? The body that is supposed to be Murdo Clarke that was on the news the other night?" she asked, fetching a packet of cigarettes and a lighter from the pocket of her apron.

Declining a fag, Baxter nodded and replied, "We're trying to trace Missus Clarke to officially inform her of her husband's remains being discovered. Do you happen to know where she might be living now?"

"No," she thoughtfully shook her head, "no idea, hen."

Lowering her voice as though afraid of being overheard, she continued, "You have to understand Stacey Clarke was a stuck-up cow who thought she was a cut above everybody else. Mind you, though I hate to admit it," she scowled, "she was a right good looking woman, but one of they people who can cut you in half with a glance, you know?"

"Had she any friends among the other mothers, someone who you think might know her current address?"

"Stacey Clarke?" McCracken looked at her as though she were mad. Resting the elbow of her right arm on her left hand while she puffed away, the older woman sighed before deeply inhaling on her fag. Turning her head to blow the smoke away from Baxter, she continued, "I was usually just knocking off from my cleaning duties for the morning. We did a split shift, to let you understand. Early into the school before the weans arrived and then back again when the weans finished for the day. When I was leaving in the morning with the other cleaners I saw it was usually him, Murdo I mean, that brought the wean to school. He wasn't a bad guy; always gave you a wee nod when he was passing by. He'd walk wee Mhari here from their house to the school, but on the odd occasion Stacey brought the wean she'd turn up in her wee yellow sports car and park right there," she pointed down the long wide stairs that led to Ardencraig Road and the school's pedestrian entrance. "Never saw her even say cheerio to that wee lassie. The wean had no sooner got her bum out of the seat than Stacey was roaring off as though she couldn't get away fast enough."

"Any idea what kind of car it was?"

"No, hen. I don't drive and I can't tell one car from the other."

Baxter thought she was again hitting a brick wall, but asked, "Do you remember when it hit the newspapers about Murdo Clarke being missing?"

"Oh, aye, it was the talk of the steamy. Castlemilk might be a big housing scheme, hen, but word gets about. Fair buzzed round here with rumours at the time. Some said that he was involved with gangsters and had been bumped off. Some even said it was Stacey that got rid of him, that she was after the insurance money. Mind you," she grinned as she nodded, "I wouldn't have put it past her, cold bitch that she was."

"I take it Mhari remained her at Miller Primary till she moved to a secondary school?"

McCracken's brow creased as she fought to recall to story then replied, "The wee lassie was off school for a time while she went to live with her granny, old Jessie Clarke who stayed in the flats in Tormusk Road, I think it was. I didn't know Jessie Clarke other than to see. Kind of kept to herself to herself, she did," McCracken sniffed her opinion of the old woman.

"She was Murdo Clarke's mother?"

"Aye, I suppose she was his mother, what with her having the same *surname*," she stared at Baxter as though the fact was obvious.

"And did Stacey live there too?"

"Stacey? No, hen," she frowned. "Stacey dumped the wean on the granny and left Castlemilk. That's right," she slowly nodded as the memory returned. "Buggered off without that wee girl."

She drew deeply on her cigarette and continued, "The word in the bowling club was after her man was reported missing, Stacey took off for the high life and left Mhari with her granny because she didn't want to be lumbered with her wean."

"When you say she took off for the high life, do you know if that was with another man?"

"That I don't know for certain, but it wouldn't have surprised me," McCracken scoffed. "Full of herself, that one was."

"I don't suppose Missus Clarke still lives in Tormusk Road?"

"No, hen," McCracken took another puff at her fag, then exhaled before replying, "Jessie Clarke died years ago. I can't remember what year it was, but Mhari would have left school by then, of that I'm pretty sure."

"So you've no idea then of the whereabouts of Mhari today?"

"Sorry, no, but I do know that she got married. I heard about it down at the bowling club a few years back. She married a local guy," her eyes narrowed as she thought. "Now, what was his name again?"

"Will you be able to find out for me, Missus McCracken? Her husband's name and if possible, where they might be living?"

McCracken didn't immediately respond, but then shrugging, offered, "If it's that important, I can ask at the bingo tonight, if you want. There's bound to be some of my pals that might know. I just don't know why the polis would be so interested in telling that cow about her man's body being dug up. From what I heard she was never that interested in him when he was alive."

She stared at Baxter and added, "She was a good bit younger than him, did you know that?"

"Any idea what age she would be now?"

McCracken blew through pursed lips, but that produced a hacking coughing fit. When she recovered, she shook her head and replied, "I'm only guessing here, mind, but she was a woman who spent a lot of money looking after herself; her appearance, you know? Anyway, I'd say these days Stacey must be maybe in her mid to late fifties."

"Well, if nothing else, we need to officially inform someone of her husband's body being recovered and if we can't trace Stacey, we should at least let his daughter know, eh?"

"I suppose so," McCracken reluctantly agreed.

"So you'll try to find out for me then?"

"Aye, hen, I'll do my best."

Feeling as though she'd lost a shilling and found a sixpence, Baxter fetched a calling card from her notebook and scribbling her name and the incident room telephone number onto the card said, "I'll be very grateful if you could phone me at this number or if I'm not there, leave the information for me."

On the way back through the school to her car, the Deputy Head Teacher, Missus Wilson called out, "Was Missus McCracken of any help, Miss Baxter?"

"I believe so, yes," she waved a cheerio and smiled but didn't stop, suspecting that Wilson would now herself speak with McCracken to find out exactly what she had told Baxter.

****

She was off duty and still in her pyjamas when her neighbour phoned her to break the news of Shona Mathieson's assault.

"And she's been taken to the Queen Elizabeth?"

"That's what I heard, aye."

"Do you know what ward?"

"No, Archie on the desk said the word is that she's not doing so good."

"Anybody arrested?"

"No, not that I heard. What do you think?"

She paused, her thoughts scrambled as she considered what to do before replying, "I think I'd better get myself dressed and go and visit her boss. It might not be connected, but he should know anyway."

"Do you think that's a good idea? I mean, what if he starts to ask awkward questions?"

"Listen, we did everything by the book, so get it together, girl. There's no comeback to us, okay?"

"If you say so," but there was a definite hesitation and concern in her neighbours voice.

"Right, I'll get off now. I've a phone call to make, but keep me informed if you hear anything else," she said before ending the call. Stood in the kitchen, she decided on a fag before phoning. Inhaling the strong tobacco seemed to focus her thoughts, what she would say.

At last, she lifted the mobile phone and searching through the directory, found the number of the office where she asked to be put through to the incident room.

"Hello, can I speak with Mister Miller, please?"

"I'm afraid Mister Miller is out of the office at the minute. I'm Alice Brookes, the office manager. Can I help you or take a message?"

Brookes heard the woman take a breath before she replied, "My name's Sergeant Pickering from the Traffic Division. Can you tell me when Mister Miller will be available or when I can call in to see him?"

CHAPTER SEVENTEEN

Her hair in disarray and barefooted, she had just dressed in an old faded pink coloured sweater and baggy jeans and kneeling on the floor of the front room, was in the middle of getting Connor changed from his jammies into his play clothes when the mobile phone in her pocket chirruped.

Glancing at the screen, she stared at the unfamiliar number and was about to delete the call, believing it to be another PPI nuisance when some inner instinct told her to accept it.

"Hello?"

"Missus Gibson? Louise Hall. We spoke the other day," the young woman politely reminded her. "My firm have been engaged by the Police Federation to assist you and I'm the lawyer appointed to deal with your father's estate."

"Oh, yes," she reached out for Connor who while his mother was distracted, squealed happily and turning quickly away from her gasp took the opportunity to run off to the bedroom and hide behind his wooden toy garage.

"Miss Hall. Sorry, I was just getting my son changed there," she struggled to her feet to pursue the errant toddler.

"If it's not convenient to speak right now I can call back?"

"No, please, it's okay," she stopped in the doorway and pretended she couldn't see the giggling Connor. "What can I do for you?"

"Actually I'm on with some good news. Yesterday at the request of a DS Mathieson from Giffnock CID, I began to process Mister Dougrie's Will relative to his estate. Late yesterday afternoon I spoke with Police Scotland's legal team. Now, because the Will names you as the sole beneficiary of your father's estate, I'm pleased to inform you that Police Scotland are in agreement that Mister Dougrie's home is no longer of any evidential interest to their ongoing inquiry and so, though the reading of the Will is still to be formalised, they have no objection to you taking immediate possession."

Stunned, she raised her free hand to her mouth, choking back a sob as tears formed.

Her son, sensing his mother's distress, slowly stood up from behind the garage and stared curiously at her.

"Missus Gibson? Missus Gibson, are you still there?"

"Yes," she sobbed, "Thank you. I…I'm…"

Connor run to her and threw his arms about her legs.

"Missus Gibson, I can hear in your voice that this is all a little overwhelming for you," Hall interrupted. "What I intend doing is having a courier dispatched to collect the house keys from the incident room at Giffnock police office and I will ensure they are then delivered to yourself. Now, remember, I'm acting for you. Is there anything else that you urgently require of me?"

"No," she managed to sob, her hand reaching down to stroke her son's head.

There was a slight pause then she heard Hall mutter, "Bugger it," before continuing, "I can hear you're upset, Missus Gibson. Do you have anyone there with you? Another adult I mean?"

"No, there's just…" she drew a deep breath to compose herself and exhaled. "There's just Connor and me. My son. He's two."

"Oh, I see. Well, look, I'll go and get the keys myself then…" Hall paused as though something come to mind and asked, "You don't perhaps drive do you?"

"I do drive, yes, but I've no car," Gibson bit at her lower lip as the tears freely flowed.

Tightly hugging her legs, Connor's lips began to tremble as he wondered why his mummy was crying.

"Right then, here's what we'll do," continued Hall. "I'm not to far away in Paisley so I'll come and collect you and we'll get the keys en route to your father's house. You just give me an hour and I'll see you then, okay?"

"Yes," her voice almost a whisper, she dropped to her knees and taking her son in both arms, openly burst into a flood of tears.

****

He opened his mobile phone to read the incoming text message from Sadie:

Taking Ella and going to mums just in case. Don't want her to be alone if a phone call comes in. Kieran's mum Sandra getting the bean after school. I'll collect her from Sandra's when I get back home. Let you know if there's any news. X

"Everything okay boss?" turning into Quarrybrae Street, Willie Baillie risked a glance at him.

"Just a personal thing, Willie," Charlie Miller replied.

"Right, this is it," Baillie stopped the CID car and switching off the engine, peered through the window of the CID car towards the four in a block cottage flats. Beside him, Charlie undone his seat belt and said with a wry grin, "He might be an old guy now, but according to his prison file this bugger has the reputation of being short-tempered and handy with his fists. If he wants to swing at anybody, your first job DS Baillie is to protect your boss."

"Aye, right," Baillie returned the grin and replied, "He'll need to catch me first, though."

It was Baillie who hammered on the chipped and peeling paint wooden door at the front of the building that led to the upper flat, then stood back when the door was pulled open with a loud squeak. The elderly, shaven headed and heavily tattooed man wearing dark coloured jogging pants, training shoes, a clean, white tee shirt that showed off his muscular physique who stood there, stared at them in turn. Settling his gaze upon Charlie, his eyes narrowed in recognition when he said, "You're the guy that was at Smiler's house."

Taken aback, Charlie glanced quickly at Baillie before replying, "And you I take it are Mister Thomas Craig? Or can I call you Tommy?"

"What's your name, pal?"

"Charlie Miller," he nodded to his neighbour, adding, "and this is Willie Baillie. Can we come in or would you prefer we do this at the local cop shop?"

Wordlessly, Craig turned and began to walk away, leaving the door wide to permit Charlie and Baillie to trail after him up the stairs.

They followed him to the front room, noticing that though the flat was sparsely furnished and sporting décor and furniture that was at least thirty years out of fashion, it was clean and tidy.

Theatrically sighing, Craig nodded to the couch and settling himself down in the facing armchair, said, "This is about Smiler's murder?"

"You said you saw me there," Charlie went immediately on the offensive. "When I left Colville, he was alive. Did you kill him, Tommy?"

Craig smiled, a beguiling smile and shaking his head, replied, "No, but I might have an idea who did."

"And are you going to tell me?"

"Can we not have a wee chat first?"

"What kind of chat?"

"I'd like to talk about who's bumping off the gang."

Bewildered, Charlie said, "I don't follow."

"Well, you've dug up that touting bastard Murdo Clarke, haven't you?"

"So, you're confirming Clarke *was* a member of your gang, then?"

Craig's eyes widened and his nostrils angrily flared. The fucker had tricked him into an admission. Teeth gritted, he tried to recover the initiative and replied, "Well, it was no great secret, was it? The papers called us the 'Four Minute Gang,' but it was Clarke that set up the jobs. Besides, too many years have passed to keep it a secret now and yes," he snarled, "Anyway," he shrugged, "Clarke *was* one of the team, but a cowardly bastard who wouldn't get involved when it came down to the nitty-gritty, know what I mean?"

"You're telling us that he never got involved in the actual robberies?"

"You kidding, pal?" Craig sneered then springing up from his armchair, walked across the room to stare out of the window to the neatly tended garden below. "Murdo Clarke's only use to us was what he found out about the jobs, though how he did that I never knew and didn't ask. Oh aye, I'll give him that," he slowly nodded as he continued to stare through the window, "he was good at setting the jobs up. Timings when to hit the places, routes to get away, the right day when the money would be worth knocking off; those sort of things."

"Didn't he *ever* go with you on any of the jobs?"

"No, never," he slowly shook his head. "We'd meet up, sometimes at Alex Murtagh's place, sometimes at Clarke's house and occasionally at mine," he paused. "Not here, though. When I lived in the Parkhead flat. But no, Clarke never came with us."

He laughed humourlessly when he added, "The bastard would only have been a liability anyway, always feart and afraid of that fucking skank wife of his."

Charlie had an idea and asked, "Tell me this, Tommy, was Clarke's wife ever at those meetings?"

"Not that I remember," Craig shook his head, then with a smirk, added, "Those were the days. Do you know we were the most wanted men in Scotland?"

Sensing Craig was beginning to boast, Charlie decided to press him for more details to fill the many gaps in his information and said, "It must have been quite an exciting time for you, Tommy. The adrenalin must have been really flowing, eh?"

He turned from the window and staring curiously at Charlie, sighed before replying, "Aye, they were the good times. You people never had a sniff of us," he sneered. "Never knew where in the country we were going to hit next. We might have got away with it for a lot longer than we did if not for him; Clarke I mean. Bastard," he sniffed.

"What about the money, Tommy? Where did that all go to? I mean," Charlie glanced around the room, "it doesn't seem to have been banked for you while you were away."

"What is it that you're really interested in, copper? Is it the money or catching the guy that did in poor Smiler and your man Dougrie?"

Charlie extended his hands and with a soft smile, replied, "I'm just trying to put all the pieces of the story together and whether or not you believe it, my priority and that of my team is finding out who murdered Murdo Clarke, James Dougrie *and* your pal Smiler."

He seemed to reflect on that and placing one hand on the double glazed window, turned swiftly on his heel and seemed about to say something, then sighed. "The money, eh? Would it surprise you to know it wasn't always about the money," he permitted himself a slow grin. "For me it was doing the job."

He returned to his armchair and sinking down into it, added, "Maybe not for Alex or John or even Smiler, but for me it was about giving you bastards the run-around."

He sniggered and continued, "Aye, the money…" he paused again, "or at least the wee cut that we took from each of the jobs, was useful at the time, but I was a single guy. I didn't have a family like the rest of them."

His face clouded over as memories came flooding back. "Like I said, we took a cut each when we did a robbery, but not all of it. Just enough to see us through till the next turn, you know? Beer money, rent money; maybe the occasional holiday to Spain or something like that. It was Smiler who persuaded us that if we started to flash large big sums of money you cops would have been down on us like a ton of shit, so we did what he said. Well," he shrugged, "the four of us did, but Clarke always wanted a larger cut even though the sod wasn't taking the same risks as the rest of us. I suppose it was his wife's doing, him wanting more money."

"On that point, Tommy, any idea where we can find Stacey these days?"

"Stacey? Why the *fuck* would you want to speak to her?"

"Well, now that we've dug Clarke up, at the material time he was reported missing she was his wife so as the next of kin we are legally obliged to inform her of the recovery of his body."

"Oh, right. No," he shook his head, "I've no idea where she is and frankly, I don't care either." His eyes narrowed and he asked, "Wasn't the money buried with him?"

Baillie coughed to hide his laugh at such a stupid bloody question, before Charlie solemnly replied, "No," then continued, "You were saying about the money. Who was the banker? What I mean is, who held on to the majority of the cash?"

"Like I said," he shrugged, "it was Smiler. He told us he had somebody he'd found a banker to keep it for us and that the money was safe with them."

His face clouded over when he added, "But to be honest I don't know if Smiler was telling the truth."

"And you've no idea who that individual was?"

He scoffed and replied, "Do you honestly think I'd be living in this shitehole if I did?"

"Point taken," Charlie smiled, but then casting a glance at Baillie he continued, "Tommy, when I interviewed Smiler, he said that at the time you guys were arrested for the Renfrew job, he thought Clarke had got on his toes and taken the money with him. Does that mean Smiler told Clarke where this safe place was or even that Clarke might have been the man holding the money?"

Craig stared back at Charlie, his eyes mean and hateful, but the vehemence wasn't directed at the detective, it was for the other three members of the gang who had kept so much from him.

At last, though it hurt him to admit it, he quietly replied, "Sometimes the rest of them kept things from me. That's why I was going to visit Smiler. I wanted to know what the fuck he knew that I didn't. I wanted to know where the money was or where it had gone to."

"Why didn't you visit him before now?"

He didn't immediately respond, but at last admitted, "Because I thought that Clarke had got away with the money," then bitterly added, "or at least, that's what the rest of them told me."

"Tommy," Baillie interjected, "you've admitted you were there after Mister Miller left Smiler's address and you're telling us that you didn't kill him. You also said that you might have an idea who did."

He stared at the big detective before replying, "What's in it for me if I tell you what I know?"

Baillie glanced at Charlie who replied, "What's in it for you, Tommy, is that we take your information and if it proves correct, you're no longer in the frame of the murder of Frankie Colville."

His voice hardened when he added, "*That's* what's in it for you, pal!"

Craig's face paled. "You think it was me who murdered Smiler?"

"I think right now from what you told us you're my first and only suspect."

He knew he was scaring the older man, but Craig's inference he had information could be crucial and so pressed home his advantage.

"Right, no fannying around now, Tommy. If you want to avoid me and my colleague lifting you out of here for the murder of Frankie Colville, you'd better tell us exactly what you do know!"

He let the threat seep in and then continued, "You said you know something and you also said the guy who murdered Dougrie probably did in Smiler, too. Let's start with why you were at Smiler's address."

If looks could kill, Charlie Miller would have dropped stone-dead, but then Craig hung his head and replied, "I'd phoned him. Told him I was coming over so he was expecting me."

"How long had it been since you'd last seen him?"

Craig's face expressed his surprise at the question when he replied, "Fuck me! How long is a piece of string? I hadn't seen or spoken with Smiler for years. Too many to remember. I didn't even know his missus had died until he told me on the phone, That's why he didn't meet me in the pub yesterday, because she'd died."

"But you remembered where he lived, remembered his phone number."

"Well, it was his wife's house. She'd kept it in on after he got the jail and as for his phone number; her number was in the telephone book. Christ, even I could work that one out," he sniffed.

Charlie suppressed a smile and asked, "And what did you want to meet him about?"

He hesitated, but realised that at some point he would have to admit it and it wasn't worth being arrested and flung into a cell when he knew he was going to tell them anyway.

"When I heard on the TV about Clarke being found buried and your man, the CID guy Dougrie being murdered…" he took a deep breath and slowly exhaled. "Anyway, it occurred to me that maybe I was being given a blinder, that Murtagh, O'Connor and Smiler knew Clarke was touting to Dougrie when we were pulling the jobs. What I couldn't understand was if they knew, why didn't they tell me!" he was suddenly angry and savagely pounded at his chest with a fist.

He paused then continued in a hushed voice as though sharing a deep and troubling secret.

"Sometimes they had their wee in-jokes and their wee secrets, you know? The three of them. I would catch them laughing about something or other and when I asked what the joke was, they'd treat me like a fucking mug, like I wouldn't understand, know? Well, that's why I was going to see Smiler. I was going to get the truth out of him, about Dougrie, about Clarke touting to you people and about the money; where it went, I mean. But the big guy I'm talking about; he got to him first, didn't he?"

"Who was this guy?" Charlie calmly asked.

"Am I going to get arrested if I tell you?"

"Not if you tell me the truth."

He snatched a glance at Baillie then slowly replied, "He came after you and the woman left in your car. I had been hiding behind the garages across the road and nipped to a café for a coffee and when I came back, he was coming out of the close. He looked in the front window of Smiler's place and then got into a black car and left."

"How long were you away getting your coffee?"

"I dunno," he shrugged and shook his head. "Maybe forty or fifty minutes?"

"And you think this man was responsible why?"

"When the guy had left, I went to Smiler's door and when I knocked on it, he didn't answer, so I tried the handle and when it opened," he paled, "I saw Smiler lying there in his hallway with a big fucking knife sticking out of his chest."

"Tommy, you've just found your pal murdered. Didn't you think to call us, the police?"

He took a deep breath and in a quiet but firm voice, replied, "No, why would I?"

"Why would you! What kind of a bloody question is that?" Charlie raged.

Craig stared at him and slowly replied, "Because the guy I saw, he was one of you. A guy in a collar and tie and a dark suit and driving a polis car. A detective."

****

DI Alan Boyle realised it was futile sitting about the hospital corridor when he could be and should be doing something more constructive.

The last text message from his office informed him the Personnel Department had sent a Superintendent and family liaison officer to break the news to Mathieson's parents of her assault and for that he was grateful.

Too many times in his lengthy career he had to disclose heart-rending news to a victim's family.

He stood to ease his aching back and turned when his name was called to see Cathy Mulgrew striding purposefully from the lifts towards him.

"Any news?" she curtly greeted him.

"Nothing yet, Mucky. The last I was told is she's still in surgery," he shook his head, suddenly aware that he had used her nickname from their days together so many years previously on the Initial Detective Course at Tulliallan.

Mulgrew smiled and with a coy expression, replied, "Nobody's called me *that* for a very long time."

"Sorry," he said, but she waved away his apology and eyes narrowing, told him, "You look done in."

"I've decided there's no point in hanging about here, Cathy. I'm heading back to the factory, see if I can drum something up, but I have to tell you the news I'm getting from my guys isn't good at the minute. The door to door isn't producing any witnesses, though I'll be sending them back later this evening to catch the locals who left early for their work. That and the SOC haven't found anything that can identify her assailant."

"The rumour mill is going full blast," she sighed. "I heard on the way over here that there's about a dozen stories circulating as to who did it and why."

He didn't ask what her source was, just accepted that it was true what was said of Mulgrew; the woman most definitely had her finger on the pulse.

"Any news of how Charlie's inquiry is progressing?" he asked.

"Nothing yet, but you know Charlie," she smiled. "He always brings something out of the bag."

"He's a good man," Boyle nodded. "If anybody will catch Dougrie and Colville's killer, it will be Charlie. Right," he took a deep breath, "Are you stopping here for a while?"

"I'll give it ten or fifteen minutes to pay my respects. If there's any update on her condition…"

"I've arranged for a uniformed police woman to come down and sit here while Mathieson's being treated and to update me regarding any developments."

"Does it have to be a police woman?" her face expressed her curiosity.

"Call me an old sexist, Cathy," he wryly grinned, "but in my experience a polis woman is more likely to be told things that a sullen faced guy won't. You women always bond and if there's a female sat here, I can almost guarantee within ten minutes the nurses will be offering her tea and toast and chatting away. Oh aye," he nodded, "a police woman will learn about Mathieson's condition and treatment far quicker than a guy."

"You're right, Alan," she smiled at him' You *are* an old sexist."
****

Alice Brookes just couldn't come to terms with what had happened to Shona Mathieson and unable to compose herself, fought the tears that constantly threatened to overwhelm her. Such was the matronly woman's open distress that more than one officer had suggested she pack it in for the day and go home.

One of those officers was the recently returned Alison Baxter who finally, to the quiet relief of the staff working in the office, took Brookes by the elbow and firmly said, "Alice, come with me, now please."

She led the unresisting Brookes to the ladies toilet where filling a basin with lukewarm water then grabbing a handful of paper towels that she thrust towards Brookes, told her, "Douse your face and if you need a good cry, go ahead. There's nothing to be ashamed of. I know that Shona was probably a good friend of yours, so…"

She didn't finish, for Brookes took a deep breath and to Baxter's surprise, falteringly interrupted, "I think I know who did it to her, who hurt her."
****

She flashed her warrant card towards the civilian bar officer and made her way upstairs to the incident room.

Opening the door, she stood and hesitantly cast a glance around the room.

"Can I help you?" the young civilian analyst glanced warily at the powerfully built woman.

"Eh, I was looking for an Alice Brookes or is Mister Miller returned from his inquiry yet, do you know?"

"Eh," the young woman glanced about her before replying, "The boss is still out I think. Alice is…ah, she's indisposed. Can I ask who you are?"

She flashed her warrant card again and replied, "Sergeant Pickering from the Traffic Department. Can I wait here for Mister Miller?"

****

Buckling his seat belt and before he started the engine, Willie Baillie asked him, "Have we done the right thing here, boss? Not giving Craig the jail? I mean, he as good as admitted he was there when Colville was murdered and then telling us that he opened the door and saw Colville's body, then buggered off without contacting anyone. What the hell was that all about? Any rational, decent person would have screamed blue murder and called us."

"Aye, like you say, Willie. Any rational, decent person, but we're talking here about a guy that served the full twenty-three years of his prison sentence in some of Scotland's roughest jails rather than admit his crime and obtain himself an early release. As he said and to be honest, my instinct agrees; Tommy Craig knew fine well if he called us he was going to be the number one suspect and an easy detection. Not that I'm suggesting he's innocent. No, not at all, for it wouldn't be the first time I've been wrong about a suspect, but something tells me that he was genuinely surprised at finding Colville's body and," he turned to face Baillie, "did you see the pleasure in his face when he told us that it was one of us, a detective that murdered Colville? I'm convinced that our Tommy believes what he saw and you saw yourself; he took great delight in telling us too."

"But he did admit that he went over there to have it out with Colville; get the truth from him about Murdo Clarke and even inferred he was prepared to belt it out of Colville."

"Yes, but he must have known by admitting that it could make him a suspect for the murder. Of course, it might be a double-bluff, but I'm inclined to believe him. You'll know from your own experience, even the bad guys tell the truth from time to time."

"And what was all that guff about? After you and Alison left the close this unknown detective in a black car turns up and does Colville in?"

"Now that's a funny one," Charlie shook his head. "Tommy obviously saw what he wanted to see; a guy in a collar and tie and wearing a suit and leaving in what he thinks is a CID car. You heard him yourself, though. He doesn't drive and can't tell one car from another. All he could say was it was black and even though he denied his eyesight is failing, you likely noticed when he was talking he squinted a lot."

"So, the vague description he gave of this guy probably isn't worth much."

"Probably not," Charlie agreed before adding, "If nothing else, though, he's gave us a better insight into the gang than we had before. He's confirmed again that Murdo Clarke was the fifth man and from the way Tommy describes it, the other three thought Tommy was a bit of a thicko and kept him out of the loop on a number of things, not least their suspicions that Clarke was a police informant."

"I picked up on that," Baillie nodded, "but what I can't get round my head is where the hell all that money went to?"

"I once heard it said follow the money and it will lead to the truth. Unfortunately," he sighed, "we're no better off tracing that than we are the killer we're after."

He glanced at his watch and pointing a forefinger towards the windscreen, added, "Maybe we should make a move, Willie, and start heading towards Govan. We've Frankie Colville's post mortem to attend."

****

Wearing a white blouse and navy blue, striped business suit with a pencil skirt and her black hair tied in a tight ponytail, the lawyer Louise Hall arrived in Tannahill Terrace in her own car, an immaculately clean and fresh smelling Ford Focus.

Seeing Jessica Gibson carry the toddler down the stairs towards the car in one arm and a folded buggy in the other, she apologised, saying, "I'm so sorry. It never occurred to me. I don't have a child seat for your wee boy."

Gibson, wearing her best skirt, a colourful blouse and a worn black nylon anorak, waved away her apology and replied, "It's no problem. I'll fasten the middle belt about him and sit in the back with him," and as if by magic produced a fudge bar from her handbag to quiet the boisterous child.

Less than fifteen minutes later and while Gibson remained in the Focus trying to entertain her lively son, Hall spent five minutes collecting the house keys from the incident room at Giffnock police office.

Now a few moments later, here they were in Belmont Drive and parked outside James Dougrie's house.

Turning in her seat, Hall pointedly ignored the biscuit crumbs on her back seat as well as Connor's fudge stained fingers and mouth and kindly asked, "Are you ready for this, Missus Gibson?"

"Please, it's Jessica," she nervously replied, for each passing mile to the house had completely deflated the the excitement of an hour ago.

Hall recognised how tense she was and suggested, "If you want to leave the wee one with me while you go in and have a look around…"

"Would you mind? I won't take long."

Forcing a smile, Hall replied, "No, of course not."

Getting out of the driver's seat, she opened the rear door and after Gibson had secured him in the buggy, said, "It looks to be a quiet road here so I'll just walk him along the pavement for a bit, keep him amused, eh Connor?" she reached for the buggy's handle and added, "Let you have some time to look the place over. Give you, say, ten minutes?"

What Hall didn't say was that ten minutes was probably all she could stand of the frantic wee bugger who immediately began to whine and tried to climb out of the buggy's restraining strap.

"Oh, the buggy. I'm sorry, but it's got a bit of a wonky wheel," she grimaced before adding, "I won't be long."

When Hall had walked off, she stared at the house, her expression one of disbelief that after all these years she was finally returning home.

That and to her relief she was getting her children out of the Ferguslie housing scheme and away from the influence of the youthful gangs and their nightly disorder and confrontations as well as the areas overwhelming social problems.

Wrapped up in her thoughts, she did not notice Hall walk off with the puzzled Connor, whose head twisted back to see where his mother was going.

She did not hear his wailing or see him try to wrestle his way out of the buggy as the younger woman determinedly leaned across to persuade him to stay where he was.

She did not see the curtains in the neighbouring semi-detached houses on either side or across the narrow road twitch as curious eyes watched her step through the wrought iron gates into the monoblock driveway and approach the white, double-glazed storm doors.

She was unaware of the tremble in her body and, as her eyes fixed upon the large bay windows with the curtains drawn back, she stared through the glass and marvelled with surprise at the size of the room beyond.

At the storm doors, her hand shook so violently she dropped the large bunch of keys.

Bending down to retrieve them, her legs felt so weak she had to place her hand upon the stone wall for balance and to prevent herself from toppling over.

Her throat was dry and she pulled sharply at the blue and white plastic checker tape with the legend 'Police: Do Not Cross' across the doorway and when it snapped, watched the two ends fall to the tiled step.

After her third attempt, she finally inserted the correct key into the lock and pushed open the storm door and baulked at the dark stain that was upon the tiled entrance.

The inner door too was locked, but she correctly guessed which key opened it and stepping warily across the stain, pushed the door open, her nose twitching at the faintly dry, musty smell as though the heating had been left on, but no windows left open to air the place. She turned and unlatched the second storm door and pushing it back against the wall, daylight flooded into the brightly painted hallway. Though she had been there just a few days earlier with the detective woman called Mathieson, it was as though she was seeing the hallway for the first time and her face lit up with a bright smile. Emboldened now, she hurried into the front lounge and stared out at the high hedgerow and the wrought iron gates, her head darting back and forth before rushing through to the rear sitting room and the wide extension that housed the large and recently refurbished kitchen, the utility room and the cloakroom toilet with the walk-in shower.

Her curiosity knew no bounds and pulling open the outsized, American style fridge, her eyes narrowed at the quantity of foodstuffs within.

She didn't bother unlocking the double glazed patio doors in the rear sitting room, but instead stared through the glass into a small conservatory that she realised must have been erected after she had been gone from the house.

She gazed with wonder at the neatly tended and spacious garden in which already she could envisage her son and daughter playing happily and more importantly, safely.

Excitedly, she raced from the kitchen into the hallway and run up the wide stairs, panting at her unexpected exertion as she breathlessly reached the half landing with the wide, tiled bathroom and up the remaining stairs to dart between the four double bedrooms.

In the room that had once been hers, she stopped dead; one hand across her stomach and the other across her mouth with the sudden realisation as to how she had come by this wonderful gift.

The murder of her father.

It was though a sudden weight had descended upon her and she felt the need to sit.

It was but a few moments that passed when lost in her thoughts, she heard her name called.

Hurrying from the bedroom that had once been hers, she took a deep breath and with one hand on the solid wood banister, forced herself to be calm as she walked down the stairs where she saw Louise Hall stood in the front doorway with Connor in her arms and the buggy parked outside the door. Descending to the lower hallway, she fought back a smile when she saw the imprint of Connor's sticky fudge fingers on the collar of Hall's pristine white blouse.

"I think he was missing his mummy," she explained as Gibson took the child from her arms.

"So, Jessica," she smiled now that the burden of the wee horror was taken from her, "have you had enough of a good look around?"

"Yes," she nodded. "I can't wait to move in."

Conscious of the time, she asked Hall, "I'm not keeping you back, am I? I mean, you must need to get back to your office, yes?"

Hall glanced at her watch and replied, "I really should be leaving, but there's no rush for you to get away. I mean, your wee girl won't be out of school, for what, another two hours or so?"

"Oh, I was hoping…no, never mind," she smiled and vigorously shook her head.

"What?"

Embarrassed, Gibson said, "I wasn't sure if you might drop me off back home, but it doesn't matter. Really. I'll get a bus or maybe even splash out on a taxi," she continued to smile and hoped because the younger woman had been so kind that Hall wouldn't presume she was overstepping the mark and abusing her kindness.

Hall stared curiously at her and shaking her head said, "Jessica. I'm so, so sorry. I'm obliged by confidentiality rules not to disclose the details of the Will prior to the official reading; however," her eyes conspiratorially sparkled, "again as you *are* the sole beneficiary, I trust that you won't report me to my firm if I leak something else." She stared at Gibson and with a mischievous smile, said, "You told me you drive. Is that true?"

"Yes, though I haven't driven for a very long time. Not since my ex-husband gambled our car away," she said with just a trace of bitterness.

"Oh, but you do have a driving licence?"

"Yes. Why?"

"Can we step outside?"

Without waiting for a response, Hall walked along the hallway and stepping out through the storm doors, turned where to Gibson's surprise, she locked arms with her.

"I should have mentioned this before," Hall said as she led Gibson and the squealing Connor to the corner of the house. Smiling, she nodded down to the end of the long driveway.

She hadn't noticed it when she had walked through the garden gates, but now Gibson's eyes opened wide when she saw the front grill of the bright red coloured car.

Her mouth dropped open in surprise and she lowered Connor to the ground to stand beside her, his grubby fingers held tightly in her hand to prevent him running off.

"It's a Nissan Juke," Hall beamed. "Just over three years old. It's part of the property of the house and according to the instructions in your father's Will and you being the sole beneficiary," she beamed, "it's now yours. As I understand it the finance was all paid off just a month ago, so the car is yours," she beamed.

She was speechless and slowly walked towards the car as sensing Hall was a little embarrassed, the lawyer said, "There is one other thing, Jessica."

"Again without actually disclosing the full details of the Will, I spoke with my senior partner who has instructed me to inform you that if you are in any financial difficulties at this time, my firm are prepared to release a sum of money to your bank account on the condition such a sum will be detracted from your father's estate. I can arrange for the release of a thousand pounds by this afternoon; in fact, as soon as I get back to my office. Might I suggest that such a sum will permit you to purchase for example, insurance for the Nissan and a car seat for the wee guy here?" she glanced down at Connor, her stomach turning in revulsion as she saw him carefully examine a fresh bogey from his nose that he held in his forefinger. Still stunned at her good fortune, she run a hand across the shining bonnet of the Nissan then heard Hall tell her in a low voice, "I brought the car keys with me just in case you fancied a wee shot of it. If you decide to drive and go to pick up your daughter from school, don't let on to anybody that you've still to get it insured in your name. Remember," she sniggered like a schoolgirl, "it's only an offence to drive without insurance…if you get caught."

****

He'd went straight back to bed without a word of explanation. Not that she expected him to tell her anything. These days other than grunting his demands or finding fault with every little thing she did, they had no contact and certainly no physical contact.

Not unless…she shuddered at his sometimes strange desires.

She knew to be quiet as she tidied around the house, for to create any noise while he was in bed was to provoke his anger and that was definitely something she could no longer bear.

That she was afraid of him was something she long ago accepted.

Carefully lifting the pail with the mop in her other hand, she carried them through to the utility room with the intention of emptying the soapy water into the large sink.

Opening the utility room door, she grimaced at the squeaking hinge, inwardly cursing that again she had forgotten to use WD40.

Idly she glanced at his clothes hanging to dry on the radiator and again she wondered.

Glancing nervously at the door to the utility room, she stepped across the floor and as quietly as she dared, closed it.

Her curiosity, though always a dangerous thing when dealing with her husband, was killing her and taking a breath, she opened the door that led to the back of the house.

She just had to know.

What *had* he been up to?

CHAPTER EIGHTEEN

Finally calming Alice Brookes down and back to some semblance of composure, Alison Baxter knelt beside the chair in Charlie Miller's office and handed the nervous older woman a mug of steaming hot tea before softly asking, "What do you mean, you think you know who might have hurt Shona?"

Brookes stared at her and with a deep sigh, replied, "I know what I said, but if you don't mind, Alison, I'd like to wait and speak with Mister Miller. There's something he should know."

Baxter stared at her and sensing the strain Brookes was under, with a slow nod arose to her feet.

"Might be an idea if you wait here till he gets back. He's at the PM just now, but I'll text him and ask when he returns to see you right away, okay?"

Brookes didn't reply, but nodded in acknowledgement.

"If anyone asks, I'll tell them you're too upset about Shona to continue at your desk. I'll see to your desk while you're in here."

With a comforting hand on Brookes shoulder, she left her to await the return of Charlie Miller.

Returning to her desk, she had just sat down when the young female analyst called out, "Alison. You had a telephone call when you were in the loo with Alice. I've left the details on your desk."

"Under my desk, you mean," she grinned and reached for the fallen sheet of paper.

"Sorry," she smiled at Baxter.

Glancing at the handwritten note, she read that Missus McCracken had instead phoned one of her bingo pals and learned that Mhari Clarke was now Mhari Fraser, having some years previously married John Fraser. According to McCracken's unnamed pal, the Fraser's son attended the same school as the pal's grandson and they lived in either Carrick Drive or one of the roads near to it.

She raised her head and catching the attention of the Traffic sergeant who was wearing plain clothes and seated at an adjoining desk reading that mornings edition of the 'Glasgow News,' asked,

"Sergeant Pickering isn't it? Can you help me out here? I'm not familiar with this part of the world. Where's Carrick Drive, do you know?"

"Eh, Carrick Drive," she repeated and closed her eyes in thought. "That's Castlemilk, I'm sure."

"Is there a police office in Castlemilk?"

"Aye, on Dougrie Road, but I'm not certain if it will be open. A lot of these wee stations are only used by the patrol officers for their breaks. Why?"

"Who would have the Voters Roll for that area?"

"Probably Aitkenhead Road office. The telephone numbers will be in the Almanac," she nodded towards a thick, khaki coloured book with string attached to its spine and hanging from a nail driven into the wall by the door.

Leafing through the book, Baxter mentally noted the number then telephoned the uniform bar where her call was answered by a bored sounding woman.

Establishing the woman's name was Liz and she was a Force Support officer, Baxter asked her to check the Voters Roll for Carrick Drive in Castlemilk for a John and Mhari Fraser and if not in Carrick Drive, also check the surrounding streets.

"I'm a bit busy here, hen," she heard Liz yawn. "Is it urgent or can it wait till sometime later this afternoon?"

"Yes, probably," Baxter brittlely replied. "I'll just let Detective Superintendent Miller know that you're too busy to assist him in his murder inquiry. Sorry, you said your name is Liz, didn't you?"

There was a unmistakable pause as the veiled threat hit home before an animated Liz answered, "Can you give me those names and the address again, please?"

****

Seated at his desk, the Chief Constable of Police Scotland, Martin Cairney, pressed the button that would summon his personal Aide, a uniformed Superintendent and asked her, "Any news?"

The dark haired woman shook her head and replied, "As you instructed, sir, I'm in contact with the Duty Inspector at Aitkenhead Road office who in turn is receiving updates from his officer at the ward. Other than the last message that DS Mathieson is out of surgery, there's been nothing further."

Cairney sighed and blinking rapidly, leaned forward and said, "Thank you, Susan. If there's anything…"

Understanding his concern, the Superintendent permitted herself a grim smile and nodding, interrupted with, "Immediately, sir."
****

The post mortem conducted on the body of Francis McGowan Colville was conducted not by Elizabeth Watson as Charlie Miller had hoped, but by her younger colleague Doctor Gemma Taylor, the raven haired pathologist who at a little under five feet tall looked like a second year high schoolgirl and to enable her to perform her examination, used a wooden box to reach the table on which the cadaver lay.

Stifling their revulsion, Willie Baillie and Tony Muirhead watched as the diminutive woman expertly wielded her instruments while performing the PM.

When the examination was completed, Taylor formally announced to them all, "My conclusion is that other than indicative wear and tear commensurate to his body as is expected of a man of his age, Mister Colville was in relatively good health. I therefore conclude that the wounds inflicted on his torso brought about his premature demise and that these wounds, seemingly inflicted by the large bladed weapon I removed from his torso, caused his untimely death. The wound on his right hand suggests it is a defence wound."

She turned to Charlie and with a tight smile, added, "In short, Mister Miller, your man here," she nodded to the corpse, "was indeed murdered."

"I don't want to put you on the spot, Doctor Taylor, but have you any idea as to the dexterity of the killer? Left or right handed?"

She pursed her lips and slowly shaking her head, replied, "The wound on the victim's right hand would seem to indicate he was reaching forward, perhaps to grasp at the murder weapon and would suggest the weapon *might* have been held in the killer's left hand. But no, I can't with any certainty say if the killer was left or right handed."

Fifteen minutes later and with Muirhead sent to the Forensic laboratory at Gartcosh with his specimens, Baillie was again behind the wheel and driving them both to Giffnock.

Charlie's phone chirruped with an incoming text message that said: *Alice Brookes in your office. Told me she has an idea who might be responsible for Shona's assault. Have kept it quiet meantime. Baxter.*

Stunned, he took a deep breath, but took the decision not to say anything to Baillie, though why he couldn't immediately explain. Before long, Baillie was pulling into the rear car park where Charlie said, "I've something to do in my office. Get yourself a coffee and try to find out if there's any change in Shona's condition."

A minute later he was opening his office door where startled, Alice Brookes rose to her feet.

He could see she had been crying and clutched a handkerchief in her hand.

"Please, Alice," he waved her backed down into her seat.

****

Pushing through the door to the incident room, Willie Baillie was met by a tall and middle-aged woman who was almost as broad as him with tight curly, light brown hair flecked with grey, wearing a blue coloured fleece jacket and baggy jeans and who asked him, "Is that Mister Miller back from his PM?"

His eyes narrowed for her face was familiar, but it was she who said, "I'm Cathy Pickering."

She smiled and seeing his confusion, added, "I'm a Traffic sergeant."

"Oh, right," he nodded in recognition, then replied, "Sorry, Cathy. I didn't recognise you without your clothes...I mean, eh, out of uniform. Aye, he's back, but he's got someone with him at the minute, Cathy. Can I help you?"

****

"So, Alice," he begun. "I got a text from Alison Baxter that said you might have some information as to who assaulted Shona? On that point, have you heard anything from the hospital?"

"The last we got," she sniffed, "was when DI Boyle phoned in to say she was out of surgery, but nothing since."

"Oh, right then. So, who or what is it that you suspect?"

Her eyes avoided his and lowering her head to stare at the floor, she swallowed with difficulty before saying, "It's about DCI Donaldson. He...he forced me to tell him what was going on in the investigation; what you were doing."

Charlie, his hands folded across his chest and fingers interlocked, stared at her, but he wasn't surprised. He'd long suspected that Donaldson was capable of such deviousness and inhaled before slowing exhaling, replied, "Go on."

"The night you arrived he phoned me at home." She raised her head to stare him in the eye as tears welled up and said, "I live with my mother. I mean, she gets a pension, but it's me who's the real breadwinner." She sniffed and dabbed at her eyes. "Anyway, DCI Donaldson told me that there's to be cuts in the civilian staff and if I didn't tell him what was going on in the investigation he would ensure that I would be the first to go. I'm sorry, Mister Miller, but he frightened me…frightens me, I mean, even though I know he's suspended. What if he comes back to work? I mean, he'll get me sacked now you know, won't he?"

"You've told me what he forced you to do, Alice, but not who you think assaulted Shona."

"Isn't it obvious?" she angrily replied. "It was him! He's the one that attacked her!"

"But why would he attack Shona? What possible reason would Donaldson have to…" he stopped and stared keenly at her. "Did he say anything to you? Tell you he did it or that he intended doing it? Threaten Shona?"

"No, nothing like that," she vigorously shook her head, "but that's the kind of man he is! Don't you see? I think that Shona might have found out what he was making me do and confronted him!"

"And what did you tell Donaldson that was so important?"

Confused, she shook her head and replied, "Nothing really. Nothing that was important. Only when you were out of the office, where you went, that kind of thing."

He imagined that Brookes must have been terrified of Donaldson, of the supposed influence she believed he had and was angry, but not at this poor woman sitting in front of him; at the cruel, malevolent and unfeeling man who had bullied so many good people.

Unclasping his hands, he leaned forward onto his desk and counting off on his fingers, said, "For one, Alice, Gerry Donaldson is no longer in a position to hurt or threaten you. For two, nothing you told him has in any shape or form altered the course of this investigation, for three, I think it's highly unlikely he had anything to do with the assault on Shona and finally; for four, I'm grateful you had the courage to come forward and admit what you did."

She stared unbelievingly at him and in a faltering voice, asked, "You're not angry with me? You're not…you're not going to have me sacked?"

He slowly smiled and shaking his head replied, "I can only imagine the unbearable burden you had working under that man. Now, I *am* going to fine you."

Her eyes narrowed as he added, "Two quid into the tea fund and we'll hear no more about it. And we'll keep this strictly between the two of us, agreed?"

The tears rolled down her cheeks, but tears of relief and standing, her lips trembling, she nodded, unable to reply.

"Now, once you've washed your face, Alice, I think you've an office to run," then pretending to be annoyed, added, "so get out of here and let me get on with some *real* work, eh?"

****

With Ella playing around their feet and seated at her mother's kitchen table Sadie Miller swapped some craic with Carol, but stopped talking when the phone rung.

"I'll get it," she began to rise from her seat, her stomach in a knot, but halted when Carol raised her hand and said, "No, hen, it'll be for me."

She watched her mother stand and walk towards the wall phone then take a deep breath before lifting the handset and saying in a nervous voice, "Hello?"

She saw Carol's eyes close and nod, then smiling turned towards Sadie to tell her, "It's okay, hen, it's Father Flynn."

Sadie breathed a sigh of relief and heard her mother tell the elderly priest, "No, Father, no news yet. Aye," Carol nodded. "The consultant said he'd phone if it was bad news, so I've Sadie and wee Ella here at the minute keeping me company."

She saw Carol listen then again nod and finishing the call with, "Yes, I will tell her," she turned to smile at Sadie. "Thank you, Father, and God bless you too."

Replacing the handset, both women stared at each other for a few seconds before to Ella's surprise, they burst into nervous laughter.

****

Willie Baillie read the note on his desk and sighed.

According to the officers from the Avon and Somerset Constabulary he had requested to interview James Dougrie's son Stephen about his whereabouts on the day of his father's murder, there was no response at Dougrie's address; however, neighbours had disclosed Mister

Dougrie was at that time with his wife and son on a Swiss skiing holiday and not due to return for at least another week.

If nothing else, Baillie lifted his pen to update the Action for the trace and eliminate, it ruled Dougrie out as a potential suspect for the murder. He also read that the English officers had thoughtfully asked the neighbours not to disclose their interest in Dougrie, believing it was not their place to inform the son of his father's death.

"Good," Baillie unconsciously nodded at their decision and made a mental note to phone Jessica Gibson and let her know that her brother was unaware of their loss and the date of his return from holiday.

He lifted the second Action from his wire tray and stared at it.

He had still to interview Missus Gibson's former husband, Peter Gibson, and wondered with a smile if Alison Baxter might accompany him.

Turning his head, he realised that Alison wasn't in the room, but before he could ask anyone where she was, he saw Alice Brookes enter the room.

Glancing at the Traffic sergeant who was still seated at the spare desk, he caught her eye and getting up out of his chair, said with a smile, "Hang on and I'll find out if the boss is free now."

Knocking on Charlie Miller's door, he popped his head into the room to see Charlie on the phone, but who waved him into the room.

"No, Cathy, no word yet." Baillie heard him say then saw him nod and add, "We're still trying to track down Clarke's wife, but I've a note here from Alison Baxter to say she's away out to Castlemilk. Apparently she's got a lead on where Clarke's daughter Mhari might be living, so it's something for the minute. Right, speak later," he said and ended the call.

"Willie," he begun. "This guy who Tommy Craig mentioned and he thinks was a CID officer that he saw coming out of Colville's close and peering through the window. Get onto the local CID at Aitkenhead Road and ask if any of their officers had occasion to call at that address yesterday. Besides that, put out a general e-mail to all CID officers posing the same question and ask for a return e-mail confirming or denying the visit. That way we can eliminate all the DO's from Craig's allegation. Mind you, I'm not convinced Craig *did* see one of our own, but we need to ask anyway, okay?"

"Right, Boss, will do. One other thing. There's a Traffic sergeant called Cathy Pickering been waiting for quite a while for a word with you. Can I send her in?"

Charlie's face creased. "Did she say what it's about?"

"I asked but she wants to speak personally with you," Baillie shook his head. "She's in plain clothes and off duty so I figure it might be important."

"Okay then," Charlie shrugged, "show her in and if there's any chance of a coffee, I'm parched after that bloody PM."

"Will do," Baillie grinned and went to fetch Pickering.

****

It had been some years since she had been behind the wheel and the first few minutes of driving the Nissan Juke had been nerve-wracking. She stalled the car twice before getting out of the driveway then turning left too sharply out of the gate onto Belmont Drive, bumped over the pavement.

Securely strapped into the middle seat in the back and thinking it was some sort of fairground ride, it didn't help her confidence any that Connor clapped his hands and squealed with delight as the car lurched along Belmont Drive.

At the junction with Orchard Park Drive, she came to such a sudden halt her forehead almost collided with the steering wheel and there was that giggling again from the back seat.

Grimly determined to master the car, she concentrated on her driving and within ten minutes the old skills returned and she was beginning to enjoy herself.

The only heart stopping moment came as she was driving on Broomlands Street in Paisley towards Ferguslie when glancing in her rear-view mirror, she saw a marked police car behind her.

Fortunately, the two officers in the car were too busy laughing at something to pay any attention to the Juke in front.

She slowed at traffic lights as they turned green in her favour and while she turned to the right, with a sigh of relief saw the police car drive off to the left.

It took her no more than twenty minutes to pack two suitcases and grab a box of Connor's favourite toys. From her daughter's room she filled a blue coloured IKEA bag with some teddy bears and a few of Amy's precious possessions.

Stuffing the cases, toys and bag into the boot of the car, she had a final look at the house and decided anything else that was needed could wait for now.

She arrived fifteen minutes early and parked in a bay near to Glencoats Primary School.

Fetching the buggy from the floor in the front passenger seat, she lifted Connor from the rear seat and made her way to the gate to watch for her daughter.

****

Following the directions voiced by her phone's SatNav, Alison Baxter turned slowly into Arran Terrace and drove down the short slope towards the cul-de-ac. She could see the four, two-storey buildings with the angled roofs before her, the buildings sheathed in the same council roughcasting and each containing six flats. At first glance the buildings seemed grim and almost Soviet in their style; however, she also saw a number of double-glazed replacement windows that seemed to indicate home ownership and that some of the residents had tried to soften the flats appearance with brightly coloured curtains that lessened their drab, dull grey coloured outer frontage.

Parking the CID car in the bays opposite the buildings, she locked it and began to count off the flats numbers, finally realising the address she sought was in the building directly opposite.

She glanced at her watch and if her timing was correct and if Missus McCracken's pal had been spot-on, Mhari Fraser or maybe her husband would be home or perhaps due to arrive home with their primary school child.

Entering the building, she found the name Fraser on a brightly polished brass plate attached to a double glazed door on the first floor.

Before knocking on the door she listened and could hear a television blaring from inside the flat.

Knocking, the door was opened by a fresh faced and attractive blonde woman in her mid thirties, her hair piled up onto a bun, who wore a bright yellow polo shirt and dark green coloured, flared, knee length skirt. She smiled and with one hand guarding the door, greeted Baxter with, "Yes, can I help you?"

"Missus Mhari Fraser?"

"Yes, that's me," Fraser's curiosity showed in her bright blue eyes, but she continued to smile.

She produced her warrant card and replied, "I'm DC Alison Baxter. There's nothing to be alarmed about, but I was wondering if I might have a word with you?"

"What about?" Fraser suddenly frowned and Baxter immediately suspected that her visit was not that surprising.

"Mummy," said a voice behind Fraser and opening the door a little further as she turned, Baxter saw a blonde haired child aged about eight who stood staring curiously, first at his mother then at Baxter.

"Away and watch the tele, Murdo, there's a good boy," his mother quietly replied and gently turning him by the shoulders, steered him towards the front room at the end of the hallway.

Her shoulders slumped and her face paled as her expression turned to sorrow and turning back to Baxter, asked, "This is about my dad, isn't it? You'd better come in."

****

Her tattered old schoolbag with the broken strap slung over her shoulder and in her free hand carrying her school blazer that was a size too small, eleven-year-old Amy Gibson was one of the first pupils who sauntered through the school gate. Heads together and deep in conversation with her closest school friend, she turned with a huge smile when she heard her name called.

It wasn't cool for girls her age to run and hug their mother, but Amy didn't care what her friends thought; her mum was the best in the world and her best friend too and so she run through the crowd and into her mother's arms while the other parents and grandparents' crowded together as heads swivelling, their eyes searched the mass of children for their kids or their grandchildren.

Throwing one arm about her mother's waist, Amy bent down to the old and worn buggy with the wobbly wheel to pat Connor on the head and like most children her age, asked the time honoured question of, "What's for dinner?"

"What would you like for dinner?" her mother returned the question.

"What I'd *like* and what I'll *get* are two different things," the wise eleven-year-old replied.

Her mother didn't move as in a cacophony of noise and like a host of buzzing bees, the crowd of children and their parents and grandparents swarmed around and past them.

"But really, what would you like for dinner?" Jessica Gibson persisted with a teasing smile.

Amy stared at her mother, wondering what game she was playing and slowly replied, "Pizza. Pizza and those little round chip things we got once when we went to the seaside for the day."

"That was nearly two years ago," her mother laughed and then as if seeing her daughter for the first time as the thoughtful and kind child she was, bent over to give her a bone crushing hug.

"Mum!" Amy protested, yet didn't resist for she was secretly pleased at her mother's affection.

"Sorry," her mother stood upright and said with a firm voice, "Then pizza it is."

She took a deep breath and pushing the buggy while carefully compensating for the wobbly wheel, said, "Right, we'd better get you home first and get you changed."

Confused, Amy lingered for a moment then turning her head pointed and replied, "But we live that way."

Stopping beside the shiny, red coloured Nissan Juke, her mother replied, "We did, sweetheart, but guess what? We're in the middle of moving house."

When her mother pressed the remote button on the car key, Amy was startled to see the lights of the red car flash and confused, her eyes widened and she said, "Mum! What…why…where did you get this? Did we win the lottery or something?"

"No, we didn't win the lottery and it's a really long story, darling," she opened the rear door of the car and bending, began to unbuckle Connor from his buggy and using her hand, swept the biscuit crumbs from his shirt and trousers as she released his straps.

"So, our first stop is to the Halfords shop in Paisley to buy a car seat for your brother, then we'll go home to our new house and while you're exploring your new bedroom, I'll order us a pizza home delivery."

****

"Please, sit down Sergeant Pickering. Cathy, isn't it?"

"Yes, sir," she replied.

"Do you mind if I call you Cathy?"

"No, not at all,"

"I understand you've been waiting to speak with me for some time. Have you had a coffee?"

"More caffeine than is good for a woman at my time of life," she gruffly replied.

"So, Cathy," he sat back in his chair. "What can I do for you?"

"To begin," she stared him in the eye, almost daring him to be annoyed at her statement, "I'm one of the two officers who arrested DCI Donaldson."

His eyes narrowed, his curiosity piqued that immediately following his conversation with Alice Brookes he was again discussing Gerry Donaldson.

"Will that be a problem, sir?" her voice flat, she mistook his surprised expression as support for his fellow detective.

He considered his reply before telling her, "In my own and very humble opinion and between the two of us sat here, I consider Gerry Donaldson to be an affront to everything good that the police stand for. His record of bullying his staff was commonly known and it's a disgrace that the senior management of Police Scotland and of Strathclyde Police before them, that nothing was ever done to curtail him. So no," he slowly shook his head, "whatever you disclose and I assume you have something important to tell me, will not be a problem. That said," he raised a warning hand, "nothing you tell me in confidence will leave this room unless it is a criminal admittance that will leave me no option other than to take some form of action; so, Cathy, do you still wish to continue with this conversation?"

The door knocked and irritated at the interruption, he loudly called out, "Come in."

It was one of the young analysts who cheerfully said, "Coffee for you, sir," then her face fell when she saw Pickering and asked, "Sorry, did you want two coffees?"

"No, not for me," Pickering waved a hand.

Handing him the coffee, the analyst left and laying the mug down onto his desk, he asked, "Well? Are we still talking?"

Pickering took a breath and nodded.

"Shona Mathieson is a friend of mine. A close friend who once got me out of a sticky situation when a female colleague falsely alleged..." she stopped midsentence and slowly shaking her head, added, "Let's just say times and mind-sets have changed a bit since then, but that's not why I'm here. Shona trusted you, Mister Miller. She trusted you and didn't want you...compromised by Donaldson."

He felt a familiar chill and asked, "How do you mean compromised?"

"Shona trusted me too and would confide in me when something bothered her. Okay," she permitted herself a smile, "we had what you might call different attitudes to our male colleagues…"

"Cathy," he held a hand up. "I have no interest in your gender preference. Just get to the point, hen. If you know something about who hurt my officer, believe me, I *am* all ears."

He saw her throat tighten and she swallowed with difficulty.

"The night before I arrested Donaldson, Shona phoned to tell me that he was blackmailing her; told her that her career was fucked unless she spied on you for him. Told her that he'd see she'd never advance in her career. Pestered her for information about what you were up to, how you were running the investigation and was looking for a way to bring you down."

She bit at her lower lip and he could see she was close to tears. Taking a deep breath, she continued.

"She tried to keep him sweet, stupid wee titbits that wouldn't harm you, but he got aggressive on the phone and she guessed he had somebody else on your inquiry keeping an eye on her and doing the same thing."

She saw his eyes widen and intuitively she asked, "You already know who that is, don't you?"

"Let's just say that particular hole has been plugged. Go on," he waved a hand at her.

"Shona told me it's no secret that Donaldson drank and drove. To be honest, sir, I'm surprised he hasn't been done for the drunk driving before, but apparently he's a fly bastard; has had his junior detectives driving for him during the day and sneaks away in his own car at different times of the evening to avoid anyone watching him."

She paused and wiped at her dry lips with the back of her hand.

He sighed, for Charlie himself was an alcoholic, though when he met Sadie stopped drinking and had been sober since that time. However, he could guess at the tricks Donaldson got up to. Christ, he frowned as he shook his head, thinking back to some of the things he did to hide his drinking; the peppermints, the mouthwashes and a host of other tricks he thought at the time fooled those around him.

She was taken aback by his grimace and wrongly believed she had in some way annoyed him, but seeing her expression he waved a hand and said, "Without going into details, Cathy, let's just say that I've had some experience of being around a functioning alcoholic. And that's exactly how you're describing Donaldson.

She nodded then continued, "Shona and I came to an agreement. She would tell Donaldson she had something important on you and that she needed to meet with him, except me and my neighbour would be waiting to breathalyse him. That was the plan and it worked a treat, but I didn't for one minute think the bugger would try to fight us. His mistake," she growled.

He saw a lump appear in her throat and her head lowered.

When she raised it, there were tears in her eyes.

"My neighbour didn't..." she paused and corrected herself, "doesn't know about the set-up. As far as she is concerned, we had a legitimate arrest and that's what she'll continue to believe. Trust me on that, sir."

She paused again to compose herself and when she spoke, her voice was breaking though not for herself, but for her good friend who lay seriously injured.

"Shona had told me to let Donaldson know it was her that set him up and when I had him alone in the back of the car..." she bit at her lower lip and unchecked, the tears began to flow. Teeth gritted, she sobbed and added, "I told him."

He knew now why she was there and so, after giving her a moment to compose herself, gently asked, "You believe it was Donaldson who attacked Shona? That he did it to get his revenge?"

She was still too upset to speak and nodded as she reached for a handkerchief from her fleece pocket.

Dabbing at her eyes, she took a deep breath and said, "I could see it in his eyes, pure hatred. Hatred not just for me, but for Shona. It's my fault. If only I'd kept my mouth shut, not did as she asked..."

"No, it is *not* your fault, Cathy. It's the fault of the person who attacked Shona and of me and every other bugger who knew he was drinking and did nothing about it!" he retorted, though his anger was directed at himself and not Pickering.

He stared at her and could see how badly this woman was hurting, for no matter what he said, she would always believe it was she who had caused Donaldson to attack her friend.

His expression was impassive when he told her, "Cathy I swear to you if it *was* Donaldson who attacked Shona, believe me, I *will* find a way to get him for it."

CHAPTER NINETEEN

Willie Baillie glanced at the wall clock and decided not to wait for the arrival of Alison Baxter, but would take young Tony Muirhead with him to track down James Dougrie's former husband, Peter Gibson.

Permitting Muirhead to drive, he said, "According to his ex-wife, Peter Gibson moved in with his father at Davidson Street over in Clydebank. I don't know where that is, but," he tapped the address into his mobile phones SatNav and grinning, added, "that's why we have the old trusted technology."

"Sure you know what you're doing there," Muirhead teased him. "I mean, you being the age you are?"

The comment earned the young detective a slap to the back of his head.

The evening traffic was beginning to build up and the expected half hour journey took them over fifty minutes.

At last they arrived outside the neatly tended garden in front of the lower cottage flat.

Ringing the doorbell, they heard a shuffling noise and the door was opened by a wizened, bald headed man wearing a faded black cardigan over an off-white shirt and black coloured jogging trousers. Leaning on a Zimmer frame, he stared suspiciously at the detectives.

"Mister Gibson?" Baillie showed him his warrant card and subtly sniffed at the strong smell of tobacco the old man exuded. "I'm DS Baillie and this is DC Muirhead from Giffnock CID. Is this the address for Peter Gibson?"

"I'm Peter Gibson," the old man barked in a voice that suggested sixty fags a day. "What do you people want?"

"Six numbers in the lottery for a start," Muirhead muttered from behind Baillie who half turned to glare at him.

"Actually," he smiled cheerfully at the old man, "the Peter Gibson we're looking to speak with is a wee tad younger, sir. Would that be your son?"

Gibson senior glared at them in turn before growling, "Why have you come here, to my home?"

"He doesn't live here then?"

The old man looked confused and said, "Of course he doesn't live here! Not for now anyway! What's this all about?"

It was evident to the detectives they weren't to be invited into the house and so Baillie replied, "We want to speak to him about his former father-in-law, James Dougrie. Do you know where we can contact Peter?"

"Is this a joke?" the old man was outraged.

"Sorry," Baillie replied and genuinely puzzled, glanced at Muirhead before asking, "Why would it be a joke?"

The old man didn't immediately respond, but then replied, "Because Peter is nine months into a two year sentence at Saughton prison for fraud!" then scowling, slammed the door shut.

"Wow," Baillie said. "Now *that* I didn't expect to hear."

"Once we get it checked, I suppose that's as good an alibi as any, eh?" Muirhead grinned.

"And that, Detective Constable Muirhead, can be your first task when we get back to the factory," Baillie grinned back at him.
****

Seated at the kitchen table, Alison Baxter watched while Mhari Fraser stood at the worktop and spooned coffee into two mugs. Through the partially open door, they could hear the sound of childish laughter at the antics of the cartoon characters.

The younger woman turned and asked, "You sure you're okay talking in here? It's just that the television can keep Murdo amused and, well, I don't really want him to hear any of this, if you don't mind."

"No, of course not," Baxter nodded in agreement, noting that Fraser apparently had named the young boy after her father.

Fraser poured boiling water into the mugs and lifted one over to the table to set it in front of Baxter.

"So, it's definitely him then?"

"I regret to tell you, yes. There's no doubt. Your father's body was confirmed by a DNA sample. When he had been reported missing,

DNA was in its infancy, but the police at that time had the foresight to take a sample of hair from his hairbrush and as a missing person, the hair was kept on file at what was then Strathclyde Police laboratory. The sample was later moved to our laboratory at Gartcosh at the time of the amalgamation of the Forces."

She moved over to the table and slumped down opposite Baxter, her lips tightly closed and tears welling up. Gently, she dabbed at her eyes with a tissue.

"Will I be able to see him?"

She hesitated before replying, "Missus Fraser. Really, I don't think that would be in your best interest. Your father was in the ground for a very long time. Of course, as you are the only next of kin that we have traced, your father's remains will in due course be turned over to you for formal interment or whatever you decide."

As gently as she could, Baxter related the circumstances of the discovery of the body of Murdo Clarke and as much as she dared about the ongoing investigation to discover who murdered Fraser's father.

"As your mother was at the time of his disappearance your father's spouse, we were legally obligated to trace the next of kin and were trying to trace your mother to inform her of the discovery," Baxter slowly began. "However, we haven't been able to obtain a current address for her and of course we now have traced you. On the question of your mother's current address," she delicately added, "we need to speak with her about your father's murder. I must emphasis at this time she is not a suspect, but she might have information that could assist us. Would you happen to have that address?"

Fraser shook her head and loudly exhaled.

"Do you happens to know what your mother's maiden name was or perhaps have a date of birth for her?"

"I know her maiden name was Morton, but I don't have a date of birth. All I can tell you is that she had me when she was twenty."

"And how old are you now?"

"I'm thirty-seven past."

"Which depending on what month she was born, would make your mother fifty-seven or fifty-eight?" Baxter mused.

"I guess so."

"And you have no idea at all where she might be?"

"You have to understand, Miss Baxter, my mother abandoned me when I was a wee girl. Left me with my Granny Clarke like I was some sort of excess baggage. It was Gran who raised me and I stayed with her till she died."

"Have you had any contact with your mother in the recent past?"

"Is it important that you contact her? I mean, from what I remember and to be honest," she sighed, "I was only nine when she left, but as I grew older and a bit wiser, I've given a lot of thought to what I do remember about when I lived in Barlia Drive."

She shrugged and added, "I think I've come to accept that my mother didn't really care that much for my dad or me either. That and from what my Gran told me though I admit," she smiled through her sorrow, "Gran *was* pretty caustic about her and sometimes it was difficult to separate the truth from her biased opinion."

"Do you know why your mother left you with your grandmother?"

Her brow creased as she remembered those painful days when she was handed over to her Gran, recalling the shouting and the awful language as she watched her mother drive away in the little yellow coloured car.

She sipped at her coffee before replying, "I didn't then, but of course, you can imagine what it was like being nine and told that your mother didn't want you anymore; or rather, that was Gran's version of events. After my dad suddenly disappeared without a word then my mum left, I just felt that I was abandoned. Don't get me wrong, though," she hastily added and raised her hand as if to stop Baxter thinking otherwise, "my Gran loved me to bits and I didn't want for anything. But it wasn't the same, living with Gran and not my dad. And my mother, of course," she almost guiltily added.

"This is a difficult question to ask of you and I apologise if it upsets or offends you, Missus Fraser, but do you recall if your mother was involved in any extramarital relationships? Was she seeing anyone else?"

She shook her head and replied, "You're not offending me, Miss Baxter, but I honestly don't remember anything like that. However, if my Gran was to be believed, my mother was an out and out slut," she smiled, but with sadness etched on her face.

She sipped again at her coffee and continued, "Not long before she died though I can't recall the date, but I remember my Gran telling me that about the time my dad went missing, my mother was supposed to be seeing somebody else. Gran said that my dad and mother were always arguing about it and that my mother intended leaving him, but he kept pleading with her to stay for my sake. Not that it made any difference," she bitterly added. "As soon as dad was gone, she dumped me, didn't she?"

"Do you have any recollection who the man was that your mother was seeing? A name or anything?"

"No," she shook her head. "Again, my Gran was so bitter about my mother that I can't even confirm if what I'm telling you is true. Not that I'm suggesting my Gran made it up, but you know how spiteful women can be," she half smiled. "Particularly if their son or daughter are involved."

For a brief instance Baxter thought of her own heartache when she discovered her husband had been unfaithful and the hurt she wanted to inflict upon him. With a soft smile, she slowly nodded in agreement, before asking, "Do you believe what your grandmother told you about your mother? About this alleged affair she was having with another man?"

Fraser hesitated, then said, "I believe *most* of what my Gran told me. Yes, she would sometimes go off on a rant about my mother, but deep down I know that most of what she told me was the truth." She raised her hands defensively and shaking her head, quickly added, "I truly believe Gran told me these things not to hurt me, no. As the years passed, I've come to believe she just wanted to explain the type of woman my mother was, that leaving me wasn't my fault, that it wasn't anything I had done. Do you understand?"

Baxter nodded with a tight smile, but also wondered just how much of those stories were true or was because it because Fraser wanted it to be true, that the young woman didn't want to believe her Grandmother wasn't simply being vindictive about her daughter-in-law.

She asked, "Is there anything that you can tell me about your mother that might assist us to trace her? Do you have any photographs of her, for example?"

"I did have *one* photo," she slowly drawled, "one that I had to keep hidden from my Gran, but I'm not certain if I still have it. Can you give me a minute?" she rose from her chair and left the kitchen.

Almost five minutes passed before she returned clutching a black a white photograph that was crumpled and had quite clearly been torn in half.

"Sorry about keeping you waiting. I don't know how my Gran come to have it. I *think* it was a photo of my dad and my mother," she explained, "but my Gran tore it in half and threw it into the bin. I got the half with my mother on it out of the bin when she went to bed and hid it. I used to look at it every night and pray that my mother would come back and get me, but she never did. I haven't looked at the photo now for years," she shook her head.

She handed the photo to Baxter who staring at the headshot of a smiling, very attractive blonde haired woman in her late twenties wearing a light coloured dress with this straps over her bare shoulders and who toasted the cameraman with a wine glass held in her left hand. What seemed to be a mans left arm, the shirt cuffs rolled back, rested protectively on her shoulders. Glancing at Fraser she said, "If you don't mind me saying, you and your mother could be twins."

Fraser blushed and resuming her seat, replied, "When my husband John saw the photo, he said that as well."

"Oh, is your husband at work?"

"Yes, he's on shift. John's a bus driver," she answered with a smile.

"Would you mind if I borrowed this photograph, Missus Fraser? I'll personally ensure that you get it returned to you."

"No, not at all. In fact, keep the bloody thing," she irately snapped, then red-faced, added, "Sorry. All this talk about her has brought up some bad memories. Deep wounds, if you see what I mean."

"But you survived and to be honest," Baxter smiled at her, "you seem to be a very down to earth young woman with a lovely home, a husband and a son that I'm certain adore you."

"That's kind of you to say and yes, I know in some respect I'm lucky, but it still doesn't take away the feelings that I have for my mother."

"What are those feelings, Missus Fraser?"

She didn't immediately respond. Baxter could see she was on edge, her throat tightening as she swallowed, then taking a deep breath, Fraser replied, "That I hate her for what she did to me and to my dad."

"I have a question to ask of you that might upset you."

"Go ahead. It can't be any worse than what we've already discussed," Fraser replied.

"We have it on record that in nineteen-eighty-seven, the police were called to your home in Barlia Drive after it was alleged your father assaulted your mother. Do you recall anything about that?"

Fraser's eyes narrowed and she slowly shook her head, but replied, "I'd be about seven at the time. I don't recall the police coming to the house, no, but I remember my Gran talking about it. She said my dad had supposedly slapped my mother because of something she did with another man. Again," she shook her head, "I don't know if that was true."

She leaned forward with her forearms on the table and staring at Baxter, frowned and added, "Because if it were true, then it was odd and contradicted everything my Gran told me about their relationship."

"Their relationship?"

"Yes," Fraser nodded. "You see, Gran used to complain all the time that my dad didn't slap her enough and tell me that he wasn't a violent man which was a pity, because because he was frightened of my mother."

****

He sat and reflected on what he had been told.

There was no evidence against Gerry Donaldson being Shona Mathieson's assailant, other than a strong suspicion and suspicion alone won't obtain a conviction.

No Forensic evidence, nothing the SOC could find at the locus and importantly, no eyes witnesses.

Not-a-bloody-thing.

He couldn't even bring the bastard in and put it to him, because to do so would only tip him off that he was suspected and Donaldson, he knew from old, was far too slippery a customer to give anything away in an interview.

Yet his gut instinct told him that Donaldson, having been told Shona Mathieson was the one who set him up for the fall, wouldn't let it go. No, he'd want to get back at her and take his revenge.

He spent several minutes wondering, if indeed it was Donaldson who attacked her, how he could go about proving it. There had to be something that connected him with the attack, something that

Donaldson would have either overlooked or taken for granted the police would dismiss.

For as long as Charlie had known him, the bastard had been a mean and vindictive individual and eyes narrowing, Charlie wondered if true to form and Donaldson was unpleasant to his staff and everyone else; how did he treat his family?

His mobile phone rung, disturbing his thoughts and glancing at the screen, saw the caller to be Sadie.

He tightly shut his eyes, angry with himself that he hadn't thought to call her before she phoned him.

Pressing the accept button, he said, "Hi, sweetheart, any news?"

"Nothing and it's gone five o'clock, so I suppose the old adage about no news being good news might just apply for today because I don't see us getting a phone call now." She paused and said, "I heard on the radio about the attempted murder of a CID officer. Anything to do with you?"

"DS Shona Mathieson, my office manager," he replied.

She had the good sense and lengthy service not to inquire about the circumstances of the attempted murder and instead said, "Oh, Charlie, I'm so sorry. How is she?"

"Not good. She's been out of surgery for a couple of hours now and I'm waiting on word of an update."

"Does she have any family?"

"She's not married, but curiously," his thoughts turned to the intimate conversation he had with Mathieson, "she broke up with her partner just a couple of days ago."

To Sadie's unasked question, he said, "The partner's been interviewed, but apparently he's got a rock solid alibi, so he's not in the frame."

"Any kids?"

"She's no kids," he replied, then added, "Do you remember Alan Boyle, used to be a DC at Stewart Street when we met?"

"Hmm, vaguely."

"He's a DI now at Aitkenhead Road. He's got the inquiry. It's a sensible decision. I'm too close to be objective and to be honest, I've my hands full right now with this investigation. He's a good man, Alan, and if there is an arrest to be made, he'll do it."

"How is your investigation coming along?"

"Frankly, it's not. There's been no new positive leads. A couple of half hearted leads, but even though the team are working flat out, we're just not getting a break."

"Do you think you'll be late again tonight?"

"Probably," he sighed. "Some of the team are still out on inquiries and I want to see them all in before I leave. That and I need to phone Cathy Mulgrew to ask a favour. In fact, if she's free I might ask her to pop by and bring me in a fish supper. Save you having to cook for me. That and before I go home I want to call in at the hospital and see if there's any update."

Sadie knew that could easily be done with a phone call, but she also knew her husband; he would need to go himself and though she was unlikely to know he was there, Charlie would want to be there anyway.

"I'm leaving my mums in about ten minutes to go home. I've still got jellybean to pick up from Sandra's house, though I expect Sandra will have fed her, so it'll only be me and Ella for dinner. Now, Miller, you're sure you'll get yourself something to eat? I don't need to worry about you fading away to the size of a bus?"

"Aye, very good," he involuntarily grinned at her cheek.

"Right, I'll see you when you get home. Love you."

"Love you too," he ended the call.

His phone still in his hand, he scrolled through the directory and stopping at Mulgrew's number, pressed the green button.

"Cathy, it's me. Are you heading home yet or can you pop by and give me a visit at Giffnock? I'd like to see you for a wee word."

"Can do. Is it something to do with your investigation?"

"No," he shook his head. "I'm still struggling with that, but I need you to do something for me."

"I've told you before, Charlie Miller, I'm gay and I won't take my clothes off for you and besides, I don't want you two-timing my friend Sadie."

"Like you'd have any kind of a chance with a right good looker like me," he retorted with a grin, then added, "I need you to bring me a personnel file, Cathy. That and a fish supper."

"What file?"

He gave her the details and then said, "Don't forget my fish supper and can you get the chippy to throw in a couple of onions too?"

"Bloody hell, Miller, what did your last slave die of?"

"She forgot to get the onions," he solemnly replied.

****

Most of the staff had gone home by the time Willie Baillie and Tony Muirhead returned to Giffnock office, though the young analyst who was working the late shift nodded through the door to the corridor and said, "Mister Miller is still in his office."

"Hang on here," Baillie told Muirhead and knocking on Charlie's door, popped his head in and asked, "Any word yet about Shona, Boss?"

"What was the last you heard?"

"She was just out of surgery."

"Then there's nothing new," Charlie sighed and nodded to the chair opposite his desk. When Baillie was seated, he continued, "According to Alan Boyle, the SIO…"

"I know Alan. He's a good guy," Baillie nodded.

"Well, Alan phoned to tell me there's no evidence at all, nothing to identify Shona's assailant. He's got a team returning this evening to the tenements around Dixon Road to knock on doors again in case they missed somebody and stopping passers-by coming from their work to ask if they saw or know anything."

He inhaled and asked, "Have you had any response from anyone about the mysterious CID man that Tommy Craig saw at Colville's window?"

"I had a telephone message left on my desk," Baillie idly scratched at his days stubble. "It was from the CID clerk at Aitkenhead Road who put the word out about my query, but nobody's put their hands up. As for the e-mail I had sent for the attention of all the detective officers throughout the Greater Glasgow Division, there's been plenty of return e-mails saying 'It wisnae me,' but if you want I can copy the e-mail to all officers throughout Police Scotland?"

"Pains me though it does, do that, Willie, and then have one of the analysts obtain a copy of serving DO's from the Personnel Department and mark off all responses. Those DO's who haven't responded by say, this time next week, will get a personal e-mail from me. I know it's time consuming and a pain in the arse, but leave no stone unturned, eh?"

They sat in silence for a few seconds, each man lost in his own thoughts, then Charlie said, "I hear you were out trying to trace Jessica Gibson's ex-husband."

"Aye, young Tony and I went to the father's house over in

Clydebank. Turns out if the old man's telling the truth that Gibson got two years for fraud and has been in the pokey for the last nine months. Tony's on the blower to the Prison Service through at Saughton to confirm the information."

"Another dead end," Charlie irritably replied.

"At least if he's inside, Boss, it takes Gibson out of the frame for Dougrie's murder. Any other developments I should be aware of?"

"Alison Baxter has traced Stacey and Murdo Clarke's daughter to a house in Castlemilk. I'm still waiting on her coming back to the office to see what the daughter had to say."

"Speaking of daughters," Baillie smiled, "I hear that Dougrie's daughter has been given the keys to the house. I don't want to sound insensitive, but if anything good comes out of his murder it's her and her weans getting out of that shitehole they were living in."

"Aye," Charlie nodded. "Sometimes I think we take it for granted because we live in nice houses and reasonably good areas, we forget what some folk have to endure from the likes of those thugs we saw running away that day we visited her. I say thugs," he sighed, "but likely most of them would turn out to be normal, decent kids if they were given half a chance. It's the conditions in which they live that turn them into packs, bonding together because they don't know any other way to survive."

Baillie stared and him then with a grin, said, "You're getting a wee bit maudlin there, Boss. Is it not about time you went home for your dinner?"

Charlie smiled and said, "Maybe you're right, Willie, but I'm expecting Cathy Mulgrew to bring my dinner in and have a wee chat, then I intend taking a turn down to the Queen Elizabeth. See how Shona's doing."

"I could drive you there. I was thinking of calling by too."

"No," Charlie shook his head. "We both know that we'll not get near her in the High Dependency Unit, so what I'll do is give you a call or a text if there's any change. Besides," he smiled at the burly man, "Alison might want to go for another curry."

Baillie had the good grace to blush and exhaling, said, "I knew you cottoned on when you saw us, I just knew it."

"Nothing to do with me how you guys spend your time," he defensively raised his hands, "but keep it to yourselves or you'll both be the talk of the steamie."

"Right, then," Baillie got to his feet, "I'll go and check how young Tony got on with that call, but unless the old guy gave us a dizzy, Boss, take it as read that Peter Gibson is out of the frame."

"Will do," Charlie nodded and then with a smile, added, "Thanks for what you're doing, Willie, and the support you're giving me and the team."

"No problem, Boss," he replied before stepping out the door, but not before Charlie had seen his face flush with pleasure.

Now all he had to do was sit back and await the arrival of Cathy Mulgrew with his fish supper, two onions and the personnel file that he was eager to peruse.

****

He hadn't counted how many times in the last few hours he had glanced from his window to the street below, but Tommy Craig knew had been up and down more times than he peed at night.

He had a curious feeling, a kind of funny sensation sweeping through him; something he had never before experienced.

He couldn't quite place his finger on what it was that was annoying him and once more without thinking, arose from the old armchair and stepped across the room to the window.

From behind the curtain, he sneaked a glance to the street below and saw that the street lighting had come on, but nothing had changed. At least nothing he could see.

What the *fuck* was wrong with him?

He had a final glance to the street below and returned to his armchair, oblivious to the chill and darkness of the room.

Slumping down into the armchair, his mind raced with the memory of Smiler Colville lying murdered, the big knife embedded in his chest.

He slowly exhaled.

As a child, he grown up in a family with nine siblings, he being the fourth boy of seven. He had taken beatings not only from their brutal father, but also his older brothers and never complained, because that's just how it was in those days and anyway; who the hell would listen?

He had seen his once vibrant and cheery Irish mother taken to her grave far too soon; worn and beaten down by life and trying to keep her children fed and clothed while her errant and workshy husband had drunk away what little money the Social gave her.

In those days he had been afraid of nothing, afraid of no one and reaching his teenage years, embarked on the physical regime that was to see him carry it through to today.

Of course there were fights, gang battles and he was never found wanting, proudly carrying his youthful scars into every pub in the Shettleston area and stepping aside for nobody; not even for the polis.

He had learned his craft in his primary school, snatching goods from the market trader's in the famous Glasgow Barra's then as he progressed through the minor criminal ranks of his area, graduated with honours from Her Majesty's Young Offenders Institute at Polmont.

From there it was a couple of spells doing time in the infamous Barlinnie, the Ruchazie Hotel to give the jail it's local *nom de plume*.

It was Alex Murtagh, the leader of the team who recruited Tommy as the muscle for the 'Four Minute Gang.'

Alex who drove him to an isolated farm out by Kilwinning and who spent an afternoon showing Tommy how to load, hold and fire the sawn-off that became his frightening trademark weapon.

Alex who introduced Tommy to John O'Connor, Smiler Colville and latterly, Murdo Clarke.

He had never trusted Clarke from the minute he met him; too nervous and always sweating when he met the team to brief them on their next job.

He was in the act of rising from the armchair when he stopped.

What the hell was he doing?

What was this compulsion he had to keep looking out of the window?

He slumped back down and to his surprise, saw his hands were shaking.

Then he knew, for it hit him like an ice-cold prison shower on a freezing day.

No longer was he Tommy Craig, the hard man.

No, his shoulders slumped.

He knew now why he was so apprehensive for he realised that no longer was he the invincible hard man of days past.

He was a sixty-nine-year old pensioner; still stocky built, but really just a shadow of his former self.

He was now just a vulnerable old man.

Thoughts of Smiler lying dead flashed before his eyes; a man who would be unlamented and was unloved by his family.

Tommy had family, but none that he kept in touch with; none who would come to grieve or care when he passed away.

His eyes narrowed as he wondered; who would mourn him?

And t*hat's* why he was so apprehensive.

He was facing the unknown, a future in which he had no control and he was frightened; frightened that the man who murdered Smiler was now coming for him.

****

She had stuck her head into the near empty incident room when she arrived back at the office and nodded to Willie Baillie who was seated at his desk; a casual nod that belied the budding relationship that existed between them, then smiled at the only other occupant of the room, the civilian analyst who was reading a report.

Now here she was sat in Charlie Miller's office briefing him on her visit to Mhari Fraser's house.

"And you're convinced that she knows nothing of her mother's whereabouts?"

"I'm certain," she replied. "Like I said, she believes herself to have been abandoned by her mother at an early age and if my assessment of her character is correct," she paused, "then I'm certain she is exactly what she seems to be; a young wife and mother making a home for her and her family."

Charlie smiled and said, "You like her, don't you, Alison?"

"Yes," she slowly replied, "I think I do like her. There was nothing false about her and during the interview she commented on a couple of occasions that though it was obvious she loved and respected her grandmother, she wasn't blind to the old lady's bias against Stacey Clarke. Mhari struck me as the sort of individual who would find it difficult not just to lie, but to prolong a lie."

She squirmed in the seat to make herself more comfortable and continued. "I'm not sure if you're aware, Charlie, but a study carried out within the recent years has suggested there are five main type of liars. Sociopathic liars, compulsive liars, occasional liars, careless liars and white liars."

"White liars?" he smiled, his face betraying his curiosity.

"Some people will lie, but do not consider themselves to be liars. They will lie perhaps in the belief they are shielding someone from harm; for example, a mother whose child is about to be inoculated and telling the child it won't hurt when the mother knows for certain the doctor is about to painfully shove a bloody great needle into their child's arm."

"Oh, well, include me in that group," he shuddered at a recent memory, a visit to the paediatric clinic with Ella. "But you believe that Missus Fraser told you the absolute truth?"

"As she knows it, yes."

"You'll need to explain that one to me."

"Well, remember she was handed over to her grandmother when she was just nine years of age. She's aware her dad has gone missing because even at that tender age, kids can be very observant and shrewd and then suddenly wham! her mother's gone too. The only real source of information she has about her parents is her grandmother who, as she admitted, had nothing good to say about her daughter-in-law. Now, any child growing up under those conditions must inevitably turn to the one constant in their life and in Mhari's situation, that constant was the grandmother. Yet even at an early age, she questioned the old lady's motives and while she admitted she didn't openly disagree with what Missus Clarke told her about her mother, I believe Mhari was an astute child and formed her own opinion about her father and mother's relationship."

She paused and her eyes narrowed, causing Charlie to ask, "What?"

"Just before I left, she did say one thing that I believe was significant. When I asked about her father's arrest for domestic abuse in nineteen-eighty-seven, she didn't recall the arrest, but admitted her gran did mention it in later years and was surprised, because it went against what her grandmother frequently told her. She disclosed that Missus Clarke used to tell her son that Stacey needed a slap now and then, but that her father was afraid of her mother. Now, doesn't that strike you as rather odd?"

"Have you met my wife Sadie?" he joked, but then more seriously, added, "Yes, it does seem a bit odd, but then again if as you were told Stacey was having a series of affairs, perhaps it's not that strange after all. Stacey might have been the driving force in the relationship."

He nodded as he asked, "Anything else of value from the interview?"

"As you are aware I tried unsuccessfully to trace Stacey under her married name, Clarke. However, her daughter told me that her maiden name was Morton, something that wasn't recorded in any of the paperwork I read and if Missus Fraser was correct, Stacey was born round about nineteen-sixty. Tomorrow, I'll get back onto the Department of Works and Pensions and ask them to try and trace her with those details."

The door was knocked and pushed open by Cathy Mulgrew who carried a brown paper food bag with steam rising from the top and a large shoulder bag in the other hand, but seeing Baxter, she apologised with, "Sorry, am I interrupting?"

Baxter got to her feet and smiling at Mulgrew replied, "I'd just finished my report, Ma'am, so no." Turning to Charlie she said, "Anything else, sir?"

"No, that's you for the night, Alison, and thanks. That was good work tracking down Clarke's daughter."

She bent to lift her handbag from the floor and was about leave the room, but stopped.

"Sorry, sir," she raised her eyebrows at her forgetfulness. Opening her handbag, she fetched out a photograph. "Missus Fraser saved this photo of her mother that Missus Clarke was intent on destroying. She believes it's the only photo of her mother that survived the purge of all her daughter-in-law's things," she joked, "and having seen the daughter, I can tell you she's her mother's image."

Laying it down onto Charlie's desk, she bid them goodnight and left the room.

Charlie lifted the torn photograph and quietly whistled, before commenting, "Looks like Stacey Clarke was a bit of a stunner in her youth."

"You'd say that about any woman. How you ended up with a good looking girl like Sadie, I'll never know," Mulgrew plonked the paper bag down onto his desk, then opening her shoulder bag, fetched out a thick cardboard file that was held together by a length of white string.

"Bloody hell, woman," he stared at the handbag. "What else do you carry in that shoulder suitcase of yours?"

She grinned and fetched out a plastic bag containing two buttered rolls, a large plastic bottle of Irn-Bru and two disposable plastic beakers.

"If we're going to have a fat boy dinner, Miller," she saucily winked at him, "we might as well go all the way."

Taking off her coat, she draped it across the back of her chair and seating herself down opposite him, fetched the suppers out from the paper bag and tapping a manicured finger on top of the cardboard file, before asking, "Now, what's this all about and this thing you want to discuss with me?"

CHAPTER TWENTY

She glanced across the yard to where Willie sat in the driving seat of his black coloured Vauxhall Mokka and waved. She had always relied upon her instincts in these matters and with the one exception, her cheating husband who had so skilfully deceived her, had always been spot-on.

She wasn't unaware of her attractiveness to men and in the recent years bedded just the two, neither of whom were in the job.

The first relationship lasted a mere three weeks while the second a little longer, almost six months and it was she who had finished it on both occasions. The first abruptly when she discovered he had lied, that he was engaged to be married and the second when she realised she liked him, really liked him, but didn't love him.

He had been hurt, having read more into the relationship than had she and she had felt bad about ending it, embarrassed when he had so publicly cried in the chic café where they met. However, feeling bad about his feelings wasn't a reason for continuing the relationship and so it ended.

She took a deep breath and for a brief second, her thoughts turned to Willie.

He didn't know, at least not yet, but she had given it a lot of consideration and now she had made her decision.

Raising the lid of the boot of her car, she fetched it out and returning to the Mokka, opened the rear door and placed it inside before getting into the front passenger seat.

Puzzled, he stared at her while she buckled her seat belt and asked, "What you got there, Alison?"

"Well, you said it's a bit late to go for dinner and I was thinking perhaps we might catch something from a takeaway and head back you your place. Or," she flashed him a quick grin, "you could rustle up beans on toast."

"I'll let you know I'm a dab hand when I'm wearing an apron," he pretended to be offended, but still wondered what was going on.

"By the way," she turned to him, "where exactly *do* you live?"

"Eh, I've got a front door ground floor flat in an old Victorian tenement over in Kirkcaldy Road in Pollokshields," he replied, his eyes betraying his curiosity. "Front facing lounge, three bedrooms, one that's en-suite," he adopted an air of snobbery, before continuing, "large dining kitchen, bathroom and…wait, why are you asking and what *is* that?" he twisted to nod at the leather holdall in the rear seat.

She smiled and reached across to gently lay her hand upon his thigh before huskily replying, "That, Willie Baillie, is my overnight bag."

****

It was over an hour and a half later during which time they ate their food and he'd updated Mulgrew on the slow progress of his investigation, that he bid her cheerio in the rear yard of Giffnock office and watched her drive off.

Climbing into his Volvo and rather than phone and disturb Sadie if she was putting the children to bed, he sent a text to let her know he was leaving the office and heading to the hospital, then switched on the engine.

His eyes narrowed when his headlights picked out Alison Baxter's car still parked in a corner for he knew that the only member of the team still upstairs was the young civilian analyst on late shift who was covering the phones and catching up on some filing.

He smiled, idly wondering where she and Willie Baillie were at and carefully drove out of the yard.

The roads were quiet that evening and twenty minutes later, Charlie was pulling into the Queen Elizabeth Hospital multi storey car park, but was fortunate to find an empty bay on the ground floor and from the absence of vehicles, guessed that visiting time had passed.

A short walk took him to the Neuro building and in the lift, he pressed the button for Ward Sixty-seven.

Exiting the lift, he followed the sign along the corridor and slowed his pace when he saw a man and woman seated on plastic chair with a young uniformed policewoman, her blonde hair knotted at the back in a tight bun, crouched down on one knee with her cap in one hand and the other holding the woman's hand.

The policewoman turned as he approached and rising to her feet, walked towards him.

"Hello, sir," she greeted him with a smile.

He didn't immediately recognise her and it showed in his face when she continued, "I'm Constable Wynd. I was at the locus of the murder in Belmont Drive?"

"Ah, yes, of course," he returned her smile and said, "Sorry, I didn't recognise you with your cap off. What's your first name again?"

"Helen, sir."

He'd already guessed, but asked anyway. "And those people you were speaking with," he tilted his head subtly towards the couple.

"DS Mathieson's parents, sir. Albert and…" she smiled, "Bert and Margaret. They've come up from Fenwick and been here all day. I tried to get them to go and get something to eat, but they won't hear of it. They won't leave."

"Oh," he sighed. The last think he had considered was meeting Shona's parents and wondered if he was ready for this.

"And how long have you been here?"

"Since just after four. I'm here to midnight and then another PW will take over. I don't know why," she shrugged, "but DI Boyle wants it to be policewoman in attendance."

"Is there any change in her condition, Helen?"

"You haven't heard? No," she blushed, "you wouldn't have asked if you'd known. About an hour ago DS Mathieson was taken back in for more surgery. I'm sorry, I don't have an update since then."

He glanced up and down the corridor and asked, "Is there a drinks machine round here? Somewhere you can go and grab a coffee or something?"

"There's machines on the ground floor by the waiting area. Do you need something, sir?"

"No, not for me, Helen. You go and get yourself a break. I'll sit with the Mathieson's and have a wee word."

"If you're sure?" he saw her hesitance at leaving her post and biting back a smile, he added, "Aye, I'm sure. If anything happens, I'll be right here and I won't leave till you get back. Promise."

She turned her head to glance at the Mathieson's and then replied,

"Okay, sir. I'll be back in about twenty minutes, if that's okay?"

"Twenty minutes," he smiled at her. "I'll see you then."

When she walked off towards the lifts, he approached the Mathieson's and lifting a plastic chair, turned it around to face them then sat down.

"Mister Mathieson, Missus Mathieson," he began, "my name's Charlie Miller. I work with Shona and I just want to let you know how dreadfully sorry that we all are that this has happened to your daughter."

The woman's eyes were red with weeping and she twisted a handkerchief in her hands while her husband's hand shook as Charlie reached across to grasp both their hands in his.

"We don't know why this happened and we don't know yet who did this to Shona, but trust me; we won't give up without finding out. The man in charge of the inquiry is a Detective Inspector called Alan Boyle. He's a good man and will do his very best to get you the answers you need."

"Thank you, Mister Miller," the older man stuttered. "We've two sons ands they're on their way here from England where they live, but Shona's our only lassie. Our pride and joy," his voice broke and he gasped.

He didn't hear the soft footsteps, but saw Mathieson's surprised glance behind Charlie turned to see the large and imposing figure of Martin Cairney stood at his back.

Dressed in a white shirt, maroon coloured tie and a navy blue pinstriped suit, Cairney placed a restraining hand on Charlie's shoulder to prevent him rising and said, "Stay where you are, Mister Miller. I'll just fetch myself a chair."

When he was seated, Charlie said, "Mister and Missus Mathieson, this is Mister Cairney, the Chief Constable of Police Scotland."

Warmly shaking their hands and with his usual booming voice lowered, Cairney softly said, "I apologise for intruding on this sorrowful time, but when I heard that your daughter was again enduring surgery, I felt the need to come here and offer you not only my support, but that of every officer and Force Support Officer who serves with your daughter. We in the police are a family and when one of us is struck down, we all feel it. Now," he glanced at Charlie, "I will assume that Detective Superintendent Miller will have assured you that everything that is humanly possible is being done and *will* be done to bring to boot the individual who did this."

"Yes," Mister Mathieson replied, his voice shaking.

Cairney nodded and continued, "While I do not personally know your daughter, I can tell you that I have read her personnel file and spoken with her colleagues and she seems to be a dedicated, remarkable and capable officer and a very popular young woman. A credit to both you and the Force she serves."

Charlie saw the comments cheered the couple a little, her fathers head rose just a touch with pride at Cairney's comments.

They sat for a while, the four of them, while Cairney regaled them with anecdotal stories of Shona and her police service, all gleaned Charlie suspected from either her personnel file or Cairney having taken the time to speak with her colleagues and once more, Charlie marvelled at the large man's care for the officers under his command.

They turned when they heard the tapping of Helen Wynd's boots on the linoleum floor as she approached them in the corridor and if she was surprised at the earlier arrival of a Detective Superintendent, she was more than shocked to see her Chief Constable seated alongside Charlie.

Pale faced, she came to attention and saluted Cairney who extending his hand towards the young officer, said, "Thank you, my dear, and you are?"

"Eh, Constable Wynd, sir. Helen Wynd," she stammered.

"Well, Constable Wynd…can I call you Helen?" he smiled as he towered over her.

"Eh, yes sir, of course, sir," she vigorously nodded.

"Well, Helen, Mister Miller and I will take our leave of you, but I'm certain Mister and Missus Mathieson will be in your good care. I assume you will contact your control room when there is news of DS Mathieson?"

"Yes, sir," she gulped as she stared up at him. "That's my instructions."

"Then we'll trouble you no further, Helen," he turned to the Mathieson's and shaking them warmly by the hand, nodded to Charlie that they leave.

With a smile and a discreet wink towards the young policewoman, Charlie followed Cairney along the corridor to the lifts.

****

They stood just outside the entrance foyer of the building, their hands in their trouser pockets and their breath making little clouds of steam in the cold air.

"It's times like this I sometimes regret giving up smoking," Cairney shook his head.

Charlie didn't believe the comment warranted a response, his attention taken by a liveried police Traffic car with two officers seated in the front seats parked twenty yards away on the access road.

Catching his glance, Cairney smiled and said, "There's little point in being the Chief Constable if I can't borrow the use of a company car for a lift now and then, is there, Mister Miller?"

"No, sir, I suppose not," Charlie nodded with a grin.

"I had Miss Mulgrew on earlier today. I gather your investigation into your cold case has ground somewhat to a halt? I say cold case," Cairney sighed, "but it's more of a multiple murder inquiry now, isn't it?"

"It's been getting that way, aye," Charlie nodded, "but I've still got a few lines of inquiries I want to pursue."

"Do you suspect you're after the same killer?"

Charlie shrugged and replied, "You know better than most , sir, that instinct isn't evidence, but to answer your question; yes, I do. I believe that even after all these years, Murdo Clarke's killer is cleaning up. Why?" He shook his head. "That I don't know yet."

Cairney nodded back towards the entrance doors and said, "I'm not surprised to see you here tonight, Mister Miller. You have an understanding of the staff who work for you that motivates them and earns their respect and loyalty. However," he lowered his head to stare at his feet, then raised it again and said, "there is a point you need to draw back. What happened to that young woman was not your fault."

Charlie almost smiled, recalling his earlier conversation with the Traffic sergeant, Cathy Pickering, then slowly shook his head and replied, "While I realise that I can't help think there is something that connects my inquiry with the assault upon her, sir."

"You know you must step back? Permit DI Boyle to deal with it?"

"I know that, sir, and yes. Alan Boyle is a good man; capable and tenacious, but if there's anything I can do to assist him, I will."

He didn't mean to sound disrespectful or so determined and when Cairney glared at him, he was about to apologise, but then the big man's face softened and sighing, he said, "And *that's* why when the body of Clarke was exhumed, I recalled you to operational duties to make the investigation into his murder for no matter what I or any other individual tell you or say, Mister Miller, you are one stubborn and strong-willed bugger. Please continue to keep Miss Mulgrew apprised of any developments in your inquiry," he unexpectedly clapped Charlie on the shoulder and turned to make his way towards the parked Traffic car.

****

Because he had turned and tossed for the early part of the night, Alan Boyle's wife had irritably banned him to the spare room, but now here he was standing in the rear porch of the house in his dressing gown having an illicit fag.

His head was spinning with the events of the day and though his team had worked their arses off, up and down the tenement closes in Dixon Road and the surrounding streets, they had not turned up one single witness who saw anything amiss on the morning Shona Mathieson had been attacked.

He hated to admit it, but he was stumped.

During his career in the CID and throughout his slow progression to the rank of Detective Inspector, he couldn't recall any inquiry where there were so few clues.

So few?

What the *fuck* was he thinking.

There were no clues at all.

If there was some indication for the motive of the attack on Mathieson, it might have given rise to who was responsible.

The obvious start was her ex-partner who she had apparently thrown out of her flat, but he was alibied by his estranged wife and teenage son, whose twin bedded room he had shared that night into the late morning.

The suspicion it might have been someone Mathieson had jailed was a reasonable start too and so he had been onto the Procurator Fiscal's office and retrieved copies of all the cases Mathieson had submitted to the PF for consideration of prosecution in the last two years and by God, there were a lot of them for it was evident she was a hard working detective.

Following that line of thought, two of his officers he had previously identified as good at paperwork spent almost sixteen hours sweating their balls off in a small office at Aitkenhead Road trawling through her cases. Everything from minor thefts to rape, housebreakings to attempted murder and even one case of abduction where the family tried to export their fifteen-year-old daughter back to Pakistan to be forcibly married off to a forty-year-old male cousin of the father. However, though some names were pencilled in for interview, there was nothing solid; no direct threats to get their revenge upon Mathieson.

He drew deeply on the cigarette, feeling the tobacco launch its way into his lungs, then spluttered for admit it or not, he wasn't the smoker he once had been. Now it was the occasional cigarette and turning to the fags only when he was worried or anxious.

"What should *that* tell me," he muttered to the night air then stubbing the cigarette out on the window ledge by the door, checked there was no update on his mobile phone and quietly made his way back to the spare room.

****

She couldn't sleep, but kept tossing and turning in the narrow, unfamiliar bed and guided by the slash of moonlight through the crack in the heavy curtain, frustratingly surrendered and got out of the bed with the intention of going downstairs to make a cup of tea. Lifting her mobile phone from the bedside cabinet, she saw it was almost two in the morning.

The bedroom, the smallest in the house but larger even than her Ferguslie homes front room, had been her brother Stephen's and remained as it was when their mother took them from the house. She reached down to switch on the bedside light with the Action Man shade and watched for a brief few seconds as the figures softly glowed. Yawning widely, she turned to stare at the Thomas the Tank wallpaper and then the the wooden toy box in the far corner with the rope handles.

She gazed with curiosity at the shelving unit that took up almost the whole of the opposite wall that was crammed with books, comics, toy cars, model planes, plastic action figures and boxes containing games; all of which were a little outdated in this IT savvy age, but eagerly reached for by the inquisitive and wide-eyed Connor.

Curiously, she had noticed that just as in her own former bedroom, there was not a trace of dust and wondered how many times her father had spent keeping both rooms so neat and tidy.

When she first led the wide-eyed Amy and the curious Connor into the bedroom her son's eyes had shone with delight, but he was soon crying then screaming for she would not for the time being permit him to play or touch the toys and he literally had to be carried from the room and the door tightly closed.

She didn't want anything disturbed till she took stock of what was there.

At least, that's what she told her daughter Amy.

The real reason was she felt like a stranger in the house that once had been her home and knew it would take time till she felt comfortable enough to make any kind of change or to disturb her memories.

In her faded Jason Donovan tee shirt, baggy beach shorts and bare feet, she tiptoed from the room into the hallway though there was no need to tread softly, for the thick, rich pile carpets prevented any noise.

The hallway was brightly lit by the upstairs ceiling light to permit some light to enter the slightly open door of her old bedroom where the children slept, for Amy did not want to be in complete darkness in the strange house.

Peeking in the door she saw Amy was fast asleep while Connor, his body akimbo, gently snored in the bed she had fashioned for him on the floor beside Amy.

She smiled, recalling Amy's fascination with the house and her pleasure when she told her that tomorrow, she needn't go to school, that with her mother they would spend the day exploring the house and the garden together and knew that Amy was desperately keen to explore the back bedroom, the room that seemed to have been used by her father as a study. Though she was not IT trained, she knew enough about computers to recognise the Apple Mac desktop and attached printer were expensive pieces of equipment, though how she was going to access the system without her father's password, she didn't know.

She turned with the intention of making her way downstairs, but some strange impulse stopped her and her eyes were drawn to the closed door of the master bedroom; the room where her mother and father shared their bed and once loved each other.

Or so she would like to believe.

She had considered immediately moving into the room, but changed her mind, telling herself that she needed to change the bedding and emptying her father's clothes from the built in wardrobe.

However, again the real reason was that she felt like an interloper. Yes, in time she would make the room her own, but certainly not for a few days or even perhaps weeks.

She had been in the room that afternoon, then closed the door over when she left so why did she have this desire to go in now, she wondered?

Stepping across the wide landing, she hesitated before opening the door and satisfied the light wouldn't disturb the children, switched it on when she entered the room, but immediately startled in fright and almost cried out in terror when she saw the figure in the window.

She breathed a sigh of relief and grinned with embarrassment when she realised it was but her own reflection in the glass.

Moving across the floor, she drew the curtains closed and then stopped dead; her eyes narrowed and her nose twitched at the unfamiliar fragrance, the faint smell of her father's aftershave that still lingered in the room.

This room, she had realised on her fist visit with the woman detective, Miss Mathieson, was changed from what she remembered and had been redecorated in bright colours.

It was light and airy with the large built in wardrobe occupying one wall, a queen size bed with a wooden slatted headboard and bedside cabinets at both sides of the bed with fashionable lamps on top. On the cabinet that was nearest the door lay a pair of reading glasses and what she guessed was a Kindle. At the foot of the bed was a wooden blanket box with a padded cushion on top. A free standing mirror was by the window and a freestanding chest of drawers with three large drawers and two smaller drawers was situated in the opposite corner.

She walked over to the chest of drawers and her fingers idly stroked at a wooden framed photograph. She involuntarily smiled. It was a professionally shot black and white photograph of her and Stephen, taken when she was aged about six years and he just four.

They were both laughing at the camera as though the photographer had told a funny story.

She couldn't help herself and felt the tears well up.

All those years her father had loved her, loved them both; loved them enough to keep their memory alive in the photograph so prominently displayed in his bedroom and wondered why he had never got in touch.

She pulled open one of the smaller drawers and saw it contained neatly folded underwear. The other drawer held socks, all paired together, though there were only about four or five pairs in the drawer and then recalled seeing the wicker basket next to the washing machine downstairs in the utility room.

He must have been intending doing his laundry, she smiled with sadness.

This is silly, she thought and shaking her head as though to clear it, was about to push the drawers closed when her eyes narrowed at the sight of a brown envelope laid flat at the bottom of the drawer beneath the piles of socks.

She was about to reach for the envelope and stopped as though she were a thief in the night.

She closed her eyes and thought, this is stupid; with her father gone, there was no reason why she shouldn't have a look inside the envelope.

Lifting it from the drawer she at first thought it empty, but then felt it contained a stiff sheet of paper.

Emptying the envelope, she saw it was not as she thought a sheet of paper, but a six by four-inch glossy black and white photograph.

Her eyes narrowed as holding the photo in one hand, the fingers of her free hand traced a line across her lips as she stared at the photograph and unconsciously backing towards the bed, sat down.

The photograph was of a couple from the waist up and she guessed was taken a number of years previously; the man in shirt sleeves with the cuffs rolled up to his forearms, his tie undone, his hair untidily plastered across his forehead and grinning drunkenly as he held a glass in one hand, a cigarette loosely held in the corner of his mouth and his other hand draped across the shoulders of the smiling woman who held a wine glass and whose eyes seemed to leap from the photo and bore into hers.

The man was clearly her father, just as she remembered him at the age when her mother took them from the house.

But who, she wondered, was the woman?

CHAPTER TWENTY-ONE

The sound of her mobile alarm going off was muffled, but still loud enough to stir her.

Slowly, Alison Baxter turned her head to stare at the sleeping Willie Baillie who lay on his back, his chest rising and dipping as he breathed and she gave a quiet thanks the big man wasn't a snorer.

Taking her time, she raised her hand to retrieve the phone from under the pillow and glancing at it, saw it was a few minutes after five in the morning and she inwardly cursed.

She had intended setting it for an hour later because she wouldn't have the lengthy journey from the police college, but in the heat of passion, clean forgot.

As slowly as she dared, she slipped from the bed, stifling a giggle at her nakedness and with a quick glance to ensure Willie was still asleep, tiptoed across the room to the door.

Wisely, she had left her overnight bag in the hallway and lifting it made her way into the bathroom.

Her toilet completed, she showered and ten minutes later was dressed in clean underwear and a fresh blouse, her collar length fair hair brushed back into a tight ponytail, makeup completed and returned to the hallway where through the slightly ajar bedroom door she could hear the electric shower running in the en-suite.

Risking a glance into the room, it was as she thought; the bed was empty.

She retrieved her skirt and shoes from the floor then stepping into the skirt, smiled and after zipping it up, knocked on the en-suite door and loudly called out, "Do you want coffee or tea?"

"You naked would be my first choice," she heard him reply, "but if that's not going to happen, tea would be nice, thanks."

"Tea it is then," she replied with a grin.

In the brightly kitchen, she stopped and glanced about her, marvelling at the neatness and style.

Willie Baillie, she decided, was a contradiction. He dressed like he was dragged backwards through a hedge, yet his home was spick-and-span and his choice of décor and furniture…well, she pursed her lips and nodded in appreciation; it was pretty tasteful and damn good for a man.

Searching through the cupboards and drawers, she found plates and cutlery and decided that some toast would do for them both.

In the middle of buttering the toast, Willie stepped in to the kitchen, his hair still damp and dishevelled from briskly rubbing at it with a towel. Wearing suit trousers, a clean white shirt with a tie hanging loosely around his neck as he buttoned the cuffs, she smiled when she saw he wore slippers.

He greeted her with, "Good morning."

She sensed he was embarrassed and keeping her face straight, said, "I take it you don't often have overnight guests?"

"Sometimes my nieces or my nephew will stay over if they've been out on the town and had a few drinks," he sat down on a stool at the breakfast bar, "and don't want to try and make their way back home to Ayrshire by public transport."

"I meant women."

"I know you did," he smiled and she was surprised to see he was...shy was her first thought.

Accepting the plate of toast, he solemnly added, "No. I do not have many female overnight guests."

"So, is that where you're originally from? Ayrshire?"

"No," he scoffed, "I'm a Govan lad born and bred. My brother and my sister moved down there when they married."

She handed him a mug of tea.

"What about you? Where are you originally from?"

The part of her that studied psychology realised what was happening.

Albeit they had just recently met, their questioning was a clear indication of their continuing interest in each other and so she replied, "My parents eventually settled in Morningside in Edinburgh. Do you know it?"

"I know of it," he smiled. "Money people, fancy houses and high tea in the afternoon with crumpet."

She slid around to his side of the breakfast bar and seductively run her forefinger along his thigh to his groin before she asked, "And am I *your* bit of crumpet, acting Detective Sergeant Baillie?"

He visibly gulped and taking a deep breath, replied, "I really, *really* hope so."

They continued to stare at each other, the silence broken when he said, "Maybe we should get a move on, eh?"

"You mean to work or in our relationship?" she teased, but was taken aback when he replied, "Work first, Alison, then I'd really like it if you would give some serious consideration to having a relationship with me. I *really* would."

****

Leaning across the bed in her cotton pyjamas, Sadie woke him with a mug of steaming hot coffee and whispered, "Try to be quiet. Neither of those wee devils are wakened yet and it means we might get ten minutes together."

He squinted through tired eyes and said, "I don't think I can manage ten minutes, sweetheart."

She grinned then pretending to scowl, replied, "It would take more than ten minutes to satisfy me, Miller, so get out of bed, drink your coffee while you're getting ready for work and I'll have some breakfast on the table when you come down."

He compliantly nodded, but his aching body really wanted to tell her that she should phone him in sick, that he needed another ten hours sleep.

When Sadie had left the room, he yawned and swinging his legs from the bed glanced at the digital clock while he massaged the stiffness from his shoulder.

"Bugger," he muttered then wearily stood and made his way into the en-suite.

Fifteen minutes later, Charlie was seated at the table while Sadie spooned scrambled eggs onto a slice of toast.

"I'm sorry I was asleep when you got in," she grimaced. "How late where you?"

"Just after two," he replied, smothering the egg in tomato sauce. "Cathy and I had fish suppers at Giffnock then I visited the hospital," and recounted his meeting with Shona Mathieson's parents and the visit by Martin Cairney.

He didn't say after he got home he'd spent another half hour reading a personnel file for he wasn't yet ready to disclose that little gem to Sadie.

"Any word how she is?"

"Hold on," he arose from his chair and going through to the hallway coat stand, fetched his mobile phone from the pocket of his jacket. "Forgot to take the bloody thing upstairs with me," he grumbled. "Maybe that's why you had a decent sleep; what there was of it, I mean," she replied.

He sat back down and opening his text messages said, "That was a text in from Alan Boyle just after four. Shona was out of surgery and back in the High Dependency, but it doesn't say how she is."

"Poor girl," Sadie sat down opposite, her hands nursing her mug. "I can't imagine what her parents must be going through."

"Are you going back to see your mum today?"

She grimaced and shook her head. "She didn't say anything, but I think my visit yesterday kept the whole issue to the forefront of her mind. I know she's got her club today at the church hall, so what I'll probably do is phone her and…" she hesitated.

"What?" he asked suspiciously.

"I was thinking of phoning the consultant, telling him my mother's not fit to receive any kind of bad news by phone and asking that when he has information, he phone our number here."

His eyes narrowed. "What about data protection? You might be Carol's daughter, but you're not the patient. He'll simply refuse."

"I *was* going to say I had her permission."

"Yeah, right," he scoffed and shook his head. "Like he's going to believe that old chestnut."

"Well, I'm going to try anyway," she huffily replied.

He grinned at her and said, "Good luck with that, but seriously. Maybe if you were to phone his secretary first for an appointment and visit him, let him know how concerned you are. You're more likely to persuade him face to face than by a telephone call."

"You think that might work?"

"I'm only presuming here, but he might want you to sign some sort of disclosure to safeguard himself about giving out his patient's information and let's face it, it won't work unless you try. Besides," he evilly grinned at her, "I know how persuasive you *can* be Sadie Miller."

She smiled and then her brow knitted when she said, "What if he wants another fee for seeing me?"

"Seriously? You're asking me to balance getting information about your mother's health against money?"

A lump formed in her throat and she knew again why she loved this man.

Getting up from her chair, she moved round to his side of the table and kneeling beside him, laid her head against him and softly said, "Try to come home early tonight, Charlie. I miss you."
****

It was Amy who holding Connor by the hand, shook her mother awake and asked, "Can I take him downstairs to the kitchen to get some breakfast?"

She guessed she had slept barely two hours, yet didn't feel as tired as she knew she should be.

Smiling at her children, she sat up and replied, "Why don't you take me as well. We've a lot to do today, haven't we?"

She reached out her hands and while the children laughed excitedly, allowed herself to be pulled from the bed and ignored the quilt cover falling to the floor.

Minutes later she sent the children to the conservatory to play and was filling three bowls with cereal.

After a quick glance into the larder cupboard and the fridge, she made the decision that other than the tinned goods, she would dump what food was there and use some of the new money in her account to go shopping.

That and with a guilty grin reminded herself to arrange for some car insurance.

Carrying the bowls on a tray through to the conservatory, she placed two on the tiled floor and settled herself into one of the bamboo chairs.

Watching her children eat their cereal, she thought again of the photograph she had discovered in the drawer.

When he had visited her at her Ferguslie home, she recalled Mister Miller the detective asking if she had any information about a woman who might have been involved with her father and made her decision.

Yes, that's what she would do, phone and speak with the woman detective called Mathieson who had been so nice and helpful to her. She'd call the detective and let her know about the photograph.
****

Feeling as though she had been given a second chance, Alice Brookes was determined that she would not let Mister Miller down, that she would strive to justify his confidence in her and her new lease of life commenced by being the first that morning into the office.

Walking around the incident room, she switched on the computers and the monitors and that done, sat down at the office manager's desk to sift through the early morning dispatches.

One brown envelope that had been sealed with sellotape she saw was marked 'Urgent' and 'For the attention of DC Baillie' with the Forensic Laboratory label stuck on the top left hand corner.

Placing the envelope to one side, she continued to check the mail.
****

He was driving to Giffnock when his mobile phone chirruped and pressing the hands free, said, "Charlie Miller here."

"Morning, Charlie. It's Harry Downes. Can you speak?"

"I'm on the road to the Giffnock office, Harry, what can I do for you?"

"I've had the press badgering me again about your officer, the lassie called Mathieson," she begun. "They're wanting to know how the investigation is going."

He was puzzled and asked, "You do know that it's Alan Boyle at Aitkenhead Road who's the SIO in that inquiry?"

He heard her express a number of expletives, mostly preceded with the word fuck, then interrupted her by asking, "Why did you think it was my inquiry?"

"Crossed wires, Charlie, but don't worry. I'll be kicking *somebody's arse!*" she bellowed the last two words and he assumed she was stood among her staff in the Media Departments general office.

"The last I heard was the receipt of text at four this morning from Alan," he said. "Is there any update on Shona's condition?"

"Not that I'm aware of. Sad to say the attack on DS Mathieson has provoked a host of interest and as usually happens in a case like this, the public wave of sympathy has caused support for the police to rise dramatically. A sort of positive PR for a very fucking negative issue. Don't ask me to explain it, but if she was an ordinary member of the public, the story would hit the headlines for a day then be forgotten, but because she's a cop…" she paused. "Well, you'll have seen it all before. The 'Glasgow News' is talking again about bringing back hanging and that's only for litter louts!"

He grinned and finished with, "That's me pulling into the yard, Harry, so like I said; Alan Boyle's your man. Nice speaking to you." As he switched off the engine, he glanced over to see Alison Baxter placing a holdall into the boot of her car and when she turned, he lowered his head and pretended to be removing the key from the ignition.

Getting out of the car he saw her striding towards him a smile on her face.

"Morning, Alison."

"Charlie," she nodded to him then in a low voice, added, "Don't take up poker. You'd be crap at it."

"Poker?"

"You're face is a dead giveaway, Mister Miller," they began to walk towards the rear entrance door. "Remember I told you about the five types of liars?"

"Yes," he slowly replied.

"Well, you couldn't comfortably fit into any of those categories," she said and stepped through the door.

****

Willie Baillie had arrived minutes before them and greeting Alice Brookes at her desk, was handed the brown envelope with his name typed upon it.

Curious, he tore it open and extracted the single sheet of paper from within.

His eyes widened as he scanned the report and slowly exhaling, he muttered, "Well, I never."

"Morning, Willie, can you…" Charlie greeted him, but stopped when Baillie thrust the report at him.

Staring at the men in turn, Alison Baxter's eyes narrowed she watched Charlie read the report, then she asked, "What?"

It was Charlie who replied, "Remember the cigarette butt that was discovered underneath Murdo Clarke's body?"

"Yes, of course."

"Well, Archie Young at the Lab managed to positively match a DNA sample to the DNA from the saliva they extracted from the butt."

"And," she could feel her stomach tense.

Charlie sighed and glancing at Baillie, said, "Frankie Colville."

****

The wall phone in the kitchen rung and answering it, she replied,

"This is Missus Donaldson, Miss Mulgrew. I'm sorry, but my husband had a late night last night and…"

"Well," she nervously replied, "if you insist. Please hang on, I'll just be a moment."

Leaving the phone hanging by its cord, her legs were shaking as she hurried up the stairs, then knocking on her husband's door, could feel her heart racing.

There was no response.

Readying herself, she took a deep breath and rushed in. The smell of whisky and body odour, mostly expelled from her husband's arse, struck her like a gloved hand and gagging, she said, "Gerald. It's the phone for you."

Flopped across the bed, he didn't stir until a little louder and leaning forward, she said, "Gerald, dear. It's the phone! Miss Mulgrew, your boss!"

"Whatsat? What?" he raised his head from the pillow and stared drunkenly at her with red rimmed eyes. He loudly burped and even at three feet, his breath was so foetid she almost gagged.

"It's Miss Mulgrew! On the phone!" she lifted the hands free and handing it to him, quickly stepped back and out of his reach.

He shook his head then slowly took it from her and said, "Hello? Who the *fuck* is this?"

"Good morning, Detective Chief Inspector Donaldson. It's Detective Superintendent Mulgrew. Are you in…" she paused, "a position to understand what I'm saying?"

Still half drunk, he was conscious enough to recognise the dig and snarled, "I'm not pissed if that's what you're fucking implying! What do you want?"

"At this time, Mister Donaldson, you have been verbally suspended. Under the terms of your suspension, you are required to sign the official personnel forms to confirm you are aware of the conditions of your suspension. Therefore, at midday today and prior to your attendance in two days at the Sheriff Court on the charges of drunk driving, assault and breach of the peace I require you to attend at Govan police office, Helen Street, to sign the said forms. Do you understand, Mister Donaldson?"

"And what if I tell you to go fuck yourself, Miss Mulgrew?"

His wife stared in horror as she listened to his vulgarity and recognised the signs that he was becoming dangerously angry.

Afraid that after the call ended she would be subjected to his violence, she turned and quickly left the room.

"Oh, I forgot," he sneered. "You're a rug muncher, aren't you Mulgrew? You don't like the cock, do you? So, as for coming in to sign some pishy forms, like I said; go fuck yourself!"

On the other end of the line, Mulgrew bristled at his crudity, but calmly replied, "I'll accept you are under stress and because of that I'll ignore your offensive language, Mister Donaldson, but just to remind you; until such times you are convicted by a court, you *are* a serving police officer. As your supervising officer, I am ordering you to attend at Govan office to sign the forms and should you refuse to obey such an order and fail to do so I will instruct that the pay office freeze your salary. One last chance, Mister Donaldson. Will you attend or do you continue to refuse my lawful command?"

His nostrils flared and his eyes narrowed.

That this fucking *split-arse* should tell him, a *real* detective, that she could order *him* about?

Bitch!

Teeth gritted, he roared, "I'll be there!" and threw the phone across the room to clatter against the door of the wardrobe where the plastic back came off and the batteries bounced across the floor.

Downstairs, his wife, listening in to the line, carefully replaced the wall phone handset into the cradle and decided that it was time to collect some shopping and stay away until he had left the house.

****

He commenced the morning briefing by disclosing Archie Young's finding of Colville's DNA on the cigarette butt.

"Right then, people," he clapped his hands together, but he already had their attention. "Let's review what we know so far. We've got Murdo Clarke murdered by person or person's unknown; however, we now know that Frankie Colville either buried Clarke's body or was present when he was buried. Was *he* Clarke's killer?"

Charlie shrugged. "If he wasn't then he most certainly did know who was. James Dougrie, Clarke's handler. Murdered the day after Clarke's body is discovered. Did he know something about the killer and had to be silenced? Was it Dougrie who murdered Clarke? Was it Colville who murdered Dougrie and if so, why and it also means there was an association between Dougrie and Colville. Can we prove that association?"

He paused to let the questions sink in then continued.

"Before we knew about the cigarette butt with Colville's DNA, he was interviewed by us as a prospective witness and possible suspect to Clarke's murder. Does the cigarette butt indicate he killed Clarke? Later that day he too is murdered. Was it to silence him to prevent him from telling us what he knew? Is there someone we have yet to identify who is killing off the 'Four Minute Gang' members? If so, why?"

He stared around the room and taking a deep breath, asked, "Well? Has anyone picked up on the little issue of Colville being the man who buried Clarke?"

The silence was broken when Alison Baxter raised her hand and nodding to her, he said, "Tell us what is now very obvious, please Alison."

"If Murdo Clarke was already dead before Frankie Colville was arrested at the Renfrew robbery, then two things occur to me. Either he provided the information to James Dougrie about the intended robbery in Renfrew *before* he was murdered and that throws Dougrie's timeline about receipt of the information into dispute or two; because Clarke was already dead it therefore begs the question…" she paused, "who provided Dougrie with the information?"

"Exactly," Charlie nodded then said, "Willie. You've something to add?"

"Didn't you tell us in your first briefing about Clarke's widow, Stacey Clarke, trying to claim the reward money for the information? And if I recall correctly, you said it was refused, that she couldn't claim it because the information was allegedly provided by Murdo Clarke. Now, it seems to me the only person who knew the truth of where the information came from *must* be James Dougrie. What's the odds that he and Stacey were colluding?"

"And that would infer that they were aware of her husband's murder and if nothing else, that Dougrie was dirty."

A further silence fell among the team, broken when Charlie, his voice lowered but still strong enough to be carried across the room, said, "We have three murders, the first twenty-eight years apart from the recent two. What we need to do is find the *recent* connection that ties the three dead men together. We also need to track down

Clarke's widow, Stacey Clarke, to find out what she knows and if she *is* the link between them."

To uproarious laughter, he grinned and added, "I don't know about you guys, but it's giving me one hell of a headache trying to keep track of all this."

He called for silence and pointing to Alison Baxter, he asked, "Want to share what you learned yesterday, Alison?"

Addressing the team, she recounted her visit to Clarke's daughter, Mhari Fraser and ended with, "…so we're looking for a woman who might have reverted to her maiden name, Morton and who if my arithmetic is correct, is about fifty-seven years of age. I'll get onto the Department of Works and Pensions and try to trace her through their records."

"Right," Charlie said, "anyone got anything to contribute or any questions?"

An analyst raised her hand and said, "It's just a thought…" but then blushed.

"Go on," Charlie smiled encouragingly at her.

"Well," the young woman nervously began, "if Stacey Clarke or whatever her name is now is over fifty, there's a chance she might have applied to the railways for her 'Over Fifty' discount card. My mum did and she had to provide her address."

There was a stunned silence, then the team broke into laughter. Blushing furiously the young analyst stared at the floor, but then Charlie raised his hands and calling for silence, loudly said, "Cracking idea."

Staring around the room, he added, "And that's exactly what I want to hear. Every option investigated."

He smiled at the young analyst and said, "Well done, hen, that's what I like to hear. Thinking out of the box, again. I want you to take that on board and telephone the railway office that issues that type of discount card with what information we have and see what you can come up with."

Wide-eyed, the young woman eagerly nodded.

Tony Muirhead raised his hand and asked, "Is it possible, sir, that the cigarette butt was deliberately left there to implicate Colville by a third party, the real murderer I mean, who dropped it in the knowledge it would incriminate Colville."

Charlie nodded before slowly replying, "I've given that some consideration, Tony, but there's two things that seem to dissuade me from that line of thought. The first is, Murdo Clarke was buried in a shallow gave in a remote field in darkest Lanarkshire. If this was an attempt to implicate Colville, I believe it would have been far easier to do so by leaving the body someplace more accessible where it would be easily discovered. My second reason is that in nineteen-eighty-nine, DNA profiling was in it's infancy and if I recall correctly, we in Scotland didn't have our own DNA database and all sampling had to be sent with a CID courier to Scotland Yard. Even then, I think it took about six weeks or so for a result, so thank God for today's technical developments," he grinned. "That and I suspect that your average ned wouldn't have known anything about DNA. How does that sound to you?"

The young detective nodded and feeling a little foolish, blushed.

"However, don't be dissuaded from questioning what seems like straight forward evidence, Tony. I like the fact that you're also thinking out of the box, so keep doing that," Charlie smiled at him. "Okay, regarding our colleague and friend, Shona Mathieson," his face was grim. "I regret there is no news…"

The phone on Alice Brookes rung and answering it her face paled and she quietly said, "Can I take your phone number, Missus Gibson and I'll get somebody to call you back?"

Meanwhile, Charlie continued with the little he knew of Mathieson's condition and when he finished, dismissed the team.

Beckoning Alice Brookes, Willie Baillie, Alison Baxter and Tony Muirhead to him, he asked them to join him in his office.

"Grab a chair or stand if you prefer," he said then lifted his mobile phone to read an incoming text that said: *You're on.*

"Right, folks, here's what we need to do today," he began.

"Before you begin, sir," Brookes had her hand raised. "During your briefing, I took a phone call from James Dougrie's daughter, Missus Gibson." Her face paled. "Actually, she asked to speak to Shona Mathieson, but I didn't say anything about…" she shrugged, "well, you know. Anyway, she's moved into her father's house and called to say she's found a photograph of her father and another woman she doesn't recognise. She wondered if it would be of interest to you."

"Did she say when or where the photograph was taken?"

"Sorry," Brookes flushed. "I didn't ask."

"No matter, Alice," he waved away her embarrassment.

He glanced at Baxter. "Alison, you and young Tony obtain an Action from Alice and take a turn up to visit Missus Gibson to have a look at the photo. Might be nothing, might be something."

"Sir," she nodded.

"Willie. I want you to concentrate today on trying to discover who this mysterious CID officer is that Tommy Craig told us about. Use any of the team who are not otherwise engaged in other Actions. If he exists, find this guy."

"Roger that," Baillie nodded, then asked, "What will you be up to today, Boss?"

Charlie stared keenly at him before replying, "I'll have my mobile phone with me in case I'm needed, however, DI Alan Boyle will be popping by. Him and I have a little job on."

****

They were in the car with Muirhead driving when he asked, "This job the Boss has on with DI Boyle. Do you think it's anything to do with Shona Mathieson?"

She considered her response, then said, "I don't doubt it, but the fact he didn't say that tends to make me think he doesn't want us to know, so the less thought I give it, the less curious I'll be."

"In other words, it's none of my business?"

"My," she smiled, "for a young guy, you're really quick off the mark."

At last they were stopped outside the house in Belmont Drive and getting out of the car, saw that Jessica Gibson was stood in the porch with the front door open.

"Morning," she smiled then asked, "I thought it might have been Miss Mathieson who was coming to see me?"

Muirhead glanced at Baxter who took the lead and replied, "About that, Missus Gibson. Can we step inside and maybe you can put the kettle on?"

Fifteen minutes later and seated at the kitchen table with a pot of tea while her daughter Amy and Connor watched cartoons in the adjacent back room, Gibson shook her head and said, "That's awful. The poor woman. I hope she pulls through. And you haven't caught the man yet that did it?"

"We don't know if it *was* a man. We're still making inquiries," Baxter replied, then wishing to divert Gibson's mind from the shocking news, asked, "How are you settling into your father's home?"

"Oh, it's all a bit strange at the minute," she sighed. "There's so much to do. Not the house," she glanced about her at the bright kitchen, "there's not a lot to do with that. I mean, well, I keep thinking it's still his house with all his things here. I suppose I'll need to start thinking about clearing his stuff away, but it seems such a heartless thing to do. Does that make sense?"

"I know what you mean," Muirhead replied for them both with a soft smile. "When my dad died, my mother resisted me and my brother and sisters' attempts to have a clear out; she felt it was kind of betraying him." He took a breath then continued, "We finally persuaded her that there are people who would benefit from his old clothes, people who normally wouldn't be able to afford good quality clothes and she finally agreed to donate all his things to a charity shop. Funny," he smiled, "after it was done, she admitted she felt a great relief."

She didn't immediately respond, but simply stared at him then said, "Thank you. I think you've just made my mind up for me."

"This photograph you phoned in about," Baxter interrupted. "Can we see it please?"

"Oh, yes, of course," Gibson got up and left the kitchen, returning a couple of minutes later with the brown envelope from which she extracted the photograph. Handing it to Baxter, she said with a touch of humour in her voice, "I found it of all places in my dad's sock drawer."

Staring at the photograph, Baxter's eyes widened and turning it back and forth, was surprised at its excellent condition and apparent newness.

She asked, "Was it hidden?"

Taken aback by the question, Gibson shrugged, "No, I don't *think* it was hidden. Put away, maybe, but if dad wanted to hide it I suppose there are better places to do that than under his socks. The furniture in my dad's bedroom isn't that old or at least it doesn't look that old. My mother hasn't been in this house for a very long time, so I can't imagine why he would even feel the need to hide the photo. Why do you ask?"

"Because, Missus Gibson, I've already seen this photograph or I should say, half of it. The woman in the photo with your father has been identified as Stacey Clarke, the widow of a murdered man called Murdo Clarke."

****

He shouted again for his wife, but there was no reply and in his dressing gown, stomped down the stairs to find her.

Continuing to call her name, he searched the ground floor rooms, but it was clear Sylvia wasn't in the house.

Bitch, he thought, snatching at the handwritten note on the kitchen worktop to read that she had gone shopping, that there was bacon in the fridge if he wished to make himself a sandwich.

Angrily, he crumpled the note and flung it to the floor.

Getting his breakfast made was *her* fucking job, not his, he fumed. After all, wasn't *he* the breadwinner in this house?

With both hands on the worktop supporting him as he leaned forward, he thought again of Mulgrew's phone call and teeth gritted, he grinned.

It was another set-up, of that he was certain, for that was why she had asked if he was sober.

His car had been brought from Govan yard by a recovery company and it now lay in the driveway, but likely Mulgrew expected him to drive to Govan office and undoubtedly on the way there, he would be pulled by a Traffic car and again breathalysed.

Well, he was too fly for the bitch and sniggering, decided he'd order a taxi instead.

But first, he stared at the kettle, some strong coffee.

****

Seated behind his desk reading the resulted Actions, Charlie Miller sighed.

There was just nothing coming in that indicated who the killer of Dougrie and Colville might be.

His mobile phone activated and glancing at the screen, saw it to be Alison Baxter.

"On your way back?" he asked.

"Not for a while, Charlie, but I have some positive news," and told him of the photograph.

"Anything on the back that might tell us when or where it was taken?"

"Nothing and that's what puzzles me," she replied, but didn't explain.

"So, it's James Dougrie who is in the missing half of the photograph we have of Stacey Clarke. Okay," he rubbed at his forehead, "it implies they were socially familiar with each other, but the photo itself doesn't confirm a sexual relationship. Were they a couple?" he posed the question. "After all, it might even have been her husband Murdo who took the photo. Anyway, you said you're not coming back for a while?"

"James Dougrie used one of his bedrooms as a study and there's a top of the range Apple Mac in there. Missus Gibson can't get it opened up, but young Tony is a bit of a computer geek and is going to have a go. They're up there the now. That and I have something I want to check out."

He didn't ask, but said, "If you believe you're on to something take all the time you need. It's about time we got a break anyway," he sighed.

His door knocked and Alan Boyle entered the room and was about to speak, but stopped when he saw Charlie was on the phone.

"Right, Alison, I need to go. Keep in touch and let me know how you get on with the computer."

"Alan," he greeted his old friend.

"I got your message, Charlie. What's going on?"

He stood and grabbing his jacket from the back of the chair, replied, "We'll take my car and I'll explain on the way."

****

Willie Baillie was seated at his desk and idly thinking of his night with Alison Baxter when a voice beside him said, "Penny for them." He turned a little embarrassed to see the young analyst at his elbow, who said, "That's a phone call for Mister Miller, but as he's not here…" she didn't continue, but stared expectantly at Baillie who sighed and asked, "Who is it?"

"A lassie from the Cooperative Funeral Service."

"What? Am I dead?"

"What?" she was confused.

"I'm kidding, hen," he smiled at her and made his way to the desk where the phone lay off the hook.

"Hello, DS Baillie," he said, the new acting rank still sounding strange when he used it.

"Hello, it's Marie from the Cooperative Funeral Service. I'm calling about the service arrangements for a Missus Elsie Colville?"

Bemused, Baillie initially thought it was a windup, but then clicked and asked, "Is that Francis Colville's wife you mean?"

"Was his wife, *you* mean," the woman replied. "The woman's dead."

"Oh, aye," he stifled a grin. "How can I help you?"

"Well, Mister Colville was making the arrangements, but our information is that *he's* now died. He was Missus Colville's next of kin and we don't have any details of any other next of kin. We were told by Aitkenhead CID that your office is dealing with his death and wondering if you might have the next of kin details?"

He recalled the son and daughter who discovered Colville's body and replied, "Well, yes, we do have a son and a daughter's name and address, but I don't have them to hand. Can you give me your phone number and I'll phone you back? Marie you said it is?"

"Aye, that's me. Bloody nuisance this is," she moaned, and rattled off the phone number.

He smiled and making casual conversation, said, "Surely in your job you must have hiccups like this?"

"Oh, all the time. Laying the deceased to rest is literally straight forward, but it's dealing with the other parties that can be a nuisance."

"Other parties?"

"Aye, you know, like the families, the ministers, the celebrants, the caterers, people like that."

"I take it by dying, Mister Colville let a lot of people down," he dryly said.

"Oh, aye, he did. I had the bloody humanist on giving me a right load of grief because when he turned up, Mister Colville wasn't in and even after he'd specifically arranged to see the man. Used to be one of your mob too, so he was."

There was a pause before she added, "Or at least I *think* he was."

Baillie's eyes narrowed and he asked, "Do you know when the humanist arranged to meet Colville? The time and date I mean?"

"No, I don't have that information, but you could ask him yourself if you want."

"You have his name and phone number?"

"Oh, aye, give me a minute."

"No, tell you what. I'll get Mister Colville's son's details and you can give me the information when I ring you back."

He ended the call and staring at the phone, wondered; could it be that easy?

****

Jessica Gibson led the two detectives into the small bedroom her father used as a study.

Alison Baxter's first impression of the room was that of a man cave, with prints on the walls that included scenes of the Coliseum in Rome, commercially printed drawings of Roman soldiers, maps of the ancient Roman Empire and framed photographs of Roman architecture. One wall was shelved and filled with dozens of hardback books of all shapes and sizes.

While Tony Muirhead leaned forward to switch on the computer, Baxter run her fingers lightly across the spines of the books, her curiosity arisen by the large volume of historical stories of old Rome, Romanic history and legendary Roman figures.

"Seems like your dad was quite an admirer of Rome," she smiled at Gibson.

"Another thing I didn't know about him," she replied with a slight trace of sadness.

Seated in front of the Apple Mac, Tony Muirhead tapped the keyboard to open the password box and biting at his lower lip, lightly run his fingers across the polished surface of the old mahogany desk.

"This is an absolute cracker," he referred to the desk.

Stood watching him from behind, Jessica Gibson and Alison Baxter smiled at his comment.

"Right then," one by one, he began opening the three drawers on each side of the desk and peering in.

"What are you looking for?" Gibson asked.

"My experience is that most folk, particularity those of a certain age," he turned and squinted at Baxter who reached forward to lightly cuff the back of his head, "tend to write down their passwords in case they forget them and stick them to the inside of a drawer. However," he sighed, "not on this occasion."

He turned in the swivel seat to face Gibson and asked, "Jessica. Spelled as it sounds?"

"Yes," she slowly nodded.

"Can never tell with names these days," he mumbled and added, 'We'll start with that."

They watched him type in 'Jessica,' but the screen failed to open. "Let's try it all upper case," but that also failed.

"Now lower case," he murmured and to their surprise, the screen opened with a panoramic highland scene and the scroll bar at the bottom of the screen. A number of folders were stacked along the left side of the screen identified with names such as 'Utilities', 'Photos' and 'Expenses' and other titles.

Muirhead grinned and inwardly surprised at his success, cockily said, "Then there's the users who choose a password that's familiar and easily remembered."

Beside her, Baxter saw Gibson pale and hug her arms tightly about her.

She placed a comforting hand on her shoulder as Muirhead continued, "I'll start with the calendar."

Opening that month's dates, he sat forward as he peered at the screen.

"It looks like your father wasn't a regular user of the calendar other than this one date," he remarked. "If you don't know this system, on that date he's marked the computer will remind you with a pop-up about your entry," he added almost to himself.

With a start, Baxter saw it was the same date that James Dougrie was murdered and said, "Can you open that date, Tony? See what the appointment was?"

Muirhead double-clicked the day and the short typed note disclosed: 15.00pm. SL visiting.

A couple of hours prior to the time of the murder, Baxter realised and seeing Muirhead's face, saw that he also realised the significance of the entry.

So, she thought, Dougrie was expecting someone to call that afternoon, but who the hell *was* 'SL?'

Muirhead clicked on the folder titled 'Photos', but to their surprise there was just one photograph in the folder; a tight group of a dozen men and women of mature years in formal evening wear smiling at the camera, none of whom were Dougrie.

"Odd," Baxter muttered as she stared at the photo.

"Do you really need me here for this?" she turned to see tears in Gibson's eyes and shaking her head, replied, "No, maybe you might want to go and see if your children are okay. We'll get on here with what we need to do."

When Gibson had left, she asked Muirhead, "If you can open the Internet will you be able to find his recent search history?"

"No problem," he confidently replied and set to work.

While he did so, Baxter glanced at the printer and then glanced at the photograph in her hand.

"Tell me, Tony," she interrupted him. "Do you think that printer has a memory? I mean, what it's recently printed out?"

"It's a top of the range bit of gear so likely it will have, yes, That," he pointed to the front of the machine, "and it's got a digital screen so it should be able to tell us what was printed. I mean like it will say doc for a document; that sort of thing."

"Switch it on and let's have a look."

Minutes later after the machine warmed up, Muirhead had a thought and leaning forward, said, "That's glossy photographic paper in there; not print paper."

She felt a tinge of excitement and replied, "Can you print out the last item that was printed off?"

"Here we go," he said and pressed a button on the control panel. Seconds later, a six by four-inch exact copy of the photograph Baxter held in her hand was discharged by the machine.

"You're thinking he just recently received that photo," Muirhead stared from the printed copy to the one in her hand.

"Yes, I do and *if* I'm correct," she stared at the computer, "it either arrived by e-mail or he's copied it from a social media site. The question now is, my geeky computer expert, can you find the photo on his computer and who sent it?"

CHAPTER TWENTY-TWO

It was just ten-thirty when he stopped in Crompton Avenue almost one hundred metres from Gerry Donaldson's red, sandstone semi-detached house and switched off the engine.

In the passenger seat beside him, Alan Boyle angrily said, "So, you're telling me, though you won't disclose how you came by this information, that Gerry Donaldson, a Police Scotland Detective

Chief Inspector is a suspect for the attempted murder of Shona Mathieson? Fuck me, Charlie, have you lost it completely?"

"All I need is for you to trust me on this, Alan. You know me from old…"

"Aye, when you were hitting the bevvy," he snarled. "Is that what this is? The rot has finally addled your brain? Jesus, Charlie…"

"Look, I know how it sounds and if it was me getting told the story…"

"What *fucking* story! You haven't told me anything other than to trust you!"

"I know, but…"

"Trust goes two ways, Charlie, so why are you *not* telling me how this guy came to be a suspect?"

"To *protect* you!" he angrily turned to face Boyle, then calmer, continued. "If this goes ape-shit, you can truthfully say that you were ordered to accompany me to Donaldson's house, that I did not explain my actions, but that you *did* question my motive. Okay?"

Boyle stared hard at him, then his face broke into a grin and shaking his head, said, "Still the same old Charlie Miller. Trying to keep everyone safe. Okay, we'll do it your way. I know that you have a good reason if you suspect this guy, so I'll go along with what you intend. However, do not expect me to fire you in if as you say this goes ape-shit and the rubber heels come knocking at my door. We've been friends for too long, Charlie, and stupid git that I am; yes," this time he nodded, "I do trust you."

Charlie sighed with relief and asked, "Do you know Donaldson?"

"Only by reputation and that's been all bad. He'd left Stewart Street before I got there."

They sat in silence for a few minutes and then Boyle asked, "How do you know for certain he is going to leave the house?"

Charlie didn't reply, but just smiled prompting Boyle to comment, "Yeah, I know. You're protecting me."

"See, I knew you'd trust me," he continued to smile at Boyle.
****

Willie Baillie wrote down the name and address and replied, "Thanks, Marie," then ending the call strode across to Alice Brookes desk and said, "Raise me an Action to interview a man called Malcolm Quinn at this address and I'll fill in the blanks when I get back."

He thrust the slip of paper at her but before turning away, added, "I'll be on my mobile if you need me."
****

She waited impatiently while Tony Muirhead worked his magic then at last he said, "Don't know if it's of any significance, but on a number of occasions in the recent past, Dougrie visited the Facebook page for his local branch of the RPOA."

"The what?"

"The Retired Police Officers Association. Are you not signed up with them already," he cheekily asked and earned himself another cuff to the back of the head.

"Hey, that's getting to be a habit with you and that big bugger Baillie," he growled.

"Then don't be such a cheeky wee shite," she responded, then leaning across his shoulder, asked, "Can you bring the page up?"

He did so and she could see that the site boasted a gallery of numerous photographs.

Pointing to the page, she selected a group and said, "Can you bring up those photos?"

Clicking the mouse, an array of photos became available and as Muirhead scrolled slowly through them, Baxter called out, "Stop! There," she pointed to a photograph comprising of a group of half dozen men and women who were all formally dressed and stood tightly together while a number of men and women, similarly dressed in evening wear, were being escorted behind the group by a liveried member of staff. According to the attached comment the photo described the group of a dozen as former Strathclyde Police detectives and was taken just over a week previously at a charity dinner held in the City Chambers in Glasgow.

"That's the same photo that's in the folder," she mused. "I wonder now, why would he keep that one separate?"

"Right now I don't know, but you away and fetch us both a coffee and let me get on with trying to find where that photo of Dougrie and Stacey Clarke came from...*mum*."

She pretended to raise her hand but that crack, she smiled, she let him have.
****

It was Boyle who saw the woman first and nudging Charlie, pointed along the road and said, "What's she up to?"

He stared to where Boyle indicated and quietly replied, "If memory serves correctly, I think that's Woodlinn Avenue she's coming out of."

His eyes narrowed as he watched the woman, then baffled, said, "I might be wrong, but it looks to me like she's hiding, the way she keeps glancing around the corner."

Minutes later, a black Hackney cab passed them by and stopped outside Donaldson's house. They heard the cab's horn sound then watched as Donaldson, wearing a dark coloured raincoat, exited the driveway and got into the cab that then drove off in the opposite direction.

Switching on the engine, Charlie said, "Okay, let's go and see...."

But Boyle placed a restraining hand on Charlie's arm and said, "Hold on a minute. Look, that woman's came from round the corner now and unless I'm mistaken, she's crossed the road and she's heading for Donaldson's house."

They watched the woman who wore a rain jacket and a headscarf and carrying a shopping bag, entered the driveway out of their sight. With a glance at Boyle, Charlie drove the Volvo forward and stopped outside Donaldson's driveway.

****

The tall, distinguished man who answered Willie Baillie's knock upon his door invited the detective into the front room of the detached house and suggested they take a seat.

Declining tea or coffee, Baillie said, "I'll get right to the point and ask, Mister Quinn. Are you by any chance a serving or former police officer?"

"No," Quinn smiled, "but I am a former fireman, Mister Baillie. Thirty-four years service and I retired as a Station Officer."

"And you now work as a Humanist at funerals?"

"I'm also available for weddings or children naming ceremony's too," he smiled before adding, "and the occasional Bar Mitzvah."

He saw Baillie's eyes narrow and grimaced, "That was a joke."

"Oh, aye, right."

"Can I ask, is that why you have called to see me? About a Humanist ceremony?"

"Yes and no," Baillie sighed. "A few days ago, did you have an appointment to meet with a Mister Colville at his home in Hardie Avenue in Rutherglen, sir?"

"Yes," Quinn frowned, "but even though he suggested the time of the visit, he wasn't at home. I have to admit I wasn't best pleased."

"And did you glance into the front window of the house before you left?"

"I did, yes. Is that some sort of problem?"

Baillie smiled then asked, "And do you own a black coloured car?"

"Yes, I do. A Ford Focus, but my wife's currently out in it, getting the shopping. What is this all about?"

"A Ford Focus, just like the models the CID use," Baillie mused. He smiled and eyes bright, continued, "There isn't a problem, Mister Quinn, but before I explain maybe I will have a cup of tea after all."

****

The consultant glanced at the note pinned to the clipboard then down at the patient.

It was the persistent bleeding that worried him.

The woman had already experienced surgery twice and it was his opinion that to subject her to a third procedure was far too dangerous.

He turned to the registrar and curtly said, "Continue with observations only."

Then to the registrar's surprise and with an uncommon display of sensitivity, the consultant leaned across and gently touching the woman's hand, softly added, "And say lots of prayers."

****

When Sylvia Donaldson answered the knock at the door, she was still wearing her overcoat.

After identifying themselves, she stared at Charlie and Boyle in turn then raised a hand to her mouth and nervously said, "My husband's not here. He's already left to go to Govan office, Mister Miller."

"It's not Mister Donaldson that we've came to see, Missus Donaldson. It's you," he replied, then with a smile, added, "May we come in?"

It suddenly occurred to her that Gerald would not be pleased that she had admitted two of his colleagues without him being present, but then with an uncommon surge of courage, she nodded and replied, "Yes, of course."

It was when the large man with the scar on his cheek stepped over the door that her courage failed her and she felt her knees weaken and holding onto the door, for one awful moment thought she might faint.

"Are you okay, Missus Donaldson?" the man called Boyle stepped forward, his hands outstretched to catch her, but she waved him away into the front room and stuttering, excused herself with, "If you take a seat, I'll just get my coat off and the kettle on."

In the kitchen as she slipped the coat off to lay across a chair, she took a deep breath, wondering why the detectives had called upon her when they must know that Miss Mulgrew had asked…no, she permitted herself a small smile, *ordered* Gerald to attend at Helen Street office.

She took a moment to calm herself and glancing at her hands, saw they were shaking. Drawing a deep breath, she filled the kettle and while it boiled, set the tray with three cups and saucers, a bowl of sugar, jug of milk and a plate of tea biscuits, all the while continuing to wonder why Mister Miller and his colleague had called to see her. Patting at her hair, she took a breath and lifting the tray, returned to the front room. Sat on the edge of the armchair nearest to the door and trying to sound as confident as she could, she said, "The tea will soon be ready, gentlemen. Now," she gulped, "what can I do for you?"

"Missus Donaldson, has your husband informed you that he is currently suspended from duty?"

Her heart raced and she held her hands tightly in her lap before she replied, "No, not specifically, though of course I knew there was something amiss. Gerald tries to protect me from his work related issues."

She forced a smile then unwilling to be caught in a lie, added, "However, I learned this morning that he was to…report," her head nodded, "into his office at Helen Street to sign some forms. I *assume* that's what you mean, Mister Miller?"

He could see she was frightened and he disliked what he was forcing himself to do, what needed to be done. Staring at her he knew the clock was ticking and he had no other option but to go for it.

"I have a very specific reason for asking this, Missus Donaldson. Has your husband ever struck you?"

Her eyes widened and she flinched as though Charlie himself had slapped her across the face.

There was now a palpable tension in the room, the atmosphere so electric that Alan Boyle dared not breathe and casting a sideways glance at him, wondered what the hell was Charlie up to?

From the kitchen they could hear the kettle whistling, but nobody moved.

"No, of course not," she stuttered then added, "Why would you say or think such a thing?"

"Then the complaint made eighteen months ago by your youngest daughter, Sally I believe her name is, of domestic abuse against you by your husband. That's not true, Missus Donaldson? Sally was lying?"

Sally!

She had threatened to report Gerald when she visited and found her mother in the kitchen with a bruised face and weeping, the evening meal splashed across both Sylvia and the wall

My God, Sally, she thought, her nerves beginning to shred; do you realise what you have done?

"Is…" she took a deep breath. "Is that why Gerald has been suspended, Mister Miller? Because if it is, that's not what happened. What happened was…"

He raised his hand to stop her and shaking his head, said, "No, Missus Donaldson, that's not why your husband was suspended. Mister Donaldson was charged with drink driving and assaulting the two female officers who arrested him."

He paused and then with his head slightly to one side as though curious, slowly and quietly asked, "He seems to have some sort of issue with women, doesn't he, Missus Donaldson?"

She was now visibly shaking and her voice low and edgy, asked, "Why are you here? Why are you telling me this? Why are you…"

He raised his hand for a second time and calmly replied, "Because, Missus Donaldson, it is my belief that your husband has done something far worse than assault you and we need your help."

****

The Hackney turned into the drop-off bay outside the front entrance to Helen Street office and stopped.

Getting out of the cab, Gerry Donaldson, still in a foul mood, threw a ten pound note through the window to the driver and snapped, "Keep the change."

Banging the door closed behind him, he didn't hear the driver mumble, "Forty pence? Aye, I'll take the wife and weans abroad for a week with that, I will and goodbye to you to, ya ignorant shite!"

Mounting the four steps to the imposing entrance, he pushed through the blue framed glass doors and into the wide entrance hall.

The face of the young and pretty red-haired female sergeant who stood alone behind the four-foot high counter that was more formally known as the uniform bar, was familiar to him.

It was Katie something he thought but he couldn't recall her surname and marching up to the counter, barked, "Open the door. I'm here to meet with Cathy Mulgrew."

The sergeant smiled and cheerfully replied, "It's Mister Donaldson, isn't it? Take a seat please and I'll inform Miss Mulgrew you're here."

"Take a seat?" he was outraged. "Do you know who the *fuck* I am?"

"Yes, of course I do," she smiled sweetly and replied. "You're the Detective Chief Inspector of this Division who is currently suspended from duty and barred from entering any police office unless specifically invited. That also means you are *not* permitted to freely wander this office, but will wait here until you are called for. So, like I said, *sir*, take a seat."

"Listen, you red-haired *bitch*," he hissed at her, "don't come your shite with me! I'm not wasting my time hanging around here, so open that fucking door *now*!"

She didn't immediately respond, but met his gaze and taking a deep breath before then slowly exhaling, the sergeant paled then replied, "You *will* take a seat until I'm ready to deal with you, you fat, drunken misogynist and if you use that kind of language against me again…" her hands were flat on the bar as she leaned forward and snarled at him, "I'll be over this bar quicker than shit off a shovel and dragging your sorry arse into a cell. Now fucking-sit-*down* when I tell you!"

Stood in the brightly lit control room that was directly behind the uniform bar, Cathy Mulgrew smiled at the CCTV monitor as she watched Gerry Donaldson's face turn crimson and for one brief second thought he was about to have a heart attack.

A moment passed then he turned and stomping back across the foyer floor, he slumped down onto a plastic chair and petulantly crossing his arms, stared at his feet.

Turning to the large, well built man from the Police Standard Unit who wore the dark grey business suit and stood behind her, she said, "Give it ten minutes, Chief Inspector, then bring Mister Donaldson to what used to be his office. Thank you."

****

She was still shaking though forced a smile for the sake of her daughter Amy who suspected that the police people who had arrived that morning at their door were not there with good news.

"Are we going to have to go back to our old house, mum?" she asked, the disappointment evident in her eyes.

"No," her mother reached for her, "of course not. This is where we live now. Whatever made you think that?"

Before Amy could respond, the door opened to admit Alison Baxter who made a comical face and said, "He's thrown me out of the room. Said if I came downstairs and asked, you might make us a coffee, Missus Gibson."

"Yes," she rose to her feet, "of course. I'm sorry, I should have asked earlier when you…"

"Are you sending us back to our old house?" Amy cut in.

Baxter stared at the little girl then turning to her mother and frowned. Returning to stare at Amy, she replied, "Why would we do that, Amy? This is your home now, isn't it? Don't you like it here?"

Amy, her eyes brimming with tears, quickly nodded.

"She's a little worried that you are here to evict us," her mother tried to make light of Amy's question.

Baxter glanced from her mother before crouching down to smile at Amy and said, "Amy, you're eleven now, aren't you?"

Again, Amy nodded.

"And I suppose your mum has told you a bit about your granddad and the bad thing that happened to him?" she turned her head towards Gibson, who tight-lipped, slowly nodded.

"Well, me and the other detective upstairs are a part of a team who are trying to find out who did that to your granddad. Please, *please*," her face screwed to emphasis her voice, "believe me when I tell you that this is your home now for as long as you and your mum and your wee brother over there want to stay here."

She smiled towards Connor who oblivious to what was going on, played happily with some action figures.

"I know you also have a big brother who is eighteen and is in the army, isn't that right?"

"Yes," Amy took a deep breath and nodding, wiped at her eyes with her sleeve. "His name's Alex and mum says we're all very proud of him."

"I'm sure you are," Baxter smiled. "Now, wouldn't it be a nice surprise when Alex comes home to find his sister knows everything about this big house and you can take his hand and show him to his own room?"

Smiling now, the little girl shrugged, the fears of returning to her old home now gone.

Rising to her feet, Baxter turned to Gibson and with a wink, said, "Why don't you get the coffee on while I tell Amy all about being a police officer."

Upstairs, Tony Muirhead had slipped of his suit jacket and tie undone stared frustratingly at the screen.

Though Muirhead considered himself to be a bit of a whizz kid when it came to computers and in time hoped to transfer to the Information Technology Forensic Unit at the Crime Campus in Gartcosh, no matter what he tried he couldn't find a way to access James Dougrie's e-mail address and finally accepted that he needed help.

Fetching his mobile phone from his coat pocket, he scrolled down to find the number of his geeky mate, a civilian Force Support Officer and fellow nerd who worked within the ITFU at Gartcosh.

"Hi, Brian? It's me. I need a bit of help, here. Have you got a couple of minutes?"

"What's doing, bud?"

Without disclosing details of the investigation, Muirhead explained his problem trying to access the Apple Mac's e-mails, but halfway through his explanation, was stopped by Brian who said, "Whoa, there, bud. Do you know what you're asking me to do? What you're asking is illegal without a warrant. For Christ's sake, I can't just give you that information and *especially* over a bloody mobile phone!"

"It's a time critical investigation, Brian," Muirhead smoothly lied, "and I have the verbal authority of the SIO, Detective Superintendent Miller."

Mentally crossing his fingers, he hoped that Brian wouldn't check that out, but was surprised when Brian, sounding a little excited and with his voice lowered, asked, "You said the SIO is called Miller. Is this about that murdered guy they dug up out in Lanarkshire, the case that's been in the papers? Bloody hell! It's the talk of the Campus here!"

Seizing on his mate's curiosity, Muirhead loftily replied, "Aye, but *I'm* not supposed to talk about it."

"You're not supposed to talk about it, yet you want me to break the sodding law?" Brian hissed at him.

Realising he had erred, Muirhead suggested, "Look, do me this one favour and we'll have a pint and I'll let you know what going on in the investigation, but you have to swear you'll keep it between us, okay?"

Holding his breath, he asked, "Deal?"

There was a distinct pause before he heard Brian loudly exhale and reply, "Okay, it's a deal, but for heaven's sake never, *ever* reveal what I'm about to do for you. Now," he could hear Brian breathe heavily, "give me your computers IP address."

Less than ten minutes later, an anxious Muirhead accepted the incoming phone call and grinning, entered the information that Brian disclosed.

Less than a minute later he began to scroll down James Dougrie's recent incoming and outgoing e-mails.

****

Feeling pretty pleased with himself that he had tracked down the mysterious detective mentioned in Tommy Craig's statement, Willie Baillie was whistling loudly to the song playing on the car radio while making his way back to Giffnock office when his mobile phone indicated an incoming phone call.

Pulling over to stop by the side of the road, he glanced at the screen to see it was Charlie Miller calling.

"Hello, Boss," he cheerfully answered the call.

"Willie? Are you out and about?"

"I'm in the car and was heading back to the factory, but I've stopped in Kilmarnock Road just about a couple of hundred metres away from Shawlands Cross. Do you need something done?"

"Right, do you know Compton Avenue in Simshill?"

Baillie's eyes narrowed and he asked, "Is that off Carmunnock Road?"

He heard the question repeated to Alan Boyle and heard Boyle confirm it was, then Charlie said, "Yes, that's correct."

"Okay," Baillie unconsciously nodded, "I've a rough idea where it is then."

"Right," Charlie continued, "for the purpose of continuity of evidence, can you get yourself here as soon as possible? I want you to take something out to Archie Young at Gartcosh for immediate analysis. I'll phone ahead and tell Archie to expect you."

Baillie glanced at the dashboard clock and said, "Depending on the traffic, I should be about ten, maybe fifteen minutes. Okay?"

"That's fine," Charlie replied. "Just don't kill yourself or anyone else getting here."

"Roger that, Boss," Baillie grinned and ending the call, pulled out into the line of traffic.

****

Sat behind the desk, Cathy Mulgrew, her long copper-red hair piled into a fashionable bun and wearing a tan coloured blouse and light grey coloured skirted suit, looked every inch like the smart and intelligent Detective Superintendent she was.

The Divisional Commander had offered Mulgrew the use of his own office for the meeting, however, she had declined. Following Gerry Donaldson's obscene description of her gender preference she had instead decided to have her own little retribution. Inwardly admitting that he had indeed needled her, nevertheless she decided to rub the bastards nose in it and humble him by having Donaldson attend the meeting in what had been his own former office.

The door knocked and she took a breath to ready herself for what she already knew would be his hostility, but paused for a few seconds before loudly calling out, "Come in."

The door was opened by the PSU Chief Inspector who stood aside to permit Donaldson to enter the room.

Indicating the chair that she had placed in front of the desk, she said, "Pleased sit down, Detective Chief Inspector."

He stared venomously at her before striding across the room to wordlessly do as she said.

The Chief Inspector moved to stand in one corner, his shovel like hands folded in front of him and close enough to move against Donaldson if he became violent, for Cathy Mulgrew was no fool. Though she did not physically fear Donaldson, she was aware that anything said or done in the room required corroboration and was not foolish enough to place herself in a situation where without such corroboration, Donaldson could make an allegation against her.

"You understand why you are here, Mister Donaldson?" she began.

"Aye, you threatened me on the phone that if I didn't come to sign your fucking form, you'd stop my salary and place me and my wife in dire straits," he snapped back at her.

Ignoring the fact that he was completely wrong, she lifted a sheet of paper from in front of her and laying it before him, continued, "I require you to read and sign this document."

He bent his head as though to read it, then seconds later snapped his fingers and holding his hand towards her, grunted, "Pen!"

She gave him that little victory and reached across the desk to hand him a biro.

She watched as he signed the form with an arrogant flourish then to her surprise, flinched slightly when he threw the pen back at her, striking her on the chest.

The Chief Inspector took a step towards Donaldson, but she quickly raised her hand to stop him.

"Anything else I can do for you, rug muncher," he leered at her.

Her face paled at the sneered insult, but she forced herself to smile and decided not to give him the satisfaction of reacting before replying, "That will be all, Mister Donaldson. You may go."

He stared malevolently at her, his hands bunching into fists and she could see the murderous intent in his face.

She continued to stare him in the eye and fought to restrain herself, her hands clasped on her lap beneath the desk, her knuckles white, for she wanted nothing more than to raise her skirt above her knees to enable her to leap across the desk and pound his fleshy face to a pulp.

Instead, forcing her voice to remain calm, she said, "Chief Inspector, please show Mister Donaldson out and by out, I mean walk him to the front door of this building and ensure he leaves Helen Street police office. A man of his apparent character is no longer welcome in this office."

It was a minor taunt, but she could see it in his eyes that her comment hit home and turning, he tried to muster some pride and swaggered out of the door.

To her surprise, the burly Chief Inspector turned towards her as he left the room and with a nod, winked at her.

When the door closed she permitted herself a smile at the Chief
Inspectors apparent approval of her restraint then lifting her mobile
phone from her handbag, scrolled down the directory for Charlie
Miller's number.

CHAPTER TWENTY-THREE

Standing in the porch of the house, Charlie Miller saw Alan Boyle
hand the ASDA plastic shopping bag to Willie Baillie, who nodded
and returned to his car.
His mobile phone activated with an incoming text that read:
On his way to you now.
Turning to Sylvia Donaldson, he said, "Your husband will be home
in about fifteen minutes, maybe even sooner, Missus Donaldson.
Can you quickly pack a bag and have you somewhere to stay
overnight, perhaps two nights?"
Her brow creased and her lips were pale with worry. Nodding, she
replied, "Do you really think it's necessary for me to leave my home,
Mister Miller?"
"I regret that your husband might not be in the best of moods when
he comes home, Missus Donaldson and I only suggest for your own
well-being…" he stopped then staring at her, his shoulders slumped
as nodding, he continued, "Yes, I believe it is necessary you leave
and right now."
He watched the indecision in her eyes then as if accepting that what
he suspected might occur to be true, she replied, "I only need to grab
some nightclothes. I mean, I can come home tomorrow or the next
day, can't I?"
"I think so, but like I said, pack for two days just in case. DI Boyle
and I will wait here and drive you to wherever you need to go."
"My daughter lives in Paisley. He won't go there. Her husband
doesn't like Gerald. He isn't…"
She stopped, realising she was about to divulge a family secret and
tell Mister Miller that her son-in-law also knew of Gerald's violence
towards his mother-in-law and he wasn't afraid of her husband, but
still that grain of loyalty to Gerald, the man she once thought she
loved, remained with her.

She swallowed with difficulty, still find it difficult to comprehend what Mister Miller had told her, at what she was doing, then nervously said, "If you can drop me at the railway station…"

He raised a hand to interrupt her and said, "I won't hear of it. We'll run you to Paisley, Missus Donaldson. It's the very least we can do. Now…" his eyes widened and taking the hint she made her way towards the stairs.

He turned at the sound of Willie Baillie driving off and was joined in the porch by Alan Boyle.

"Cathy sent a text. I reckon he'll be here in about ten minutes, fifteen at best."

He nodded to the stairs and said, "She's packing a bag then we'll run her to her daughter's house in Paisley."

Boyle nodded and replied, "God, Charlie, I'm finding it all hard to believe and already I'm trying to work out in my head how I'm going to explain this in my report."

"You've always been…," he grinned, "creative, in your reports, Alan. I'm sure you'll find a way."

Boyle returned his grin and eyes narrowing, asked, "Do you think Archie Young will find anything?"

Charlie slowly exhaled and replied, "I hope so. We've done our part, so it all hinges on him now."

He glanced at his wristwatch and then walking to the bottom of the stairs, placed a hand on the banister and called out, "How are you getting on, Missus Donaldson?"

"Be with you in a a couple of minutes," the faint voice called down. Returning to stand with Boyle, the DI growled, "She's cutting it bloody fine."

"I know, but we can't leave her here."

A few minutes later she appeared at the top of the stairs.

Hastily Boyle joined her when she was halfway down to take the black coloured, rigid plastic cabin suitcase from her and usher her down the stairs.

"I'd better lock up," she began to fumble in her handbag for her house keys, but then Charlie asked, "Does your husband have his house key with him?"

Her eyes narrowed in thought, but then widened when she said, "I was out at the shops, so he must have them because the door was locked when I got home."

"Good," he snapped and taking her by the arm, hurried her along the driveway to the Volvo parked outside.

Opening the rear door, he helped her into the seat while Boyle, lifted the suitcase and placing it in the boot and out of her earshot of Sylvia Donaldson, hissed, "Must have brought the bloody kitchen sink too." Charlie sniggered and getting into the driving seat started the engine and pulled away from the kerb.

As he increased speed he saw a black Hackney cab in his rear view mirror and as he watched, saw it stop outside the house.

With relief he muttered, "We cut that fine," before adding, "Right, Missus Donaldson. Where to?"

****

Called back to the study by his shout, she peered at the screen over the top of Alan Muirhead.

"I found this e-mail with the photograph of Dougrie and Stacey Clarke as an attachment," he smugly told her.

Patting him on the shoulder she replied, "I'm impressed. How the hell did you manage to get in?"

"Oh, it was a wee bit difficult, but nothing I couldn't handle," he boastfully lied, deciding the less Alison knew, the better.

"Right, let's see," she murmured. "The date confirms he received the e-mail a couple of days before he died and the sender is…" she paused, her eyes narrowing as she read:

reliquitutebatur@hotmail.com

"I don't know what went wrong," he pointed to the sender's address and said, "but it looks like the name of the sender has been corrupted."

"No," she slowly shook her head and smiled in understanding, "it's not a corruption. I left my handbag downstairs. Give me your pen and a piece of paper."

Puzzled, he did as he was asked and leaning onto the desk, Baxter wrote: '*reliquit utebatur*' and showed him what she had written.

"Oh, you think it's two words. What does it mean?"

"Well, my Latin's a bit rusty," she grimaced, "but if I recall correctly from my Catholic schooling and unless I'm way off the mark, it means left-handed."

"Left-handed? What kind of name is that?"

"I don't think it's a name. I think it's a description," she sighed and glancing at the books of Rome on the shelf, added, "and again, unless I'm mistaken, it's a description that James Dougrie would recognise."

She slapped him on the shoulder and with a smile, told him, "You did well to get his e-mails open, Tony, but will you be able to track who sent it?"

He shook his head and replied, "Sorry, but that kind of skill is way beyond me, Alison. If the Boss wants to progress it any further, he's going to have to get a warrant and turn it over to the IT Forensic boys at Gartcosh."

"Pity," she shrugged, "and you were doing so well."

A thought occurred to her and narrowing her eyes and twisting her mouth in concentration, she said, "There *is* one more thing I'd like you to check, Tony. Can you bring back that Facebook photograph, the one of the retired police officers at the City Chambers?"

"Yes, but why?"

"Just a feeling," she replied.

He did as she requested then Baxter asked if he could enlarge the photograph. Copying it to the desktop, Muirhead was puzzled and said, "What is it? What do you see?"

She leaned closer and with a satisfied smile, pointed a manicured finger at the photo and said, "There."

****

Passed quickly though the Gartcosh security doors by the uniformed commissionaires who were expecting him, Willie Baillie hurried up the stairs to the Forensic laboratory with the ASDA bag clutched firmly in his hand and panting furiously, rung the bell at the lab door.

It was Archie Young himself who opened the door and staring at the plastic bag, asked, "Is this pizza a home delivery?"

"Aye, very good," Baillie breathlessly replied and added, "and this time I'll be hanging on to take the stuff back with me, so I suggest you get a move on, pal."

****

After leaving Alan Boyle at his car in the yard, Charlie Miller made his way to the incident room to be greeted by Alice Brookes who said, "There's an update for you, sir, from DC Baxter. She requests that when you're at your desk, you give her a call on her mobile."

"Right, anything else?"

"Willie Baillie phoned in a few minutes ago to say he's got the result you wanted and is en route to Aitkenhead Road to drop the stuff off, but didn't say what it was. He said you'd know?" her face expressed her curiosity.

She jumped back in alarm when Charlie punched the air and shouted, "Yes!" then his face reddening, with a broad smile he apologised.

"Eh, I'll be in my office if you need me, Alice," he left her wondering what was going on.

His first call was to his wife, Sadie, who reminded him that no news was good news and admitted her phone call to book an appointment with the consultant was a waste of time.

"The first appointment was in two weeks' time, but by then mum will have had some sort of result, I expect," she huffed.

"Well, look on the bright side," he tried to sound cheerful. "The consultant told your mum if the lump proved to be malignant, he'd phone right away. This is the third day and she hasn't heard anything; so, isn't that good news?"

"I suppose so," she quietly replied before asking, "How are things with you?"

"Getting better," he cheerfully said then finished with, "Got to go, sweetheart. I'll try to get home a little earlier this evening."

"If you can, please do. I miss you."

"Miss you too and give the weans a hug from me," he ended the call. His next call was to Cathy Mulgrew to inform her about the visit to Sylvia Donaldson.

"Was it worthwhile?" she asked.

"I believe so, yes. One of my guys, Willie Baillie, is now heading back from Gartcosh and on his way to Aitkenhead Road to meet with Alan Boyle, so hopefully you will hear from Alan a little later this afternoon."

"You have no idea how much I look forward to his call," she replied. He grinned and asked, "Was it difficult?"

"Very," was all she said before ending the call.

Scrolling down the directory, he phoned Alison Baxter and asked, "Looking for me?"

"Yes, sir," she formally replied and he realised she was travelling in a car and presumed with young Tony Muirhead.

"I've placed you on speaker, sir. We're on our way back to the office, but I thought you might be interested to know that the photograph Jessica Gibson discovered of her father and Stacey Clarke was sent in an e-mail to Dougrie a couple of days before he was murdered."

"You managed to get into his e-mails?" Charlie was impressed.

"Actually, it was good work by Tony, sir," she glanced at the young detective. "Our problem is that we don't know who sent the e-mail and according to our resident geek here," she reached across to ruffle Muirhead's hair, "we'd need a warrant to obtain that information."

"Yes, of course," Charlie agreed, but inwardly thought damn, before asking, "Is there any indication who might have sent the email? Any previous e-mails from the same address?"

It was Muirhead who replied, "No, sir, but Alison had an idea and I checked through Dougrie's outgoing e-mails and the day before he received the photograph, he sent a *different* photo to a company website; a photograph that he had in a folder on his computer. I've printed off a copy of the photo and I've got the company's details as well. We're bringing them back to the office now."

"What's the significance of the photo and the company?"

There was a pause before Baxter replied, "We'd like to explain that when we see you, sir."

"Then I look forward to your return, DC Baxter," he ended the call and smiled in anticipation.

If Alison Baxter thought it important then fingers crossed, it was and again was pleased that though she had no previous CID experience he'd the foresight to bring her onto the team.

****

The three detectives had been sitting in the chill of the CID car for over an hour, waiting on the go ahead from their boss.

"I'm bursting for a pee," said the brawny detective in the driver's seat.

"You shouldn't have drunk all that coffee right away," his neighbour in the passenger seat nodded to the extra large, now empty McDonald's disposable cup at his feet. "You'll need to hold onto it. You can't go ducking into any hedges around here. You'll have the polis on us," he grinned at his own humour and continued to sip at the hot coffee from his own regular size beaker.

In the back seat, the third and youngest member of the team of three grunted in his sleep, then loudly passed wind.

"Dirty bastard!" the front seat passenger used a folded 'Glasgow News' paper to fan the foetid air then coughing, gave in and opened his window.

The mobile phone in his jacket pocket rung and squirming in his seat to fetch it out, he inadvertently knocked the newspaper against his McDonald's cup, spilling some of the scorching hot liquid onto his thigh.

"Shit!" he almost jumped from the seat while the younger man stifled a grin.

The commotion woke their colleague in the back who drowsily asked, "What the fuck's going on?"

The call stopped then almost immediately rung again, but this time with his phone in his hand and dabbing at his soaked thigh with his handkerchief in his other hand, the detective answered, "DS Graham, go ahead."

His two colleagues sat in pensive silence and when the call ended, he glanced at them in turn and with a grim smile, said, "Right, it's a go. Let's go and get him."

****

Willie Baillie knew that he really should be getting back to the factory, but decided to linger in the CID office at Aitkenhead Road, sponging coffee and biscuits from the CID clerk while he waited and sharing some craic with the inquiry team assigned to catch Shona Mathieson's assailant.

An air of expectancy hung in the air and even though some of the team were now off duty, they were reluctant to go home and either found excuses to stay on or just simply refused to leave.

The phone on the clerks' desk rung and the room fell into silence as the male and female detectives watched him snatch at it.

"Yes," they crowded around and heard him say, then saw him nod. Replacing the hand set, he turned to the room and smiled, "They've got him. He's downstairs going through the charge bar and being signed in on a Section 14 detention."

****

Equally pensive about what was happening in Aitkenhead Road, Charlie Miller wished he was there, but knew that staying out of it was the correct thing to do; it was Alan Boyle's inquiry and as the SIO, Boyle had primacy in all aspects of the investigation.

His thoughts were disturbed when his door knocked and opened to admit Alison Baxter and Tony Muirhead.

"Okay to come in, sir" she asked.

After waving them both in and indicating they sit, Alison began by handing Charlie the photograph of James Dougrie and Stacey Clarke.

"And you say his daughter found this," he waved the photo, "hidden in his sock drawer?"

"Yes," she nodded.

His eyes narrowed as in thought, he asked, "If Dougrie lived alone, why would he feel the need to hide this photo?"

Baxter shrugged before replying, "I don't think he placed it in the drawer to hide it. I believe he just wanted it out of his sight."

"What do you mean?"

"Well, if he wanted to hide it or even dispose of it he could have done a better job, but I'm of the opinion the photo reminded him of a shameful period in his life and for reasons better known to himself, he decided to keep the photo handy, perhaps to bring it out now and again to look at and to punish himself. I mean, every time he opened the drawer the photo was there to remind him of what he did."

He stared keenly at her before replying, "You mean you believe he was having a clandestine affair with Stacey Clarke and the photograph is a reminder of that? An affair he was ashamed of? An affair that cost him his marriage and his children?"

"That's my considered opinion, yes," she nodded.

Baxter continued, relating how Muirhead had successfully broken into Dougrie's Apple Mac computer and of learning that on the day he died, Dougrie had a 3pm appointment that afternoon with an 'SL', though there was no further information about either who 'SL' was, why or where the appointment was to take place.

She related Muirhead's success in opening Dougrie's e-mails and discovering the photograph sent from the Hotmail address *reliquit utebatur* and her translation as left-handed. Continuing, she told him of Dougrie's apparent fascination of all things Roman and her belief the Latin phrase would have been easily translated by him and thus it was likely he would have known or at least have guessed the identity of the sender.

"Go on," Charlie nodded.

"Tony?" she turned to the younger man.

Trying to curb his enthusiasm, he laid a photograph in front of Charlie and explained, "This is a photograph of a group of retired Strathclyde Police detectives attending a charity dinner at the Glasgow City Chambers and taken about a week before James Dougrie was murdered, sir."

"Yes, I see that," Charlie agreed, recognising some of the the municipal building's famous marble and granite pillars in the background of the photograph.

Muirhead's excitement was infectious as he continued, "After we discovered the incoming e-mail with the photo of Dougrie and Stacey Clarke, Alison had me check Dougrie's outgoing e-mails and I discovered that the photograph of the retired detectives had been sent a day earlier by Dougrie to a company's head office e-mail address," and almost with a flourish, laid a piece of paper on the desk in front of Charlie with the company name written upon it.

"Unfortunately," he frowned, "we don't know the recipient was in the company that the e-mail was intended for."

Peering at it, Charlie raised his head and staring at Baxter, he asked, "This word, 'Sinistra'? Is that the name of the company?"

"Yes, sir, it's Latin again," Baxter smiled. "It means left."

"Left," he slowly repeated, before asking, "What kind of service does this company provide?"

Acting almost like a double act, it was Muirhead who replied, "The e-mail address gave me a website address and we discovered the website is for a chain of hairdressing salons that according to the website are located throughout the central belt of Scotland."

Charlie's eyes widened. "And Murdo Clarke's widow Stacey, we were told, was a hairdresser."

He glanced from one to the other when he asked, "Do we know anything about this company from the website? Who owns it or anything like that?"

Muirhead shook his head before replying, "The website gives information about the services provided and their salons, sir, but no personal information about management or employees. However, we have their head office details here in Glasgow city centre, but," he glanced at the wall clock, "I expect they'll be closed for the day now."

"It's interesting though that this 'Sinistra' is a hairdressing company," Charlie mused, "that we know Stacey Clarke is or *was* a hairdresser and though maybe we're jumping the gun a bit here, there's the strong possibility that the killer of Murdo Clarke and the killer of James Dougrie was left-handed."

He stared at them in turn and with a slow smile, said, "Good work, you two."

"Oh, we're not finished, sir," Baxter grinned widely and glancing at Muirhead, nodded that he continue.

The young detective, trying hard to contain his excitement, said, "Alison asked me to blow up the Facebook photograph of the retired detectives, sir, and this is what we found."

Muirhead had discovered larger size photographic paper in the lower drawer of the desk and laid an A4 photograph in front of Charlie.

Leaning forward, Charlie could see that it was a cutaway section of the of the City Chambers photo of the retired detectives, but enlarged and showed the faces of only three of the detectives.

Muirhead added, "The quality of the print is excellent and though I'm no photographic expert, I can only suppose the image resolution is because it's an Apple printer."

With a tolerant sigh, Baxter muttered, "He's a computer geek, Mister Miller, just ignore him."

Puzzled, he glanced at the photo then back at Muirhead who grinned and suggested, "Ignore the detective's faces, sir. Check out the other guests behind them."

Charlie again examined the photo and peered at the heads of some of the guests passing behind the detectives. His eyes widened and he nodded in understanding.

The glamorous blonde woman who smiled as she turned her head towards the cameraman was an older woman, perhaps in her mid to late fifties, but the years had been kind to her for she was still very attractive and looked remarkably like the woman in the black and white photograph he had seen of Stacey Clarke.

He took a breath and said, "I'm surmising you believe Dougrie has been trawling the Facebook photo's and seen the woman who he thought was Clarke in the background of the retired officers photograph?"

It was Baxter who took up the explanation when she replied, "Yes, sir. Before we came back to the factory, I phoned the City Chambers and spoke with their administration office. We had the date of the charity function from the Facebook photograph and we learned that tables for that evening were purchased by a number of companies as well as groups like our retired detectives. It was a long shot we thought, but asked for the names of the companies who had purchased tables for the function. Among the companies was notably 'Sinistra' and of course we recognised the name from the outgoing e-mail."

"Did the woman intimate if Dougrie or anyone else had also asked for that information?"

She smiled and replied, "It seems that a Detective Inspector Wallace from Stewart Street police office, or so the caller had claimed to be, called a couple of days after the event to make that very inquiry."

Charlie nodded as he smiled. "You're going to tell me there is no DI Wallace at Stewart Street?"

"Correct," she nodded.

She permitted the information to sink in then continued, "According to the woman I spoke with she has a list of the company personnel whose names featured on the booking list. It's our assumption that Stacey Clarke was one of the guests at the 'Sinistra' table and we also believe that the woman in the group photo is in fact Stacey."

She paused then continued, "When I asked the woman at the City Chambers for the name of the 'Sinistra' individual who *booked* the table, she told me it was she who took the booking and was able to recall it was booked by a member of the 'Sinistra' staff on behalf of a Missus Livingstone."

"Livingstone? Not Clarke?"

"No, sir," she shook hear head, "which made us wonder how Dougrie came to associate Clarke with 'Sinistra'?"

He sighed and replied, "I presume when he was provided with a list of the company names, *you* believe that Dougrie recognised the name 'Sinistra' and with it being a Latin word and translated as 'left,' you also believe he associated it with this woman he thought was Clarke."

He chewed at his lower lip before adding, "And that seems to indicate Dougrie *did* recognise her as Stacey Clarke and sent the e-mail to the company with the group photograph as what, bait to let her know she'd been spotted and to elicit a response?"

"That's our assessment, yes, and hence the return e-mail with the photograph of them both. Perhaps as a reminder of happier days," she shrugged.

He paused then muttered, "Livingstone. The 'SL' appointment for the day he was murdered. Stacey Livingstone perhaps?"

She glanced at Muirhead and nodded, "We were thinking the same thing."

"Well," he glanced at the wall clock, "there's no point in continuing to guess when we can go tomorrow morning to visit 'Sinistra' and find out."

He suddenly grinned and added, "Did I say earlier good work? I should have said outstanding work. Now, get yourselves out of here and be bright and early tomorrow morning, for you're both coming with me to find out exactly who this Missus Livingstone, query 'SL' is."

****

He sat behind the desk in the square, windowless and claustrophobic interview room, ignoring the tangible smell of body odour and other bodily secretions that seemed to permeate the very walls.

Idly he glanced at light grey painted walls, the paint peeling from the corners and the dull unpolished linoleum floor and wondered how many hours through his career he had spent in such rooms.

He licked at his dry lips and realising he was parched, was about to loosen his tie and open the top button of his shirt, but stopped. He did not wish to present himself as fatigued, aware the man he was preparing himself to face was a man well used to such places as this foul room and who Charlie Miller had described in three words as arrogant, conceited and cunning.

A man who would see any sign of weakness as an opportunity.

And so, parched or not, he would for now tolerate the insufferable heat.

His eyes narrowed with the realisation that this interview was likely to be one of, if not *the* most important interview of his career and he was determined it would be short and very positive.

When the door knocked he took a breath before loudly called out, "Come in."

The door was opened by DS Mark Graham, a rugby playing monster of a man who greeted him with, "I have Mister Donaldson with me, sir, if you're ready."

Stepping into the room, Graham beckoned forward Gerry Donaldson while the detective behind Donaldson remained in the corridor as Graham closed the door.

"Good evening Mister Donaldson," he stared up from his chair and and greeted him. "Please take a seat, sir."

"This is a fucking outrage," Donaldson hissed at him, his eyes bloodshot and bubbles of spit sliding from the corners of his mouth. "How *dare* you send three of your goons to my home to bring me to this shithole! I might be suspended but I'm still a Detective Chief Inspector and you *will* stand when I'm addressing you! What the *fuck* were you thinking of?"

His nose twitched for he could smell the alcohol as soon as Donaldson had entered the small room and determined that he would not retort to any abuse, for he knew it was a tactic and to do so would disrupt his planned interview.

While Donaldson continued to stand, DS Graham stood behind him and ready to intervene if he became violent.

He ignored the sullen man and pressed the button that started the tape machine then calmly intoned, "I am Detective Inspector Alan Boyle of Aitkenhead Road CID."

He continued with the time and date and gave the names of both Donaldson and Graham as being the others present in the room.

To Donaldson's surprise, Boyle then recited the common law caution and saw Donaldson's eyes narrow, before continuing, "I understand, sir, that at the charge bar you refused the services of a lawyer?"

"Why the *fuck* would I need a lawyer?" Donaldson consented at last to slump down into the chair opposite and grinning, clasped his fingers behind his head as though he had no care in the world, though Boyle suspected his cavalier attitude was more due to his alcohol intake rather than his disdain for the procedure.

"Now, what's this all about?" he asked then, as if seeking to resolve this apparent trivial matter, then staring at Boyle before the DI could respond, quickly asked, "What's you name again?"

He ignored the attempt to distract him and tapping a forefinger on the sheet of paper with the prepared questions, said, "As the Detective Chief Inspector in charge of the Govan CID, You were the senior supervising officer for Detective Sergeant Shona Mathieson, sir. Is that correct?"

"You know it is which reminds me, how is the wee lassie? Bad thing that happened to her, wasn't it?" he pursed his lips and frowning, slowly shook his head.

"When was the last time you saw DS Mathieson, sir?"

"Why? What's that got to do with anything?" he replied and Boyle was certain there was a definite slur to Donaldson's voice.

"Please just answer the question, sir."

"I don't recall. Oh, wait," he slapped with the palm of his hand at his forehead as though suddenly recalling. "It was the day that bastard Charlie Miller took over my murder inquiry. Now, what day was that again?"

Boyle ignored Donaldson's attempt to become the interviewer and asked, "And you did not see DS Mathieson on the day an attempt was made to murder her?"

"Of course not," he sneered. "Is that what this is all about then? Some bastard is trying to stick that to me as well as a trumped up drink driving charge?"

He suddenly placed both hands flat on top of the desk and rising from his chair, leaned towards the tape machine causing Graham to reach for him, but the big DS stopped and backed off when Boyle raised a hand as Donaldson shouted into the machine, "I'm being set up here and it's that *bitch* Mulgrew and her lapdog Miller that's doing it!"

He grinned menacingly at Boyle and slowly sunk back down into his chair, but his eyes flickered when he saw Boyle smile and just for an instant, the Detective Inspector saw apprehension in Donaldson's eyes.

He didn't immediately react to Donaldson's outburst, but then quietly said, "I have information that on the morning of the attempted murder of DS Shona Mathieson, you left your home just after five o'clock that morning and returned home a few minutes before nine o'clock. Can you please tell me, where did you go to?"

His face paled and his lips tightened.

The only person who could *possibly* know that was Sylvia!

How the hell…what could she have told them?

His brain reacted to the question and experience warned him a no comment response would seem suspicious.

As casually as he dared, he replied, "That was the morning after I was suspended from duty. I was distraught and I could not sleep and went for a drive. Nothing more," he flatly added.

"Having mentioned you were suspended from duty, Mister Donaldson, for the benefit of the tape am I correct in saying the suspension was for a suspected drink driving charge?"

There seemed little point in denying it and so he nodded.

"You're nodding your head in agreement, sir. For the benefit of the tape, are you agreeing I am correct?"

"Yes," he irritably snorted, "you're correct."

"And while you were being charged with the alleged drink driving, sir, did you provide a blood sample?"

"Of course I did and willingly so," he lied. "The officers made a mistake and I can only presume their breathalyser machine was fault. I'm confident a court will clear me of the charge and I *will* resume my duties as a Detective Chief Inspector," he glared threateningly at Boyle before adding, "so let's not forget that, eh?"

Boyle ignored the implied threat and continued, "And as a police officer with a lengthy service record, sir, you are aware that these days DNA can be extracted from blood?"

"Of course I'm aware. Everybody and their bloody auntie is aware! Why do you ask?" he wondered where this was going.

"Returning to the subject of your early morning drive, sir. Can you recall where you drove to?"

"No," he shook his head.

"Did you drive to Dixon Road where DS Mathieson resides in a flat?"

"No, of course not," he stared suspiciously at Boyle though his tone now implied he was becoming bored with this questioning.

"Did you enter the tenement close where DS Mathieson resides and wait till DS Mathieson vacated her home and in the common close on the ground level, did you assault DS Mathieson by striking her on the head with an object and cause her to fall to the ground?"

"No, of course not," Donaldson scoffed and shook his head, but the sheen of perspiration on his forehead didn't escape Boyle's attention.

"And when she was knocked to the ground, sir, did you kick her in the face as she lay helplessly on the ground?"

"No," his stomach began to churn for didn't like this, not one little bit.

"Did you strike her with such force with your feet that her head cannoned off a wall and resulted in DS Mathieson sustaining a serious head injury and the effusion of her blood?"

"No!" he growled.

"After assaulting DS Mathieson and attempting to murder her, did you then leave her in a seriously wounded condition and left the close without calling for medical assistance for DS Mathieson?"

"No! I'm telling you, I did *not* assault that woman!" he snapped.

But Boyle wasn't done.

"After having attempted to murder DS Mathieson," he stared Donaldson in the eye as the tape recorder continued to silently whirr, in a monotone voice asked, "Did you then return home where at the hosepipe attached to the wall at the side of your house you did attempt to destroy evidence of the attempted murder of DS Mathieson by running water over your blood-stained shoes and your blood-stained trousers and blood-stained socks?"

Donaldson swallowed hard, but his mind was racing as he fought to recall exactly what he had done and knew then he had been betrayed; his *bitch* of a wife had betrayed him and after all he had done for her and that's why she was gone when he had got home from the Helen Street office!

Breathing heavily now, his voice faltered as almost in a whisper, he replied, "No."

Boyle stopped speaking and paused for a few seconds as he stared at Donaldson, then reaching down to the floor he lifted a clear plastic bag and placed it with a thud on to the desk.

To Donaldson's horror, he saw it contained a pair of heavy, black leather brogue shoes.

His shoes.

"I am showing Mister Donaldson a pair of shoes that were handed to me by his wife, the witness Sylvia Donaldson, who has provided a statement that confirms these shoes are the property of Mister Donaldson. "Do you recognise these shoes, sir?"

"My wife's mistaken. I have never seen them before in my life," he glanced away.

"According to the information I have, sir, on the morning of DS Mathieson's attempted murder, you were wearing these shoes when you returned home just a few minutes before nine o'clock and while wearing these shoes you run your feet under the tap on the side of your house. Mister Donaldson," he stared at him, "Forensic analysis has proved that not only is your DNA on these shoes, but so also is the blood and DNA of DS Mathieson. Can you explain how that could be, sir?"

He almost choked, but at last managed to gasp, "I'm being set up. You've put her blood on the shoes!"

Boyle reached down and lifted two more plastic bags, one that contained a pair of navy blue suit trousers and the other a pair of black coloured socks.

"Do you recognise these trousers and these socks, sir?"

"Don't be stupid," he scornfully sneered. "Why would I recognise a pair of breeks and a pair of socks?"

Boyle stared at him before replying, "On the said morning, sir, my information is that these items of clothing were damp at the material time you handed them to the witness Sylvia Donaldson to be dried, then cleaned. For the benefit of the tape, I am showing Mister Donaldson a pair of his suit trousers and a pair of his socks, both items which again are Forensically proven to have his DNA upon them as well as DS Mathieson's blood and DNA."

"Even if these things *were* mine, remember your training," he blustered. "You have no legal authority to remove them from my home without a warrant!"

"As a police detective with a lengthy service record, Mister Donaldson, I am certain you will be aware that I do not require a warrant to seize clothing or any item that is surrendered to me by a witness."

He needed a drink and thought he was going to faint, but then mustered enough breath to wheeze, "Get me a fucking lawyer! It's all lies! You're out to get me! I'm a *real* detective, not like you poncey bastards!" then grunted, "I'm saying nothing else."

Lowering his head, he tightly crossed his arms.

Glancing at Graham, Boyle took a deep breath and bracing himself, formally said, "In light of the evidence and the witness statement; Gerald Donaldson, I am arresting you for the attempted murder of Detective Sergeant Shona Mathieson…"

****

Locking the door of the Volvo, Charlie Miller was making his way across the driveway when his mobile phone activated.

"Alan," he greeted the caller, who replied, "It's done. He's in a cell and charged with Mathieson's attempted murder. I'm just about to give Cathy Mulgrew a call, but thought I'd give you the heads up first. Thanks, Charlie. I can't imagine how you cottoned on to

Donaldson and frankly, as you said it's probably better I don't know."

"No worries, Alan, and thank you for the call."

He made his way to the front door where it was pulled open by Sadie who holding Ella in her arms, was brushed aside by Geraldine who clasped her arms around his waist.

"Daddy!" she cried out while Ella reached for him.

"Aye, that's right," Sadie grinned and rubbed her hand through the wee girls tousled hair. "I feed you, do your washing, tend to your needs but when your daddy gets home, I'm abandoned like the skivvy I am."

Laughing and giggling, the four of them finally bundled their way along the hallway into the front room where Charlie deposited the squirming two girls onto the couch while Sadie said, "You have ten minutes with them while I get the dinner ready."

He distracted the girls by switching on the Netflix cartoons and making his way into the kitchen, sneaked up on Sadie and wrapped his arms about her waist.

"I take it when I didn't hear from you there was no news about Carol?"

She continued stirring the stew before replying, "Nothing yet. I phoned her half an hour before you come home to ask if she wanted to come over for dinner, but she told me that she'd a busy time at her club and she intended getting an early night."

"If you want to go after dinner, I'll put the girls down and you can pop over to her place for a visit."

"No," Sadie nodded and turning to him, seductively smiled as she replied, "This is the first night in the last couple of days I've had you home early, Miller, so no. Once the girls are down, I'm having a bath, a glass of vino and then stepping into that black negligee you bought me. Once I'm tarted up, I'm going to seduce you then we're having an early night too, okay?"

He felt himself become aroused and was about to reply when his mobile phone in the front room activated.

With a sigh, he stepped away from Sadie and smiling, said, "Hold that thought."

Returning to the front room he found Geraldine stood at the door and solemnly waiting to hand him his phone.

"Thank you, Miss Miller," he ruffled her hair and accepting the call, stepped back into the hallway before he said, "Hello?"

"It's me," Cathy Mulgrew greeted him and he could hear she was calling from her car. "Did Alan Boyle phone you?"

"He did," Charlie confirmed.

"I'm heading to the Chief's office in Dalmarnock to meet him and Harry Downes," she continued. "This is going to be a bloody PR disaster when the media get hold of the news."

"Still," he replied, "Alan Boyle did well and if nothing else, it not only solves the attempted murder on Shona Mathieson, but gets rid of a really bad policer officer too. That said," he almost allowed himself a grin, "I wouldn't like to have been present when the Chief received the news."

"Yeah, well at least he has something now to tell the poor girls parents. Anyway, what you up to? Are you at home?"

"Yes, I'm just about to sit down to dinner, Mulgrew, so bugger off and give me some peace."

"Lucky you. Jo told me that if I continue to keep these bloody hours…well, let's just say I'm grateful to have her."

Promising to give him a call the next morning to inform him how her meeting went, she ended the call a minute before she pulled into the Dalmarnock office car park.

Locking her Lexus, she heard then saw Harry Downes' Vauxhall turn into the car park and stood waiting for Downes at the front entrance.

Watching Downes getting out of her car, Mulgrew could see that the Media Department boss had obviously come straight from home and was dressed in a light coloured floral dress and a yellow coloured cardigan.

"I got a call from the Helen Street control room to attend here pronto," Downes began. "Is this about the Mathieson girl?"

On the way through the building to the chief's office, Mulgrew apprised her of the latest development.

"Shit! And him a DCI?" Downes was aghast, already envisaging the press response and them having a field day over the news.

At the Chief's office, they could see his secretary had finished for the evening and walking through the outer office, knocked on his door.

"Come in," Martin Cairney loudly called out and entering, they saw him stood by the window, informally dressed in a brightly patterned plaid shirt, light coloured chinos, brown brogue shoes and with his hands clasped behind him.

Mulgrew was about to speak when to her surprise, she saw his face seemed almost grey.

"Thank you for coming in at such short notice, ladies," he sombrely greeted them then reaching towards his desk, handed Mulgrew a page torn from a notepad.

"I received this communication just five minutes ago from the Divisional Commander at Aitkenhead Road," he began. "Half an hour ago, Detective Sergeant Shona Mathieson succumbed to her injuries."

CHAPTER TWENTY-FOUR

Alison Baxter rolled over into Willie Baillie's arms and smiling, softly whispered, "This is getting to be a habit."

He hugged her tightly and replied, "But a good habit, yeah?"

"So far," she mischievously grinned at him then sliding from the bed, added, "While you're in the en-suite, I'll nip into the bathroom and meet you in the kitchen for breakfast."

"Deal," he called out and headed for his shower.

Fifteen minutes later and ready for the day, she was piling her hair up into a tight bun when she got to the kitchen.

Dressed in his suit trousers, white shirt and red and black striped tie that was Windsor knotted, Baillie was stood leaning across the worktop with his hands laid flat on top and his head bowed while the radio quietly played in the background.

She could see it in his face that something was wrong.

He lifted his head and turning to stare at her, said, "It was on the seven o'clock news. Shona Mathieson died last night."

Shocked, she stepped over to where he stood and laying her head on his back, wrapped her arms about him and hugging him to her, said, "I didn't know her like you did, Willie. I'm so very sorry."

"Well," he exhaled and turning around to take her in his arms, replied, "I'm glad I waited at Aitkenhead Road to hear the bastard was arrested, though of course now Alan Boyle will amend the charge to murder. Poor Shona," he sighed, "I can't imagine how her family must be feeling."

His eyes narrowed and staring at her, said, "I feel awful, like since Charlie Miller made me the acting rank I've jumped into her shoes before she was even dead."

"Then you shouldn't feel that way," she pretended to scold him. "Miller made you acting DS because he needed someone to do the job and he believes you to be that person. What *you* need to do now, Willie Baillie," she poked him in the chest with her forefinger, "is prove to him that you *are* that person. You've told me that though she was young, Shona was a good supervisor and looked after her troops. Now you need to live up to her standard and be as good if not better than she was. Can you do that?" her eyes challenged him.

He stared thoughtfully at her then broke into a smile when he replied, "If I know that you're behind me, then yes, I can."
****

When Tony Muirhead arrived at the office that morning there was a quiet, sombre atmosphere, for the news of Shona Mathieson's demise had been echoed not only on the morning radio and television news, but also headlined in every newspaper.

Hanging his jacket on the back of his chair, he sidled over to Willie Baillie's desk and quietly asked, "Is it true what I'm hearing? That the suspect the papers are reporting was arrested is Gerry Donaldson and that he's been charged with her murder?"

"It's true," Baillie sighed with a nod and though he didn't voice it to the young detective, thought that at some point last night or earlier that morning, a police officer somewhere who had the same information about Donaldson's identity, whether for cash or not had knowingly or unwittingly mentioned it to a reporter or to someone who in turn had contacted the press.

The bloody polis, Baillie knew from bitter experience, could not hold their water.

They both turned when Charlie Miller entered the room and called out, "Right people, gather round, please."

As the team crowded forward Charlie took a deep breath and confirmed what had at that point been the unofficial news; that DCI Gerald Donaldson was in custody for the murder of their colleague, DS Mathieson.

He stared around the faces and continued. "There will be much speculation as to why Donaldson killed Shona; however, let me quite categorically inform you now that no matter what scurrilous rumours or accusations might be made about Shona and Donaldson, she was nothing other than a victim. I repeat," he stared pointedly at the faces, "a victim. For some reason known only to himself, Gerry Donaldson had seemingly developed a deep rooted hatred for Shona and speaking as an individual who only knew her slightly, I can only assume that while he was a pathetic excuse for a detective and a supervisor, he saw her as I did; a bright, intelligent and successful young woman who had a glowing career ahead of her and was jealous."

There was a murmur of consent among the team, some of whom Charlie saw nodding for it was easy for those who knew the vindictive Donaldson to imagine what he said to be true.

"I am informed this morning by Detective Superintendent Cathy Mulgrew," he continued, "that details of a service of remembrance and funeral ceremony for those colleagues and friends who wish to attend will be issued at a later date."

He inhaled and slowly exhaling, realised the team needed their spirits uplifted and said, "Right now though folks, the best way we can honour Shona is to continue what she was part of and find the killer of *our* victims. So," his eyes sought out Tony Muirhead and he wickedly smiled. "Our very own DC Muirhead and his colleague, Alison Baxter had a constructive afternoon yesterday and I'm turning this briefing over to him to update you all about what they accomplished. Let's hear it for young Tony!"

Astonished and taken aback at being singled out, the blushing Muirhead was greeted by good natured handclapping and a few cheers while Alison Baxter, stood at the rear of the room and realising what Charlie was doing, caught his eye and gave him a thumbs up.

****

Later in his office with Willie Baillie and Alice Brookes, Charlie began by congratulating Baillie on tracking down the mysterious man who was seen by Tommy Craig at Frankie Colville's window. "And he wasn't a CID officer after all? How the *hell* did you manage to track him down?" he stared in bemusement at Baillie.

"Just first class police work on my part, Boss," Baillie grinned before self-consciously admitting the phone call from the Cooperative funeral service.

"Well, it's nice to get a wee break now and then," Charlie smiled. Turning to Brookes they spent some minutes discussing the outstanding Actions before he instructed her to raise an Action for him, Baxter and Muirhead to visit the head office of 'Sinistra' in the city centre.

"Now, an issue of a more personal nature," he glanced at them in turn.

"While I'm away, Willie," he frowned, "I regret as my deputy I need you to go through Shona's desk and remove all her paperwork to another room so the team don't see what you're doing; go through it and reallocate any outstanding inquiries she might have that are currently active. I know it won't be easy," he shook his head, "but you'll either need to take them on yourself or if there are to many, reassign them to other members of the office. I know you and Shona were probably friends, so I'll ask you; are you okay to deal with that?"

"I'll manage, Boss," Baillie replied.

"Alice," he turned to the matronly woman. "I assume Shona had a locker here in Giffnock?"

"Yes, sir. There are lockers for the female staff downstairs next to the muster room."

"With respect to your maturity and undoubted friendship with her, can I request of you that you empty Shona's locker. Anything of a personal nature that you believe might be of value to the family we can arrange to be forwarded to them at a later date. Any items that you deem to be disposable, I'll leave you to decide what to do with them."

It wasn't his intention to upset her, but saw the tears forming in her eyes as she nodded.

"Okay then," he grimly smiled and arose from behind his desk, "I'll be with young Tony and Alison Baxter, so if you need us, we'll be on the mobiles."

****

Returned from dropping her daughter at the school, Sadie Miller finished her phone call to the Inspector, grateful that he understood her predicament and with sympathy, assuring her that she could add a further two days of her leave entitlement to her current time off.

She had barely finished the call and was about to take Ella upstairs to get her ready for her morning at the nursery when the phone rang. "Hello?"

"Hi, darling," her mother chirpily greeted her.

"Hello, mum," she smiled, but then thought she detected a forced cheeriness and asked, "Is everything okay?"

There was a definite pause before her mother replied, "That was the consultant on the phone. He's asked that I go and see him today. This afternoon."

A cold hand gripped at Sadie's chest and she asked, "Did he say why he wanted to see you?"

She heard Carol give a quiet sob, then listened as her mother took a deep breath and said, "He told me it's not good news."

****

Languishing in his cell, his stomach aching and his bowels threatening to explode as the lack of alcohol shredded his nerves, Gerry Donaldson could not believe the turn of events that brought him to this.

There had been no witnesses, of that he was certain. He had entered the close at the rear and left by the rear and left no evidence of his presence there.

Nothing.

After it was done, no one had seen him return to his car parked two streets away.

No one.

Then how, he wondered, did they come to suspect him?

His mind had raced through a sleepless night as he struggled to remember; those backstabbing individuals who set him up and starting with his slut of a wife, the woman who betrayed him after all the years he had supported her. The woman who couldn't provide him with a son, but produced two wastrel daughters who when they were old enough, took off without any thanks for the time and money he had spent raising them.

His problem, he snarled and now realised, was he hadn't beaten enough respect into the three of them like he should have.

"Hey, Jimmy, hey you in the peter over there," the voice from across the corridor called.

"Jimmy, you in the peter across the way. You there?" it called again. His body aching, he raised himself from the concrete bed to his feet and stepped over to the open hatch in the grey painted steel door.

The man had called the cell a 'peter,' so Donaldson realised he must be a former con.

"What!" he snapped, aware that with the charge amended to murder and because protocol demanded it, a young uniformed constable was on prisoner watch to prevent any attempt he might make at suicide. Sitting at the end of the corridor he heard the constable getting out of his seat and his boots now lazily walking towards Donaldson's cell door.

The man in the opposite cell, in his fifties Donaldson thought, had been hauled in during the early hours of the morning shouting and screaming obscenities at the arresting officers.

"Are you the polis that's dubbed up for the murder, pal?" the man asked.

He scowled and angrily replied, "What's it to you?"

The man giggled and said, "I heard the polis talking at the charge bar when I got lifted. Lifted for *fuck all*, by the way." The man paused for breath. "You're a copper, aren't you, pal? Well, see you, pal, see when you get to the Bar-L, pal, you're in for a fucking roasting, you are. See when the cons get told you're a copper, your arse is going to be ripe, so it is. See you, ya *bastard*," the man was shouting now, "If they don't put you in for segregation, you'd better get yourself a bucket of Vaseline because you're going to get yourself shagged rotten, so you are!"

Stunned and now visibly shaking, Donaldson backed off from the door as wordlessly, the constable slammed the hatch shut then heard the other hatch also being slammed shut.

The man continued to scream abuse and though Donaldson slapped his hands over his ears, he could still hear the mans rage and in his minds eye, already envisage the horror of what was to come.
****

With Charlie in the front passenger seat and Alison Baxter in the rear, Tony Muirhead drove the CID car towards Glasgow city centre.

"Remind me," Charlie turned to Muirhead, "where is this head office again?"

"Bath Street, sir. I had a quick look on their website and the office is located on Bath Street to the east side of Blythswood Street."

"I know the buildings," he nodded, recalling his time as a DS at Stewart Street. "Right, here's the plan. We've no direct evidence against Stacey Clarke or whatever name she's calling herself these days, but we have the blow-up of the City Chalmers photograph, so no matter what name she's using, if she's employed there we should be able to identify her. At the minute we're looking at Stacey as a witness, but I don't intend interviewing her in the comfort of their head office or wherever the company employ her. We track her down and take her to a police office, whichever one is local to where she works, okay?"

"Sir," Baxter replied while Muirhead nodded, then with a curious frown, asked, "Is she our suspect for the murders, sir?"

Charlie glanced at him and slowly replied, "Let's just say right now, Tony, we've more questions than answers and if Stacey gets any of them wrong, she might very well be, son. Okay?"

"Okay, sir," the young detective nodded.

Several minutes later Muirhead, driving westwards on Bath Street, pulled into the side of the road and stopped behind a UPS delivery van on a single yellow lane in front of a blonde sandstone, two-storey Georgian building.

"That's the head office back there, sir," he turned his head to nod.

Charlie and Baxter turned their heads towards and saw a bay window with a sign that said, 'Sinistra' in large letters.

"I'll stick the car log book in the window and hope the yellow peril don't hand us a ticket," Muirhead grimaced.

"If they do, you're paying," Charlie subtly winked at Baxter.

Entering through the front door into a plush outer office, it seemed evident to them that a lot of money had been spent decorating the place.

A young auburn haired receptionist who could have been no more that twenty years of age and dressed in a tight fitting blouse and short black skirt, sat behind a glass topped desk.

The girl was startlingly beautiful and looked like she had just stepped off a Vogue shoot.

Charlie was conscious of Muirhead taking a sharp intake of breath and resisting a grin, was about to speak when he glanced at the outsized, gilt framed photograph hanging on the wall behind the receptionist; a photograph of a glamourous looking middle-aged blonde woman sitting behind a desk who smiled at the camera and in common with such photographs, pretended to be caught in the act of signing a document.

"May I help you?" the young woman asked, her accent what Glaswegians customarily describe as 'pure West End.'

None of the three immediately responded and the girl smiled a little nervously, curiosity on her face as she stared at them in turn; the large, lumpy man with the scar on his cheek, the smartly dressed and attractive blonde haired woman and the younger man who stared longingly at her and whose jaw was hanging down.

It was Baxter who finally asked, "Can you tell us who the woman in the photograph is?"

She didn't turn around, but smiled and with admiration, replied, "That's Missus Livingstone, the CEO and founder of 'Sinistra'. Is that who you are here to visit?"

"That's her, isn't it, sir?" Muirhead turned to Charlie. "Stacey Clarke."

Then as though a light had been switched on, he added, "Stacey Livingstone. The SL in James Dougrie's calendar for the day he was…"

Charlie cut him off with a scowl and still staring at the photograph, took a breath and muttered, "Aye, that's her Tony, but what do you see?"

"Eh," Muirhead was puzzled and was about to ask Charlie what he meant, when Baxter interjected, "The pen, Tony. She's holding the pen in her left hand. She's left-handed."

****

They were back in the car within minutes and after fastening himself into the seat, Charlie dialled Willie Baillie on his mobile phone.

"Boss," Baillie answered the call almost immediately.

"We're just pulling away from Bath Street, Willie, and heading for…" he glanced at the note in his hand and read aloud, "Braehead Road in Thortonhall. That's up by East Kilbride, apparently."

In the back seat, Baxter was typing the address into her mobile phones SatNav and addressing Muirhead, said, "Head for East Kilbride, Tony, and I'll update you with directions as we get nearer."

"What's going on, Boss?" Baillie asked Charlie.

"We've just called into the head office of 'Sinistra' to find Stacey Clarke, now calling herself Missus Stacey Livingstone, is the owner of the company. According to the receptionist we spoke with, Stacey didn't arrive for work yesterday and phoned in yesterday afternoon to say she was taking a couple of days off."

"Are you on your way to visit her at home?"

"Yes, the lassie gave us her home address. I want you to contact the PF's office and have them draw up a Sheriff's search warrant for the address we're going to. That's…"

"Occupied by Stacey Livingstone, Braehead Road in Thortonhall. Yes, I've taken a note of it. I'll check the local voters roll and confirm the number. Anything else?"

"Willie, if you recall Clarke and Dougrie's post mortems about the killer…"

"There's a suspicion the killer is left-handed," Baillie finished for him, causing Charlie to smile and inwardly pleased that Baillie justified the confidence Charlie had in promoting him to the acting rank.

"Exactly," he finally said, "and we've just seen Stacey in a photograph holding a pen in her left hand. Now, her receptionist told us that it was unusual for Stacey to take any time off work, so we must assume she's spooked and if she is, she's got more than a full day's start on us. However, here's what I need you to do. In the likelihood she's making a run for it, contact the Ports Coverage Unit at Glasgow Airport and request that they issue an all points bulletin UK wide to stop any woman around the mid-fifties age using a passport in the name Stacey Livingstone. Alison took a company brochure from the receptionist that features an up to date photograph of Stacey so once we've been to the house and if she's not there, we'll get the photo issued to the PCU. It might be she's already away," he exhaled, openly irritated that Stacey might have stolen a march on him, "but we need to cover our options."

"Right, Boss, I'll get it done. Can you ask Alison to photograph the brochure photo on her camera and send it to me? I can get started with a script for the PCU and include the photo."

"Good thinking, Willie," Charlie grimly smiled, then turning to Baxter, he saw her nod as she said, "I heard."

"Anything else, Boss?"

"Can't think of anything, but hold on. Tony?" he turned to the younger man.

"No, sir."

He squirmed in his seat. "Alison?"

She shook her head, but called out, "Sending you the photo now, Willie."

"Right, Willie, we'll give you a phone when we get to the house," he ended the call.

****

It took a frustrating thirty minutes through roadworks to get to Stacey Livingstone's house in Braehead Road in Thorntonhall and finally they stopped in the quiet country road outside the house that was surrounded by a eight foot wooden fence. Though the wrought iron electric gates had a lattice of thin wire across the bars, it still permitted a view of the large, detached home.

The two garage doors were closed and the only car in the driveway was an old style, but highly polished and seemingly cared for Mercedes saloon.

On the grassy verge twenty feet from where they had stopped was parked an eight-year-old silver coloured Vauxhall Corsa with a dented and rusting nearside wing and a 'Baby on Board' sticker on the rear window. In the absence of any other house being close by, Charlie assumed the Corsa's driver was in the house.

Muirhead, staring at the house, was clearly impressed before whistling and remarking, "Blinking heck, this is some upgrade from a council mid-terrace in Castlemilk, eh?"

They were about press the call button on the post by the gates when they saw a young woman in her late twenties, her dark hair pulled back into a loose ponytail and wearing an navy blue anorak, blue jeans, brightly coloured training shoes and carrying a plastic bag in her hand that seemed to be heavy, emerge from the door of the large detached house and walk towards the gate.

The woman at first seemingly oblivious to their presence, stopped to fetch a cigarette pack and a lighter from her anorak pocket and lit a fag. Inhaling deeply, she continued towards the gate then saw them and warily approached. With the gate still closed, she glared suspiciously at them and said, "Can I help you?"

"Is this the Livingstone residence?" Charlie asked.

The woman stared at him then broke into a wide smile. "You'll be the polis then, aren't you? This is about Stacey, isn't it? Well sorry, pal, but you're too late," she nodded back towards the house and added, "She's gone."

"Gone where?"

She shrugged and reaching to a keypad just inside the gate, pressed four digits before replying, "No idea."

As the gates slid noiselessly open, Charlie asked, "And you are?"

"According to him," she nodded back towards the house, "I *was* the cleaner before he told me to fuck off. All I know is that Stacey left me a generous three month's wages and a note telling me that I wouldn't be needed again. That," she grinned and lifted the plastic bag, "and enough hair products to last me a year."

The gate slowly opened and stepping past them towards the Corsa, the woman cocked her head and asked, "You're the CID, aren't you?"

Charlie nodded.

"Aye, he said you'd be coming. Hope you get more out of him than I did, the drunken git. Bye," tossing the plastic bag onto the passenger seat, she got into the Corsa and as they stared at her, she drove off.

"Sir, shouldn't we have got a statement from her?" Muirhead asked.

"To tell us what? She cleaned for a woman she apparently liked and didn't like him, whoever he is? No," he shook his head, "I don't see Stacey confiding her sins to her cleaning woman, can you, Tony?"

"No, sir," he sheepishly grinned.

"Right then, let's go and introduce ourselves to him indoors."

****

They didn't bother knocking, but entering the large hallway heard a noise from a lounge and entering, saw a man slumped in a leather armchair, a table at the side with an empty whisky bottle and a half full second whisky bottle. Lying flat on the floor beside the table was a second empty whisky bottle. In his hand the man held a chunky crystal glass that was almost full.

Barefooted, both the mans white dress shirt and light grey coloured slacks bore whisky stains and it was obvious he was extremely drunk.

"Mister Livingstone, I presume," Charlie asked and rolling his eyes at his inadvertent pun, shook his head at Baxter's smile.

"Who the…Oh, you're the detectives, yeah?" the man asked in a heavily slurred voice, his eyes heavy and it seemed to Charlie he was about to pass out.

"Can you tell us where Stacey has gone?"

"Stacey? My wife?" the man drunkenly giggled and trying to raise the glass to his lips, slopped some of the liquid across his shirt before taking a large gulp.

"Gone," he replied at last. "Fucked off. Said you'd be coming for her."

Glancing about the room, Charlie could see numerous photographs of Stacey and the man in different situations; some of the couple obviously taken abroad in sunnier climates, some in formal dress at functions. As he stared at the photos, it seemed to him that though they were taken over a number of years and while Stacey seemingly hardly aged, her husband had faded from the dark haired and athletic man he once appeared to have been to the grey headed, potbellied man he now was.

"What's your name, sir?"

"My name?" he stared in confusion at Charlie, then burst into laughter. My name," he repeated, before replying, "is *Mister* Stacey Livingstone."

Charlie turned to stare at Baxter and Muirhead and like him, saw neither got the joke.

"What's your first name, sir?"

The man sighed and mumbled, "Eric. Eric Livingstone. But most of our friends just call me Stacey's husband," then laughed again.

Stepping closer to Charlie, Baxter whispered, "I think what he's trying to tell us is that his wife wore the trousers. Looking at the photos when he was younger. I'm guessing back then he was the eye candy."

"Eye candy? Oh," Charlie suddenly realised and nodding, softly replied, "You reckon she was the brains behind the marriage?"

"And likely everything else, I'm guessing," Baxter agreed.

Turning to Muirhead, he said, "Find the kitchen and start a pot of black coffee. Other than that we do nothing till the warrant gets here."

Baxter and Muirhead stared at him when he smiled and shrugging, added, "Nothing *official* that is, but Alison; while Tony's getting a brew on for our friend here, why don't you and I ensure there is nobody else in the house and if we do happen to stumble across any kind of travel documents…"

****

Within minutes of her mother's phone call Sadie Miller had Ella strapped into the child seat and was haring out of the driveway on her way to Carol's house.

Fretting with the knowledge her mother would be distraught, Sadie drove too fast and without thought and it was when she failed to stop at a busy junction and almost collided with a bus at a junction, she came to her senses.

She could see the bus driver angrily mouthing obscenities as he pulled away.

Shocked and with the car engine idling, she startled at the sound of the horn behind her and pulling round the corner into the main road, stopped in a bus layby.

Her body shaking, her hands felt as though they were welded to the steering wheel. Slowly, she lowered her forehead onto her hands and started to sob.

In the child seat, Ella realised there was something wrong and began to whimper.

****

Shaking hands with her daughter's new head teacher and entrusting Amy to her new classroom teacher, Jessica Gibson pushed her son Connor in his new buggy out of the front entrance of the primary school towards the parked Nissan.

She stopped and staring back at the building, marvelled that in just a few days her life and that of her children was in the process of irrevocably changing.

Now here she was on her way to the lawyer Louise Hall's office in Glasgow Road in Paisley to hear her father's Will read and the legal documentation that would confirm her inheritance of his house and property.

Thirty minutes later with her strong-willed son wisely strapped into his buggy and fumbling with his action toys, she was being shown into Hall's office where the young woman greeted her warmly, though missed the look of wariness Hall cast towards the sneaky Connor.

"There are a number of formalities to be observed," said Hall, who as the executrix-datives, legally confirmed Gibson's identity from the documents she produced.

"Did you get insurance for the car?" Hall grinned as an opener.

"Yes, finally," Gibson admitted with a smile.

"Right, down to business then. The Will. It's really pretty straight forward," Hall assured her and began by reciting the items that her father had listed in his Will as his property.

However, when Gibson watched the lawyer tear open a brown envelope and after glancing at the single sheet within, turn pale, she asked, "What? Is there a problem?"

"Something that I regret I didn't pay too much attention to when I hurried through the details," Hall honestly replied, holding her hands defensively in front of her before continuing, "It's a letter from a Spanish bank that has a bank account in your father's name. I truthfully didn't give the Spanish account much thought simply because these days it's not uncommon for retired people to open bank accounts in Spain and the usual practise has been to deposit a few pounds to keep the account open in the event the account holder decides to retire there."

Hall sat back and rubbed at her forehead before she continued. "With the view there might be some money in the account, I applied for a confirmation document from the Sheriff Court that will permit you upon production of the confirmation document and your father's death certificate, to claim such monies that are currently in the account."

She paused and took a breath. "Acting on your behalf, I'd been in communication with the bank to inform them of your father's death and of course as most communications these days are completed electronically, I did think it a little unusual that the banks response was forwarded by a courier when it arrived this morning. I didn't think to open the letter immediately, having decided to wait till the reading of the Will. However, now that I have opened the letter, it details the savings in your father's account in both Euros and Sterling."

She stared at Gibson and hesitantly asked, "Do you follow?"

"I think so, yes. What you're telling me is with this court document and my father's death certificate the bank will release the funds in the account. What's the problem?" she shrugged. "I mean, my father was a police pensioner and yes, I know that the mortgage was paid off and he owned the car. I can't imagine he would have much left over from his monthly outgoings to save in a Spanish bank. I mean, surely his pension can't have amounted to that much?"

"Missus Gibson…" Hall hesitated and handing the letter across the desk, suggested, "Perhaps you'd be better reading it yourself." Puzzled, Gibson took the letter from Hall and her stomach clenched. Swallowing with difficulty, she said, "If you don't mind, Miss Hall, when we're done here I think I'd better take this letter to the police."

CHAPTER TWENTY-FIVE

During their brief and quite illegal search of the house, either Charlie nor Alison Baxter discovered anything that indicated where Stacey Clarke or Livingstone had fled to, though it was obvious from the dishevelled state of the opulent bedroom that she had packed in a hurry.

"I'm no expert, Charlie," Baxter lifted a cocktail dress from a pile of abandoned clothing that was strewn about the room, "but I'd guess this is a two or three hundred quid frock I'm holding here."

"If the paintings and the art is anything to go by, there's certainly a lot of money been spent on this place," he sighed.

He turned when Tony Muirhead appeared in the doorway to tell him, "I've taken the booze off her husband, sir, but the guy's wasted. I've tried to get him to drink black coffee, but I'm worried he's going to chuck up all over the place."

"Okay, Tony, give it a rest for now."

They all heard the sound of a car stopping outsider the house and making their way to the front hallway, saw Willie Baillie, followed by two of the team, making his way up the steps to the door.

In his hand he clutched a sheet of paper and called out, "Sorry about the delay. The duty Sheriff was at lunch and the bugger refused to be disturbed till he'd eaten," he shook his head in disgust. "Anyway, it's signed now."

"Right," Charlie addressed those present, "apart from Alison, the rest of you are looking for anything that connects Stacey Livinsgtone to Stacey Clarke or any of our victims. Paperwork, photographs, anything like that. Let me say from the outset I do not expect you to find a murder weapon, but if you do," he wryly grinned, "you're getting a week off work and it *won't* be from your leave entitlement."

Laughing, Baillie led the team into the house while Charlie turned to Baxter and said, "I know he's well and truly pissed, Alison, but see what you can get from him about when he met Stacey, where he met her and what he knows of his wife's history before they married." She nodded and made her way into the lounge to interview the drunken Eric Livingstone.

While the detectives began their search, Charlie walked through the house and used his mobile phone to update Cathy Mulgrew with what they had so far discovered.

"And you suspect she might be trying to flee the country?"

"That's my first thought, yes. Somehow she knew or suspected that we might be getting close and has taken off."

"Any suggestion she was tipped off by someone?"

He knew what was going through her thoughts and shaking his head, replied, "No and I've no worries about any of my team, either. If she *was* tipped off that we were looking for her it can only have been someone who knew about her current life. The obvious suspect would have been her daughter Mhari, but from what Alison Baxter told me, it's unlikely that the daughter knew about her mother's whereabouts. No," he grimly shook his head, "I'm more inclined to believe she simply got cold feet and decided to take off before we found her."

He glanced at the pictures spread throughout the house. "That and I believe if the daughter was in contact with her mother then Stacey would probably have had family photographs, perhaps of her grandson, in the house, but there's no trace of anything like that."

"What about her husband, this man Livingstone?"

"Well," he slowly replied, then smothered a snigger, "Our first impression is that he's her trophy husband, but we'll need to get him sobered up to find out what their relationship was like."

"Can't have been that great if she's buggered off without him."

He smiled and replied, "There's a lot of photographs about the house that indicate he and Stacey were a handsome couple when they met, but remember; she's in the beauty industry so as the years passed it certainly seems that Stacey worked hard at keeping her looks, but he's definitely let himself go."

"Says God's gift to women," she dryly replied.

He grinned and said, "I'm only trying to explain why she might have left him behind."

"What's your next move?"

"As I said, I've had the Ports Control Unit alerted, but I feel it in my bones she's on her toes. What I'm intending is commencing my case to Crown Office and when I've got it written up, take a copy to the Chief for his attention."

"You sound like you're almost certain she is gone, Charlie."

"That's the way it's looking, Cathy," he replied and ended the call.

Minutes later he was checking on how Alison Baxter was faring, then seeing Livinsgtone dozing in his armchair, she grimly shook her head and gave him a thumbs down.

Rising from her knees by Livingstone's chair, she said, "He's too far gone at the minute. We need to let him sober up before we can properly interview him, but from the little I did get out of him and I won't include the expletives," she sighed, "it seems he had no idea of Stacey's past. When he met her she was Stacey Morton and didn't know or recognise the name Clarke."

"So when she left Castlemilk and her daughter behind, she reverted to her maiden name," Charlie nodded in understanding.

"Livingstone told me he met her in a city nightclub. He was a croupier and says it was her money that started the business, that she told him the money was inherited from a deceased husband, that she controlled all the income and he was paid a monthly allowance."

"Which might explain where some if not all the stolen money went."

"When I asked him about kids," she continued, "she told him she couldn't have any and he went along with that."

"I wonder how her daughter would feel if she knew that," he sighed. "Is he involved in the business?"

"No. When I asked him he just laughed and said he was a kept man, but inferred in the recent past Stacey was seeing other men. Her flings, he called them. He's obviously drunk and I have no reason to say this other than my gut feeling, but he doesn't strike me as a particularly bright man."

"And he's no idea where she went? They didn't have a place abroad or anything?"

"That occurred to me, but he said no."

"What's your gut feeling, Alison? Drunk as he is, do you believe what he told you?"

She didn't immediately respond, but arms crossed her chest, said, "There is a saying that a drunk mind speaks a sober heart. According to a French enlightenment philosopher, most individuals when drunk will lose their inhibitions and tend to disclose their true thoughts and feelings. Now, I don't know this man Livingstone, but you are asking if I believe what he told me. If my psychological studies taught me anything, it is to be circumspect when dealing with someone who perhaps has something to gain by lying. However, in this particular case and right now perhaps because he *is* so drunk, I am of the opinion that Mister Livingstone in there would find it difficult to lie. So, to answer your question, Charlie, yes; I believe he is telling the truth as he knows it."

"As he knows it?"

"I say that because he is telling us what he believes to be true; what Stacy Clarke told him."

"Ah, well, perhaps…"

He was interrupted by his mobile phone ringing it and glancing at the screen, said, "It's Alice Brookes."

"Hello, Alice."

"Sir, are you in a position to return to the office?"

"Why, what's up?"

"James Dougrie's daughter has arrived here and says it's vital she speaks with you. She's a bit upset and says it's something about her father's Will. I've given her a coffee and sat her in your office, if that's okay?"

He glanced at his watch and said, "Yes, you did the right thing, Alice. Give me fifteen or twenty minutes to get back to the office," he added, then ended the call.

Calling through to Willie Baillie, he said, "I'll take Alison back to the factory with me, Willie. You and the lads finish up here, but before you leave," he cocked a thumb over his shoulder towards the lounge, "ensure Mister Livinsgtone in there knows someone will be back to see him when he's sober."

****

She had arrived at her mother's home determined to be if not cheery, then optimistic, but when Carol opened the door, Sadie was unable to hide her feelings and hugging her mother, the tears freely flowed while a confused Ella stared from one woman to the other..

It took several minutes for Carol to calm her daughter and ushering Sadie off to the bathroom, told her, "I'll attend to the wee one while you go and wash your face, hen."

Returning to the kitchen few moments later, she saw Ella in the high chair making short work of a slice of bread and jam while Carol stood at the cooker brewing a pot of tea.

Sitting herself down in a chair, Sadie asked, "So, what did the consultant say?"

"Well," she turned with the teapot and pouring the scalding liquid into two mugs, replied, "the first thing I told *him* was to explain it in simple English so a wee woman like me who lives in a council house will understand it. Then after telling me it was not good news, the next thing he told me was not to worry."

"Not to worry?" Sadie was aghast.

"Aye," Carol smiled at her. "Said that the lump seems to be isolated and explained that in most cases, breast lump removal is done at an outpatient surgery."

"Did he say if it is malignant?"

"He'll need to carry out further tests," she shrugged. "Told me I'll be given a local anaesthetic and the operation will take about an hour or two at the most. Said it will be pain free, but they always tell you that, don't they?" she sniffed disbelievingly before continuing. "Once he has performed the procedure he'll send the lump for immediate analysis and then we'll have a definite answer as to whether or not it is malignant."

"But I thought that was why you went through the examination when we were there the other day?"

"Apparently not," Carol sighed, then staring suspiciously at Sadie, asked, "Do you think this bugger is trying to screw more money out of you and Charlie?"

"He better not if he wants to continue walking with his balls still hanging between his legs," she grimly retorted.

"Sadie!" her mother snapped at her ripe language and nodding to Ella, added, "The wean, for heavens sake!"

"Sorry, mum," Sadie sheepishly grinned, then said, "Well, at least it's not the worst news."

"I'm sorry, hen," her mother stepped around the table to cradle her daughter's head against her breast. "I wasn't thinking straight when I phoned you. I must have given you a hell of a fright."

"Aye, you did," Sadie quietly replied, then added, "but I'll forgive you if you stick on some bacon for a sandwich. I'm starving."

****

Alice Brookes met Charlie in the corridor and in a low voice, said, "Missus Gibson's in your office. She has her son with her, but I've persuaded her that you'll want her undivided attention and one of my girls is taking the wee boy for a walk in his buggy."

"Good thinking, Alice," he was about to turn away, but she raised a hand to stop him and said, "I've popped my head in a couple of times to make sure she's okay, but she's still a bit upset, sir. I'll let you get your coat off and bring you both in a cup of tea."

He smiled and pushing open the office door, greeted her with, "Hello Missus Gibson. Nice to see you again. How are you settling in at the house?"

Hanging his jacket on the hook behind the door, he stepped behind his desk and sitting down, saw that when she nodded her greeting, she was pale and nervous.

"Now," he opened the discussion, "I understand you wanted to speak to me about something?"

She nodded and began, "I was at the lawyer's office this morning to speak with Miss Hall about my father's Will. She's the woman from the firm the Police Federation use. Anyway, she said the reading of my dad's Will would be relatively straight forward," Gibson shrugged, "but then she opened a letter from a Spanish bank."

"A Spanish bank?"

"Yes. Apparently my dad opened the account with this bank a long time ago. Anyway…"

"Sorry to interrupt, but do you know when the account was opened?"

"Oh, the details are here in the letter they sent," she fished in her handbag for the envelope.

She handed him the envelope, but before he opened it, he said, "Go on."

"Anyway, Miss Hall told me she had found out in my dad's Will about the bank account and contacted the bank, but when the reply arrived this morning she didn't think to open the letter prior to the reading of the Will. She said she didn't believe it would contain very much money, but knowing I'd probably want to withdraw the money…I mean, what would I want with a Spanish bank account?" She stared at him then blushing, said, "Sorry, I'm raving here. Anyway, she applied for something from the court that I'd need, something called a 'confirmation.' Please," she pointed to the envelope, "read the letter and you'll see what I mean, why I'm here."

The door knocked and was opened by Alice Brookes who placed a tray with two cups and saucers, milk and sugar onto the desk and with a smile, left again, closing the door quietly behind her.

Charlie slid the A4 sheet of paper from the envelope and opening it, saw the Spanish bank logo on the top right hand corner of the sheet. The letter, typed in faultless English, was a response to Ms Louise Hall's inquiry regarding the savings account of James Martin Dougrie and listing the home address in Belmont Drive, included formal regret about the news of Mister Dougrie's death.

He read the account was opened…his eyes widened…in February 1990; roughly two months after the disappearance of Murdo Clarke. As his eyes scanned the letter he unconsciously inhaled for he saw the savings described in the account now totalled in Sterling, over five-hundred and fifty thousand pounds.

He glanced at Gibson, her lips tightly set and asked, "Do you know if your father ever had any kind of inheritance or came from, how can I explain this, family money?"

"No, not to my knowledge," she replied, her voice almost a whisper.

He sagged into his chair, for now there was no doubt in his mind. James Dougrie had been dirty and the money, excluding the interest on the account that had been accumulated over the years, was part of the proceeds of the 'Four Minute Gang' robberies.

But how could that be proved.

He glanced again at the young woman in front of him and deciding that Jessica Gibson was an innocent in her father's affairs, there was no need to burden or distress her with his suspicions.

"May I keep this letter, Missus Gibson? For now, I can have a photocopy made for you."

"Yes, of course, but…" she hesitated and staring into his eyes, said, "You know something about this money, don't you, Mister Miller?" Before he could respond, she took a deep breath and asked, "Was my father a dishonest policeman?"

"I have no proof of that," he truthfully said, but realising that she needed an honest answer, added, "I'm still making inquiries. However, believe me when I tell you if I do prove your father was corrupt, I will tell you the truth."

"And what about that," she pointed to the letter, "the money, I mean. What do I do now?"

"I'll ask you to give me a little time to permit me to make inquiry into its origin and again, when I discover anything, I'll be the one to tell you. How does that sound?"

She stood, prompting Charlie to also get to his feet.

"Thank you, Mister Miller. I can't ask for anything fairer than that." Turning towards the door, she smiled and said, "I think I'd better rescue your young lady because no doubt my son will be howling his head off by now."

He watched her leave and resuming his seat, read through the letter again before dialling the number for the Fraud Squad.

****

Willie Baillie returned with the other detectives to Giffnock and reported to Charlie Miller that they had been unsuccessful, that there was nothing they could find that implicated Stacey Clarke in the murders of her husband Murdo, James Dougrie or Frankie Colville or indicated where she might have fled to.

"How was her current husband when you left?"

"Zonked," Baillie grinned, "but I've left a note indicating that we'll be back to formally interview him." He screwed his mouth and continued, "Maybe not strictly legal, but before we left I took the precaution of lifting this as a wee bit of insurance in case he tried to be wide and bugger off too," and from his jacket pocket produced Eric Livingstone's passport.

"Any entry or visa stamps in there that might give us an indication of their country of choice?"

Baillie shrugged and replied, "As you know, the European countries seldom stamp the passports these days and though there is some entry and departure stamps, the only thing that seems of real interest is what I found inside the passport wallet. It was a duty free receipt issued two years ago at the, pardon my pronunciation," he paused and eyes narrowing read out, "Sir Seewoosagur Ramgoolam International Airport, wherever that is. Hold on, Boss," he opened the door, "I'll Google it and see what I can find."

He returned minutes later and grinning said, "Mauritius. He visited Mauritius two years ago…"

"So it's reasonable to assume his wife went with him," Charlie interrupted, "if as he claims, she holds the purse strings."

"Right, Willie," his face twisted in thought, "if nothing else this receipt is a starter for ten. Get onto the PCU and ask them about flights to Mauritius. I don't expect there will be direct flights from

Glasgow, so they might have to check flights and time relevant CCTV recordings from Glasgow or Edinburgh via London. Those guys will be used to this sort of request so be led by them."

"On it, Boss," Baillie replied and was out the door.

****

Cathy Mulgrew was in conference at Coatbridge office with DCI Lorna Paterson and her DI, Billy McKnight, discussing the ongoing inquiry at the Bellshill nursing home when her mobile phone activated. The screen indicated it was Martin Cairney, the Chief Constable.

Excusing herself, she stepped out of Paterson's office into the corridor and said, "Sir."

"Miss Mulgrew, I understand that was a good piece of work by DI Alan Boyle at Aitkenhead Road. What evidence does he have?"

She read into the question and replied, "Sufficient DNA evidence to place Donaldson at the locus and with DS Mathieson's blood and DNA on his footwear and lower clothing, sir. That and a statement from his wife that confirms his indisputable ownership and wearing of the clothing items at the material time of the assault."

"His wife," Cairney slowly repeated. There was a definite pause before he continued, "Dare I ask how Donaldson came to be a suspect?"

"Perhaps we should mark it down to good police work, sir," she tactfully answered.

"But you can assure me that the evidence as it stands will convict Donaldson?"

"Absolutely, sir."

"I heard a whisper that our friend Mister Miller might have had a hand in identifying Donaldson."

She grimaced for it was well known among his senior staff that Cairney had informants placed at different ranks throughout the Force.

"As I said, sir, the evidence against Donaldson will convict him, of that I have no doubt."

"So, Miss Mulgrew, when I visit DS Mathieson's parents later this evening as I fully intend to do, I can assure them that the man who murdered their daughter will go to prison?"

"Yes, sir, you have my word on that."

"Thank you, Miss Mulgrew. Is there any word on Mister Miller's own investigation?"

"I understand there has been a development, sir, but I am not fully *au fait* with the circumstances; however, he did tell me that he intends commencing a report to Crown Office and will visit you with a copy."

"I look forward to reading it. Thank you, Miss Mulgrew," he ended the call.

She stared for a few seconds at her mobile phone, then slowly exhaling, returned to Paterson's office.

****

In the incident room, Charlie faced the team and said, "As you are aware, we have finally located and identified Murdo Clarkes widow, Stacey, and discovered she is now Stacey Livingstone and the successful and wealthy owner of the 'Sinistra' hairdressing salons that I'm certain some of you lovely ladies will know," he tightly smiled.

"At this minutes, there is no direct evidence against Stacey, however, we have discovered she is left-handed and you might recall we suspect the killer of Murdo Clarke and James Dougrie also to be left-handed. We have obtained a partial statement," he glanced at Alison Baxter, "from Stacey's current husband that when they met she was in possession of a large sum of money. How much," he shrugged, "we do not know, but it seems to have been of a sufficient sum to enable her to start her own company. Remember, ladies and gentlemen, this was a woman working as a hairdresser and from a council background, so we ask ourselves; where did this money come from? Is it part of the 'Four Minute Gang' haul?"

He paused before continuing, "Our efforts to interview Stacey have been thwarted for it seems she somehow came to suspect she is the subject of police attention and apparently fled, we believe somewhere abroad. Willie," he nodded to Baillie, "is currently making inquiry with the Ports Coverage Unit to find out if they can trace her point of departure and destination."

He stared around the room and his tone serious, continued, "This information does not leave this room, however, you will have gathered from what I have told you that as of now, albeit we have only circumstantial evidence, Stacey Clarke or Livingstone as she is now, is our number one suspect for the murders."

A ripple of excitement run through those present.

"It is my intention to report what we know to the Crown Office and ask that they consider issuing an arrest warrant to enable us to formally interview Stacey about the murders. However," he sighed, "if the bugger has left the country that might not be for quite a while."

He paused again then said, "In the meantime ladies and gentlemen, we will continue with what Actions we have outstanding, but I believe once I have reported the facts and at the discretion of Crown Office, we will be standing down as an investigation. One other thing, before we finish for the day. As you will know, Gerry Donaldson has been locked up for Shona Mathieson's murder. I am aware that Shona was not just a colleague, but a friend to many of you. I am impressed that though you were distressed at what Shona suffered, you all continued to work to the best of your ability. Good effort, everybody, and thank you."

He stepped back and beckoning Alice Brookes and Willie Baillie to him, said, "I'm about to lock myself in the office and start this report. I'll leave you guys to attend to anything that comes in. One thing I'll ask of you, Willie," he smiled at the big guy. "If you're staying on for a couple of hours and if you're getting some food for yourself, you could grab me a bag of chips?"

CHAPTER TWENTY-SIX

Three days had passed since the negative search for Stacey Clarke at her home address.

After several drafts and corrections during those days, it was just after eleven in the morning when Charlie Miller read through the final draft and was satisfied that his final report to the Crown Office contained all the relevant information he and his team had acquired. Phoning ahead, he made an appointment to meet with the Chief Constable at his Dalmarnock office prior to his submission of the report to Crown Office.

When Charlie arrived, Martin Cairney was standing in his office with a pile of reports clutched in his hand. On the coffee table that sat in the middle of a ring of four easy chair lay a tray with an aromatic pot of freshly brewed coffee and two mugs.

"Mister Miller," he greeted Charlie and striding across the large office to lay the reports down upon the desk, returned to the coffee table and handed him a poured mug of coffee. Nodding to his desk, he joked, "You'd think that now I've reached the top position in this job I'd have someone who could deal with this lot."

"The job's never done till the paperwork's finished," Charlie grinned the old adage at him, then as both men sat down in opposite armchairs in front of the coffee table, he continued, "I'm on my way to the Crown Office through at Gartcosh, sir, to deliver my report, but I wanted to present you with my findings and a copy for your own perusal."

He handed a buff coloured folder to Cairney who glancing at it, laid it down onto the table, then folding his shovel like hands across his chest, said, "While of course I fully intend reading your report, Mister Miller, please take the time to summarise it for me, for I expect that you will have thoughts that must be difficult to express on paper. I am told though you do have a suspect?"

Charlie stared at Cairney then slowly nodded before he began.

"I'm certain you understand, Chief Constable, that what I am about to relate is based on my assessment of the information and the very few facts that my team and I have so far discovered."

"I believe it has been a trying time for you," Cairney replied, but Charlie thought there was an underlying knowledge in Cairney's comment and briefly wondered if he was subtly referring to Charlie's domestic concern with his mother-in-law, Carol.

"To begin, sir, the so called 'Four Minute Gang' were in fact a gang of six. I am of the opinion that the unofficial leader of the gang was Stacey Clarke, the wife of Murdo Clarke. I believe that Stacey was the driving force behind the robberies, that it was she who selected and drew the four men together and it was she who persuaded her husband to participate by reconnoitring the banks and building societies that were robbed. He did this reconnoitring, as you are already aware, by using his company issued pass to travel the length and breadth of Scotland to survey and plan the robbery locations. According to what Clarke's daughter, the witness Mhari Fraser, was told by Clarke's mother and from my interview with the witness Thomas Craig, it seems Clarke was a timid man. It is my belief that

Murdo Clarke, if not frightened of Stacey, then certainly did not fully trust her for she seems to have been and by all account continues to be a very strong-willed and manipulative woman. It's conjecture on my part, but I believe that Stacey used her womanly wiles, perhaps even offering sexual favours, to keep the gang in line."

"And you believe this why?"

"Her current husband, the witness Eric Livingstone, has admitted in his statement that throughout their marriage and even at her current age, Stacey has a voracious appetite for men, but always favours men she can control; no matter their age, no matter their circumstance."

"Go on."

"I'll remind you of the alleged wife assault that occurred in nineteen-eighty-seven that brought the Clarkes to the attention of the police. That incident introduced Stacey to DS James Dougrie, later DI Dougrie, and brought her a rare opportunity; the chance to bring a police officer into her web."

"You make her sound like a Black Widow spider, Mister Miller," Cairney smiled.

"Well, it's an apt analogy and I don't think you're too far off the mark, sir," he replied. "Stacey was an extremely beautiful woman as well as being very calculating and I think before long, Dougrie found himself in a relationship with her he could neither control nor get out of."

Cairney took a deep breath and his face darkened when he snapped, "So you're saying Dougrie *was* a corrupt officer?"

"If I may continue, sir?"

"I'm sorry, Mister Miller. Forgive me for interrupting," he raised a hand to apologise.

Charlie nodded and said, "The photograph we have obtained and though it isn't dated, quite clearly shows a relationship between Stacey and Dougrie, though where or who took the photo isn't known. There's a copy for you in the file there," he nodded to the brown folder. "Again though I have no evidence to substantiate this, I am of the opinion that this relationship was sexual and ultimately was the cause of the break-up of Dougrie's marriage that led to him losing contact with his children; a blow that I believe he never truly recovered from and which affected him deeply."

He paused and sipped at his coffee before continuing.

"Now, to Murdo Clarke. As I said the witness Thomas Craig, a former member of the 'Four Minute Gang', has stated that Murdo Clarke was afraid of becoming involved in the violence of the robberies. I'm sure Stacey must worried about her husband's weakness for violence and perhaps foreseeing the gangs run of luck coming to an end, decided her husband was becoming a liability."

"You think she had him murdered?"

"Actually, I think *she* murdered him. The PM suggested Clarke was probably drunk at the time of his murder, knocked on the back of the head and then stabbed to death by a left-handed killer. And of course we have the opinion of the pathologist, Doctor Watson, who has in her professional judgment opined the killer was likely left-handed; as is Stacey. I am aware this of course is only circumstantial evidence."

He sipped again at his coffee.

"While court records suggest the deceased Alex Murtagh, who died in prison, was the 'Four Minute Gang' leader, as the true leader of the gang I surmise Stacey took responsibility for the money that was stolen. I also believe she did so because the four gang members who participated in the robberies had previous convictions and if the police came calling; well," he smiled, "none of the four would have had reasonable cause to explain their possession of such large sums of money. Because of the money laundering legislation in force at that time too, any attempt by them to deposit the money into a bank would have rung alarm bells at the banks. I can only surmise that Stacey persuaded the four gang members that at the end of their run she would equally divide the money. This unique position of power enabled Stacey to use the gang members as she saw fit and thus after Murdo was murdered, enabled her to persuade Frankie Colville to dispose of Murdo's body, hence the cigarette butt we discovered in the grave with Colville's DNA."

"Hold on a second," Cairney's face clouded over. "If Clarke's body was buried by Colville *before* he was arrested, then that means…"

"Clarke was already dead and unlikely to be the informant who tipped off James Dougrie about the robbery," Charlie nodded as he finished for Cairney. "It also adds weight to my suspicion that Dougrie was given the information by Stacey and adds to my belief that they were colluding together."

"And do you believe Dougrie knew about her murdering her husband?"

"Perhaps not immediately, but in time, yes; I believe he knew."

"My God, Mister Miller," Cairney rubbed at his jaw, "what a cunning and unscrupulous woman this Stacey is."

"Oh, aye, sir, you said it," Charlie agreed with some feeling.

"To continue," Charlie took a breath. "With the exception of Tommy Craig who seems to have been kept out of the loop on a number of issues, I do not believe the other two gang members, Alex Murtagh and John O'Connor, knew of Murdo's murder. My gut feeling is they likely died believing Clarke had informed on them and escaped not only justice, but with their share of the stolen money too and that this information was fed to them by Stacey."

"Do you think the gang members knew of Dougrie's involvement?"

"No," he shook his head. "I think Dougrie's participation in keeping the gang apprised of police inquiries into the robberies was known only to Murdo and Stacey. I'll explain as I go on, sir."

"Of course," Cairney waved a hand before asking, "But getting rid of Clarke's body. Why would she trust and collude only with Colville?"

"Again, Stacey being the clever and manipulative woman she is and whether by sexual favour or sheer force of her personality, I think she persuaded Colville to do her bidding. I also suspect she kept her interaction with Dougrie, Colville and the other gang members separate; compartmentalised them if you will. Knowledge of course is power and while Stacey ensured some of them knew a little of what was going on, she knew everything. I also believe it was Stacey who fed the gang the information that Clarke informed on them to Dougrie, thereby deflecting any suspicion from her and providing the gang someone to focus their suspicion upon; her husband Murdo Clarke."

"But back to the money. Surely Colville, having disposed of Clarke's body, would know that Clarke had not stolen the money?"

"Again, it is my belief that Stacey forced his silence by persuading him that if he opened his mouth he would go down for Clarke's murder and so he kept his mouth shut."

"So, DI Dougrie," Cairney snorted. "Tell me what you suspect of his full involvement with this woman."

"As you know, sir, Dougrie retired three months after Clarke was reported missing and six years short of his thirty years. That means he didn't receive a full pension, yet our inquiries indicated shortly after he retired, he was able to pay off his mortgage and live a relatively quiet life on his pension without seeming to be too well off. I believe the mortgage repayment was courtesy of Stacey and some of the stolen money."

Cairney stroked at his jaw again and asked, "After murdering Murdo Clarke, their man who did all the reconnoitring, I'm guessing you believe that was why the gang were arrested? They no longer had access to the same information about their targets?"

Charlie didn't immediately respond, but then said, "I think that Stacey realised they'd had a good run, but Dougrie has probably tipped her off that the police were amassing a lot more information about them than was comfortable and as I said earlier, she worried the gang were in danger of soon being arrested. Now," he sat forward and stared at Cairney, "this is simply speculation on my part, but here's what I think. Stacey and James Dougrie were in a sexual relationship driven by her. She decided Clarke, probably by now a nervous wreck and going to pieces, was increasingly becoming an inconvenient liability and that's when she decided to murder him. Where," he shrugged, "I don't know, but I suspect from what his PM seemed to indicate, she got him drunk and that made him vulnerable. Though Dougrie must have later been aware or at least suspected she had murdered Clarke, somehow she persuaded Dougrie to inform his superiors that it was the now missing Clarke who told him about the plan to rob the Renfrew building society. It's likely she forced Dougrie who probably believed himself to be too involved with the gang and thus unable to resist her instruction for fear of himself being arrested."

He licked at his lips and continued, "I believe it was Stacey's idea to have her associates arrested knowing that if she was holding the money, none of them would disclose anything about her part in the robberies for fear that if she too were arrested, they stood to lose everything they had stolen. Of course, other than Colville, the other three members of the gang still believed Stacey was in possession of the money only to be told later be told Clarke had run off with it."

"One thing puzzles me. With Colville knowing Clarke was already dead and if as you surmise it was the wife who murdered him,"

Cairney shook his head. "How do you imagine this bloody woman induced him to bury the body for her?"

Charlie shrugged and replied, "I can only assume she had some sort of hold over him; sexual perhaps? Without any direct information, we can only guess, sir."

Then permitting himself a smile, he added, "Some day I hope to ask her that very question."

He sipped again at his coffee. "However, as you know the information provided by Dougrie resulted in the arrest of the four members of the gang. Being the type of men they were and presumably believing that Stacey would hold their individual share of the stolen money for them, they categorically refused to cooperate with the police investigation and likely expected to be rich men when they'd served their sentences."

"Good heavens. Then, you must believe Stacey kept all the money for herself?"

"Were it that simple, sir," he sighed. "Upon his death Dougrie's daughter, the witness Jessica Gibson, inherited the house and his possessions then at the reading of his Will discovered that he had a Spanish bank account with over five-hundred and fifty thousand pounds in it. Excluding the interest that was accrued over the last twenty-eight years since the account was open, the initial sum deposited was close to half a million pounds. I am of the opinion this was paid to Dougrie by Stacey to keep his mouth shut about what he knew and included the murder of her husband, Murdo Clarke. That and of course were he to admit his knowledge of the gang's crimes, he faced not only imprisonment, but his family would be without a husband and father and likely not just lose their home, but be destitute too. Splitting what was then a fortune, Stacey in effect bought Dougrie's silence. Interestingly, since the date the money was deposited by Dougrie, there has been no withdrawals."

"None?" Cairney was visibly surprised.

"None, sir," Charlie shook his head and added, "I think Dougrie was ashamed at what he was part of and didn't want to be associated with the money. Then again, though it's speculation on my part, perhaps after the murder of Murdo Clarke and his involvement with the gang, his conscience finally caught up with him."

"After all these years, will you be able to prove this money in the Spanish account was the stolen money?"

Charlie pursed his lips and knowing how Cairney would react, didn't immediately respond, but then said, "I've been in discussion with the Detective Superintendent in charge of the Fraud Squad and regretfully no, we will never actually *prove* it is stolen money."

Outraged, Cairney replied, "You're telling me, Mister Miller, that Dougrie's daughter will inherit this money! This *stolen* money!"

Sighing, Charlie nodded and replied, "I am quite satisfied that his daughter, Missus Gibson, is an innocent in all this, sir. I've spoken to her and made her aware of where I suspect the money came from. She quite adamantly tells me that she is ashamed of what her father did and is prepared to hand the money over to whoever has legitimate claim to it. At Missus Gibson's instruction, her lawyer is currently negotiating with the Spanish bank to recover the money that will be handed over to the Crown Office who will ensure those companies who have a legitimate claim will be made aware of the return of the money. However," he stared at Cairney, "there is the issue of the interest that was accrued."

"How so?" Cairney stared suspiciously at him.

Repressing a smile at Cairney's obvious annoyance, Charlie explained, "My discussion with the Detective Superintendent of the Fraud Squad has indicated that because we cannot definitively prove the money in the account to be from the robberies and as Missus Gibson is being so fully cooperative and handing over the bulk of the cash, it is likely Crown Office will permit her to retain the accrued interest that amounts to a little over fifty thousand pounds; less tax of course when HM Inland Revenue get to hear about it. In short, the accrued interest is *not* stolen money."

"Well, I never," Cairney shook his head and peering closely at Miller, asked, "You are the appointed Senior Investigating Officer, Mister Miller, so I will bow to your decision. Do *you* believe that to be fair?"

Charlie shrugged and replied, "The young woman knew nothing of her father's involvement with the gang and is deeply upset at what she has been told. She is in fact surrendering half a million pounds that she can quite legally keep, so yes, sir," he pursed his lips and nodded, "I believe it's fair. I must also add she does not yet know of the Crown Office's decision."

"So, in conclusion, Mister Miller?"

"In conclusion, sir, my official report is that Stacey Clarke was the leader of the so called 'Four Minute Gang,' a devious and manipulative woman who corrupted a previously hard working police officer and in doing so destroyed his family. I believe she murdered her husband and in an attempt to reinvent herself, abandoned her child. I believe she set up her associates to be arrested and stole the proceeds of the robbery. I further believe to keep James Dougrie quiet, she shared the money with him and probably reminded him too that any attempt by him to expose her would result in his own downfall. Colville excepted, she likely informed the three other members of the gang her murdered husband stole their ill-gotten money. Keeping it the remainder of the money and reinventing herself as Stacey Livinsgtone, she went on to open a successful beauty business. However, when Murdo Clarkes body was exhumed she must have been deeply worried that both Colville, who did know of the murder and Dougrie who, if not knowing then suspecting she had murdered Murdo Clarke, were now potential witnesses against her."

He paused for breath before continuing. "Added to that it was her misfortune and even after all these years, James Dougrie recognised Stacey in the background of a photograph he viewed on the Retired Police Officers Association website that had been taken within the past few weeks in the City Chambers. Being a former detective, it didn't take him long to discover her new name. Contacting Stacey via the Internet at her business address, she returned him a photograph, the one in the file," he nodded to it.

"I can only assume the photo was to remind him of their relationship all those years ago. I assume one of them suggested they meet, presumably Stacey who turned up at his house earlier than the appointed time where she stabbed him to death. However, when Frankie Colville learned about Dougrie's murder he recognised the name. When we interviewed him he confirmed to us that at the time of their arrest, he and the other gang members suspected Clarke was touting to Dougrie. Like I said, I believe Colville was probably told that by Stacey. He also said he had never met Dougrie and that seems to confirm my hypothesis that Stacey was a past master at keeping all the parties separate and juggling the lies to avoid suspicion falling upon herself. When we disclosed to Colville our interest in tracing Stacey what we didn't know was he knew how to get in touch with her. How he knew where to find her, I never discovered; however, I can only assume he contacted Stacey to tell her we were looking for her and that's when she realised he was another loose end and decided to murder him too."

"Did Colville benefit from the money that was stolen?"

"Given his living situation, I don't believe so. I have to confess," he shook his head, "I have no idea what lie she told him about where the money went to, but it seems evidently clear he did not benefit from the robberies."

"A busy woman, then," Cairney shook his head, then cocking his head to one side, asked, "What of this woman's current husband? This man Livingstone?"

"The day after we searched the house looking for Stacey, we interviewed him when he'd sobered up or as near as damn was sober. I'm quite satisfied that Mister Livingstone had no knowledge of his wife's history and has no idea where she might have gone to. Frankly, he is at a loss what to make of all this. It seems that he was kept on a tight leash and has no income of his own. Even the house and both cars belonged to Stacey, as did the business. What will happen to the property and the business is now of no concern to us for without a conviction, the Crown Office will not be able to issue any seizure order. Mister Livingstone did however intimate he'd engage a lawyer to try and get everything signed over to him. I informed him that he cannot cite the police to assist him with his claim."

"I agree. His claim will undoubtedly be through a civilian court and we cannot disclose details of any current case we might bring against his wife," sighed Cairney.

"Indeed, sir."

"Right, Mister Miller, you've given me the story as you believe it occurred, but have you enough evidence to arrest this woman?"

Charlie slowly shook his head and replied, "I regret, sir, that there is no hard and convincing evidence at this juncture to arrest and convict Stacy Clarke. The case I intend reporting to the Crown Office will request a warrant be issued to arrest her for interview regarding the murders, but I am of the opinion that as most of the report is speculation and conjecture, that warrant will *not* be granted. The best I can hope for is that she will remain a person of interest in the investigation that will, for the time being, remain open and unsolved."

"Yet you are in no doubt she is your killer?"

"I'm in no doubt of that, sir, but knowing of her guilt and proving it..." he opened his hands.

"Do you have a notion as to where this woman has gone?"

"With the information we provided, the Ports Control Unit at Glasgow Airport successfully identified Stacey boarding an Emirates flight to Dubai. That and her Mercedes Coupe was later discovered in the short stay car park at the airport. The flight ticket was one-way and as likely you are aware, Dubai is the hub for almost everywhere in the African mainland, the islands off the African coasts or onwards to the far east and to Australia and New Zealand. One of my team did find evidence that two years ago Stacey and her husband holidayed in Mauritius, but there's nothing definite to suggest she has returned there."

"A can of worms, indeed," Cairney sighed. He stared at Charlie then continued, "I set you an almost impossible task, Mister Miller, yet though the suspect has fled and you freely admit we have almost no evidence against her, you have proved to me that the murderer of Murdo Clarke and latterly of James Dougrie and Francis Colville, has been identified. I agree from what you have related that as there is a lack of substantive evidence it is unlikely Crown Office will issue you with an arrest warrant; however, you have fulfilled your task."

He rose from his chair and extending his hand to shake Charlie's, added, "For that I am grateful."

Cairney's eyes narrowed and stroking at his chin, he continued, "Though it pains me to admit it, with this bloody woman making off and therefore unlikely there will be a public trial, the corruption and collusion of former Detective Inspector Dougrie with the 'Four Minute Gang' will thankfully remain confidential."

He stared Charlie in the eye and added, "As you are aware, we have quite enough of this ongoing PR disaster with the murderer of our colleague, DS Mathieson, being himself a senior police office."

He slowly exhaled and with a tight smile, said, "Now, is there anything else that you wish to apprise me of?"

"Not at the minute, sir," he began to reply, but then stopped and added, "That said, I'd like you to know that I believe the actions of some members of my team might be worthy of bringing to your attention. I appointed DC William Baillie as acting DS when Shona

Mathieson was so cruelly struck down and he impressed me with his tenacity and determination."

"You'd like to see his acting rank confirmed?"

"Yes, sir," he nodded, "I would."

"Anything else?"

"Alice Brookes, the senior civilian HOLMES operator took on the role as my office manager. She did a grand job and it occurred to me that in future you might wish to consider such a role for suitably qualified civilian staff. If nothing else, it would free up more Detective Sergeants to participate in the inquiries. As you yourself so often comment," he gave Cairney a wry smile, "solving crime isn't the prerogative of just the police."

"I'll give it some thought," Cairney smiled and narrowing his eyes, added, "What about you, Mister Miller? How did you cope being back on operational duty?"

"I have to admit, sir, it was a nice break from the training establishment," he grinned.

While walking him to the door, Cairney said, "While I do not wish to hear details, Mister Miller, I am aware that you were also instrumental in identifying DS Mathieson's killer, our former colleague Donaldson."

Taken aback, Charlie replied, "Ah, well, the credit must go to DI Boyle, sir. It was after all his arrest."

"Of course it was," Cairney returned a knowing smile.

With narrowed eyes, Cairney watched Charlie return along the corridor as he headed towards the stairs and decided then that his Detective Superintendent's time at the Training Department was very soon coming to a close.

****

Sadie Miller restlessly sat in the comfortable chair with the magazine in her hand, but no matter how many times she glanced at the page, she didn't remember what she had just read.

Fetching her mobile phone from her handbag on the floor, she texted her friend Sandra to inquire how Ella was behaving and almost immediately received a response that read:

She's a wee dream. No worries. Any word yet? X

She responded with a text that read:

No. Still waiting.

Her eyes kept glancing towards her mother who slept peacefully in the hospital bed and Sadie wondered what was going through Carol's mind; was she having a restful slumber or did the nightmare of cancer pervade her very dreams.

She felt weary and for a moment, just a short moment she thought, closed her eyes.

She abruptly awoke when the magazine slipped from her fingers and with a soft slap it hit the floor. Bending to pick it up, she heard her mother say, "Are you okay, hen?"

"Mum," she quickly moved from the chair to stand by the bed and take her mother's hand in hers. "You're awake."

"I have been for a wee while," Carol smiled. "I opened my eyes and saw you sleeping so I didn't want to disturb you."

"Oh," Sadie smiled and stroking her mothers hair with her free hand, said, "I didn't even realise I'd dozed off. How are you feeling?"

"If I'm honest," Carol grunted, "a wee bit sore. Has there been any word yet?"

"No, nothing yet," Sadie sighed, "but the consultant told me that the biopsy could take several hours and it will be him that comes and tells us the result," she forced a smile.

Carol was no fool and with a grin, replied, "You mean you told him it had *better* be him who comes with the result?"

"Something like that," her daughter grinned back.

"So, we just need to wait then?"

"Aye, nothing else for it," Sadie nodded. "We just need to wait."
****

Willie Baillie glanced at the phone's screen and smiling, said, "Hi, babe. How's the first day back at the course treating you?"

"Oh, a bit boring after what we've been doing over the last week. Charlie Miller arranged for me to start with the new batch, so I've six weeks of lectures. But," she smiled, "it's a five-day week during the course so I have the weekend off. What's your plans?"

"Well," he drawled, "I'm planning a wee bit of a celebration for Saturday evening."

"Oh, yes; what's that for?"

"I had a phone call from the Divisional Commander. I'm on the promotion parade next week."

"Willie! That's great news! Congratulations! Have you any idea if you're returning to uniform or staying in the CID or where you'll be posted to?"

"I'm not supposed to know, but shortly after the Div Comm phoned me, I got a call from Charlie Miller. Told me to keep it to myself, but it seems I'm staying in the CID and taking over Shona Mathieson's job at Giffnock."

"How do you feel about that?"

There was a definite pause before he replied, "I really don't know, to be honest. I liked Shona and we got on well together. I kind of feel that I'm…" he stopped and sensing his hesitation, Baxter replied, "That you're stepping into a dead woman's shoes?"

"Something like that," he unconsciously nodded.

"Well, try not to think that way. You're good at your job and from what some of your colleagues at Giffnock told me, you're long overdue that promotion. Now," she exhaled, "any news about Shona's funeral?"

"Yeah, this coming Monday. Can you make it?"

"I'll speak to the DI, Mark Bennett and ask him for the time off. I don't think it should be a problem if the boss is going too."

"Okay, well if he agrees, when you come through on Friday after your course, you might as well stop over till the Monday and we can travel together."

"Oh, bit presumptuous there are you not, DS Baillie," she teased. "What makes you think I'm coming through on Friday evening?"

He didn't immediately respond, but then said, "Because Saturday's celebration wouldn't be a celebration without you being here."

"That's as good a reason as any," she grinned before ending the call.
****

After handing over his typed report to the Crown Office at Gartcosh, Charlie Miller met with Willie Baillie at the entrance gates to Rutherglen Cemetery in Broomieknowe Road.

Getting into the front passenger seat of the Volvo, Baillie said, "I got a lift here, Boss, so if it's okay, can you drop me back at the factory when we're finished?"

"Not a problem," Charlie agreed and asked, "Has the cortege already arrived?"

"Just a couple of minutes ago. They'll be up at the lair now. There were two hearses so I'm guessing Colville's getting buried with his missus."

"Right, let's get up there," Charlie nodded.

Moments later the two detectives were stood thirty yards back from the two dozen mourners among whom Charlie recognised Colville's son Joseph who in turn, saw him and gave a slight nod of recognition.

After the bodies were laid to rest, Joseph Colville made his way through the throng of mourners towards Charlie and Baillie and extending his hand, said, "Thank you for coming, Mister Miller and you too, Mister Baillie."

"I won't keep you, Mister Colville," Charlie began. "I've just returned from the Crown Office at Gartcosh where I delivered my report on the murder of your father."

"You know who killed him then?" Colville's eyes angrily flashed.

"We have strong suspicions as to who the murderer is," Charlie carefully replied, "and the individual concerned is also being sought for the murder of a retired police officer, James Dougrie. However, I have to inform you that we have very little evidence against this individual and…"

Colville's face paled and he bunched his fists.

For a split second, Baillie, who took a step forward, thought the younger man might become aggressive when Colville replied, "So, what you're telling me is you can't do a fucking thing about my father's murder?"

"We're not the bad guys here, Mister Colville," Charlie grimly replied. "The rules of evidence limit me in what information I can disclose to you, but hear me when I tell you this; your father was murdered by a close associate from his criminal days and for something he did in his past. With the limited information and the evidence I do have, if your father had not been murdered by his associate he would likely have been in the dock with his associate for a number of charges that include murder!"

He stopped to take breath before continuing, "As it is, Mister Colville, you can bury your father without your family again having to suffer him being dragged through the courts and likely awarded a sentence that would have seen him die in prison!"

He slowly exhaled and his tone softened when he added, "I do not know what kind of relationship you and your brother and sisters had with him or the relationship you have with each other, but you are the eldest of his children so can I suggest that you simply tell them that the individual who killed your father has for now escaped abroad, but we will *not* stop hunting that individual."

Colville stared at Charlie then visibly relaxing, slowly nodded and wordlessly turned away.

Watching him re-join his family, Baillie asked, "What do you think he'll do, Boss?"

"What I think, Willie, is that we'll get the blame; he'll tell the family that we've fucked up and let the killer of his father get away. However, for all that he seems a decent enough young man and he'll probably also consider that he'll not want his own family and those of his brother and sister's families to be tarred with their father's criminal past. He'll also not want their families being subjected to any media attention and while they might be confused and angry, I think in time they'll try to comes to term with what happened."

"But, we'll always be the bad guys?"

"I'm afraid so," Charlie sighed, "but better that than…"

To their surprise, they saw Colville returning to them and stopping in front of them, he said, "You would let me know if you catch whoever did it?"

"Of course, Mister Colville, but I won't lie to you. While he did not deserve to be murdered, your father was not a completely innocent man."

"I'm not stupid, Mister Miller. I know my dad was a robber and he hurt people, but what I can never forgive him for was hurting my mum. No," he shook his head, "he didn't hit her or anything like that, I mean, but the time he spent in the jail away from her and us too; well," he shrugged, "he did more damage to us than he could ever know. One thing I'd like to ask you though. You said the person that killed him, they also killed the retired detective. Was that the story that was in the newspapers?"

"Yes and we believe your father's killer to also be responsible for the retired detective's murder."

"And do you think my dad was involved in that murder too?"

"No," he slowly shook his head, "I don't believe your father was involved in *that* murder."

"So it was someone else who was murdered?"

"I can't disclose too much. I'm sorry."

"Okay," he sighed, "I understand." He glanced behind him at his family who were watching from a distance. "We won't make waves, Mister Miller, because I think you're being honest with us, but if you do find the killer…"

"You have my word you will definitely be informed."

"Thank you," he replied and held out his hand.

Making their way back to the Volvo, Baillie said, "James Dougrie's funeral tomorrow, Boss. His in the morning and the interment of Murdo Clarke in the afternoon. You attending them?"

"Yes, I feel the need to be there and I'd like you to accompany me. It'll be a busy day, so keep it free."

"No problem."

He had momentarily dropped Baillie off at Giffnock office when his mobile phone activated with an incoming text:

Opening the message, he read the text that simply said:

Non-malignant

and exhaled with relief.

CHAPTER TWENTY-SEVEN

Driving to the Linn Crematorium, Charlie Miller felt refreshed and relaxed, grinning as he wondered what a psychiatrist would make of those emotions when he was attending a cremation.

He turned into Drakemur Drive and was surprised at the number of vehicles parked close to the cemetery entrance.

He was a little early, having arranged to meet Willie Baillie at the gates and together they would walk to the crematorium in the grounds.

Getting out of the Volvo, he saw Baillie speaking with two men in dark suits who nodded as they left and walked up the incline.

"Couple of retired CID guys I know," he nodded at the departing men before smiling a greeting at Charlie "Apart from yourself as the SIO in the investigation, Boss, will there be any senior management here today?"

Charlie shook his head and replied, "The Chief Constable has privately made it known to the senior management that because of Dougrie's involvement with Stacey Clarke and the 'Four Minute Gang,' there will be no official representation from Police Scotland. However, because it will not be made public about Dougrie's past, he has no objection to any serving personnel attending here for personal reasons."

"There's a right load of old cops here, most likely from the RPOA," Baillie nodded to the building as they approached and to Charlie's surprise, he recognised many former colleagues, some of whom greeted him with handshake, smiles and nods.

"Any word how Alison feels about being back at Tulliallan?"

Baillie blushed and with an embarrassed grin, replied, "She's settling down to her six weeks, but not too happily. I'll hear more on Friday. She's coming through to mine and then we'll go for dinner of Saturday night to celebrate my promotion. She's hoping to get Monday off for Shona's funeral, too." He turned to Charlie and with a smile, said, "And as for my promotion; thanks for that, Boss. I'm really grateful."

"Nonsense, Willie, you've earned your stripes, but don't sit back on them. You've more in you than settling for the DS rank, believe me."

"Is that true what I hear about Alan Boyle? He's getting the DCI post at Helen Street?"

"Bloody hell," Charlie was surprised. "The jungle drums aren't slow, are they?" then nodded. "It's not official, yet, but he'll be on the same promotion parade as you, so he'll be your new boss."

"Good," Baillie was genuinely please, then asked, "What about you? Back to the Training Department at the college?"

"I expect so," he grinned and unaware of the Chief Constable's plan for him, before shrugging, "If nothing else, it's a five day week."

They stood back at the sight of the cortege arriving and to their surprise, saw that Jessica Gibson and her two young children were assisted from the black coloured Daimler by a smartly turned out young soldier.

"Seems like she managed to get her son home for the funeral," Baillie nodded towards the teenager.

Glancing at the crowd, Gibson smiled nervously, but then seeing Charlie and Willie Baillie, handed her son Connor's hand to Amy and approaching the detectives, said, "I'm so glad you came."

To their surprise she leaned forward and kissing each man on the cheek, in a quiet voice added, "Thank you both, for everything."

****

Later that afternoon, the burial of Murdo Clarke at the same cemetery was a muted affair and among the few mourners were his daughter, Mhari Fraser, her husband Michael and Charlie Miller who again was accompanied by Willie Baillie.

When the short ceremony concluded, Charlie approached to introduce himself and Baillie. Initially stunned at the startling resemblance of Missus Fraser to her mother, he smiled at the young woman and said, "I regret DC Baxter was unable to attend. She's currently on a course in Fife, but she asked me to convey her apologies and her condolence," he added, then politely asked, "How are you?"

Fraser smiled and poignantly replied, "I lost my dad a long time ago, Mister Miller, but at least I now have closure."

She sighed and added, "And of course now I know he didn't simply abandon me, not like her." She stared curiously at him before asking, " Have you managed to find my mother, yet?"

"No," he admitted with a shake of his head, then added, "but we remain optimistic."

As the two detectives walked the couple back to the funeral car, she asked, "Was it my mother who killed my dad?"

He stared at her and though bound by the rules of evidence, decided this young woman deserved the truth.

"We have no proof it was your mother, but if you were to ask my opinion, yes; I believe it was your mother who killed your father."

He watched her face pale and with a frown, she replied, "I used to dream that someday my dad would turn up at the door and we'd be a family again; but finny enough, I never dreamed that of my mother."

Taking a deep breath, she continued, "I'm glad I'm nothing like her," she almost spat out, then sighing, added, "I'm glad too he was found. Now," she turned to glance back towards the grave, "I've somewhere to visit."

With a nod to the detectives, she climbed into the rear of the large, black coloured car.

They watched the car drive off then turning to Baillie, Charlie said, "Let's grab a coffee and to celebrate your promotion, I'll let you pay."

****

The evening sun was slowly setting on Le Goulet Beach and created a dazzling display of light on the still water.

The palm trees hanging across the beach café bar cast their shadows almost to the wide expanse of the hot sand to the water's edge where the small fishing craft floated on the tranquil sea, yet still the air retained the humid heat of the day.

Most of the café's patrons had by now returned to their villas or hotels for their evening meal and so, with a subtle glance about her, saw at last she alone remained.

She had known he was watching her, could almost feel his eyes upon her.

She had always been aware of the interest she provoked in men; the desire to possess her.

Though now in her late fifties, she had maintained a strict regime that kept her body supple; her breasts firm, her skin taut and her shoulder length hair was the best blonde colour that money could buy. With deliberate casualness, she slid the light coloured robe to one side to reveal smooth and shapely legs that glistened with suntan oil.

For the past hour she had allowed the loose fitting robe to slip down from her shoulders and expose the low cut cleavage and the black coloured swimsuit that clung to her body and showing off the provocative figure of eight shape beneath.

Lying on the shaded sunbed, she watched from behind gold framed sunglasses the dark skinned waiter Francois carry his tray as he moved gracefully among the tables to lift the empty glasses and thought him to be in his early twenties.

His hips swaggered as he walked, the close-fitting white tee shirt showing off bulging biceps and the denim shorts so tight she thought with an inward smile they must surely constrict his manhood.

She suspected he knew she was watching him, for his lithe movements were without a doubt a calculated performance.

He manoeuvred his way to her and with a smile and teeth so white they almost dazzled her, asked politely in accented English, "Does Madame require another drink?"

Leaning a little closer, he stared meaningfully at her full breasts while adding, "Or any other service Francois can provide?"

"And how much would this other service cost Madame?" she teased him with her own perfectly white toothed smile.

He shrugged as though the cost were irrelevant and replied, "A lady as lovely and as obviously wealthy as Madame. What does money matter?" he shrugged. "Here in Mauritius we do not care for such detail. It is the loving that matters and I, Francois," he said with a slow grin, "am told that I am very capable at the loving."

She sat upright and raised her hand to him.

When he took it she said, "My villa is a short step from here, sonny. Why don't you walk with me there and we'll discuss your other service in a little more detail?"

"You know me as Francois," he helped her rise from the sunbed, "but how shall I address Madame?"

She smiled and reaching forward to pat him gently on the cheek, said, "Call me…Madame Stacey."

****

Firstly, thank you for your support in reading this book.

Needless to say, this story is a work of fiction and none of the characters represent any living or deceased individual.

As readers of my previous books may already know, I am an amateur writer and self-edit, therefore accept that all grammar and punctuation errors are mine alone. I hope that any such errors do not detract from the story.

If you have enjoyed the story, you may wish to visit my website at: www.glasgowcrimefiction.co.uk

I also welcome feedback and can be contacted at: george.donald.books@hotmail.co.uk

Kind regards,
George Donald

Printed in Great Britain
by Amazon

27923190R00203